Fearless

By
Tawdra T. Kandle

Printed in the United States of America

Copyright © 2012 Tawdra T. Kandle

ISBN-978-1-68230-269-9

All rights reserved.

Without limiting the rights under copyright reserved above, no part of this publication may be reproduced, stored in or introduced into a retrieval system, or transmitted, in any form, or by any means (electronic, mechanical, photocopying, recording, or otherwise) without the prior written permission of both the copyright owner and the above publisher of this book.

This is a work of fiction. Names, characters, places, brands, media, and incidents are either the product of the author's imagination or are used fictitiously. The author acknowledges the trademarked status and trademark owners of various products referenced in this work of fiction, which have been used without permission. The publication/use of these trademarks is not authorized, associated with, or sponsored by the trademark owners.

Dedication

In memory of my parents,
Robert and Jeanne Thompson.
And with gratitude and thanks to my family,
Clint, Devyn, Haley, Catie, David, Greg,
Robyn, Chris, Sean and Kaden.
All of whom taught me how to be…

fearless

Acknowledgements

One person can create a story, but it takes a team effort to birth a book. I would like to thank Mandie O'Steen Stevens for more help than I can ever properly acknowledge, Elizabeth Sharp for her amazing cover design and Julie Titus for her patience and excellence in formatting. My wonderful writer friends at A Writer's Block, particularly Marcie Bridges, Deana Barnhart and Andrea Chapman, have offered invaluable encouragement and suggestions. Closer to home, my husband, Clint, exhibited superhuman patience in helping me with web design and a myriad of other details, and my very particular daughter, Catie, displayed tremendous editing and photography prowess! Thank you, thank you, thank you.

Chapter One

New girl. She doesn't belong here. Doesn't fit in here. Not one of us.

I jerked my head toward the sound of the voice before I realized that no one was speaking aloud. None of the students in the Chemistry classroom were paying any attention to me, the new girl, standing up front at the teacher's desk waiting for a textbook and a seat assignment.

I bit my lip and kept my eyes glued to the floor. This wasn't the first time I'd mistaken someone's thoughts for spoken words. Sometimes the voice was so clear in my head that I could swear I actually heard it, just another benefit to my particular talent.

I wondered which of my new classmates was already thinking about me in such glowing terms. I'd had more than my share of first days at new schools. I was used to the gamut of reactions, from warm welcome to a sort of benign neglect, but I hadn't had anyone hate me right from the beginning. Until today.

Before I could begin to brood in earnest, the teacher handed over a thick hard cover book and looked at me appraisingly.

"Tasmyn..." She pronounced my name very exotically, and with more of a *z* sound than the softer *s* that I used. I detected a slight accent in her words. "Very different. And quite lovely." She gazed at me with frank curiosity. "May I ask what your science background is?"

What was this, an interview? Did I have to qualify for this class?

"I took Physical Science when I was a freshman, and Biology last year," I answered. "And actually, it's Tasmyn. Rhymes with... has-been," I added with a self-conscious laugh, shifting from one foot to another and wishing I was anywhere but here.

Ms. Lacusta stood, and I saw that she was shorter than me by several inches. She couldn't have been much more than thirty-five or so; her jet black hair was long and curling, offsetting nearly translucent skin and flashing dark eyes. She wore a white lab coat over black cotton pants and a flowing turquoise shirt.

She examined me in silence for a moment and then nodded. "Fine, *Tasmyn*. You probably won't have any difficulty with this class, then." Her eyes scanned the classroom briefly, and I knew she was looking for a place to seat me. "Why don't you join Liza at her table? She's in need of a lab partner. Right there, behind Nell and Casey." She gestured to an empty seat on the left side of the room.

Liza was a cool blonde, with lightly tanned skin and blue eyes. As I approached the table, she looked at me with cursory interest before turning back to the conversation she was having with the girls in front of us. Perfectly manicured fingernails tapped absently on her open notebook as she listened to the other two girls.

They were both turned slightly in their seats, facing our desk. Casey had light auburn hair, cropped short around her small face. She was very animated, and as she spoke in a low voice, her hands never stopped moving.

In contrast, her lab partner—I thought her name was Nell—sat quite still. She was about my own height, with hair nearly as dark as our teacher's. It was long and waved about her shoulders. Her complexion was olive-toned, and her eyes were a very pale blue. The striking differences in her hair, skin and eye color were startling enough to be attractive. She appeared to be listening to the other girls, but I noticed that her eyes slid to me speculatively for a moment.

I sat down next to Liza and tried to be as inconspicuous as possible. Glancing around the room, I noticed with a little bit of surprise that most of the students were girls. There were only two boys, sitting in the back. This was an upper level Chemistry course; I would've expected it to be a little more testosterone heavy.

First day jitters made it harder for me to maintain my mental block. I struggled to keep out the floating thoughts in the room by focusing on the front of my new textbook; filling my mind with anything else, concentrating hard, sometimes helped me mute the voices. It wasn't working at the moment.

Hope she doesn't call on me... didn't get that homework... look at Casey's shoes, wish I could buy stuff like that... don't care what anyone says, she's weird... who wants to be in that stupid chemistry club anyway... meeting at the clearing tonight, what will she teach us?

A blood sacrifice. It has to be a blood sacrifice.

A chill ran down my back, and I scanned the room in alarm. A *blood* sacrifice? Someone had actually been thinking that? It was impossible for me to tell whose thought it was since I didn't know anyone yet. Sometimes I could zero in if I were concentrating on a particular person or familiar enough with a mind—like my parents. It was easy to recognize their thinking after seventeen years of hearing it—or trying not to hear it. But here it could have been anyone.

My palms were damp, and I forced my hands open,

rubbing them against my jeans. There had been malice in that thought, a palpable cruelty. I usually picked up on emotions and feelings even more easily than I did on thoughts, and the evil I perceived now was chilling.

At the front of the room, Ms. Lacusta began her lecture. The girls in front of me turned around, and next to me, Liza busied herself with finding a pencil. I tried to steady my own hand as I got ready to take notes, and the minds in the room receded to a steady hum.

It had to be a mistake. Or a misunderstanding. There must be a perfectly good reason why one of my new classmates was considering a blood sacrifice.

Chapter Two

I was still pretty shaky when I left Chemistry forty minutes later. As I walked toward the door, someone bumped me from behind, hard enough to make me stumble.

"Sorry!" The voice was low and intense and sounded everything but apologetic. *Watch where you're going* was what I heard, and the thought was accompanied by a nasty tone as the girl who sat in front of me stared me down.

"I was—I mean, no problem." I concentrated on answering only what Nell said aloud and tried to get out of her way.

Unfortunately, she followed me through the door and into the open-air walkway. I was more used to a traditional school building with hallways linking classrooms, but apparently in Florida, the classroom doors opened directly to the outside. Covered sidewalks took the place of the tiled hallways, and lockers were against the stucco building between the brightly colored doors.

I fumbled with my bag, trying to find the paper that told me where I was supposed to go next and hating first days at new schools with a renewed passion. I knew Nell was still standing behind me—I could hear the low rumble of her mind—but I pretended that she wasn't there.

"Where did you come from?" Her question was clipped and abrupt. I decided to pretend that she was asking it in friendly interest.

"Uh—well, the last place I lived was Wisconsin. We just moved down here. I really like Florida—"

"Why are you taking Chemistry?" Nell demanded. There

was another flare of animosity in her thoughts.

"Because the guidance counselor said so?" I didn't mean it to sound like a question, but it did.

"I think you'd be happier in another class," Nell announced. She glanced around us, as though she didn't want anyone to overhear what she was saying. I didn't blame her. I wouldn't want anyone to hear me being a bitch, either.

"Um—Nell? That's your name, right? Did I do something to offend you just now? Did I kick your chair or breathe too heavily? Because I can't think of any other reason for you to say that."

She raised one perfectly groomed eyebrow and pinned me with a stare that I assume brought other people to their knees. I could hear the fury churning in her mind; it kept me from making out any particular thought.

"We're very selective about who joins this class. Ms. Lacusta isn't a typical teacher, and it's—it's a very demanding course. I think if you go to the office and tell them you want to transfer to botany or astronomy or whatever, they'll take care of it."

"What if I don't want to transfer?" I countered. I wasn't usually able to stand up for myself like this, but something about this girl just got under my skin.

"I think you'll live to regret it." Nell all but hissed this last line. She sounded like the villain in a bad melodrama, and I stifled a completely inappropriate giggle.

"Hey—what's going on?" Nell and I tore our eyes away from each other to glare at the boy who had interrupted our conversation. Nell looked away again quickly, but I didn't. In fact, I didn't look away at all.

He was taller than me by a good half a foot, and he had

light brown hair that hung just a little long over his ears and forehead. But the eyes that held mine were what made breathing tough. They were huge, deep green and framed by the most improbable lashes I'd ever seen on a boy. And they were fastened on me, filled with an expression I couldn't quite read.

Impulsively I pulled the focus of my mind away from Nell's and aimed it toward the boy. I only picked up a few stray phrases over the buzz of the people pushing around us.

...the girl... beautiful... wonder what... her name... Nell up to her...

"Michael, this has nothing to do with you," Nell said smoothly. "Leave us alone." She gave him the same stare she'd given me a few moments before. He only rolled his eyes.

"It sounds like you're giving her a hard time." Michael jerked his head in my direction. "Wouldn't it be nice to let the new girl settle in before you begin the torture?"

The temperature around us seemed to suddenly drop several degrees. Nell took a step closer to Michael. "It's *none* of your business. Leave us alone."

"Not going to happen." Michael stood relaxed in front of Nell, but I sensed the subtle alertness lying just beneath the surface. Nell might have realized it, too, because she gave a slight shrug.

"Whatever." She flicked her eyes across my face. "We'll talk again later. You might want to give some thought to my advice." She walked away from us without looking back.

I watched her go, still more than a little mystified by the hostility. A sudden tingle jolted my attention back to

Michael; he was touching my shoulder, looking down at me with concern.

"Are you okay?" he asked. "Don't worry about Nell. She's that way to pretty much everyone. It's not just you."

"I guess that's a relief," I said. "She's a little intense, isn't she?"

Michael laughed, and my heart flipped over about ten times. "Just a little. What happened to set her off?"

I liked that he didn't assume it was something I did. "I don't know. She wants me to drop Chemistry class. She said it was—exclusive or something. No, she said the teacher was *selective*. That's kind of weird, isn't it?"

He shrugged. "Typical Nell." He waited a beat, as though to let that subject drop completely. "By the way, I'm Michael Sawyer. This is your first day here, isn't it?"

I nodded. "Yeah. Tasmyn Vaughn. I just moved here. Thanks for stepping in with Nell. I appreciate it."

"No problem. Try to stay out of her way, and she probably won't bother you again. She's kind of a bully." He hesitated again. "You're a junior, right? You have lunch sixth period?"

"I *am* a junior. I have no idea about lunch—I'm just taking it class by class." I waved the paper schedule that was my lifeline for the day.

"Well, all the juniors and seniors have sixth period lunch. If you want someone to eat with, look for my friends and me. There's room at our table." He glanced over his shoulder, and I realized that the walkway was almost empty. I was going to be late for my next class, and I didn't even know where it was.

"Thanks. Um, I have a class called speech and debate

next." I scanned my schedule quickly. "Room 32? Can you point me in the right direction?"

Michael grinned. "Sure. Go to the corner of this building and make a left. Should be just a little way down." His eyes lingered on me just a moment longer. "I hope I'll see you at lunch." He turned and jogged away from me.

I hoped so too.

Chapter Three

The cafeteria was located near the center of the school. There was indoor and outdoor seating, and at the moment I approached, a long line of students snaked out the doorway.

I joined the throng, looking around for Michael. I didn't see him, but it was so crowded, I could have easily missed him. Having so many people around me was also making it hard to keep up my mental walls, and I frowned in concentration. The last thing I wanted was a headache with my lunch.

I finally made it through the doors. It was a typical high school cafeteria. Long tables with attached benches were set up along the walls. I saw another door leading to the outdoor eating area. Immediately in front of me were the tray pick up and the food line. The room was filled with milling students, choosing their food and then their seats. The tables were nearly all filled, and I began to panic not only about finding Michael, but about finding a place to sit at all.

As my eyes swept the room, I saw Nell sitting at a table, along with Liza and Casey and four other girls. Ah, yes, I thought, that would be the in-crowd right there: Nell and her posse. She was clearly the center of the group, leaning on the table in the bored, self-assured attitude of one who was positive of her place in the world. I sighed at the injustices of life.

"Hey, you made it!" I heard Michael's happy thought before I saw him. He was smiling and holding an overflowing tray in one hand.

"Yeah, here I am..." Well, that was a truly inspired

reply. I tried not to wince at my own lameness.

"We're right over there." With his free hand, he pointed to a table in the corner, where two other boys and two girls were sitting. They were all watching us with great interest.

"Are you sure there's room for me?" *Oh, please say yes,* I begged silently.

Michael's thoughts were a warm and happy buzz in my mind, but I focused on listening to his spoken reply. "Oh, yeah, plenty of room. Grab your food and come on over. I'll save you a spot."

My hands were still shaking as I picked up a tray. My experience with boys was fairly non-existent. It was all part of the blend in, fly under the radar and don't make a fuss theory of life to which my parents subscribed, at least when it came to me. Michael was not only a boy, he was an incredibly hot one who actually seemed to be interested in me.

I made it through the line, grabbing only a small salad, a pack of crackers and a bottle of water. Holding the tray in a death grip—what would be worse than to drop it at this point?—I carefully wended my way through clumps of people who were trying to find seats themselves. When I finally reached Michael's table, he slid along the bench and patted the spot he had just vacated.

I put my tray on the table and dropped onto the bench, still warm from Michael. My heart was pounding so loudly in my ears that between its noise and the crowd of thought voices, I could barely hear Michael introducing me to his friends.

"Hey, guys, this is Tasmyn. She's new."

They were all looking at me already, and the rush of

attention brought their minds into sharper focus for me. I couldn't quite pick out who was thinking what.

Michael, with a girl at the lunch table...pretty... what was her name? ...Hey, she's in my speech class... oooh, Michael has a girlfriend!

I flushed and frowned, trying to concentrate on keeping my wall up and the voices out.

"Are you okay?" Michael dropped his voice low and looked at me with concern.

I forced a smile and nodded. "Yeah, sorry. Just—you know—a little headache. I'm probably just hungry."

Michael's expression cleared, and he turned back to the rest of the table, dropping a hand on my back. I smothered a gasp as a surge of electric feeling shot through me. I was immediately feeling everything he was feeling, and it was dizzying.

He pointed to the opposite bench. "So, over there, that's Dan, Brea and Jim." They each smiled in turn, and the girl, Brea, sketched a small wave. "And here on this side, Craig and Anne."

Anne leaned over and beamed at me. "Don't worry, there's no quiz on this stuff. You'll figure us all out sooner or later."

One of the boys sitting across from me nodded. "Yeah. So where are you from?"

I kept the smile pasted on my face, trying hard to focus on the conversation and not on Michael's hand—still on my back—or the curious thoughts buzzing around the table.

"I've lived all over, actually. We move about every two years. This last time, we came down here from Wisconsin."

The boy at the end of my bench snorted. "That's gonna

be a change. So which are you, a skier or a surfer? Are you going to miss the cold or love the heat?"

I shook my head. "Not at all. I was really over the whole snow thing. I like the idea of year-round summer."

There were snickers all around the table, and I realized I had just fallen into the typical new Florida resident trap.

Michael dropped his hand from my back and shot a mock-angry look at his friends. "Cool it, guys. We've all lived here forever. Tasmyn hasn't had a taste of—uh, year-round summer yet."

I ventured a glance at him. "Really? You've all been here always?"

"Yup." Michael nodded. "At least, in Florida. Craig, Anne and I have been together since kindergarten, and everyone else came to King at different times."

"That must be nice." If my voice held just a touch of envy, Michael ignored it. He smiled and then looked at my tray.

"Where's the rest of your lunch?"

"What do you mean?" I was lost.

"You're going to eat more than a salad and water, aren't you? You can't get through an afternoon on just that."

"I think I'll make it," I answered, not even attempting to hide my amusement.

He shook his head and shoved a small paper container of French fries toward me. "Here. Eat these at least. I don't want to hear about you passing out in—whatever class you have this afternoon."

I picked up one fry between two fingers and nibbled on it delicately. First days always gave me a queasy stomach, and I didn't want to tempt fate.

"What *do* you have this afternoon, anyway?" Michael asked.

I pulled out my schedule and scanned it. "American History and Trig."

"Cool. I have English and Botany."

I raised my eyebrows. "Botany? Really? That's not your typical high school Science class."

Michael grinned. "It's an elective for seniors. Retired professor from University of Florida teaches it."

"You're a senior?" I hadn't picked that up in his mind. Which of course isn't surprising; who goes around thinking of their vital statistics all the time?

"Yup. We all are here." He indicated the table with a flip of his thumb.

I managed a crooked smile. "Does being a junior mean that I get tossed off this lunch table?"

Michael laughed. "Nah, we don't discriminate against age."

I clapped my hand to my heart and feigned a swoon. "What a relief!"

He smiled again, but his eyes—those deep green eyes—stayed riveted to mine. And then suddenly I could hear him, as though he were whispering into my ear.

Don't want to come on too strong. Ride home? Maybe. Work today... but it could happen...

Too late, I realized I was staring. Michael's expression had turned quizzical again, and I tried to remember the last thing he had said aloud. Before I could figure it out, he spoke again.

"Do you drive to school? I mean, if you need a ride... I live way outside town, so pretty much every neighborhood is on my way home." He was trying to sound nonchalant, but even without hearing him think, I picked up the eagerness. It made my heart start flopping all over again.

"I didn't drive. Actually, my mom is picking me up." I felt the redness creep up my neck. Could I sound any more like a five year old?

But Michael didn't even blink. "Okay, maybe another time. If you needed a ride to school or home or whatever. I'm just saying it's on my way."

The girl on the other side of Michael leaned around him, mischief dancing in her eyes. "What he's trying to say is that he has a really cool car that he likes to show off, and you'd be doing him a favor if you let him drive you somewhere."

Michael rolled his eyes and gave her a gentle shove. "Shut up, Anne. You're just jealous because I don't let you drive her."

Anne laughed. "See that? '*Her.*' His car is the real love of his life."

The bell sounded, interrupting any comeback Michael might have made. Everyone stood up, grabbing books and any trays still left on the table. Michael took mine along with his, stacking and carrying them on one arm.

I took a deep breath. "Well, here I go. Nice short afternoon, anyway."

Michael grinned and followed me as I pushed through the crowd. At the door, I paused and looked up at him.

"I think I need to go this way," I said, pointing to the left.

He nodded. "Sounds right. I go in the opposite direction." But he didn't turn away.

"Well... thanks for letting me sit with you guys today.

It's one of the hardest parts of a new school, you know—having someone to eat with."

"I hope you'll sit with us permanently. I mean, all the time. You're welcome to, anyway."

"Thanks." I drew in a deep breath. "I guess I'll see you later?"

Michael's eyes were drilling into mine once again. "Definitely." He turned and disappeared into the throng of people on the walkway, and I stood watching after him.

Chapter Four

My afternoon didn't hold any real surprises. I liked my History teacher right away; he was an older man with a wickedly dry wit. I knew his class would be a challenge, but at least I wasn't going to be bored.

Math was a different story. Anything with numbers was an anathema to me. The teacher didn't seem too bad; she was young and energetic, and assured me with a snap of her fingers that I would "catch up just like that!" I didn't share her optimism, but I smiled and nodded anyway.

I recognized some faces from my morning classes in History and Math, and some of them even nodded to me vaguely. I wasn't exactly thrilled to see that Nell was in my History class. This time she was on her own, with none of the girls from Science or lunch surrounding her. She sat aloof, her eyes forward, and she didn't even blink when I walked past her to my seat. I made a concerted effort not to pick up any thoughts or feelings from her direction.

I lingered for a few extra minutes at my locker, pretending that I was searching for a book. I didn't even admit to myself that I was hoping to see Michael again. But when someone tapped me on the shoulder, my heart did give a little leap, and I turned expectantly.

But it was not Michael. My Chemistry teacher, Ms. Lacusta, stood behind me, her eyes bright and somehow knowing.

"Hello, Ms. Vaughn. And how was your first day in King?"

I frowned. I couldn't hear anything coming from the

teacher's mind, just some odd kind of static. It made me dizzy, as though I had expected solid ground and instead had stepped into emptiness.

"Uh—good. Thanks. It was good."

Ms. Lacusta smiled, and a chill snaked down my backbone.

"I'm glad. I think King will prove to be very interesting to you. If you need anything—any help in adjusting—please, don't hesitate to come and see me."

I didn't know how to answer, so I just nodded and stuttered my thanks. After a moment, Ms. Lacusta turned and glided away.

That was weird, I thought as I slammed my locker door and headed toward the parking lot. I'd heard of involved teachers, but there was just something a little off about that woman. I shivered even as the mid-afternoon sun beat down on me.

My mother had parked near the front of the student lot. As I walked toward her, squinting in the glare of the sun, I picked up a loud thought at the same time that I heard my name.

"Hey, Tasmyn!" A light blue older model car slid up alongside me. It was a convertible and the top was down. Michael smiled up at me from the driver's seat.

"Hi," I answered. From across the parking lot, I could feel my mother's shock and trepidation and from the car, I could feel Michael's warm interest. It was like being pulled in opposite directions.

"Did you have a good afternoon?" Michael's eyes were hidden by sunglasses, but I could just imagine the kindness there.

"Um, yes, I did. How about you?"

He shrugged. "Not bad. So, your mom's here?"

I gritted my teeth and nodded. "Yeah, she's over there." I waved vaguely in her direction and struggled to save myself from total humiliation. "She doesn't usually drive me to school, but since it was my first day here—and I didn't know how long it was going to take—"

"Hey, it's cool! My mom or dad drove me to school for years. We live too far outside of King for me to walk. And then my sister drove me once she got her license."

"But now you've got your sweet car." I touched the door. "It's—is it an antique?"

Michael slapped a hand to his heart and feigned a look of horror. "Don't tell me you don't know what kind of car this is."

I felt the flush returning to my cheeks. "I'm not much of a car expert."

"Well, let me educate you. This, my dear, is a 1965 Mustang, the best car that ever rolled off a line in Detroit or anywhere else."

"It's... nice." I knew I sounded lame, but I couldn't think of anything else. The pressure of knowing my mom was watching this whole scene unfold was making me panic.

"Nice." Michael rolled his eyes. "Let me take you for a ride soon, and I bet I can get more than '*nice*' out of you."

"Sorry." I glanced over my shoulder at my mother, who was sitting with her hands folded over the steering wheel. Michael followed my gaze.

"No, *I'm* sorry. I'm holding you up, aren't I?"

I shrugged. "Just—it's my first day here, and she probably wants to know how everything went."

Michael's voice was very low when he answered. "I didn't mean to get you in trouble. Is she—will she be mad?" And beneath the words, I could hear his churning thoughts and realized that he had misunderstood completely.

"No! I mean, she's not that way. It's just—" This was going to be mortifying, but it was better than Michael believing that my mom was going beat me when we got home. "I don't usually talk to boys—they don't talk to me—and she's probably wondering what's going on. I'm an only child. My parents can be a little overprotective."

"You don't talk to boys?" Now Michael was totally confused, but this time, what he was thinking made my heart flutter. *A girl like her? Thought guys would be all over her. Can't believe she doesn't have someone already...*

"I guess I tend to be a little shy." That was an understatement. "Listen, I'm sorry, I don't want to be rude, but I really do need to go. Can I—I'll see you tomorrow?"

"Sure." Michael leaned back in his seat and grinned again. "See you then."

I stepped back from his car as he pulled away, but I didn't move toward my mom until he had turned out of the parking lot.

With a deep breath, I opened the car door. "Hi!" I wondered fleetingly if I could distract her with talk about the rest of my day. "Sorry about that. I had a really good first day, though—"

"So it would seem." My mom's voice was dry, and I felt the conflict of emotions rolling from her. She was both pleased and disturbed that I was talking to a boy. She was excited and frightened for me at the same time. I didn't know which to address first, and neither did she. We were both quiet as she turned onto the street.

"It's nothing big, Mom," I said at last, affecting the best careless tone I could manage. "He was just being nice."

"Are you cheating?" Her tone was only mildly accusing. I knew she was talking about the agreement we had made years ago, when I was very small: no listening in on parental minds. It was a hard agreement to keep: the two people in the world I was closest to were also the easiest for me to hear. But I had learned early on that I didn't really want to know what my parents were thinking, and so I tried to block them pretty consistently.

"No, I didn't need to listen to your mind," I answered. "I could feel you from all the way over there. Plus, I know you. You're already freaking, trying to figure out how to deal with this."

"I'm not freaking!" Her voice rose an octave. "You've got to understand, this is new territory for your dad and me. I know most girls your age have boyfriends, and it's completely fine. But you—Tas, you know you're different. You're special. We have to take special care..."

"I get that!" My voice rose too, despite my efforts to keep it even. "I understand. But I also know I need to have a life. And a life might include friends, and yes, even boyfriends. I don't even really know Michael yet. Maybe he's just a nice person who will turn out to be a good friend. But I won't find out if I don't—if you won't trust me a little, give me a little space."

"Michael?" She was a bit calmer. "That's his name? How old is he?"

"Yes, Michael Sawyer. And he's a senior."

"You got all that from a five minute conversation at his

car?" She already suspected the answer.

"No. I met him earlier in the day, and I ate lunch with him—and his friends."

My mother's concern ratcheted up a couple of levels. "That sounds like someone interested in more than just being nice."

I blew out a breath between clenched teeth. "I told you, I don't know yet. There was a girl giving me a hard time, and he kind of stood up for me. And then he asked if I wanted to sit with him at lunch, so I did. I liked not having to sit by myself for a change."

My mom winced. "Tasmyn, we don't make these rules because we want you to be lonely. We make them to protect you." We pulled into our driveway, and she carefully put the car into park, engaged the brake and fiddled with the keys. "We only have your interest at heart, you know that. It's so hard to know whom we can trust. Daddy and I realize how difficult this is for you."

"I don't think you really do," I shot back. "I've been in seven schools in twelve years, and I've never had any friends. You always tell me how special I am, how I have to be careful. But I can't live the rest of my life worrying about being taken advantage of. I just can't. I need to be able to get to know people, to make some real friends. You and Daddy have each other. I have no one."

I jumped out of the car, grabbing my backpack and slamming the door. Tears were threatening, and I wasn't going to break down out here. I held myself stiff as my mother unlocked the front door, and I followed her inside, going directly to my room.

I threw my bags on the bed and then dropped down next

to them, curling up with my head buried in the pillow. I had never been a dramatic teenager. My parents had gotten off pretty lightly when it came to adolescent angst. But right now, it felt as though all the injustices of the world were crashing down on me. Any other normal girl could talk to a boy in front of her mother without said parent envisioning doom. Why did I feel so guilty?

I sulked in my room until my mother called me for dinner. At the table, the tension was painfully thick. My father broke the awkward silence about half way through the meal.

"Your mother tells me you met someone today," he began. "That must have been nice."

"It was a change, anyway," I muttered.

"Well, you're a beautiful young lady. I'm only surprised this hasn't happened before now." I knew what this was. This was the praise that was supposed to make me feel good about myself before they lowered the boom of whatever came next.

"But…?" I prompted.

"But what?" My father was all innocence. "I was just commenting."

"Really?" I broke off a piece of meatloaf with my fork and toyed with it. "So you'd be okay with Michael driving me home from school?"

My mother nearly choked on her green beans, and my father put down his knife with a deliberate clunk. They both gawked at me as though I'd grown a second head.

"Driving you home? When?" My mother found her voice first.

"I don't know. He just mentioned that he could. Or would. Some time." I was hedging.

"Why would he do that?" my dad demanded.

"I don't know, maybe because I'm—what did you say? A beautiful young lady?" I bit back a smug smile.

For a few minutes, the silence returned. My father took a bite of his roll, chewing slowly. I didn't cheat and listen to him, but I couldn't block his swirl of annoyance, worry and fear.

When he did speak, his voice was serious.

"Tasmyn, we have been given the job of protecting you, all your life. Not only because of your—your gift, but just because you are our child. No matter what the circumstance, we would be very cautious about entrusting your safety to someone we don't really know."

"I understand that. But I also know that I'm seventeen years old, and I've never given you reason to believe that I'm anything less than trustworthy. We're talking a drive from the school to here, less than ten minutes. I'd probably be safer that way than walking home, which was what I'd been planning to do, now that I know the way."

Neither of them answered me immediately. I knew they were struggling, and in some ways, I felt guilty for being the cause of their distress. I inadvertently picked up a few phrases floating in their heads... *she's still so young, she doesn't know... how do we know if this boy can be trusted...* But still I stayed stubbornly quiet, my eyes glued to the table.

Finally, my mother spoke. "So, you really think it's safe for you to ride to school with someone you've known—what, a day? Not even?"

I shrugged. "It's not like he's asked me out on a date. He just offered me a ride. I'd like to know I could say yes without you guys freaking out or getting mad."

My father scowled at me. "I don't think either of us has freaked out. We've expressed our reservations to you. If I'm going to be honest, Tasmyn, I'll admit that I'd be more comfortable with you not getting involved with this boy. You might think it'll all work out, but it's going to be hard for you to be his friend without giving away your—what you can do."

"I can do it. I've lived with this my whole life. I think I can handle it."

My mother sighed heavily, and my father shook his head. "Tas, obviously your mom and I have serious reservations about this whole idea. But we do trust you. If you want to ride home with this—what's his name? Mike?"

"Michael," I answered, almost giddy that they were going to give in.

"Okay, Michael. If you feel that it's safe for you to ride home with him, I guess it's all right. But you need to take things really slow, understand? Be very, very careful."

"I will. I promise." They both looked so doubtful that I added, "I can do this. I know I can."

Chapter Five

"I'm a little worried."

We were driving to school, and my mother broke the silence. I was preoccupied with thoughts of the coming day, and I glanced up at her in surprise.

"About what?" I wondered if she had picked up more about yesterday than I had shared. The thing about my particular talent is that sometimes, I don't really buy that others cannot hear *my* thoughts. There have been many, many times that I was sure my mom was tapping into my mind, even though she claimed it was only mother's intuition.

"You didn't say anything about what everyone was wearing yesterday. That's not like you."

"Oh." Relieved, I thought about the fashion scene at school. "Well, you know, it wasn't that big a deal. Most girls were wearing shorts or cropped pants, jeans and that kind of stuff. I saw a couple of cute little sundresses. I think I'll be okay with the summer clothes I have for now, although I might need a few shirts and maybe some jackets. The classrooms can get kind of cool, with the air conditioning."

"All right. Should we plan a shopping trip this weekend then?" She turned onto the main street of town and glanced at me expectantly.

"Um... sure, I think that sounds good, as long as I don't have too much homework."

My mom nodded. "Okay."

I could feel her reaching out to me tentatively, but I continued to stare out my window.

"Are you still upset because I wouldn't let you walk to school today?"

I shrugged. "No. It's okay."

"You know it's not that I don't trust you. I just—"

"—want to keep me safe. I know."

She sighed then and all the stress I'd caused her in the last twenty-four hours was heavy in that one breath.

"It's not just from teenage boys that I want to protect you. You're not used to Florida yet. There are alligators in the lakes, and water moccasins, too—"

Now I did turn from the window. "Are you serious? In *every* lake?" We just happened to be driving by a park that bordered an expanse of crystal blue water.

"Yep. Your dad told me that any standing water in this state can potentially have gators in it—even ditches."

I shuddered. Maybe having my mom drive me to school wasn't such a bad thing after all.

We pulled into the school parking lot, and I scooted out with a quick wave to my mother. I hated when things were tense between my parents and me; it made me feel off balance and cranky, probably because it happened so rarely.

I wandered toward the school building. It was still a little early, but I figured that I could find a bench and do some extra reading. There were a few other kids standing at lockers, but thankfully, their thought noise was muted this morning. I could easily handle blocking small numbers.

Although I didn't even admit it to myself, I was keeping my eyes—and my mind—open for Michael. I had lay in bed the night before, envisioning different scenarios for today, imagining how I could let him know that I was free to accept a ride home from school. I didn't want to be too pushy; what if he didn't really mean it? What if he was just trying to be nice to me because I was new? What if he totally ignored me today? I had to be cool and not expect anything.

By the time I got to my locker, I had convinced myself that I probably wouldn't even see Michael today. He had felt sorry for me yesterday after my run-in with Nell Massler. He was a senior, he already had a group of friends, and there was no good reason in the world for him to be interested in me.

At my locker, I swapped out books, taking what I needed for morning classes. My speech notebook was caught on something in the back, and I stuck my whole head in the locker, trying to pull it loose.

"Hi. You trying to climb in there?"

I jerked my head out, banging it against the top of the locker in the process. Michael was leaning against the wall, looking at me speculatively.

"Ouch." I rubbed the top of my head, still seeing stars.

"You didn't knock anything loose, did you? Should I get the nurse?"

Someone thought he was a comedian, I thought crossly. Hitting my head always made me grumpy.

"I think I'll live. You just startled me. My notebook is stuck back there, between the side and the back." Some part of my mind was noting in astonishment that this unbelievably attractive boy was paying attention to me—again—but somehow I was able to speak.

Michael leaned into the locker, and I moved out of the way. He glanced back and smiled full on at me. I felt my legs melting and wondered how I was still upright.

"Allow me." With a theatrical flourish, he reached in and pulled out my notebook, intact and unharmed, and presented it to me triumphantly.

This was the goofiest behavior I had ever seen, so why on earth was I ready to swoon at his feet?

"Thanks." I took the notebook and tucked it between my French and Chem books and decided to play along a little. I glanced up at him from under my lashes and smiled. "My hero."

I heard him suck in breath. "Jeez, you've got a killer smile. Wow. Listen, do me a favor and don't smile today, okay?"

I felt a little dizzy. "Why not?"

"Just a request. No smiling unless you're with me. I really don't want to have to fight off other guys. I could, of course—" he flashed a smug, self-assured look, "—but I'd rather not."

I closed my locker and stood there just looking at him.

"What?" he asked, in mock bewilderment.

"I just—listen, you don't need to worry about it. Guys falling all over me have never been a problem, and I don't think it's going to start today. And why do you care anyway? Are you the King High School Welcome Wagon?" I didn't want to be rude or unfriendly, but I was confused. No one ever paid this much attention to me.

I shouldn't have worried about being unfriendly. Michael didn't look fazed at all. He smiled at me again, and his eyes never left my face.

"I don't think I believe you about guys not paying attention. And I care because—" he hesitated and for the first time seemed a little unsure of himself. "I don't know that I can explain it right now. You might think I'm crazy."

I raised my eyebrows and just shot him a silent look.

"Oh, too late, huh?" His humor and self-confidence were back. "Let's just say I *am* the Welcome Wagon—your own personal Welcome Wagon. And part of my duties are to make sure you eat lunch with me again today."

I flushed. While I wanted to eat lunch with him almost more than I wanted my next breath, I didn't need a pity date, and I had to be sure he wasn't asking me out of some strange sense of obligation. But as I opened my mouth to say as much, Michael put out his hand to stop me.

"For me, okay? I'm not on some do-gooding trip. This is purely selfish." He gave me a mock glare. "Indulge me. Please."

I didn't know what to say, so I just nodded. "I've got to get to class."

"Where are you going? What's your first class?"

"French. Building 2."

He made a face. "I've got European History in a satellite classroom. Opposite direction, and even I can't move that fast in time. So—" he began walking backwards away from me, "—see you at lunch. I'll meet you outside the door to the cafeteria."

Still somewhat speechless, I nodded again, stood for a puzzled moment watching him go, then turned toward French class.

I was preoccupied during French, which was not a good thing. It was a small class and thus impossible to be inconspicuous. Since it was my second day, I was still trying to make a good impression on the teacher. I managed to fake it until she asked me to orally translate a passage from English into French, and I realized that I had no idea where we were in the book. I flushed in embarrassment when the teacher sighed her long-suffering impatience.

But I couldn't help it. Although I wanted to concentrate, my mind kept wandering to Michael and our exchange this morning. And then I would think about lunch, and my heart beat just a little faster. I created a thousand scenes in my head, each one more improbable than the last.

Fortunately, my daydreams kept me from worrying about Chemistry. I didn't have time to dread it until I walked through the door and saw Nell.

Actually, I didn't see her before I heard and felt her. There are people whose minds are so loud and strong that blocking them is very difficult. Nell was clearly one of those people.

She was sitting in the same spot she had occupied the day before, talking to the same three girls. And she was not thinking very pleasant thoughts about any of them.

Liza is so stupid, she makes me want to gouge out my own eyes. Will she never shut up? On and on and on... better than Casey who thinks she knows everything.

I knew the minute she spotted me, as I lingered in the doorway. Her animosity and fury surged, and her mind narrowed to a single focus.

HER.

My throat tightened. The hatred struck me like a blow to my head, and I struggled not to recoil. Instead I gripped my books and walked to my seat as steadily as I could manage.

Liza glanced at me curiously and shifted her notebook away from my side of the table. Casey stopped talking as she realized that Nell was completely ignoring her.

"What are you doing here?" Nell asked, her voice tight with intensity.

I swallowed and tried for an off-hand tone. "This is where I sit. Ms. Lacusta assigned me this seat yesterday. Don't you remember?"

Sense of humor clearly wasn't one of Nell's strong points. "What are you doing in this class? I thought you were transferring out."

"No, you *told* me I should. *I* told *you* I need this class." A few other girls were beginning to turn and stare at us, and I lowered my voice. "I don't know what the problem is here, Nell. If I've done something to bother you, I'm sure we can—"

"*I don't want you here. I want you gone.*" Nell was losing what little control she'd had. "You don't belong. I told you—"

"Nell!" Ms. Lacusta had entered without either of us hearing, and she swept down on us, adding her own anger to the cacophony of fury that was nearly choking me. "What do you think you're doing?"

Nell's eyes darted from me to the teacher, and I felt her momentary indecision. "Just clarifying a few things for the new girl," she said finally.

"It did not sound like clarification," Ms. Lacusta remarked. She pinned Nell with a steely glare for a moment. None of us moved until she added, "I don't have time for this now, Nell. We have a lab today. I will see you after school, and we can discuss whatever might be troubling you." It was clearly a command, and Nell's face flamed.

I mentally rolled my eyes. I understood that Ms. Lacusta was probably trying to help me, but getting Nell in trouble was not going to make her the president of my fan club.

There was a swell of whispering that ended abruptly

when Ms. Lacusta stood at the front of the room, facing the class. Unlike most teachers, it seemed that she did not need to call for attention or even clear her throat for silence. Her eyes roamed over all of us, missing nothing. When she did speak, I detected again that musical quality that her accent gave her voice.

"Today's lab is a relatively simple one. We will be working on identifying an unknown solution. This solution, which we will refer to as Solution X, contains a cation belonging to the alkaline-earth family and an anion belonging to the halogen family. By observing the ionic reactions between solutions of each of the cations with solutions of selected anions, you will be able to compare Solution X's reactions with the same anions."

Ms. Lacusta began walking down the rows between the desks. "If you turn to page 57 of your textbook, you will find the procedure for this lab. While none of the solutions in this experiment are dangerous, I will remind you of our laboratory safety rules. It's a good idea to get used to assuming all substances are potentially dangerous, since as we know—" her eyes slid to Nell's, "—even the safest solutions can become quite dangerous if combined with the wrong elements or handled carelessly."

She paused for a moment before adding, "You may begin now. I will be strolling around observing. Raise your hand if you need help."

Next to me, Liza flipped open her textbook. When I didn't move, she glared at me. "Are you doing this or what? If you're going to be my lab partner, you need to keep up. I'm not getting in trouble because of you."

Obviously either Nell's attitude was contagious or none

of her friends were willing to cross her. I didn't bother answering Liza. I found the lab in my book and read aloud as she began pulling out test tubes and beakers.

"Put about ten drops of sodium carbonate in each of the three wells of row A, the same amount of soda ash in three wells of row B, point two five milliliters of sodium oxylate in row C and point one milliliters of chromium potassium oxide in row D."

Liza reached for the labeled beakers without comment. She was operating on the principle that if she ignored me, I didn't exist. It was fine by me; I just wanted to get through the class in one piece.

That line of thought reminded me of the day before and the troubling words I'd overheard about blood sacrifice. In all the excitement of Nell expressing her hatred and my first meeting with Michael, I had shoved that memory to the back of my mind. Now a dark suspicion began to grow as I considered who might have been most likely to be thinking about spilling blood.

"Hey! What's wrong with you?" Liza's annoyance was a huge suffocating cloud as she snapped her fingers in my face. I blinked and shook my head.

"Sorry. Just zoning, I guess. What next?"

Nell half turned in her seat and raised one eyebrow as she smirked at me. "Maybe you should reconsider my suggestion. If you can't keep up with a simple lab like this, I don't know how you'll handle the rest of the class."

I felt the heat of a flush creep up my face. "Thanks so much, Nell, but I think I'm okay." I turned back to Liza. "What do we do next?"

"I was saying, you need to fill row B. Ten drops in each

well. Measure carefully, I don't want to do this twice." She shoved a glass beaker filled with some kind of clear liquid in my direction. I picked it up and looked around for the droppers. They were in a stand across the table, and as Liza was studiously looking away from me, I stifled a sigh and stood to reach carefully around her.

    I caught the movement out of the corner of my eye at the same time I heard a malicious cackle coming from Nell's mind. Both came too late for me to move out of the way as Nell slammed the back of her chair against our table, knocking me over in a spray of chemicals and broken glass.

Chapter Six

My first thought was that I was glad I hadn't worn the white t-shirt I had considered that morning. My second thought was that I was pretty sure that the solution all over me wasn't dangerous. And my third thought involved inflicting bodily injury on Nell Massler.

"What's going on over here?" Ms. Lacusta was instantly standing over me, annoyance crashing off her in overwhelming waves. I tried to tune it out, but in my current state of anger and embarrassment, it was hard to control or block anything.

"*She* seems to be having a little trouble with the lab," Nell replied in a smug, laughter filled voice.

Ms. Lacusta's face remained expressionless, but she turned to look at me.

"Miss Vaughn? Would you like to tell me what happened?"

I swallowed hard. I was in a no-win situation. I wouldn't make any friends by implicating Nell; at the risk of sounding like a five-year-old, no one likes a tattle tale. On the other hand, I sensed that the teacher already knew what had happened. I could feel the challenge in Nell's gaze, and I kept my eyes steady on hers as I answered Ms. Lacusta.

"I was filling the wells, and I needed the dropper. I went to reach for it, and I guess I lost my balance."

Ms. Lacusta reached over to brush some shards of glass from my jeans. "Are you cut anywhere?"

I moved cautiously and checked my hands, which had taken the brunt of the fall. "I don't think so. I don't feel anything."

She sighed and shook her head before offering her hand to pull me to my feet. "Would you like to go to the nurse? Nothing that we were working with is dangerous, but if you'd like…"

"No, thanks, I'm okay." I didn't particularly care for school nurses.

"You cannot finish the school day in those clothes. You're soaked." Ms. Lacusta pursed her lips before gliding to her desk to scribble a note. "Here. Take this to the office, and they will see that you can get a change of clothing." As I began to pick my books and notebook out of the mess of wet and broken glass, she added, "Please have the custodian sent down to us as well."

I barely made it out of the classroom before hot tears ran down my face. Nell's hostility, both the outward expression and what I heard her think, stressed me to the point of exhaustion. I was still shaking from the fall, and the intensity of my anger meant I was hearing minds even more clearly, a confusion of noise that made me hold my head.

I managed to stagger around the corner, out of sight of the Chem classroom. Somewhat hidden from the main walkway, which was mostly empty at any rate, I collapsed against the rough stucco wall and slid down to the cold concrete. A sudden breeze made me shiver; the air was warm, but my t-shirt and jeans were both sodden and cold against my skin.

I just needed a moment to recover, away from the speculative minds and mean-spirited glee that abounded in the classroom. I had to calm myself before I went to the office. I hugged my arms tightly to my ribs and focused on the painstaking process of rebuilding my mental walls.

I hadn't gotten very far when a shadow fell upon me, blocking the little bit of sun that shone through a gap in the walkway roof. I felt Michael Sawyer before I saw him or heard his concerned voice.

"Tasmyn? Are you okay?" Panic tinged his words, and I picked up some of the fleeting images in his head—he thought I'd been attacked. Well, he wasn't that far off.

I blinked up at him, not quite able to speak yet. He sank to his haunches next to me, laying a hand on my shoulder.

A zap of electricity—or something very like it—ran through me, and I jerked my head up, my widened eyes meeting Michael's bright green ones. For a moment, his thoughts were so clear that I couldn't distinguish them from my own.

She's hurt, who did this? Need to get help—can't leave her—call 911—

"No!" I managed to choke out one word. "No. Don't call anyone—I'm okay, just shaken up—it was an accident..." My voice trailed off as Michael's face fell into lines of confusion.

"How did you...?" he began as mortifying realization dawned on me.

I had just broken one of the first rules my parents had taught me. I'd reacted to and answered Michael's thought, not his words.

My heart pounding, I mentally scrambled for a logical explanation, and I remembered what my father always told me. *People will believe the simplest rationale for something they can't understand.* Maybe if I just pretended that it never happened, he'd forget about it.

"I'm okay," I repeated. "It was just an accident in Chemistry, and I ended up wet. I'm going to go call my mom and ask her to bring me some dry clothes, but I just needed to take a minute."

Michael's hand tightened on my arm. "What kind of accident? What's all over you—are those chemicals?" *And how did she know that I was thinking of calling someone? Lucky guess... maybe...*

I concentrated on his spoken words. "Yes—whatever we were using for our lab. Nothing dangerous, though. Just—" I pulled my soaked tee away from stomach," —wet."

"How did it happen? Did you drop something?"

I shivered again and drew my knees against my chest, moving carefully so that Michael wouldn't take away his hand, still on my arm. "Kind of. I had some help. Nell knocked me over and I ended up on the floor in the middle of lots of glass and liquid."

Another shock surged through me and my mind jumbled again. *Nell... what the... what's wrong with her... I'll take care of Nell, she won't mess with her again... she looks so pale, is she really okay... get the nurse...* Images from Michael's thoughts flashed into my throbbing head. I screwed up my eyes and dropped my forehead down on my knees, trying to dull the pain. I needed to separate what he was thinking from my own mind, but at the same time, I didn't want to do it. I wanted to pull him in closer and savor the connection.

Going to get help...

"No, don't go!" I burst out before I could stop myself. "Don't leave me here."

Michael frowned down at me. "I didn't move." He

released my arm and brushed my hair away from my face. "But I think we should get you to the nurse. You're shaking."

"I'll be all right in a minute. I'll go call my mom." I pushed up to my feet, and Michael took a step back. His thoughts were whirling suspiciously, and I couldn't meet his eyes.

"Can you make it to the office?"

I nodded, still staring at the ground. "I think so."

"See you at lunch?"

I ventured a glance up. "Are you sure you still want me to eat with you?"

He didn't answer me right away. I couldn't read his expression, and his thoughts were so jumbled that it was hard to get a fix on them, either.

Then he reached out and touched my cheek with the very tip of his finger. With the vaguest ghost of a smile, he answered, "Of course. I'll see you then."

Chapter Seven

By the time my mom arrived at the school with a dry pair of jeans and a fresh shirt—and not a few questions about how I had ended up wet—Chemistry was over and English had begun. I tried to slip unobtrusively into the classroom, but it was not to be. Mrs. Cook stopped lecturing when I opened the door; I meekly handed her the pass that excused my tardiness and sat in the first empty desk I spied.

As she resumed teaching, I scribbled some notes that I hoped would eventually make sense. When the bell rang, Mrs. Cook called me to her desk.

"You'll need to copy the notes you missed from someone," she said, her eyes roving over the last students in the classroom. "Ah, Amber! Could you come here, please? Can you lend Tasmyn your notebook?"

She addressed a girl who had been sitting diagonally across the aisle from me. I hadn't really noticed her before this; Amber was the kind of girl who blended into the background easily. Her hair was brown, a little darker and straighter than mine. She was pretty in a very low-key way, wore no makeup that I could see and kept her hair in a simple ponytail low down her back. She wore jeans and a pale pink t-shirt and was not a little flustered to have been singled out by Mrs. Cook.

Amber ducked her head and nodded in response to the teacher. She flipped her notebook open to the needed page and handed it to me. I caught her eye and smiled.

"Thanks. I really appreciate this." Amber stared at me for a moment, then nodded again.

"I can copy the notes over lunch and get them back to you before the end of the day, if you'd like," I added.

"No rush," she mumbled. "You can just bring the notebook to class tomorrow. I won't need it until then."

"Okay," I replied. "Thanks again." I watched as she left the classroom, looking like she was in a hurry. I thanked the teacher and headed toward the cafeteria.

As much as I had been looking forward to lunch earlier, I was kind of worried about it now. With some time to think about what had happened this morning, would Michael have figured out anything? Would he think I was crazy or some kind of freak?

All the way from my locker to the lunchroom, I prepared myself to be cool and collected, as self-assured and blasé as Nell was. No matter what Michael had to say, I would deal with it. I might even be able to play off this morning's events. After all, I hadn't told him anything. I could explain away nearly all of it. My parents would expect me to do that. It would be so much easier to simply deny everything, to play dumb.

Yet... I was surprised to realize how much I wanted to share it all, every detail, with Michael. The urge was amazingly strong. I wanted to tell him all the stories that had lived only in my mind for so long, all my memories, things I hadn't even shared with my parents. It occurred to me in a sudden and painful way how solitary and lonely my life was. I had always known it had to be this way, so it didn't even cross my mind to mourn what might have been. But now the longing to connect was consuming, as though part of me had been waiting for Michael all along.

He was standing outside the cafeteria as he had

promised, which I decided was a good sign. He was talking with another boy, a tall and thin red haired guy I recognized from lunch yesterday. I knew the minute that Michael caught sight of me, because he pushed away from the wall and moved toward me, even as his friend continued to talk. The other boy looked at him, confused, until he saw me, and then I saw him grin and shrug as he went through the doors into the cafeteria.

"Hey," Michael stood in front of me, his eyes never leaving my face. "You look... drier."

I looked down at myself as though checking on my condition. "Yeah, I decided the wet look was over-rated." I gestured to where he had been standing. "I think you blew off your friend."

He looked over and shrugged. "Nah, he's cool. He knew I was just waiting for you."

"Really?" I thought most guys played it cooler than that. Michael continued to be an enigma.

He grinned and guided me toward the doorway and the lunch line. We didn't speak as we chose food, although I saw Michael roll his eyes at my choices, and I clearly heard him thinking.

Is that seriously all she's gonna eat? Get a quiet table, talk about this morning. Got to figure it out and see... just see...

I wasn't surprised then when instead of heading for his friends at their normal table, Michael guided me toward the doors that led to the outdoor eating area.

"Do you mind?" he asked. "I know it's kind of hot, but I wanted some... privacy."

"No, that's fine." Privacy was abundant out here; I saw

another couple sitting across the yard, but other than that, it was empty and quiet.

We stopped at a table that was partly in the shade. I looked at Michael's tray as he set it down. It held two pieces of pizza, a plate of fries, some carrots and celery, two cookies and two cartons of chocolate milk. No wonder he thought I ate like a bird.

"That's as much as I eat in a day. Where do you put it all?" I looked at him in amazement.

"I guess I burn a lot of calories." He took a huge bite of pizza and shook his head as I picked at my fruit bowl.

"So…" he swallowed and took a swig of his chocolate milk. "You want to tell me about what happened in Chem today?"

I was taken so completely by surprise that I actually dropped my fork onto the table. I had expected questions, but not about that.

"What do you mean?"

"I mean, how did you end up soaked?"

I tore open my cracker pack and nibbled on one of them. "I thought I told you. I was doing a lab and I lost my balance and fell."

Michael gazed at me steadily. "That's not what I hear. And it's not what you told me this morning."

I tried to remember what I'd told him. What I had said was all jumbled in my mind with his words and thoughts. "What do you mean?"

"It's a small school. People talk. Everyone's saying that Nell Massler knocked you over on purpose in Chem, and that it was pretty nasty."

I bit my lip. "Yeah, I guess that's pretty accurate."

"What did you tell the teacher?"

I cast my mind back. "Same thing I just told you. I was reaching for a dropper and I fell."

Michael frowned. "Why didn't you tell her the truth? Nell needs someone to stand up to her. You can't let her get away with that kind of crap."

"I didn't want to make it a big deal, okay? For some reason, Nell doesn't seem to like me. At all. I don't know why. But I can deal with it." I gave up on the main part of lunch and moved onto dessert, breaking off a piece of cookie. "I'm not really sure why you're even asking me about it. I thought you'd want to talk about... something else."

He smiled slightly. "Like what?"

I rolled my eyes and sighed. "I don't know. Let's see, you know next to nothing about me, and I don't know anything about you except your name, your car and that you have a weird thing about welcoming new people to the school. You asked me to have lunch with you today. I thought it was so we could get to know each other. Or maybe talk about—what happened this morning after my Chem accident. And instead you're interrogating me about Chem and what happened... and hey, speaking of that, how did you happen to be out of class at the same time I was this morning? Just coincidence?"

I expected him to be offended, but he merely smiled and polished off his fries. "I do want to get to know you better. I expect to do that. I don't know that this is the place to do it. I thought you might like more privacy for that. I know I would. I can tell you anything you want to know about me. Just ask. Oh, and the reason I was out there today was I saw you walk past my physics class, and I asked for a bathroom pass. You looked like something was wrong, and I was worried."

I didn't really have any reply. The idea that he had been actively seeking me out to offer me help or comfort... that was astounding.

"So here's my story, in condensed version. My name is Michael Sawyer, like I told you. I'm almost eighteen—my birthday is at the end of November. I've lived here all my life—in the country, outside of town. I have an older sister who is in college in Virginia." He paused for a minute, thinking. "I don't play football or baseball, but I run track. I'm a pretty fair student. I like to learn, so I usually like school. Did I forget anything?"

I tilted my head, considering. "You said something yesterday about a job. Where do you work?"

Michael's forehead wrinkled as he frowned at me again. "I said something about work? I don't remember."

I nodded. "Yeah, when you were asking me if I had a ride home..." Suddenly, I couldn't remember if he really *had* mentioned a job or if he only thought it.

He was looking at me oddly again, and I felt the same speculation from this morning. And once again, I heard him loud and clear.

I don't think I said anything about work. Did I? It's almost like she can...

I couldn't help it. I flushed before he could finish that last thought. His eyes were fastened on my face, and I looked away quickly as my cheeks burned.

His next thoughts were so deliberately organized that I would have known he was testing if even the words hadn't confirmed it.

That's it, isn't it? You can read my mind. You know what I'm thinking. This was followed by a huge wave of doubt as he began to second-guess his own intuition. *Am I crazy? She's gonna think so. Sitting here staring at her... psycho nut job...*

I dropped my head onto my hand and closed my eyes. The smart thing here would be to say something, anything, that would convince Michael he was wrong. I could just go on about the job, make him feel ridiculous for his insane suspicions. Keep him at a distance, don't let him know for sure... that was my typical modus operandi. That's exactly what I should have done.

But I didn't.

Instead, I raised my head and met his eyes. I nodded, just once, barely a movement.

Michael released the breath that he had been holding. "No way," he murmured. "No freaking way."

"I'm sorry!" The words burst from my mouth before I could stop them. "I didn't mean to listen to you. I'm sorry—"

"Shhh." Michael stopped me, raising his hand. "It's okay. I think. I'm just—geez. Kind of—trying to figure this out."

I stared unseeing at the brown grass beneath our feet and focused with all of my might on not hearing Michael's mind. I owed him this small gesture of privacy at least.

"This is crazy," he said finally. "You really can...?" When I nodded, he drew in a deep breath and smiled wryly at me.

"So you've been reading my mind since we met yesterday?"

"No!" I shook my head and met his level gaze. "I don't

try to hear thoughts—I really work hard *not* to hear them. I accidentally picked up a few things from your mind—but when I get upset, it's harder to block. Sometimes I can't tell what I'm hearing and what I'm—" I tapped my forehead, "—*hearing*."

To my utter relief, Michael looked more interested than horrified. He opened his mouth to say something else, but before he could speak, the bell buzzed, signaling the end of lunch.

He ran a hand through his hair and scowled. "I want to talk about this more. But we can't do it here." He stood up abruptly, grabbing our trays, and I struggled to my feet, still feeling shaky.

Michael dumped our trash into the nearby garbage can and set the trays in the slot on top of it. He turned back to me with another smile and reached out to touch my shoulder. I felt the same zing as before and sucked in a breath. If Michael noticed, he didn't react.

"Is your mom picking you up today?" he asked.

I shook my head, and Michael's smile widened.

"Then can I give you a ride home? We could talk a little more, maybe."

"That would be great. Thanks."

We both hesitated a moment more before Michael turned to lead me through the now emptying cafeteria and back to the main walkways, crowded with students. I turned to look up at him, to say goodbye, but my breath caught at the expression in his eyes—a mix of question and longing. I could feel the same mixture coming off him in waves, and when he gripped my shoulder again, I was nearly overwhelmed by the flood of emotion.

"Are you okay?" Michael asked in alarm. "You just went white."

"Yeah." I pulled in a breath. "Sometimes touch makes the connection stronger." I covered his hand lightly with my own. "It just took me by surprise."

Michael nodded, his eyes never leaving mine. "Okay. I'll see you at your locker after school." He turned and joined the crowd, disappearing from my sight.

Chapter Eight

I don't think too much happened in class that afternoon, but I really couldn't swear to it. I was completely and totally in another world. Mr. Frame lectured on something that happened in the early nineteenth century, and the Trig teacher spent the whole class period wrapped up in a concept I could not even begin to comprehend. All I knew for sure was that they left me alone to think.

When I wasn't with Michael, I could think rationally, and I could plan carefully. I knew that it was absolutely ludicrous to believe that this person I had known for barely two days could be so important to me already, and it was even more impossible that *I* could mean anything to him. I thought about each time we'd been together... but I couldn't remember them in too much detail or I lost any of that rationality.

I came down to one conclusion: it didn't make any sense. Michael had so far offered no explanation for why he was spending this much time and energy on me. If I had a suspicious mind—which I did—I might worry that it was my unique talent that drew him to me, but if I was looking at things logically, I had to admit that he had sought me out before he knew about my ability. So it was pretty far-fetched that he liked me for my freakish mind.

Far more frightening was considering my own reaction to him. I couldn't look into his eyes for any length of time without losing all sense of reality. Each time he smiled at me, my insides begin to melt away. My whole being hummed with gladness when I knew I was going to be with him, and I felt every sense sharpen when we were together.

This was so new to me. In the past, I had found boys attractive. I could look objectively at a cute guy and admire him. I had even had a few small crushes on classmates—crushes that never had amounted to anything more than me sighing to myself when that boy passed me in the hall or fleetingly caught my eye. I never pursued those feelings, because they weren't that important.

This situation was so radically different that I couldn't even compare it. I wondered, though, what would have happened if Michael had never made a move to talk with me. What if I had just seen him in the cafeteria on the first day and that had been the end of it? Would I still be hung up on him? Or was it that he *had* reached out to me, had made it a point to talk to me, that made him so attractive?

At the end of two class periods, I didn't have the answers. I knew that Michael was already more important to me than anyone except my parents. I knew that I trusted him. Beyond that, I was going to have to do something I rarely did: wing it.

I hurried to my locker after the final bell, anxious and ready to go. Michael was already there, leaning against the wall... He smiled as I rushed up with my books falling out of my hands.

"How was your afternoon?" he asked, as he watched me open the locker and juggle books.

I stepped back and spread my arms. "Well, I'm dry, so that's one good thing. It was pretty uneventful. How about yours? And how did you get here so fast?"

"Mine was boring. English and Botany. And I got out a little early because we had a quiz in Botany, and I finished early. No more Nell issues?"

He had changed the subject so quickly I had to pause to think before answering. "No. She's in my History class, but she pointedly ignored me." I slammed the locker shut and turned to face Michael fully. "What's her deal, anyway? I mean, I get that she's the queen diva around here. I saw that right away. But usually those types don't bother with anyone who doesn't threaten them."

Michael's eyes were speculative. "Maybe you threaten her."

I laughed. "Oh, that's possible. No, I don't think that's the issue."

"I've known her for as long as we've been in school. She's always been someone you don't want to mess with. Some of the guys can deal with her, but most of the girls steer clear, unless she chooses them to be in her little group."

I laughed. "I don't think that's a concern of mine. I'll be happy to be among the steering-clear crowd, if she leaves me alone."

Michael smiled, too, ruefully. He glanced at his watch. "Are you all set?"

I nodded. "Ready to experience the wonder of your amazing cool car."

He rolled his eyes. "She doesn't appreciate sarcasm. Remember, she's my best girl, so you'll want to make a good impression."

I giggled as we started toward the parking lot. Michael glanced sideways at me. "Assuming you do make the cut, do you think your mom would let me give you a ride to school? I drive in every day, and I could stop to pick you up… if you wanted."

I did want, more than I could even express. And since my parents had—no matter how grudgingly—given their consent to rides *from* school, I decided that being driven *to* school couldn't really be that different.

"Yeah, I think that would be fine," I answered finally. Michael's smile was nearly as staggering as the explosion of feeling that poured out toward me. I concentrated on keeping my steps steady.

We reached his car, and Michael opened the passenger door for me. I swung my backpack into the rear and sank into my seat as he sprinted around to his side.

I examined the interior carefully. "I like your car. It's in very good shape for such an old... vehicle."

Michael shook his head in mock despair. "It's not old, it's antique. And it's been lovingly maintained. This car has been in my family since it was brand-new. That's very unusual."

"Really? I don't know very much about cars." I ran a finger over the chrome detail on the dashboard. "I mean, I can drive, and I do, but not that often. My mom usually needs the car during the day."

Michael snuck a glance at me as he turned the key in the ignition. "Do you want to drive my car some time?"

Taken aback, I scrutinized his face to gauge his seriousness. "Are you kidding? You'd let me drive your antique?"

He laughed. "It's a car, Tas. Yes, I am pretty fond of it. It was my uncle's, then my dad's, then my sister's and now it's mine. And I'd love for you to take it for a spin, if it would make you happy."

Now I was more than surprised, I was touched. "Thank

you," I murmured. "I'd really like that."

He grinned. "Of course, I should probably warn you... once you drive the 'Stang, you'll be spoiled for anything else."

"I guess I'll take my chances." The car was meticulously maintained, and only a little bit of wear indicated its age. I looked at the vintage radio, the huge steering wheel... and the stick shift. Grimacing, I shook my head.

"Your car. It's manual. I mean, stick shift."

Michael turned in his seat, looking through the rear window as he began to back out. "Yup, it is." He put his hand on my headrest as he did, and his wrist was nearly touching my face. I couldn't breathe. I leaned my head back and closed my eyes, just absorbing his closeness.

"You okay?" I heard the quizzical concern.

"Yes." I opened my eyes but didn't move my head. "But I can't drive your car. I never learned how to drive manual."

Michael moved his hand to the gearshift and the car slid forward smoothly. "Seriously?" I shook my head. "Well, when we have time, I'll teach you to drive stick, so I can keep my promise, okay?"

The idea that he was making plans with me—even as incidental as a driving lesson—made me glow all the more. I closed my eyes again; with my head swimming, my blocks were worthless, and I could hear him so clearly.

... Pushing? Am I coming on too strong? Moving too fast... She makes me feel—I can't even think about how she makes me feel... like I could conquer the world when she's with me... but what if she doesn't want me around?

I opened my eyes abruptly and sat up. Michael glanced over at me. "You okay? I thought you had fallen asleep.

Which would have made it hard to get you home, since I have no idea where you live."

I looked out the window as we drove through town. "No, just thinking." I gave him the general location of my house and then gathered up my all my courage and continued, feeling my face heat as I did. "A driving lesson would be great. And I wasn't trying to listen to you... but you're not being pushy. And—" I took a deep breath, "—And I never don't want you around me."

Michael's face was a study in confusion. I didn't blame him. I usually spoke clearly, but for some reason, it was easier just now to say what I didn't want—his absence—than it was to say what I did want—or need: his presence.

"So if you don't not want me around, is that the same thing as wanting me around?"

I knew my face had to be flaming. "Yes, I guess that's what it means," I whispered, my eyes fastened on the road.

We were turning onto my street, where I was certain my mother was waiting by the front door, making sure I hadn't come to any harm. Michael slowed the car and pulled up just out of sight of the house. Turning in his seat, he put a finger beneath my chin to raise my face, forcing me to look into his eyes.

What I saw there was steady and bright. He was smiling that wonderful smile, and when he spoke, his voice was low.

"I don't not want you around either," he said. "And I know we haven't had the time or privacy to talk this through, but just so you don't worry—this is not the norm for me. I don't give girls the rush. I've dated a little—taken girls to dances and the movies with a group of friends—but I've never had anything like—you—happen to me."

I was already shaking my head. "Me neither."

He looked at me a minute more, and his finger moved from my chin to the side of my face, stroking lightly just along my hairline. He didn't say anything, and I was able to keep whatever he was thinking from reaching me.

At last, regretfully, he dropped his hand and coasted the car to the front of my house. Before I could even turn, he had jumped out and come around to open my door for me, helping me get out my bag, too.

I could feel my mom was lurking beyond the front door, but I couldn't go in without bringing up what I'd expected Michael to ask since we'd met at my locker.

"You didn't mention—what happened at lunch." It was a statement, but Michael answered the question he heard behind my words.

"I know. Car ride wasn't long enough. I was thinking—I'm working tomorrow, but would you be able to hang out after school on Thursday? We could go out to Lancer Park and just... talk."

I wasn't sure I could endure two more days without clearing the air, but I nodded. "I think I can. I'll have to ask my mom. Is the park in town?"

"Just outside. Would it be better if I asked your mom?"

"No!" I was quick to answer. If my mom sensed that Michael knew that I could hear minds... well, I wasn't sure what would happen, but it wouldn't be good. "Thanks. My parents can be a little overprotective. Part of my whole. . deal." I made a face, but Michael only smiled.

"Okay. I'll leave it to you then. I'll be here tomorrow at seven-thirty to pick you up, all right?"

I smiled back at him. "I'll see you then."

Chapter Nine

Getting permission from my parents to go to Lancer Park with Michael wasn't as difficult as I had anticipated. There was the expected flare of surprise and the same predictions of disaster if I slipped up and revealed my ability. I was able to avoid out and out lying, since they didn't ask me if Michael already knew about it. Eventually, they acquiesced, with lots of warnings to be careful, to keep up my blocks and my guard.

I was waiting by the door the next morning when the powder blue Mustang slid down the street at a safe and respectful speed and pulled up in front of our house.

"Mom! I'll see you after school!" I called. My heart was pounding. I grabbed my bag and concentrated on walking calmly and coolly out the door.

Michael was out of the car and opening the door for me. I noticed, for the first time, how he was dressed. It seemed before I had never looked away from his eyes. Today he was wearing faded but decent looking jeans and a gray t-shirt. He smiled as I approached.

"Good morning, " he greeted me, and I shivered at his voice. What was it, I asked myself, that made me feel this way? All I had to do was see him and I felt swoonish, if that was even a word.

"Good morning," I answered. "Looks like it's going to be a pretty day."

Michael glanced at the sky through the windshield as he climbed into the driver's seat. He smirked at me. "Yep, it's Florida. Pretty days are the rule, more often than not."

I cringed inwardly. What a trite, stupid thing to say, talking about the weather of all things!

But Michael didn't seem to notice my embarrassment. "Guess it's a lot more of a sure thing here than it was in Wisconsin."

I was surprised that he remembered the last place I had lived. "That's not saying much, but yeah, it is."

We were both quiet, then I ventured, "I really do appreciate the ride. You're possibly saving me from a horrible fate, if I had to walk."

Michael laughed easily as he turned a corner. "Oh, yeah? What's that? Blisters?"

"No!" I answered, my eyes widening. "You know, all the wildlife danger. Scorpions, snakes and alligators! Oh, and those biting ants, too."

This time he laughed in earnest. "You're not serious, are you?"

"Of course I am. My dad told me all about everything that lives down here. He said not to go near natural bodies of water, and I'd have to walk past a lake on my way to school."

Michael shook his head, looking at me sideways in mock pity. "Sad. Do you really think there's gators just roaming the streets?"

"There might be," I replied darkly. "Who knows?"

He was still chuckling as we turned into the parking lot and found a spot. We climbed out of the car, Michael waiting as I slung my backpack over my shoulder.

"So, are we on for tomorrow afternoon?" he asked. I could tell he was trying to keep his tone casual.

"Yes! My parents said it was okay, as long as I was home by dinner and..." I altered my voice to mimic a parental tone, "be very careful and smart."

Michael shot me a quizzical glance. "What does that mean?"

"It means my parents don't want anyone to find out about what I—what I can do." I kept my voice down. There weren't many people near us, but I'd been well schooled in caution.

"It's a secret, then?"

We had reached Michael's locker, and we stopped there while he swapped books. I raised my eyebrows.

"Well, yes. No one knows. Just my parents and me... and now you. And they can't know that *you* know, or they will really freak out, and probably send me away to military school."

Michael slammed his locker shut. "Seriously?"

I shrugged. "No, it wouldn't be military school. Probably we'd just move out of state and they'd home school me for the rest of my life."

"No, I mean, no one else knows? And they'd be mad if they knew I knew?"

I shuddered. "Mad doesn't begin to cover it. Mostly they'd be frightened, I think. Their worst fear is that someone finds out about me and then... I don't know, they have all kinds of dark scenarios in mind."

"Hmm." We moved down the walkway toward my locker, and it was my turn to root through my books. Michael leaned against the wall, and I could feel his eyes on me before he spoke again. "So do you think you can keep yourself dry and out of trouble this morning?"

I rolled my eyes. "That doesn't seem to be asking too much, does it? Sometimes I think I'm missing some essential element I need to be part of things. I'm always the invisible girl... unless I'm in Chemistry here, then I'm the girl with the target on her."

"I don't think it's you. We get a certain amount of transient kids in King... you know, they move here for a year, then they're gone. I guess it does take a while before people really open up." He shrugged. "Like I said the other day, I've been in this area, at King schools, all my life. So I don't know for sure."

"Small towns are always harder to break into," I agreed. "I thought Florida would be different, *because* there are always people moving in and out, and all the tourists, too."

"King is a little bit of an oddity, though," Michael remarked. "There are a few old Florida families, and sometimes they act like they're royalty. Not all of them, but there are some odd ones."

"King has been here a long time?" I questioned as I closed my locker.

"Haven't you heard the history of this town?" Michael asked. "It's kind of cool, I guess, if you're into that sort of thing."

"What sort of thing?"

"Oh, you know, history, magic, legends, all that paranormal stuff."

My spine tingled. "Some people would say I am very into paranormal stuff," I murmured softly, just for Michael's ears.

He smiled gently. "Not like this. Gravis King was a carnie. Actually, he owned a big carnival, one of the largest in the south in the late nineteenth century. He retired down here, bought land, and brought his whole carnie family down to live here, established this town. Said they all needed a place to make a fresh start.

"Lots of people who still live in town can trace their family trees back to King's carnies. If you go downtown and walk around, you'll see shops with some of the carnie names up there. People trying to play on their heritage, I guess. Makes a good draw for tourists, and we get busloads every year. Whatever works." He shrugged.

"That's very interesting," I mused. "Is yours one of the families?"

"No way!" he laughed. "My parents settled here as a compromise. My dad came from the panhandle, my mom came from south Florida, so they agreed to live here as a half-way point. And they're not much on the mystical elements people in town play up. My mom says it gives her the creeps. So we don't live in the town, we live just outside, like I told you."

The first bell rang, and I looked up, startled. I had been totally absorbed in our conversation.

"Gotta run," Michael sighed, regretfully. "See you at lunch. Stay dry!"

It was hard to believe it was only my third day at King High School. I managed to keep it relatively uneventful. In Chemistry, I slid into my assigned seat as quietly as I could, but I needn't have bothered. Liza, Casey and Nell were all in full ignoring mode, not even bothering to acknowledge my presence. I was perfectly okay with that. I took notes on Ms. Lacusta's lecture and kept my eyes on my notebook.

When the bell rang, Ms. Lacusta called me to her desk and handed me several papers stapled together.

"These are the notes from the lab you missed," she

explained. "And there is a summary worksheet on the back page. If you complete it tonight, I will make sure you receive full credit for the lab you missed." Her eyes were very perceptive as she gazed at me. "I don't believe that you were at fault yesterday. I should have kept a closer eye on the situation, especially considering the... personalities involved."

I wasn't sure what I should say at this point, so I just nodded and murmured my thanks. As I turned to go, Ms. Lacusta said softly, "Tasmyn... tread carefully. And please, do feel free to let me know if there is anything I can do to help you feel more settled and at home here. I think I could be very helpful to you."

Her words were kind enough, but quite suddenly, I sensed a very different feeling pulsing from her mind. It swirled around me, almost like a tangible mist, and it was not pleasant. Rather, it was cunning and nearly—I struggled for the word—painful? No, not quite. Dangerous, that was a more accurate description. Like a beautiful snake that might lull its victim into admiration before it struck with deadly venom.

I took an involuntary step back from the desk and nearly stumbled. I mumbled another incoherent word of thanks and fled the room as quickly as I could. I spent most of Speech and Debate trying to shake off the sense of foreboding Ms. Lacusta had triggered in me.

In English, I returned Amber's notebook to her with another word of thanks. Again, she didn't respond to my efforts to start a conversation; she just took the notebook back with a nod and never even met my eyes. I stifled a sigh, wondering what I could have possibly done to offend yet another girl by my third day of school.

The rest of the morning passed quickly, and I was so glad to go to lunch that I felt like skipping the whole way. Michael was waiting for me in the same spot outside the door, and his smile upon sighting me lit his entire face.

The idea that I was the reason for that incredible smile was intoxicating. I really couldn't understand why he sought me out, why he wanted to be with me, but I wasn't going to press my luck and ask too many questions, lest he figure out that I wasn't worth the effort. I was surprised and not a little scared to realize that Michael Sawyer was already so important to me.

As he had the day before, Michael opened the door and followed me inside. But today, he was taking a personal interest in my lunch. He added a plate of fries to my tray (which held a cup of soup and a salad) and made me take two cookies instead of just one. When I protested, he just shook his head and moved me forward.

"You cannot make it through an afternoon on just rabbit food and soup," he told me firmly. "Besides, I'll help you eat them."

Everyone at our lunch table greeted me warmly as we sat down. I tried to keep up with the conversation that flew around us… If I kept my concentration on just one person at a time, I was able to tune out most of the thoughts. Fortunately, the few I did pick up were positive and friendly.

Michael made sure that I kept eating throughout the talk. He sat next to me today instead of across the table, and he angled his body so that I felt protected and safe, even as he encouraged me to talk to the others. I realized that he was giving me another gift: he was sharing his friends with me.

It was toward the end of lunch that Anne mentioned Nell Massler's name. She rolled her eyes as she told us that Nell had joined the Harvest Moon Dance Committee. Across the table, Brea sighed in a show of empathy.

"I just don't get it. She's very popular, but she is *so* intense. We were having a meeting, and she gets all wrapped up about the dumbest things. I can't believe how many people are listening to her. Drives me crazy!"

I was quiet. I had just met these girls, and I didn't want to chime in on something negative.

Michael moved slightly closer to me and leaned to whisper in my ear. "Why don't we beat the rush and go to our lockers now, if you're finished eating?" He glanced down at my tray and sighed. "You didn't finish your cookie."

"I'm full," I answered. "I'm ready to go."

Once out in the hallway, Michael walked alongside me in silence. "I thought maybe the Nell talk was making you uncomfortable."

I glanced at him sideways. "Are you sure you aren't the mind reader here?"

He looked at me in surprise. "Pretty sure. I just try to be observant." We stopped at his locker first, and as he twirled the combination, he said quietly, "You talk about it so casually. But I thought—what you can do was a big secret."

"It is. I mean, it always has been. I don't—" I struggled to put what I was feeling into words. "I've never been able to say those casual things to anyone but my parents. I guess it's just really freeing. I'm sorry if it makes you uncomfortable."

"No, it doesn't." Michael closed the locker. "I was just surprised." He stood looking down at me so intently that I flushed and dropped my eyes. "There were some times at lunch that you seemed to be listening really hard. You were just looking at Anne and Brea—I don't know, like you were concentrating intensely on what they were saying." He hesitated, and I sensed that he didn't want to say anything I might take the wrong way. "Were you... were you *listening* to them? You know, to more than what they were saying out loud?"

My face grew even warmer. "No! I don't do that, not on purpose. Sometimes things slip in..." I was getting upset as I tried to explain. "What I was concentrating on so carefully was *not* listening. I work very hard to keep up the walls that block other people's thoughts."

Michael closed his eyes and leaned back against the wall. "I didn't mean that to sound—accusing. I was just wondering. I've been worrying about what you might be reading in my mind, that you might not like it. I didn't even think that you might be trying not to know."

His admission took my breath away. *He* was worried about what *I* would think? That was insane. I was the freak, the one who was made wrong. And he thought I would read his mind and not like it?

I took a steadying breath. "I haven't heard anything from your mind since yesterday in the car. And I wasn't trying then. It happens. I try to keep it from happening, but it does."

Michael pushed off from the wall. "Tasmyn, I promise you, I am not mad at you. I wouldn't have been angry if you had been reading my mind or the girls' minds. I just didn't know." He put his finger under my chin to lift my face. "Please don't be upset," he murmured.

My eyes were caught in his, and I couldn't look away. I could feel his warm finger just grazing my face. My wall slipped a little, but I could only interpret earnest, intense feelings from him—no specific thoughts. And then just for a split second, I saw my own face, looking up at him, the way he was seeing me, and I was completely blown away. I knew it was my face; I recognized the long brown hair and saw my own hazel eyes, but it didn't look like the image I saw in the mirror each morning. It was beautiful.

The bell rang and the walkway filled with people. We were no longer alone, but Michael stood still. I was the first one to move.

"We have to go to class," I said, although I had no idea how my voice was working.

"I know." He breathed deeply and ran his hand over his hair. "I know. This is," he shook his head, as if to clear it. "Okay, I'll see you at your locker after school."

"I'll be fast. I don't want to make you late."

"You won't. See you." He took off around the corner and I wondered how I was going to move myself to class when my legs were suddenly made of rubber.

Chapter Ten

I spent another afternoon zoning through my classes, thinking only about Michael. When the final bell rang, I knew I had to get to my locker fast; Michael had to get to work, and I didn't want to make him late.

I ran to my locker, already holding the books I would need to drop off and mentally listing the ones I needed to grab. Michael was there waiting, his eyes focused on the paperback book he held in one hand.

"Hey—I'm sorry you had to wait, I'm hurrying. She always keeps us in Trig until the last minute."

He held up his hand. "I just got here. Take a breath. I wasn't going to leave without you."

I shoved my books into the locker and rooted for one I needed. Glancing back over my shoulder, I inquired, "What are you reading?"

He held up the book so that I could see the cover. "John Keats. We're reading him in English and I needed—" he broke off for a minute, not meeting my eyes. "I was kind of preoccupied in class today, and I need to be more familiar with some of these. This kind of stuff doesn't come as easy for me as Math and Science."

I closed the locker. "All set. I love Keats. I wrote my sophomore lit paper on *Ode on A Grecian Urn*."

Michael grimaced. "That makes me feel so much better, thanks."

"No problem. You can do the same when I tell you that my Trig teacher was speaking in a foreign tongue today." We were walking toward the parking lot, and I looked up at him, smiling a little. "At least I think she was. I was a little... preoccupied too."

He blew out a breath. "Nice to know I'm not the only one. I was beginning to think that maybe I was."

"Was what?"

Michael didn't answer me as we headed toward the parking lot and climbed into his car. He remained silent while he started up the car and then turned to me. "What I meant before was that I worry that I'm the only one who gets preoccupied. It's crazy. It makes no sense. But sometimes..." His voice trailed off again, and he shook his head, looking down. "You probably think I'm insane."

"I don't. Not at all."

Michael shifted into reverse and then pulled out onto the road. He kept his eyes on the road even as he prompted me. "But...?"

"But nothing. This is all so new. I've only known you for three days, and like I told you yesterday, I've never..." I drew in a deep breath. "I don't have any experience with boys. At all. I feel totally comfortable when I'm with you, but then when I stop and think about it, the whole situation seems unbelievable. Like I must be crazy."

"Well, that's it then." Michael shot a quick bright smile at me. "You need to stop thinking. And so do I."

"Really?" I cocked an eyebrow at him. "We need to stop thinking?"

"Yup." Michael nodded. "Or maybe we need to stop *over* thinking. When we're together and talking, I don't have any doubts that—well, about us. I like you, Tasmyn. And there's more than that to it... more that we need to talk about. Not today." He ran a hand through hair and scowled. "I don't have time before work."

"You never did tell me where you work," I remarked. "When we were talking about it yesterday, we kind of got side-tracked."

Michael laughed. "Yeah, we did. I work for my parents. They own a nursery and landscaping company, and I work there three days a week and most weekends."

I was impressed. "Wow. I don't know anything about plants. Do you like it?"

"It's cool. I like working outside, and my parents are pretty flexible. But I don't like to take advantage of them." He pulled up to the curb in front of my house. "So as much as I'd like to stay with you and talk now, I need to just drop you off and get moving."

I hopped out of the car. Michael met me at the sidewalk and handed me my backpack. I slung it over one shoulder and turned to look up at him.

He was looking down at me with such intensity that I couldn't breathe, and for one moment I was sure he was going to kiss me, right out here in the open. But he only squeezed my arm.

"See you tomorrow morning," he whispered. And as he left, I wondered how on earth I was going to make it until then.

Chapter Eleven

I was up early again the next day. When I opened my eyes, I had a delicious sense of anticipation—remembering that something good was going to happen but not quite grasping what it was.

"Oh!" I sat straight up in bed. Today was park day, when Michael and I would have an entire three hours of uninterrupted time together without worrying about classes or other people. A wave of pure joy washed over me, and I jumped up onto my feet, turned on my music and dashed into my closet. I looked around for a minute before I ran back out and clicked on the computer to check the day's weather. What I saw their inspired a little impromptu dance: sunshine, temps in the mid-eighties and virtually no chance of rain. That meant I could definitely wear the sweet little sundress I had been considering.

Even though I took much more time than usual with my primping, I was ready early. My mother had made pancakes, and I managed to eat one and drink a glass of juice before my stomach refused any more.

When I saw the Mustang turn onto our street, I called a goodbye to my mother, promising once again that I would be home by dinnertime. And then I was out the door.

"Good morning!" I fairly sang as I met Michael at the car.

He was grinning and looking at me with undisguised admiration. He whistled low.

"Wow."

I stifled the urge to laugh and twirl around to further

show off. "Is 'wow' good?" I questioned teasingly.

"Wow is… very good."

"Well, I do try to dress decently every once in a while."

"It's not the dress—not totally, anyway. It's you. You look—" he paused and scrutinized me. "All lit up, kind of." He helped me into the car, and his eyes were still warm when he climbed into his seat.

"I do like the dress, too," he added.

I laughed. "Thanks. It's a beautiful day and… I'm happy." It was true, I realized as I said it.

Michael smiled at me so brilliantly that I felt my heart leap into my throat before it broke into an unsteady rhythm.

"I'm very glad that you're happy. I'm happy, too." He glanced at me slyly as we turned the corner. "The park should be nice today."

"Where exactly *is* Lancer Park?" I asked. "My dad seemed to know what I was talking about when I told him where we were going. I know you said it was right outside town."

"Yup, right on the Lancer Lake," Michael answered.

"The lake? Where the alligators and the aggressive water moccasins live?" I wasn't going to let a little thing like death-threatening creatures spoil my good mood, but it was wise to be prepared.

"I promise, no harm will befall you. People go to this lake every day, Tas. No one has ever been attacked by wildlife. At least no one in my lifetime…" He raised his eyebrows and looked at me meaningfully.

"Thanks," I said. "But guess what? I am not going to think about that. I am in much too good a mood to think about creatures who are waiting to eat me at the park."

"Water moccasins don't eat you. They just bite you."

I rolled my eyes at him. "Whatever. Not thinking about it. Not thinking about Nell either. Only happy thoughts today!"

We pulled into the parking lot, and as we walked toward the school, Michael looked thoughtful. "How about we eat outside today?"

"Really? Outside in the heat?"

"It's not that hot today, and hardly humid at all. And that way we can talk in private without having to be social with everyone else."

I frowned slightly. "I thought we were going to the lake to talk privately."

"We are. But at the lake, I want to hear about you. I was thinking that in order for you to be honest with me, I need to explain some stuff about me. I told you yesterday that there's more we need to talk about. So that's the agenda for lunch today." He looked determined, and for the first time, my happy mood faltered a bit.

"Is this stuff you're going to explain good or bad?" I asked cautiously.

He smiled at me, assuring. "I think it's good, but you'll have to be the judge of that, after you hear it. It's nothing that big, just me getting some things out there that I think you need to know. Okay?"

I took a deep breath. "Okay. So we're eating outside. Sounds like a plan."

"I'll go ahead and get a table, since I always get to lunch before you. Oh, and don't worry about getting any food, I'll get your lunch along with mine."

"Meaning there'll be enough for a small army?"

He assumed an innocent face. "I don't know what you're talking about."

I think I floated through that morning. French was a pleasure, one of those classes where it seemed I could do nothing wrong. I translated a passage from our book, reading it aloud, and the teacher actually complimented me on my accent. She passed back homework we had turned in the day before, and I had earned a perfect grade. It was gratifying to feel that I was finding my rhythm in a few classes, at least.

And then on my way to Chem, one of the girls from the lunch table, Anne, called my name and greeted me with a warm smile.

"I love your dress! It's so pretty. I could never wear it, but it looks wonderful on you." Anne was several inches shorter than I was and curvy in all the right places.

"Thank you," I replied, sincerely flattered by her words.

"See you at lunch today?" she asked.

I hesitated. "I think—Michael said something about eating outside today."

She smiled knowingly at me. "He wants you all to himself and doesn't want to share! Well, I guess we'll let him go for today, but you make sure he doesn't hog you all the time. I enjoyed talking with you yesterday."

More happy warmth spread through me. "I enjoyed it, too," I told Anne. "I'm sure I'll see you at lunch tomorrow."

"Okay!" She slipped past me with a quick wave and smile as I continued on to class.

I was so far into my happy place that I didn't even spare Nell and company a glance when I entered the chemistry classroom. I put my books down on the table and then walked to the front of the room to hand in my missed lab assignment worksheet. Ms. Lacusta took it absently from my hand; she seemed absorbed in something else on her desk, and I was happy to slip away without more interaction.

When I returned to my seat, though, my books were no longer piled neatly on the table; they were spread open and face down all over the floor in the aisle. I hadn't heard a sound, so I assumed the three girls had worked together to quietly and quickly displace them.

Immediately I gathered the books and put them back on the table, taking my seat. Nell was turned sideways in her own chair, and in striking contrast to the previous days, she was staring insolently at me.

"All dressed up today, aren't we?" she mused. "What's the occasion?"

I was determined to keep things as peaceful as I could, and I answered her coolly but calmly.

"Nothing special. Just a pretty day. Oh, and I saw on the schedule that there's no lab today, so I decided I was safe from having chemicals thrown at me."

Nell rolled her eyes. "Oh, isn't she dramatic!" she exclaimed, addressing Liza and Casey. She turned back to me. "No one threw anything at you. Your own clumsiness is what got you wet. Isn't that what you told Ms. Lacusta? And if you had just taken my advice and dropped this class, maybe even that wouldn't have happened."

A day earlier, Nell's words would have crushed me or at least angered me beyond the ability to reply, but in my current near-euphoric state of mind, I found I was able to respond.

"We all know what happened here, Nell. You can think whatever you like, but the next time you want to get nasty during a lab, I'm taking you down with me. Literally."

Nell's eyes flared at me, and she opened her mouth to say something, but at that moment, Ms. Lacusta began lecturing. With one final glare, she turned around. The atmosphere around us was tense, and I could feel the antipathy pouring off Nell.

Actually, I was amazed at myself. I had no idea where those words had come from. I never stood up to anybody. For that matter, I had never been in a position where I needed to stand up to anybody. But somehow the words had come, and it dawned on me that I had just threatened a girl who seemed to be a fairly powerful force in my new school's social system.

And she wasn't going to let it go. From the bits of loathsome feeling and waves of hate I was picking up, I knew that Nell was not one of those bullies who would back down when someone stood up to her. No, she was more like a black widow spider that would strike with deadly accuracy when I least expected it. I was going to have to watch my back.

Chapter Twelve

I hurried my way to lunch and flew through the cafeteria doors, slipped past the people waiting in line and straight across to the second set of doors leading outside. I blinked in the bright sunshine and spotted Michael just setting two trays an empty table.

"Hey!" I greeted him. And then stared at the food on the table. "I thought it was going to be just us for lunch today."

He looked at me in surprise. "It is. Why?"

"You cannot seriously imagine that the two of us are going to eat all of that. I could sit here for hours and not make a dent in it."

He rolled his eyes at me. "You underestimate my appetite. And you have to eat up, because…" he dropped his voice and leered at me. "The gators at Lancer Park are expecting a good meal this afternoon. I'd hate to disappoint them."

I just looked at him, evenly. "Oh, funny. You know, you probably don't want to mess with me today. I stood up to Nell in Chemistry, and I am feeling pretty invincible."

Michael feigned shock. "Really? Is she still giving you trouble?"

"I think she'll leave me alone just long enough to think of something horrible to do. But I don't want to talk about Nell." I settled myself into my bench seat. "I'm here to listen to you, remember? All mysteries solved and so on?"

He laughed, and I glowed inside. "I don't know about all mysteries. Here, eat some of this hamburger." He pushed a plate with the sandwich and a stack of fries on it toward me.

"Okay, okay, I'm eating." I took a bite of the burger and was surprised how good it tasted.

"So..." Michael fidgeted with the silverware on the tray and scowled at it. It dawned on me that he was stalling... he was nervous. Again I felt such an overwhelming tenderness toward him that my heart seemed to swell.

"You know, you don't have to talk about anything you don't want to," I said, swallowing another bite of hamburger.

"It's not that. I'm just trying to decide how to start."

"Why don't you begin with my biggest question: why me? Why do you care about what I think or do or how I'm adjusting here, or if I need a ride to school? I'm not saying that I don't like it," I hastened to add. "I'm just not used to it. You—you look after me. It seems like you really do—care."

"I do," he vowed, his eyes intensely serious. "I guess that's the biggest thing I want you to believe. I know this is very fast and very sudden to you, but to me—" he took a deep breath before continuing. "I've been waiting for you all my life."

My heart pounded and I couldn't answer.

"When I saw you that first day in the hall, with Nell going at you, I couldn't believe it. I just looked at you and I knew. I don't know how I managed to make any kind of sense to you or Nell, because it felt like all the words were jumbled around in my head. I would have stood up for anyone Nell was picking on, but when I saw it was *you*—it was like..." He closed his eyes and drew in a deep breath. "Like finding what I didn't even know I'd been looking for. And I was so rattled that I couldn't even figure out what I was saying."

"*You* were nervous?" I was incredulous. "I wouldn't

have guessed. You just seemed so sure of yourself."

"I guess I'm a good actor," he laughed. "I was glad I thought to mention lunch, because then I knew I'd see you again. All I wanted to do was talk with you alone, get to know you, but I didn't want to scare you off. I thought eating with my friends would make it easier on us both, but that whole time, I just wanted them all to leave us alone. I was kicking myself afterward, wishing I'd managed to talk to you by myself a little more.

"And then I saw you in the parking lot that afternoon. I had been looking for you, but I had to get to work. When you looked up at me, before I even called you…" Michael took another deep breath. "I knew, for sure."

What he was saying was heady stuff, but I needed some clarification. "You said that before—that you *knew*. What did you know, exactly?"

Michael set down the cookie he'd been eating. "This is what I've been… uncertain about saying. I don't know what you're going to think."

This time it was my turn to say it. "You can trust me, Michael. Whatever you tell me, it's not going to change what I—think of you." I had been about to say, what I *felt* for him, but at the last minute I lost my nerve. It was the first time that I was in the position to assure him that it was safe to open up to me; up until now it had been the other way around.

He looked at me steadily, holding my eyes with his in that devastating way he had. My whole body was instantly tingling, electrified.

"I *knew*… that you are the girl I've been waiting for, since I became old enough to realize I *was* waiting. I've liked other girls, as friends. I've even thought some of them were pretty. But you—ahhhh." He exhaled in frustration. "I can't explain it the right way. I'm eighteen, or just about, so it's going to come off like I'm some kind of nut, or like I'm just giving you a line. If I were saying this ten years from now, it might seem reasonable. But right now, it sounds like a page from a bad romance novel." He narrowed his eyes at me. "Not that I've ever read a bad romance novel. Or any romance novel at all."

"Of course not," I murmured.

"When I saw you that first day-was it only three days ago? When I saw you then, you took my breath away. You—you're so beautiful. And when I got to talk to you, I knew right away you were just as gorgeous on the inside, too. The *real* you, I mean. Who you are."

I couldn't reply, mostly because I had stopped breathing and my throat had closed. I was mortified to realize that tears were lurking at the back of my eyes. Michael's words and the obviously deep feeling behind them stunned me.

"So... are you completely freaked out? Ready to take out a restraining order?" His words were light, but his eyes were worried.

I shook my head slowly, and I found somehow I could breathe again. "No, that never crossed my mind." My thoughts were swirling, not making sense, and it was growing harder to keep Michael tuned out. I could feel his nervousness and his fear, but even stronger than that was his ringing sincerity. And then bits and pieces of real thoughts began to fly out at me. *This is it, what she thinks and how she reacts, that's all the matters. What if she doesn't really... what if she can't feel the same way or if she's spooked by what I'm saying... I don't know what I'll do.*

I closed my eyes abruptly and turned my head away, concentrating hard on not listening. After he had essentially bared his soul to me out loud, it seemed a petty intrusion to hear his thoughts.

At the same time, I knew I had to reassure him. Keeping my eyes closed, I murmured, "I'm sorry. When things get—intense, like this, it's harder for me to respect the privacy of others. I'm just working on not hearing."

My eyes flew open when I felt his hand against my face. His fingers firmly cupped my jaw and his thumb brushed one eyelid gently. "Don't," he said softly. "Don't shut me out. I promise, there's nothing I'm thinking that I don't want you to know."

Another first. Never in my life had anyone offered me an open pass to his mind. I expended so much energy and attention keeping up my mental wall that the idea of letting it down was a little daunting, even while it was freeing.

"Thank you," I whispered. "You don't know how much that means to me. But I won't abuse your trust."

"I know," he smiled. "That's part of the whole you being gorgeous on the inside, too. I have faith that even if you did hear something you weren't meant to, you wouldn't use it against me."

I sighed. "That's the one flaw in your line of reasoning. I don't think you're a stalker, I don't think you're just handing me a typical guy line. I believe that for some insane reason, you really do feel the way you just told me. But I still don't get the why. I'm so not worth the trouble that comes as part of the package."

"Well, there you're wrong," he said with absolute certainty in his voice. "About the trouble and the worth, I mean. The bigger issue is whether or not *I'm* worthy of you. That's my real doubt. And since I'm not a mind reader—" he smiled slightly, "—I have no way of knowing your feelings on that."

"You mean, unless I tell you."

He nodded. "I'm not trying to force you into some big confession of—anything. I wanted you to know where I was coming from before we talked this afternoon. I have lots of questions for you, and I want you to feel comfortable with answering them, knowing how I feel about you."

I wasn't sure I could handle giving him a reply yet. What had I expected him to tell me today? His actions and words all week had pointed to the fact that he was interested in me. That was as far as I had been willing to take this in my mind, afraid that even considering anything more would hurt when it didn't materialize. But what he had told me was completely beyond my hopes. He had trusted me enough to open himself up to possible rejection or ridicule; although I was afraid I wore my feelings for him in plain sight, he seemed to be as unsure about me as I had been about him.

I took a deep breath and took the plunge before I could think myself out of it. "I have no idea why you feel for me what you do, because I'm nothing special. I have a special gift, or talent or whatever you want to call it, but you didn't even know that at first. I believe you, I believe all you told me today, but I still don't understand the *whys*.

"It's incredible to me that you do—feel that way. It would be immensely flattering under any circumstances, but it's more than that now. Because from what I've read or seen, this—" I pointed at Michael and then back at myself, "—rarely happens." I swallowed hard before continuing, because tears were threatening again. The tender feelings rolling off Michael weren't helping.

"What I am trying to say, and not very well, is that—one of the reasons I believe you is because—it's how I feel, too." For the first time since I began speaking, I looked up from the table and into Michael's eyes. They shone at me with such depth of trust that I was momentarily lost. I struggled to continue.

"That first day, in the hall, I could hardly talk to you. But for me, that's not unusual. I never talk to boys, and I don't even have that many conversations with girls, either. When I saw you at lunch, I was grateful to you, but still pretty confused about why you bothered. And then after school that day, when you stopped me as I was leaving—it was like the sun broke across a gray sky.

I smiled, shaking my head. "I know. Lame, isn't it? But it's true. You think you've been waiting for *me*? My life has been..." I sucked in a breath as I considered my next words. "Empty. It's been me and my parents, and my mom and dad have each other. I never had anyone to talk to about how I hate moving all the time, because it would make them feel guilty. I don't talk much about my—what I can do, because I know it makes them crazy. They like to stick to the illusion that I can control this, that it's not a big deal. Well, it is a big deal, and I've been very lonely.

"So even if you had turned out to be just a good friend, that would've been something. But I knew from that first afternoon, to me you were something more. I was smiling inside for the first time, maybe ever. And then when I blew my cover with you, and you didn't freak out or tell anyone, that made it even better, because not only were you kind to me, now I could talk to you, really talk, and not hold anything back. And that is something I haven't had with anyone outside of my family. Ever."

This was a very long speech for me, and I ventured another look at Michael to make sure he wasn't bored. His eyes were fastened on my face, and he seemed alert, so I continued.

"You said you *knew*. Well, maybe I wouldn't have put it quite that way, but I think it's the same thing. I... *felt*." I laid a hand over my heart. "For the first time, I felt connected and—that I mattered to someone. I knew that I cared for you way too much, way too soon, but I couldn't talk myself out of it." I took another long breath. "So there you have it."

Michael didn't say anything. He reached across the table and took my hand from where it lay and twined his fingers through mine, then raised our joined hands together to his lips, brushing across my knuckles like a whisper. My heart skittered again, and this time I couldn't blink back the tears that filled my eyes.

The bell rang shrilly, and we both jumped. We were the only ones left outside.

"We are so going to be late," I moaned.

He grinned at me and jumped up, releasing my hand. "No, we're not. I'll take care of the trays. You go on to class. I have a sub for English today anyway." He grabbed my arm as I turned to leave and brushed a hand over my hair.

"I'll see you at your locker after school," he reminded me. "Have a good afternoon."

As if any alternative was a possibility.

Chapter Thirteen

Lancer Park was about ten minutes outside the King town borders. I saw the large lake before we even turned into the park and tried not to think of what lived in it.

We parked on the grass at the edge of the beach and walked toward the lake. The water sparkled innocently in the late afternoon sun, but I was still wary. Michael took my hand and pulled me down on the sandy lakeshore.

"You're safe here. Nothing's going to jump out of the water and get you."

I raised an eyebrow skeptically. "It's on your head if a gator grabs me by the leg and drags me out to the middle of the lake."

He smiled slightly. "I'll take that responsibility." My heart beat a little erratically as my cheeks felt warm. Without meaning to, the wall I kept between us slipped slightly, and I heard, "*So pretty... what am I doing here with a girl like her? She's going to see that I'm not good enough for her...*" I pulled my gaze from his face and concentrated on not listening.

"What's wrong? Are you really that freaked? We can go if you want."

"It's not that. I am just trying... not to listen. Sometimes it's hard when it's a more one-on-one situation."

This time it was his face that reddened. "Are you hearing something you don't like?"

Oh, great, Tas, I thought, way to help things out here. I decided it was better to lighten the mood.

"Not yet, I didn't. Maybe I wasn't listening hard

enough?" I put my fingers to my temples and struck my best mind-reader pose.

It worked, and he laughed, bumping his shoulder against mine in a friendly way. I did notice, though, that he was still holding my hand from when he had pulled me down onto the sand. He followed my gaze.

"Does it bother you?"

I didn't have to drop the wall to know what he meant. But I couldn't quite articulate with my heart thumping and my throat suddenly feeling tighter. I just shook my head. He smiled then, and gripped my hand just a bit tighter.

We looked out over the water in silence for a few minutes, and then he began hesitantly, "Can I ask you a few things? About... you know, your talent."

"Sure. Ask away. I don't know how much I can explain, but I'll try." I bit the side of my lip and frowned slightly. I saw a reflecting frown on Michael's face and his brow was furrowed.

"I don't have to ask anything. You don't have to tell me anything. We can just hang. It's cool. I don't want you to be uncomfortable." I could feel waves of uncertainty coming off him—he thought I was afraid he couldn't be discreet.

"It's not that. It's not that I don't trust you to keep it to yourself. It's more—" I took a deep breath. "It might change how you feel about me. You could start seeing me differently. Acting differently around me."

He was silent for a moment. I could tell that he was thinking about what I said, and it was a relief that he didn't just offer me assurances.

"I don't think it will make any difference. I already know the biggest part—I think, anyway—" he threw me a swift glance and I nodded in agreement, "—and it doesn't make me like you any less. I just kind of want to know... more."

I nodded again and took a deep breath. "Okay, so fire away. Unless you want me to just pick the questions out of your mind?" I meant the last part to be said flippantly, and he rolled his eyes at me.

"No, let's do this the old-fashioned way, if you don't mind. So, how long have you been able to read minds?"

"First, I'll tell you it's not really mind-reading. It's more like hearing. Reading implies will; you don't just walk around accidentally reading stuff, but you can definitely hear things you might not mean to hear. That's more what it's like with me. And it's been all my life. As long as I can remember."

His eyes widened. "Really? So even when you were a little kid? What was that like?"

I laughed without much humor. "It was just how I was. For me, it was normal. It was what I knew. So I don't know what to say to that. I don't remember any time when I couldn't hear people."

"How did your parents figure it out?"

I sighed. "It wasn't easy. I wasn't born with it stamped on my forehead, so my parents didn't really figure anything out until I was old enough for it to affect my behavior. Although my mom thinks in hindsight there were clues when I was a baby."

"What kind of clues?"

I stretched out the hand that wasn't being held and used it to support myself as I leaned back a bit. "I guess, when I would cry, I would quiet down as soon as my mom would get up to get me—before I could even see her, but she was probably thinking about me and somehow I heard that. And also if she woke up in the middle of the night, hoping I would stay asleep, right after she thought about me, I would wake up. My mom figures I could hear her thinking my name and it woke me up."

He laughed then, delightedly. "Your poor parents. They must have loved that."

I chuckled too. "Let's just say they never meant me to be an only child, but my early childhood was such a challenge that they decided I was enough for them."

"So when did they realize that you were not the average kid?"

I felt the familiar pain from those early years. "It didn't take too long. I talked really early, probably because I was hearing so many more words than other toddlers. I started to repeat things that my parents had never said to me, and they had no idea where I could've picked up the phrasing, the words. And... I was very easily upset. I could pick up all my parents' thoughts about me and about each other, and believe me, you don't want to know what parents are thinking all the time. It wasn't bad, but if they were the least bit impatient or tired or whatever, I knew that, and it upset me, because I didn't know how to process what I was hearing.

"And then I started having trouble sleeping. My parents would get me to sleep, but I would wake up, screaming, probably because I heard them thinking, or I heard the neighbors thinking or whatever. I didn't have any way to tune it out. And the lack of sleep, and dealing with what I was hearing all over the place—it didn't make me a very pleasant toddler. The worse I got, the more my parents worried, and then I picked up on that, too." I swallowed hard, unable to go on for a moment.

He squeezed my hand for just a second and then raised our joined hands to my face. I was surprised to feel that my face was wet.

"I'm sorry," he murmured. "If you want to stop…"

I shook my head. "No, it's just difficult. These aren't really *my* memories, or even totally things my parents told me. They're more the memories I've picked up from them over the years, and they're kind of painful ones." I took a deep breath. "Okay, I'm all right. So there I was, a troubled two year old. My parents didn't know what to do. They took me to doctors, had me tested, and basically, they were told it was either a phase I would grow out of—or it was more serious. One doctor told them that he was sure I was emotionally disturbed, that I would probably end up living in some kind of group home for kids who were violent. That about killed my mom and dad. I think it was then they realized they couldn't have any more children; some of the doctors were warning them that I might be physically abusive to any siblings."

He whistled softly under his breath. "That must have been tough on them. What finally clued them in?"

I smiled shakily. "My grandmother figured it out. I spent a lot of time with her. She was the only person my parents would leave me with, and when I stayed there, I could actually sleep. See, she lived out on a farm, pretty far from her nearest neighbors, and she lived alone—my grandfather died before I was born. So it was very peaceful with her. She was a calm and restful person. And because of that, I was a calm and restful child when I was with her.

"She figured out gradually what I could do. She said there were lots of hints, and when she finally accepted that I could hear her thinking, it seemed the most logical answer."

"Wow, what did she do? Was she freaked?"

I shook my head. "No, she wasn't. She just dealt with it. My parents were harder to convince, but she asked them to hear her out and not jump to any conclusions. And to their credit, they did just that. I think they were so relieved to have an answer that didn't involve me being in an institution, they would have accepted just about anything."

"What happened next? Did they go back to the doctors?"

"No, because they knew the doctors wouldn't listen and then the more they thought about it, they were afraid people might be interested in me for other reasons than to help me. So they kept it quiet, and they just started to focus on ways to deal with my issues. Like the sleeping. My mom started playing music in my room at night to block the thought noise, and they also started giving me a light sedative, just until I was old enough to learn how to deal on my own."

"Did that help? The sleep, I mean?"

"Oh, it made a huge difference. So did the fact that my parents were so happy now and that they understood me. They worked, too, on ways to block their minds from me—trial and error, of course. And that helped. Immensely."

I was finished for now, and he was quiet. I waited, wondering, and tempted more than I usually was to cheat and hear what he was really thinking. I didn't, more out of cowardice than manners.

Again he tightened his grip on my hand, and again he raised our two hands. But this time, instead of bringing them to my face, he pulled them to his own, turned them over and brushed his lips over the back of my hand, as he had today at lunch. I shivered, even in the warmth of the late afternoon sun.

"I'm sorry," he whispered, still holding my hand near his face, so that I could feel his breath against my fingers.

"Don't be," I breathed, still not sure why he was sorry.

"I don't feel sorry for you, not now. But I am sorry for the little girl you were, and it makes me sad to see you remember, and hurt."

"Thank you," I murmured. I cleared my throat. "So, what else do you want to know?"

He cocked his head, thinking. "Can you hear everything, all the time?"

"If I just opened myself up and let it be, I would be able to hear a low buzz that would be the thoughts of everyone within a certain radius. I'm not sure how big a radius that is, but the closer people are, the more clearly I can hear them. I don't test it often, at least not on purpose. If I'm startled or stressed, sometimes the wall drops suddenly, and then I get a rush of noise. And as you learned, if I'm very emotional, sometimes I can't distinguish between the spoken word and the thought word."

"How did you learn to block it all?"

"My mom and dad taught me, as much as they could. They figured out when I was concentrating, I didn't hear so much. We practiced, and they also taught me that it was impolite to listen in on other people who hadn't given me permission. They made me realize that private thoughts are just that. And that even if I did accidentally hear something, I shouldn't respond or comment, because that wasn't polite or safe."

"Safe? So you really think you could be in danger from this?"

I hesitated. "Maybe. I don't want to sound all *X-Files* or anything, but even if you're not talking government stuff, there are companies that would be very interested in someone who could give them that edge. Anyway, I don't want to open myself up to anyone who might exploit me, at all."

He gazed at me intently, silently. He still held my hand near his face, and now he shifted to wrap it tightly in both of his, subtly pulling me slightly closer.

"I would never, never violate your trust in me. I want you to know that."

I wanted to make a silly reply, lighten the mood, but I couldn't pull my eyes away from his. I nodded, barely. "I know."

We were quiet for several minutes. The sun was slowly going down, still warm against our backs. Twilight had settled across the lake.

"Is there anything else you wanted to know?"

He pulled in a deep and slow breath. "Hundreds of things. But nothing that can't wait. This has been a lot for you today."

"I'm not used to it. I *don't* share—I just don't. And I don't even talk much about this stuff with my parents."

"Why not?"

"Unless there's a problem, there really isn't any need to talk about my—gift. I guess no more than you would talk about being blind or deaf. It just is, and we deal with it."

"And no one else has ever guessed or figured it out?" He was lightly running his fingers back and forth over the back of my hand, but his eyes were squarely on my face.

"No, not ever. I try not to get into many situations where someone might get suspicious."

"That's the whole staying aloof thing. You said before that you didn't have many conversations with girls *or* boys."

I nodded. "And it's not hard. When you have to concentrate on not hearing everyone, it can come off like you're stand-offish or stuck up. Or even something else." I smirked a little, remembering.

"What?" he demanded. "What's funny?"

"I was just thinking about my last school, in Wisconsin. There was a rumor going around that not only was I a snob, I didn't like boys either."

He raised his eyebrows. "Seriously?"

I laughed at the disbelief in his eyes. "Well, people look for an explanation for what they don't understand, and I guess that was the best they could come up with for why I wasn't interested in any of the local hotties."

A smile curved his lips, and for the first time in over an hour, he released my hand. I felt oddly bereft for just a moment, but I didn't have a chance to dwell on that, as he leaned closer to me and brushed the hair back from my face.

"How about here?" he murmured, so close to my ear that I shivered even as my face grew hot again. "Are there any local hotties you're interested in?"

My heart was thumping so hard and fast that I could hardly hear my own reply. "Maybe," I breathed. And my concentration slipped so suddenly that it seemed I could hear him shouting, "*Do I kiss her? I don't want to push. But maybe...*" I closed my eyes briefly and shut it all out, but I knew I couldn't be anything less than honest.

"I'm sorry," I murmured. "I could hear you, just now.

It's harder to concentrate when I'm—flustered, I guess."

He didn't pull back, didn't seem at all upset that I had violated the privacy of his mind. Instead, he slid his hand from my hair down to my neck and cupped it softly. He leaned even closer to me, resting his forehead on mine.

"Why don't you *not* concentrate for a minute? Why don't you relax... and listen?"

My eyes widened as I realized what he was doing. This was such a rarity, that someone would willingly invite me to listen to their thoughts; seldom did even my parents condone it. I closed my eyes, breathed deeply and carefully lowered the wall.

"*Tasmyn, trust me. I won't hurt you, ever, and if it's in my power, I won't ever let anyone else hurt you, either. I've never felt this way about anyone before. May I kiss you... please?*"

I was shaking ever so slightly as I nodded my head, barely. A smile spread over his face as he brought his other hand to my neck and gently tilted my head back. His lips brushed mine, and it was so tender and innocent that I felt tears spring to my eyes.

He kissed me again, deeper this time, and I moved my lips against his, lost in the sensation even as I heard him in my mind. "*So sweet, so soft. Tasmyn...*"

I don't know how long we sat there, but at some point he lowered his hands to my shoulders and was holding me closer. I was so involved in the kiss that I barely even heard the quiet murmurs his mind was making. Suddenly I heard a loud, "*STOP!*" and I jerked back in surprise.

His breathing was ragged, and his eyes were closed. "Sorry. I didn't mean to get so carried away."

I was somewhat breathless, too. "I only—you know, stopped, pulled back, because I heard you. You thought *STOP* really loud, you know that?"

He looked at me for one solemn moment, and then with a shout of laughter, threw himself back onto the sand.

"What? What's funny?" I was just a tad defensive.

He was still lying back, shaking with laughter. But I could feel that it wasn't derisive or mocking; rather it was joyous.

Finally he lifted his head and looked at me, still sitting as he had left me. He dropped his head and chuckled again. "You. That you exist. That I found you. That I…" He raised his head again to look at me, but this time the laughter was gone. "That you let me kiss you. That you trust me."

I had no words to reply, and the feelings rolling off him were too strong for me to comprehend at the moment. He sat up slowly, his gaze never leaving my face.

"Are you still listening to me? You know, like, *listening*, listening?"

"I'm… not getting precise words from you. Not complete thoughts, because I'm tuning into what you're saying verbally. That's normal. But I'm still getting waves from you."

"Waves?"

"Yeah, even if I'm doing a good job of blocking actual thoughts, sometimes I still get these waves of feelings from people. Especially if they're particularly strong feelings."

He smiled broadly. "And what kinds of waves are you getting from me right now?"

I giggled. "Are you sure you want me to tell you?"

"No, on second thought, there are some things better left

unsaid, right?" He stood up then and stretched. The sun was sinking ever lower behind us, and the puffs of breeze actually carried some chill. "Come on. I'd better get you home before the gators come out for their night time feed." At my expression of abject terror, he laughed again. "Kidding, just kidding."

He pulled me to my feet then, squeezing my hand as he gazed down at me. Hands still linked, we set out for home.

Chapter Fourteen

As we drove toward my house, Michael glanced at me with a twinkle in his eye.

"So," he announced, "I just remembered that I actually do have some more questions for you."

I might have been worried if I didn't hear the direction of his thoughts. I looked at him expectantly. "Okay, shoot."

"Do you always go by Tasmyn, or does anyone use a nickname?"

I laughed. "I can't believe that's what you want to know. Okay, well, most people just call me Tasmyn, but my parents call me Tas sometimes. I answer to either one."

He nodded seriously. "Good to know. And by the way, you didn't ask, but I only answer to Michael. My parents named me after an archangel, and they felt it was only right that I use the whole name all the time."

I raised my eyebrows. "So no Mike or Mikey or Mick?"

He shook his head. "Never. You said you moved around a lot. Where have you lived?"

I cast my eyes upward thinking of the list. "Hmm... well, you know about Wisconsin... going backwards before that it was Texas, Massachusetts, California, Missouri, Texas again, Delaware, Washington State, Minnesota, Virginia..."

"Wow," he whistled. "How come you've moved so much? Is your family military?"

"No, but my mom says we might as well be, with as much as we relocate. My dad is an engineering troubleshooter, and he works for a company with lots of different holdings, all over the country. They send him to a new location every time one of the plants is having a problem, or if they're getting ready to update systems, stuff like that. It works out to be every two years or so, but sometimes less, sometimes more, depending on the work needed."

"Huh." Michael looked impressed, I thought. "That makes it tough on you and your mom."

"I guess, sometimes. My mom is a freelance artist, so her work can be done wherever we live. And I just kind of go where they tell me we're going."

"Still." Michael shook his head again. "Sometimes I wish I could get away from central Florida, but I like knowing where my home is, having those roots." He reached over to take my hand and squeeze it gently. A steady warmth flowed into me.

I was still glowing when we pulled up to my house. I turned to Michael. "Would it be asking too much for you to come inside and meet my parents? Do you have time?"

Michael pulled up on the brake and turned off the car. "Absolutely. I would love to meet them. And I think it's a good idea. I want them to trust me and feel comfortable when you're with me."

I led the way through the dwindling light to the front door and went inside. I could smell my mother's spaghetti sauce from the kitchen.

"Mom!" I called.

"In here," she answered, her voice coming from the back of the house.

Michael followed me into the kitchen. My mother was at the sink, rinsing a pot, and she looked up when we entered.

"Tasmyn—oh!" She saw that I wasn't alone, and I felt

her surprise as she turned, drying her hands. "Hello. You must be Michael."

I had my mental guard down with Michael, and now it wasn't back up quite yet. I could clearly hear my mother's flustered thoughts: *I'm not expecting company! Did she invite him for dinner? She looks happy, though... so good to see her really smile... has she ever been happy like this?*

I decided to be merciful. "Mom, I wanted you and Daddy to meet Michael. Is he here?"

She smiled at us, almost shyly. "Yes, he's sitting outside, in the back. Why don't you go on out and see him?"

My father was sitting in his lawn chair, a book draped over his lap. He turned as we came outside. I saw his eyebrows rise when he spotted Michael.

I plunged right into it. "Daddy, this is Michael Sawyer. He wanted to meet you." I wondered if there were something else to say, but I couldn't think of anything.

My dad was on his feet, holding out his hand. "Michael. Good to meet you. Rob Vaughn."

They shook hands in that sober and purposeful way that men have, and I tried to hide my smile. My father was attempting friendliness and welcome, but what I was feeling was suspicion.

"Thank you, sir, for letting Tasmyn come to the park with me today. I appreciate it."

"Well, thank you for bringing her home safely. So you live here in King?"

Michael smiled. "Actually, we live right outside town. My parents own a nursery."

My father nodded. "Well, that's wonderful. Good business to be in down here. You're a junior?" Mentally I rolled my eyes. I knew I'd told them Michael was a year ahead of me.

Michael shook his head. "No, sir, I'm a senior this year."

My dad's eyes widened. "That right? You making plans for next year then?"

I decided the third degree had gone on long enough. "Daddy, you can quiz Michael another time. I'm sure he needs to get home. His parents are expecting him."

My father waved us off, "Sure, okay. We'll talk another time, Michael. Looking forward to it. Nice to meet you. Thanks for stopping in."

My mother, having recovered from her surprise, stuck her head out the door.

"Rob, Tasmyn, dinner's ready. Michael, would you like to join us? It would only take a moment to add another plate to the table."

Michael hesitated, and then shook his head again. "Thanks, really, Mrs. Vaughn, but my mom and dad will be waiting for me to eat, and I have a test in English tomorrow that I should study for."

My mom smiled. I knew she was relieved. "Well, another time, maybe?"

Michael smiled back at her, and I saw my mom's mouth drop a little. Apparently, susceptibility to Michael's charm wasn't limited to one generation of the Vaughn family.

I walked Michael to the door and out onto the porch. "Thanks for a beautiful afternoon," I said quietly.

"And you didn't even get eaten by any horrible creatures," he teased. He glanced at the door, but my parents were still in the kitchen. I could hear them rattling pots and pans.

Michael reached his hands to my shoulders and drew me near. He leaned his forehead against mine, and I closed my eyes, letting my mental block drift away.

Thanks, Tasmyn. You'll never know what this afternoon meant to me. Your trust in me... it means the world. May I kiss you good night?

My mouth curved and instead of answering, I moved my face up, so that my lips touched his. He held my face very gently and kissed me with such heartbreaking tenderness that when he released me, I was breathless.

He traced one finger around the curve of my cheek down to my chin, and then kissed me very briefly again.

"Good night," he whispered. "See you in the morning."

Chapter Fifteen

Friday was a day I thought would never end. I had my first three-minute speech due in the class of the same name, and since I hate public speaking, this was not my idea of fun. Somehow I got through it with dignity intact. The teacher gave me the same nod he did the rest of the class, so I assumed I hadn't bombed completely.

Michael and I ate lunch inside again, and Anne teased him about wanting to keep me to himself. He didn't deny it; he only laughed and rolled his eyes at her.

"Of course I want her all to myself. We have a lot to talk about, stuff to catch up on. You," he pointed at her. "I've known since we were in kindergarten. We're talked out."

Anne stuck out her tongue at him but winked at me behind his back. Michael shook his head in mock disapproval.

"Sorry about her. She's always been incorrigible."

Anne laughed. "He's just still mad that I won the hamster care award in first grade."

"Hey! I had that thing sewed up until you took Mr. Whiskers home and gave him a makeover."

"See?" Anne looked at me triumphantly. "I rest my case."

"Whatever." Michael deliberately turned his back on her and addressed me. "So... would you be interested in coming out to the nursery tomorrow? I have to work in the morning, but I could pick you up at lunchtime, and you could spend the afternoon with me. I think you'll like it... and my parents want to meet you."

It had all sounded so promising until that last part.

"Why? Why do your parents want to meet me?" Panic drove my voice up several octaves.

Michael remained serenely calm as he took a bite of a huge lunchmeat sandwich. He regarded me with amused eyes as he chewed and swallowed.

Anne popped her head around his back. "Don't worry, Tasmyn, Michael's parents are the absolute best. I love them. His mom is so cool."

I wasn't worried about loving them. I was worried about *them* loving *me*.

Michael had already figured that out. "They want to meet you because I talk about you all the time at home. They're curious. And they will adore you. Trust me."

"You talk about me? All the time?"

"Pretty much." He shrugged. "I talk to my parents. I tell them things. If that makes me weird, well..." He spread out his hands in a take-it-or-leave-it gesture.

"That's not what I mean. But what if they expect to meet the girl you've been talking about all week?"

Michael's eyes narrowed and he frowned. "Now I'm confused. What are you talking about?"

I sighed, patiently and sadly. "What have you been telling them about me?"

Brow still furrowed, he considered. "Just...good stuff. The truth. I told them that you're gorgeous, smart, friendly, kind... funny..."

I nodded knowingly. "I was afraid of that. See, now they're going to *expect* me to be what you said. And just think of how disappointed they're going to be when I turn out to be plain and ordinary." I thought for a minute, biting my lip. "Of course, you've known me less than a week, so maybe they'll realize that your descriptions weren't exactly dependable."

"I doubt it. *They* trust me."

I blew out a breath. "Point taken. I'll try to relax and be charming and gracious. What should I wear, though?"

"Why would that matter?"

Anne leaned around Michael again. Obviously she had been following the conversation more closely than I had thought. She shook her head and pointed at Michael. "He's a male. He has no clue about these things. I can help you, though. If there's room for me in Michael's car today and if you don't mind me inviting myself over, I'll come home with you after school and we'll put you all together.'

To say I didn't mind would have been a gross understatement. One of my fondest dreams, borne out of dozens of teen novels and sitcoms, involved having a girlfriend come over to play dress up and make up. I had spent the majority of my teenage years doing that by myself, and the idea of living my fantasy was thrilling. I couldn't even modulate my excitement as I answered her.

"Really? You'd do that?"

Anne laughed. "Of course. It'll be fun."

I could feel her anticipation. She was just as excited as I was, and that made me even happier. And Michael was looking at me with a combination of pride and smugness. I knew even without listening to him that he was glad I was making friends.

When I walked into History after lunch, I wasn't thinking of much beyond my afternoon plans. Which could have explained why I found myself sprawled flat on my face, books scattered, between the desks.

Or it might have had something to do with the elegantly sandaled foot that was placed directly in my path.

My face burning with embarrassment, I struggled to my feet and pulled the closest books toward me. There was a low level of derisive laughter and a buzz I knew was the thought noise of my classmates. In her seat just behind me, Nell lounged, one foot crossed over the other, a small mocking smile playing on her lips.

"Really, Tasmyn," she murmured, just loud enough for me to hear her, "you must be more careful. I see you on the floor more than I see you on your feet."

The day before I had been able to play verbal war games with Nell, but today that power was lost. I glared at her in silent fury and sat down at my desk. Mr. Frame entered the room at that moment, and I was forgotten as he announced an impromptu Friday quiz.

"We've been talking about how the Civil War actually had its roots in the earliest days of our country. I want you to take just one of those causes and write me a one page essay on how that cause evolved to help bring about the war. You'll have 30 minutes." He looked around at the room of dismayed faces. "And people, I don't think I need to say it, but no open books during this quiz."

There were groans all over the room, but I had already pulled out a piece of notebook paper and begun writing. This was my type of quiz; I could express myself without worrying about ambiguously written multiple-choice questions.

I covered one page and half of another in about fifteen minutes and carried it to the front. Mr. Frame grinned at me.

"You didn't groan," he observed to me in a low voice. "I think you were the only one."

I smiled back and replied in the same quiet tone. "I like this kind of quiz. I only hope I didn't write too much."

His eyes scanned the pages. "I'm looking forward to reading it." He winked at me as I returned to my seat.

We only had time for our weekend assignment of reading by the time all the quizzes were completed and turned in. Trig went by relatively quickly, if painfully; I sensed my peppy teacher's enthusiasm for my talent in Math was diminishing quickly.

By the time I made it to my locker, both Michael and Anne were waiting for me. "I'm hurrying," I promised.

"Don't worry. If I'm late for work, I'll just blame you. That'll make my parents' expectation more realistic, right?"

I grimaced at him and ran my eyes over my books. I needed Trig and History; I'd already finished my English and French reading, and nothing was due in Speech or Chemistry.

Slamming my locker shut, I turned. "Okay, all set."

Anne climbed into the back seat of the Mustang and flipped the seat back into position for me. "Are you sure you don't want sit in the front?" I asked for the third time.

Michael sighed in exasperation. "Tasmyn, let her sit there. I want you next to me." As he turned to back out, I glanced down at the gearshift. He followed my gaze. "I was thinking that maybe tomorrow afternoon we could work on your driving lesson. Lots of country roads out by us."

Anne let out a squeal in the backseat. "Tas, you don't drive?"

"I've never driven manual, only automatic," I corrected.

"Oh, you'll have fun," she assured me. "My dad made

me learn to drive on his truck. And Michael is probably a better teacher than my dad."

We pulled up in front of my house, and I slipped out, then moved the seat so Anne could exit. She started up to the porch. "I'll just wait up here while you two say good-bye," she said, looking at us meaningfully. "Make it snappy, Michael."

I leaned back into the car. "Have fun at work." I was still too new at this to initiate any physical contact.

Michael smiled at me. Keeping one hand on the wheel, he used the other to frame my face and leaned in to kiss me quickly. My heart thumped in response as I heard him think *Wish I could stay... tomorrow, tomorrow, tomorrow.* I grinned back at him.

"Yup, tomorrow," I whispered. He laughed before he stole one last kiss.

"Go," he instructed. "Before Anne comes back and drags you out. See you tomorrow. Have fun!"

Other than the most obvious surprise—my special talent—I had been a fairly predictable child for my parents up until our move to King. But this last week had definitely tested my mother's capacity for absorbing shock. I thought of this with some amusement when I went into her office, Anne trailing in my wake.

My mom was sitting at her drawing board, with several pages pinned up on the walls around her. She was completely caught up in her work and had barely noticed that I was even home.

"Mom," I called from the doorway. "Can I interrupt for just a minute?"

"Sure," she replied, still not looking up.

"We have company."

That caught her attention. "What? Oh!" She had finally noticed Anne. "I'm sorry, I was just... in another world, I guess."

"Mom, this is Anne Lewis. She sits at our lunch table, and she came home with me today to..." Suddenly it occurred to me that I hadn't asked yet about my trip to the nursery tomorrow. "Michael asked if I'd go out to the nursery tomorrow, to meet his parents. And Anne offered to help me find what I should I wear."

My mother looked at both of us skeptically. "You need help to figure out what to wear to a nursery?"

Anne jumped in here. "It's nice to meet you, Mrs. Vaughn. Tasmyn's just worried about meeting Michael's parents, and I'm here to calm her nerves."

"Ah..." My mother nodded in understanding. "I see."

"It *is* okay if I go tomorrow, isn't it?" I asked.

"I think so. But I thought we had a date at the mall."

"Oooh... I forgot about that." I felt guilty for blowing off my mom and our planned trip. Then I thought of something. "Why couldn't we get up early and go first thing? Michael's not picking me up until lunchtime. We could be back by then."

My mom laughed. "Okay, that sounds good. Do you girls want anything to eat or drink?" I noticed her eyes were straying to her board, anxious to get back to work."

Anne answered for me. "Don't worry about us. If we need anything, Tas will take care of it. I'm going to haul her off to her room now for some serious clothes talk, and we'll let you get back to work. It was good meeting you!"

I led Anne into my room and was pleased to notice that

she looked around approvingly.

"You're lucky to have a room of your own! I've shared with my younger sister forever. One of the perks of being an only child, I guess."

"I guess." I looked around the room myself and thought of how often I had wished for a sibling of any kind. "I think you're lucky to have the sister."

Anne laughed and flopped onto my bed. "Okay, so the grass is always greener. Open up the closet and let's get to work."

For the next hour, I had more fun than I could remember having—maybe ever. Anne loved my closet, and I was impressed by her sense of style. We finally settled on a pair of dark denim capri pants, a pretty cotton shirt that was several steps up from a simple t-shirt but wasn't *too* dressy, and a pair of flat, sturdy sandals. The shoes gave us the most trouble.

"You don't want anything too good that could be ruined," Anne explained to me. "After all, it's a nursery. You're going to be walking around in dirt. But you also can't wear anything too dressed down with this outfit."

We accessorized next, choosing a delicate gold and silver entwined chain for my neck, simple gold hoops for my ears, and a silver bangle bracelet.

"Now, if you were Brea, I'd have to do a make-up consult," Anne mused "But I like what you do—you always look good without being overdone."

I was sitting on the floor with my knees drawn up, while Anne lay on her stomach on the bed, idly waving her feet.

"I have to confess, I'm a little bit of make-up and skin care junky," I told her. "It's my guilty pleasure."

Anne leaned her hand toward me in high-five position. "Me, too! My mom is a hairdresser, so I get all the samples and fun stuff. I spent most of my Saturday nights in freshman year doing facials on myself and messing around with makeup."

"I can't imagine that. You must have had a waiting list for your Saturday nights."

Anne twirled a lock of hair around her finger. "Nah. I didn't have a boyfriend at all until last year. Thank goodness for our lunch table crowd. We've been friends for so long, they kept me from being a total social outcast."

I was really surprised. Anne was so pretty and vivacious that I assumed that she had always been popular. I knew she wasn't dating anyone at the moment, but I had seen the admiring looks that several interested seniors threw her way.

"As a matter of fact," she continued, "I really don't deserve how well they treat me. I pretty much blew them off last year when I started dating Nick."

I cast my mind around, trying to place Nick. Seeing my frown, Anne laughed joylessly. "No, you don't know him. He graduated last May. Made me all kinds of promises, how we were going to stay close, stay together when he went off to Florida State. Then the second weekend he was there, he wrote me a Dear John email."

The pain and hurt rolled off Anne in strong waves. My heart ached for her.

"I'm sorry," I murmured.

"Yeah, well… that's how it goes, right? I should've seen him for what he was. All my friends did. Jim—" she was referring to another one of our lunch table crowd "—told me right off that Nick wasn't good enough for me. He knew he was a user, he said. But I'd never had a boy pay attention to me the way Nick did, so I told Jim to mind his own business.

"They never said I told you so. When I came back this year, and I knew Brea had told them everything that had gone down with Nick, no one said anything. Michael punched me in the arm and asked when I was coming back out to the nursery, and Dan teased me about something..." She frowned a little, remembering. "Only Jim isn't really the same anymore. He still kind of treats me... differently. I don't know, maybe it's just my guilty conscience!" She gave me a half smile.

"Everyone at the lunch table has been really nice to me. I don't know them that well, but they've all been kind. I think it's because of Michael."

Anne smiled at me. "Maybe when he first brought you over, but I think they like you now for who you are. Even though it's only been a few days, we can tell. Plus, Michael likes you. We've never seen him this way about a girl, ever. And believe me, there's been plenty of opportunity."

"Really?" I was quite curious about this.

"Oh, yes. Haven't you noticed the glares you've been getting from a large segment of the senior girls? All these years they've been flattering him, following him around, making eyes at him... and you come in and have him in a day—with not that much effort."

"Try no real effort," I muttered.

"What was that?" Anne asked.

"Nothing. What about Nell Massler? Was she ever after Michael?"

Anne wrinkled her forehead, thinking. "No... not that I remember. Nell has always been sort of an anomaly, if you know what I mean. If everyone else was doing it or liked someone, Nell didn't. She's definitely more of a leader than a follower. And she's a major pain in the neck," she added. "None of us can really stand her. She surrounds herself with girls who think she's amazing, and every now and again she chooses some boy to date. It never lasts, but it gives her someone to take her to dances or whatever. Last year it was Kyle Dannon. He stuck with her longer than most of them. Then she got all involved in that chemistry club stuff and the new teacher, and she dropped Kyle because he said the teacher gave him the creeps."

Ah. Some pieces were beginning to fall into place for me. It wasn't a surprise that Nell and Ms. Lacusta were pals—or at least that Nell saw things that way. It fit with the vibes I'd gotten from both of them in class.

"Well, I don't think I have to worry about Nell in that way. She hates me. I don't know why. I haven't done anything to her."

Anne nodded. "Nell's always been that way. If she takes a dislike to someone, it's not pretty. And sometimes there's no rhyme or reason as to why she doesn't like a person. She used to target girls in elementary school and junior high—and it was ugly." She shuddered slightly. "She never bothered with any of us—we were older, we didn't much care—but the girls in her own class and below—oooh. I used to feel so sorry for them." She looked at me with a mix of sympathy and compassion. "I hope she gets tired of picking on you soon. I'd tell you to just ignore her, but the normal stuff never seems to work with Nell. There's a girl in your class—Amber Cole—Nell started harassing her in grade school and never stopped.

"I'd love to see someone stand up to her," she finished, looking at me hopefully.

I laughed without much humor. "I don't think it's going to be me," I told her. "My mind doesn't move as fast as hers does. And you're right—she's nasty." I shared my tripping story from History.

"That's classic Nell," Anne said. "And it'll escalate until she finds someone else or gets bored."

"I'm hoping for the boredom," I replied, standing to stretch. "I think my mom has chocolate chip cookies she made yesterday in the kitchen. Are you interested?"

"Chocolate? Cookies? I'm in," Anne rolled off the bed to stand. "I shouldn't. I can't carry it like you can—they'll show on my hips in five minutes. But who cares? You only live once."

Chapter Sixteen

I really love shopping with my mom. We work well together, and we know when to team up and when to split off. We found several sales racks full of cropped pants and capris, and I was able to choose a few serviceable zip up sweatshirts and jackets.

But my nerves about the afternoon were playing havoc with my good time in the morning. The whole time we were out, I was fidgety. In the dressing room, my fingers fumbled with buttons and zippers. I tried not to snap at my mother as she wandered through aisles and flipped hangers along a rack. I even let down my guard to probe her mood a bit, trying to gauge how much was real desire to shop and how much was deliberate dawdling. Her vibes were serene, which irritated me all the more.

Finally, she looked up at me, smiling as though she were oblivious to my impatience. "Well, are we done here? Do you think you're set?"

I tried to keep my voice light. "I think so." And so we were on our way home.

Once there, I grabbed my bags and flew to my room. I dropped my purchases on the closet floor and grabbed the outfit that Anne and I had selected. Somehow everything was pulled together before Michael arrived in front of the house half an hour later.

He came to the door this time, dressed in jeans and a t-shirt with the words SAWOOD NURSERY splayed across it. He smiled when he saw me at the door.

"Hey! You look great. I guess you and Anne had a good

time?"

"Thanks, and yes, we did. It was so much fun." I could feel ebullient waves of excitement bouncing off him. "So did you try to prepare your parents to be disappointed? Did you tell them maybe your earlier descriptions weren't so accurate?"

Michael rolled his eyes at me. "They're excited about meeting you. I told them you were nervous, and I think they found that endearing."

I groaned. "Oh, great."

"Tas? Is that Michael?" My mother appeared. "Hello," she smiled in greeting. "Are you two heading out now?"

"Yes, if that's okay." Michael addressed my mother with a mix of respect and deference. "And my mother wanted me to ask if it was all right for Tasmyn to stay for dinner tonight—that is, if you want to?" He turned to me, and I nodded, glancing at my mom expectantly.

She hesitated only a moment before nodding her approval. "But not out too late, please," she added.

I called good-bye to my father, kissed my mother's cheek quickly and pulled Michael out the door before there could be any more small talk.

As he got into the car, Michael looked at me and laughed. "You look like I'm carrying you off to your execution."

"No, really, I'm looking forward to it," I assured him. "We'll hang out at the nursery, and I'll get to see where you live. It'll be fun."

"Keep saying that, maybe you'll convince yourself."

"Tell me about your parents. I want to know what to expect."

Michael looked thoughtful and then smiled. I could see the love he felt for his mother and father in that smile.

"Well, they're pretty cool. They love what they do, they love each other, and they love my sister and me. Matter of fact, I was going to tell you their story when we got to the nursery, but it might make you feel better to hear it now."

"That sounds a little ominous. Don't tell me they hear minds, too?"

He gave a shout of laughter that echoed in the car. "No. At least not that I know about. Although sometimes my mom makes me think she does."

I shook my head. "Mine does the same thing. It's just a mother thing. So tell me the story."

He glanced at me sideways, and I sensed that he was slightly apprehensive about sharing something with me. "I was going to tell you this the other day, but I was afraid it really would send you running."

His concern was so sweet that I was suddenly brave enough to reach out to him. I touched his arm gently. "I'm not going anywhere, really."

Michael smiled appreciatively. "Good. Okay, so you remember what I told you, about when I first saw you on Monday? That I knew, right away?"

I grinned. "I don't think I'm likely to forget that."

"I hope you don't. Well, it turns out it's actually not such an aberration. It might be... genetic."

"Genetic?"

He took a deep breath. "Yeah. A family... thing. My mother grew up in south Florida, on the beaches down there. Her parents owned a hotel in Deerfield Beach. When she was fourteen, she went to visit her grandparents, who lived in a small town on the Panhandle. And while she was there, she met a sixteen-year old boy who had spent his whole life in that tiny town. He saw her, and he knew that she was the girl for him. According to my mother, she wasn't much to look at in those days—all gangly legs, frizzy hair and braces on her teeth—but my father thought she was the most beautiful girl he'd ever laid eyes on. She thought he was crazy. And don't get me wrong, nothing happened between the two of them then. The summer ended, and my mom went back to Deerfield Beach. But my dad knew that she was his future.

"So he got a job, and he worked hard for the rest of his time in high school. And he wrote to my mom. Every day. At first, I think she was flattered, then maybe a little worried he was a wacko, but he kept his letters pretty light—nothing too stalkerish. And whenever he could manage it, he'd drive down to Deerfield to see her."

"What did her parents think?" I was imagining the reaction of my own mom and dad under similar circumstances.

"Well, of course, they were worried, but then they got to know him and realized he was steady, serious and sane. My mom's grandparents knew the family, of course, so that was a help. And after a while, it was just... normal.

"When my dad graduated from high school, he got a scholarship to a small school that specialized in agriculture. It was close to the college where my mom intended to go. He kept working hard, saving money, seeing Mom when he could. When she graduated and started college, they got engaged and when he graduated they got married. After my mom finished college, they moved up here because it was half way between both of their family homes. My dad worked for a local nursery for a while, then they opened Sawood. It's a play on their names—my mom's maiden name was Wood.

"So that's my parents' story. And I wanted you to know it, because maybe it makes me seem a little less crazy."

"I keep telling you, I don't think you're crazy," I insisted. "Delusional or misinformed, maybe, but not crazy."

"Oh, that makes me feel so much better," he answered dryly.

We had turned off the county highway onto a smaller two-lane road that curved through empty fields and patches of forest. I saw a yellow diamond-shaped sign with a small black figure in the middle of it. Squinting, I tried to figure out what was on the sign.

Michael noticed my attention had been drawn out the window. "What are you looking for?"

"There was a sign—it looked like those deer crossing warnings? But I don't think it was a deer on this one."

"No, you're right. It wasn't. It was a bear."

"A *bear*?" I squeaked in alarm. "Are you serious?"

"Yeah. We have bears out here. They don't bother with us, but we see them from a distance sometimes."

"Oh." I couldn't manage more than that. "So, add something else to the list of creatures lying in wait for me in Florida. Alligators, deadly snakes, and bears."

"You forgot Nell," Michael commented. I stuck out my tongue at him, and he grinned.

We were slowing down, and I saw a wooden sign reading, "SAWOOD NURSERY". Beneath the large print were the words, "Landscaping, Retail and Wholesale" written in smaller flowing scrip. We turned at the sign onto a dirt road. Columns of trees surrounded us before they opened into two endless fields, dotted with rows of bushes and smaller trees. I could see several greenhouses in the distance.

"Wow," I breathed, "this is huge."

Michael looked around as if seeing it for the first time. "The original nursery was smaller, but when some land next to us went up for sale, my parents bought it. We expanded about eleven years ago."

The dirt road ended in a parking lot that backed up to two buildings. Michael pulled between the buildings and followed a smaller driveway into the woods, which opened to reveal a log cabin.

"We'll park here, but we're not going to the house yet," he announced to me. "My dad is in the fields somewhere probably, but I think my mom should be in the shop or in the greenhouse." He paused before opening his car door. "Tell me the truth. Did I spook you with the story about my parents?"

I thought about it for a few minutes before answering. "No, I don't think so," I said slowly. "It does make me wonder, though."

"Wonder what?"

"Well, I assume you grew up hearing the story about your father and mother. So what if... maybe in some part of your mind, you *expected* it to be the same for you. And then your subconscious just played into it."

I expected him to vehemently deny this idea, but instead, he seemed to consider it. For the space of several heartbeats, fear gripped me as I wondered why on earth I had mentioned this possibility. After all, what if he decided I was right? In my terror, I slipped down the wall and listened to him.

No, it's not just subconscious expectations. Doesn't she think I wondered about that? But how to convince her it's real, that's the problem. How to make her see that we belong together no matter what happened to make it that way.

Relief washed over me. He wasn't thinking of a way to let me down easily.

"A couple of things wrong with that theory," he said, choosing his words carefully. "First, let's say I did expect it to happen to me the way it did with my dad. I haven't exactly been a hermit all my teenage years. I've met girls. I've even kind of liked some girls. Nothing serious," he assured me quickly. "But still, I thought some girls in school were pretty or were fun. So if I were looking to be like my father, why wouldn't my subconscious have jumped on the bandwagon at that point? Actually, that would have made more sense. I knew those girls better than I knew you. Some of them I'd known since kindergarten. Look at Anne, even. Why not her?

"Second, and you didn't know this, so I can't blame you for thinking the way you did, this isn't just a two-generational thing with my family. It actually goes pretty far back."

"What do you mean?" Now it *was* beginning to sound strange.

"Before my dad met my mom, his father, my granddad, had experienced something very similar with my grandmother. They met and married within a week. They celebrated fifty years together last spring.

"And *his* father, that would be my great-grandfather, saw his wife-to-be across a crowded ferry boat. He lost her when they were getting off the boat, and he waited at the dock every day for three months until he found her again. They were married a month later."

"Aren't there any exceptions?" I asked curiously.

"I have a great uncle who never married. He says it's because he still hasn't met the one yet. He's sixty-four years old. Still looking for her every day."

"So… you're saying that if by some twist of fate, my father's company hadn't moved us to Florida, you would live out the rest of your life single?"

Michael was very serious as he took my hand. "If I hadn't met you, yes, I would still be waiting. I have to believe that there's something bigger than fate controlling this, though. I have to believe that if you hadn't moved down here, we would've ended up at the same college or met on a trip somewhere—something like that."

I was silent, thinking. Michael released my hand and leaned over to kiss me lightly on the lips. "Come on. My mom probably saw the car when we went past the greenhouse and she's in there thinking I'm taking advantage of you back here."

"Really?" My face flamed, mortified at the thought Michael's mother thinking we were doing anything inappropriate in the silence of these woods. But Michael just laughed at me. He slammed his own door shut and then came around to pull me out of the car.

"I'm just teasing you. She won't think that at all. She's going to love you."

Chapter Seventeen

To my complete surprise, it seemed as though Michael was right. His mother did at least appear to like me. And to me, she was amazing.

We found her in the middle of a greenhouse, working with some kind of plant. Clueless as I was about anything pertaining to gardening, I didn't know what she had in her hand. But she seemed to know what she was doing.

"Hey, Mom," Michael greeted her. "How's it going?"

She looked up, and instantly I knew where Michael had gotten his gorgeous green eyes. The smile that curved her lips stretched to those eyes, and she put down her tools and the plant.

"Hello!" She welcomed me warmly. "You must be Tasmyn. The way Michael has described you, I would know you anywhere."

"Yes, well, about that... I'm not sure how accurate Michael's other descriptions were..." I murmured. He laughed out loud.

His mother ignored him completely. "I am so happy to meet you, Tasmyn. I'm Marly."

I don't know what I expected Michael's mother to be like, but it wasn't this beautiful young woman in slim jeans and a tank top. Her hair was a little darker than Michael's chestnut brown, and although I guessed it was quite long, she wore it in a messy ponytail, with tendrils curling around her face.

The jitters about meeting Michael's parents must have made me more susceptible to sensing moods and feelings.

Wave after wave of happiness and welcome shone from this woman and made me feel joyful, too.

"Thank you," I answered her. "I appreciate you inviting me out to the nursery. It's just beautiful."

She sparkled even more at that. "We do love it. It's so rare in life, I think, that you can find something you enjoy doing and are allowed to indulge yourself. I never really saw myself working with plants, but watching Luke, I got curious... and twenty-plus years later, here we are. And I wouldn't change it at all."

I looked around the greenhouse, interested. There were tables holding what looked like identical plants up and down the sides of the building. Closer to us, I saw the beat-up wooden table where Marly had dropped her tools. It held a few small pots and some additional gadgets I assumed had something to do with her work.

I also noted a newer model radio with an MP3 player attached to it. I wondered what she listened to out here, working among all the greenery.

Marly saw the direction of my gaze. "Do you enjoy horticulture?"

"I love *looking* at beautiful plants and flowers, but I know nothing about them. My dad gardens a little, but I never really got into it. It always seems that we just get our yard perfect and then it's time to move."

Marly twisted her mouth into a sympathetic face. "Michael said you've moved a lot. That's got to be challenging."

"It's got its pros and cons. I've been happier to leave some places than others."

She reached over and grabbed my hand, again reminding

me of her son. "We hope you're here in King for a good long while. Michael, did you ask Tasmyn about dinner tonight?"

He was standing alongside of me, looking at the two of us smugly. "Yes, I did. And I asked Mrs. Vaughn if it was all right, too. It's fine as long as we don't keep her out too late."

Marly laughed. "Okay. Well, Tasmyn, we don't eat too fancy out here. I'm better in the greenhouse than I am in the kitchen, but Luke runs a mean grill. And all of our vegetables are fresh from the garden."

"That sounds wonderful," I replied, and meant it.

"Michael, are you going to give Tasmyn the grand tour? Don't forget to take her through the Christmas trees. The scent is incredible," she told me as an aside.

"Yeah, we're heading out there, if you feel sufficiently introduced."

She raised one eyebrow at her son. "Tasmyn and I haven't even begun to know each other. But give us time. We'll talk more at dinner, and I'll feel less distracted." She gestured vaguely toward her plants.

"Cool. That's our cue to leave, Tas, and let her get back to her tinkering."

Marly smiled at me. "Enjoy yourselves, you two. Dinner around six-thirty or so. Tasmyn, it was truly a pleasure to meet you."

"Thank you, Mrs. Sawyer. It was lovely to meet you, too."

We walked out of the stuffy warmth of the greenhouse into the relative cool of the outside air, and I took a deep breath.

"I know, it gets kind of oppressive in there, doesn't it? I

don't know how my mom stands it. I like to be outside in the air. By the way, she really would rather you call her Marly. She still thinks Mrs. Sawyer is my grandmother."

"Okay, I'll remember that. Sorry."

"Tas." He stopped walking and turned to me, putting both hands on my shoulders. "Stop stressing. This is not an audition or an interview. My parents are generally good, easy-going people. My mother already loves you, couldn't you tell?"

"I didn't listen to her, if that's what you mean."

He sighed in long-suffering patience. "I didn't think you did. I meant, couldn't you tell by her *verbal* clues that she likes you?"

I pursed my lips thoughtfully. "She was putting off some pretty happy vibes. And yes, she is a very warm person. I liked her, a lot," I added.

"I'm glad," he said. "It would definitely make things easier if the most important people in my life get along."

"Am I one of the most important people in your life?" I asked wonderingly.

He smiled at me, his eyes crinkling in the corners, and leaned into my ear. "You are," he whispered.

The moment seemed to freeze as I looked into his eyes. "That might be the most wonderful thing anyone has ever said to me," I told him softly. "Thank you."

"I only speak the truth." Michael dropped his hands from my shoulders and took my hand in his. "Ready for the tour?"

Sawood Nursery was a fascinating place. Michael took me into the small shop first, and I was charmed by the garden accessories and assorted knick-knacks.

"The shop was my sister Lela's idea, and it's still her

baby, more or less," Michael told me. "She does most of the buying, even now that she's in college."

Next we walked out into the fields that were adjacent to the parking lot. Michael pointed out plants to me as we wandered through, the names rolling off his tongue with ease.

"How do you remember all these?" I marveled. "Some of them look the same to me."

"I grew up with all of this," he reminded me. "This is how I learned to read. It's in my blood." He winked at me, and I giggled.

"So are you going to teach me?"

"Sure. We'll work in a botany lesson right after the driving lesson."

I groaned. "You're seriously planning to try to teach me to drive shift? You don't know how bad a driver I am. Even on cars without the extra pedal and the shifty thing." I gestured with my hand, imitating a gearshift.

"I trust you. And I am an excellent teacher, so there's no problem. Come on, let me show you the trees."

We walked through the rows of citrus trees first, and I breathed in the heady fragrance. The ground was covered with black plastic, which made it easier going here than in other areas of the nursery. Michael noticed me enjoying the scent.

"My favorite thing to do is to stand over there—" he gestured widely, "—between the citrus field and the Christmas tree field. You get the pine and orange smell all mixed in—it's the best."

We made our way toward the evergreens. I noticed that they looked much different than the Christmas trees my parents and I chose each year.

"Do you have Douglas firs?" I inquired.

"No, that's a northern tree. We import some of them already cut from North Carolina every year. Same with the frasiers. These in this field are native to Florida. The ones here—" he pointed to the row closest to us, "—are spruce pine. Then we also have sand pine and two other species of spruce. We encourage people to tag and cut their trees, because it's better, both ecologically and economically."

"Why is it better to cut down a tree? I would think ecologists would want people to *not* cut down trees."

"Well, first, we grow these specifically to be cut. And the benefit that the trees offer while they're growing is substantial. Also, remember having to transport the trees from out of state adds to air pollution, not to mention the cost of having to truck them here."

I was silent, looking at the endless rows of beautiful trees. "Will you save me the best of the bunch this year?"

"Sure. I'll tag it for you at Halloween. We don't let anyone else tag until the weekend before Thanksgiving."

"Thanks. Is that one of the benefits of being an important person in your life?"

"Definitely." We were hidden from the rest of the nursery, standing in the midst of the evergreens. Michael pulled me close to him, drawing my two hands behind his back and linking his hands around my shoulders. "It's very private here."

"It is." All of a sudden, the relaxation I had enjoyed while touring the nursery had dissipated, and I was having trouble maintaining my mind block.

"Tas... chill. Really. I can feel you tensing up. And I bet

part of that is because you're working hard to keep your wall up, isn't it?"

I flushed. I wasn't accustomed to being so easily read; usually I was the enigma who knew what the rest of the world was thinking.

"I thought so. Don't try so hard. I told you before, I don't think anything that I wouldn't want you to hear."

I swallowed over the lump in my throat. "This is all very new to me. Not only the... extra kind of sharing that I can do. But the whole—the dating thing." I had dropped my head and couldn't meet his eyes in my mortification.

"Hey." Michael moved one hand to lift my chin. "Don't be embarrassed about sharing that with me, about sharing anything with me. Okay?"

I nodded, but my eyes were still fastened firmly to his shirt, not his face.

"Tasmyn, remember, I'm new to this too. We'll get through it together, but we have to be open with each other." And then my wall totally slipped, and I could hear him continue. *How do I convince her that I'm as nervous as she is? I've never kissed a girl before her. I've slow-danced a few times, but I've never touched a girl, in any other than a casual, friendly way. I want her to realize that... I cherish her, that I won't do anything to lose her trust.*

I realized that having listened in on his mind, I owed it to Michael to be at least as honest as he was.

"I'm sorry. I know it's weird for a girl to be as old as me and not have any kind of—of experience." Again my face flamed. "I know how I feel about you, and I trust how you feel about me. You have to understand that." Finally I lifted my eyes to meet his, in an effort to underline my sincerity.

"But I also know I'm not ready yet for any extreme level of-of physical relationship. I just wanted to be clear about that, so you didn't feel like I was sending you the wrong message." I took a deep breath. "Oh, and I just heard what you were thinking, too. Sorry."

To my surprise, he wrapped his arms around me and pulled me flush against him, and I thought I felt his lips brush the top of my hair.

"Nothing to be sorry about. I told you that. And Tas, you don't need to be embarrassed about being who you are. I'm happier than I can tell you that you're not more—what did you say, experienced. I don't have any practice there, either. We're on a level playing field, okay?"

I smiled broadly against his chest and lifted my head slightly. "So we're both freaks?"

"Well, not me. I'm just very, very selective." With lightening speed, he moved his hands from around my back to under my ribs and tickled me until I was gasping with laughter. Before I could catch my breath, he had my face in his hands and was kissing me silly.

"I'm not pushing, Tas," he murmured against my lips. "And I think we need to be very cautious about being in situations where we're—well, let's just say where there's too much privacy. You *are* gorgeous, seeing you *does* make me crazy... and I don't want to put too much temptation on my plate." He kissed me again, this time a quick caress. "But I do want to say something, right now, while we're alone. And I don't say this lightly." He smoothed his hands over my hair. "Tasmyn, I love you. You don't have to say anything back. I'm not saying this to push you. But I think it's important to be up front about how I feel. I have never said that to anyone other than my parents and my sister. And I mean it, with every fiber of my being."

I was so completely overwhelmed that words were impossible. I could still hear Michael's mind, but it was in essence repeating and confirming everything that he was saying out loud, so I didn't listen very closely. The depth of the emotion emanating from him nearly knocked me from my feet.

I took a deep breath and tried to make some order of my thoughts. I knew how I felt; I'd known since Tuesday, at least. But saying it was so much harder than I'd ever guessed. Telling Michael how I felt would be surrendering any advantage I had in this relationship. Somehow this didn't matter to me anymore.

"If I say it now, will you believe me or will you think I'm just being nice?"

I could feel Michael's laughter shake his body, as his arms were securely around me again. "Well, I'd have to ask you—will you mean it, or *are* you just being nice?"

I tilted my head back to look him fully in the face. "I wish you could hear me as well as I can hear you. Then there wouldn't be any question, would there?"

He chuckled again. "No, since I'm frankly amazed you didn't hear me think it before today. I've been thinking it every day this week, just about."

"Well, I guess now *you* have to trust *me*." My heart was pounding, and I knew I had to say it before I lost my nerve. "I love you, Michael Sawyer. I may not know things the way you do, but about this, I'm as sure as I can be."

We stood in the midst of the evergreen field for another few minutes, wrapped in each other's arms and lost in the moment we had just shared.

Chapter Eighteen

My driving lesson went better than I expected, although I realized with some chagrin that it was mostly an exercise in amusement for Michael. We stuck to the dirt roads on the nursery property, and I was pleased that I managed not to crash into anything. However, I also found it nearly impossible to get the car into first gear.

"I can get from first to second and second to third," I pointed out to Michael indignantly when he was doubled over with laughter after I stalled yet again.

"That's great, but you can't consistently get from a stand-still to first gear," he answered, gasping still.

I made a face at him. "That's why normal cars don't have that extra pedal down there. Why would they make it so you have to let up on one while you press down on the other? I'm not that coordinated. I don't think anyone is."

"How do you explain the millions of people who successfully drive a standard transmission every day?"

"Freaks of nature," I informed him loftily. "Anyway, I'm finished for today. It's almost six. Shouldn't we go help your mom with dinner?"

"She's probably still in the greenhouse, but my dad might be starting up the grill. Let's go see. Here, switch seats with me. I'd have you drive us down to the house, but we'd like to eat before midnight."

I made another face at him that sent him into more shouts of laughter.

His father was indeed at the grill when we arrived at the house. Michael led me directly around to the back when he smelled the coals. Luke Sawyer was built very much like his son. His hair was blonder, and his eyes were brown, but he had the same charming smile that so captivated me in Michael. He was dressed in faded jean shorts, scruffy-looking sneakers and a t-shirt that had seen better days. He was poking at the coals in a large stainless steel tub with a thick, round stick as we approached.

"Something smells good," Michael called.

His dad's head jerked up in surprise, then his face relaxed into a smile.

"Hey," he greeted us. He laid the stick across the tub, rubbed his hand across his shirt as though to wipe it off, and then extended it toward me. "I'm Luke Sawyer. You must be Tasmyn. I'm really happy to know you."

I shook his hand and smiled, and he grinned at me in return. "Thanks, Mr. Sawyer—Luke. I'm glad to meet you, too. I had a wonderful time exploring your nursery today. It's just awesome."

His smile was sweet and mellow. "Thanks. We like it here, too. I hope you'll feel welcome enough to come back anytime." He poked his son in the ribs with his elbow. "You don't even have to bring this one if you don't want."

Michael feigned offense. "Better watch it, you'll lose your most dependable employee," he threatened teasingly.

"Maybe we'll trade up," his father replied. "Tasmyn, what do you say? Are you interested in a job in horticulture? Might be cheaper to pay you than to feed him."

I laughed. "If I learned anything today, it's that Michael's got it all over me when it comes to plants and trees. I am really impressed with his knowledge."

Luke fairly beamed. "We raised them talking the talk

and walking the walk. Michael has an affinity and talent for the growing end, like his mom and me. Lela takes more of an artistic bent—did you get to see the shop?"

"I did. It's lovely."

"And she does flower arranging, too. We're very proud of both of our offspring," Luke told me, hugging his son around the shoulders.

"Okay, enough of the sweet talk," Michael laughed. "Are the coals ready? Can we bring out the meat?"

"I have strict instructions from your mom not to put Tasmyn to work. She told me that you're to show her the house, get her something to drink and sit out on the deck until dinner is ready."

"Oh, no," I protested. "Really, I don't mind helping at all."

"Hey, when Marly gives me an order, I don't second-guess it. Go show her around," he told Michael. "I'll see you out here when you're done."

The Sawyers' home reminded me of the family themselves: Straightforward and welcoming. We went in through the back deck, entering a warm and open living room. The furniture was soft, in muted brown tones, with splashes of bright color coming from knit blankets and afghans tossed casually over the back of chairs and couches. The rounded coffee table in the center of the room was covered in magazines and books.

A hallway led off the living room, and Michael led me toward it. "This is my parents' office," he said, throwing open a door. "You can see their organizational styles are a little different." One side of the room was neat, with hanging folders, a bulletin board and shelves. On the other side, the desk was covered with papers, magazines and pictures, spilling over onto the chair.

"Believe it or not, my dad is the organized one," Michael chuckled. We moved down the hall, and Michael pointed out the bathroom, his parents' room and his sister's room.

"What about you?" I teased. "Do they make you sleep in the garage?"

He grinned. "Nah, actually I have the best room in the house. Come on."

Pulling me by the hand, he led me back out through the living room to a set of stairs that I hadn't noticed before. They opened to a huge loft, with a high, beamed ceiling and wide windows. A simple bed stood in the corner, and along the wall were a dresser and wardrobe. The floor was hardwood, with a few throw rugs scattered here and there. There was a desk in the corner opposite the bed, and a worn-looking sofa and chair were nestled on the far side of the room.

"It's amazing… how did you score such a great room?" I marveled. "I'm surprised your sister didn't want it—or did she?"

Michael laughed. "No, she didn't want it. First, there's really no privacy to speak of up here, and I guess girls like to be able to close a door. It doesn't matter to me because no one comes up here anyway, and my parents have always respected my need to be alone sometimes. And second, there's no closet in here—and Lela likes a good closet. So this has always been my space."

"Have you lived here all your life?" I asked, looking out the windows at the view below.

"No, when my parents first came here, they had a little

house not too far away. That's where they lived when Lela and I were born. But when they acquired the additional property, they decided it made more sense to live on-site, and they used some of the extra space to build what they always wanted—a log cabin. We moved in when I was in second grade."

"A second-grade boy would love all this space," I mused.

"You know it. At one point I had a hockey net and basketball hoop set up in here. My mom hated it, because of the noise it made downstairs, but she let me do it anyway." He smiled, remembering. "My parents have always been pretty tolerant and supportive."

"I guess so!" I laughed. Michael was looking at me steadily. "What?" I asked, mystified. "Why are you staring?"

"I was just thinking that this is one of those situations I have to beware of," he admitted. "The most beautiful girl in the world, the only one I love, alone with me in my bedroom… well, it's dangerous."

I felt my face heat. "Then maybe we should move along downstairs. Didn't I hear your dad say something about a cool drink on the porch? That sounds like heaven."

He rolled his eyes at me, and then laughed in resignation. "You're right, of course," he assured me, taking my hand and twining our fingers. "Doesn't make it any easier, but you're still right. Let's find you that drink."

Chapter Nineteen

Dinner with the Sawyers was relaxed and fun. I felt comfortable enough to laugh along with them at their stories of the day at the nursery, and Michael kindly shared the high and low points of our first stick shift lesson. He and his dad got another good laugh at my expense.

Marly shook her head in mock severity at both her son and husband. "I think it was very brave of Tasmyn to try something new," she proclaimed. "You two should be ashamed of yourselves for laughing."

"You weren't there, Mom. It really was funny," Michael informed her.

After dinner, I insisted on helping with dish cleanup. When Marly protested, I gathered my courage and replied, "If you really want me to feel at home, you have to let me help. I'm not used to being pampered. I'd like to help."

I saw Marly shoot Luke a secret smile before she answered me. "Thank you, Tasmyn. I would love to have your help—and your company—in the kitchen."

We worked together with the same sort of light chatter I shared with my own mother. I was enjoying myself immensely, to the point that I lowered my perpetual guard and before I knew it, I was hearing Marly.

...Like her so much... sweet girl, but something different about her too, just what Michael needs. Someone to keep him on his toes... so glad that he chose someone I can love, too. Wonder what Lela will think of her... she's been the princess around here so long...

I frowned in concentration and with effort pulled the

wall back into place. Marly, who I noticed was as perceptive as her son, saw my face.

"Are you all right?" she questioned, concern tingeing her voice.

"Oh, yes, thank you. This whole evening—afternoon, day—has been such a treat for me. You have a beautiful home, and a wonderful family. Thank you for letting me visit."

"Tasmyn." Marly laid her hand on my arm. "I don't say this lightly. You are welcome here, anytime. We love the fact that Michael's friends consider the nursery a second home, and they're here, frequently. But you're special. I hope that you'll visit often, and that you'll look at our home as yours, too. And on Luke and me—well, not as parents, certainly, but as friends, I hope."

"Thank you," I murmured. "You can't know what that means to me."

"I think I can understand a little," she answered. "Michael told us that moving your whole life forced you to be a little isolated. That's hard for me to truly understand, because I lived all my life in one place, until college and then until Luke and I lived here. And once you've found the person you're meant to be with, it doesn't really matter where you live, because where *he* is becomes home. But I can imagine that for a child—and an only child, at that—it must have been quite lonely."

I nodded. "I don't think I realized *how* lonely until I moved here—until I met Michael and found out what I had been missing," I confessed.

Marly smiled and gently hugged me to her. "As far as I can see, loneliness isn't going to be a problem anymore," she promised. "Matter of fact, you might get tired of all of us and need some time on your own. That's fine, as long as you know that we're here for you, whenever you need us."

Chapter Twenty

My first month at King High School passed much less eventfully than my first week. I fell into an easy rhythm of classes, homework—and Michael. My friendship with Anne continued to blossom, too, which I think made my parents feel slightly better about the amount of time I spent with Michael, either at home, at school or out at the nursery.

It was a new way of life for all of us, as I watched—and felt—my parents adjust to the reality of me having a boyfriend. That Michael continued to be respectful and responsible seemed to ease their minds. And Anne, who often spent afternoons at our house when Michael was working and I was free, spoke of him with such obvious affection that my parents couldn't help but be impressed. She shared the stories that Michael never would have; tales of his kindness to her and to others over their years in school, how hard-working he was, and that he had already been offered several scholarships and early acceptance to two colleges.

The idea of college and Michael going was something that hadn't really occurred to me until Anne had mentioned it. The thought of him leaving King—and me—caused such a choking panic in my heart that I could hardly breathe.

For the most part, though, I was more relaxed and happy than I had ever been. What surprised and somewhat dismayed me was that the more comfortable and settled I became in my new life, the harder it was to keep up my mental wall. It seemed that it was impossible to relax one part of me without letting down all my guards. It was frustrating to hear so much more than I wanted to know, not to mention the constant base of chatter that filled my head whenever I was in school.

On the bright side, Nell's open enmity toward me seemed to have settled into a seething hate. For the most part, she ignored me completely, as did the rest of her crowd. Occasionally she would throw a stinging barb my way, but if I failed to rise to the bait, she let it go at that. More troubling was that my lowered mental block meant that I could hear and feel even more of Nell's dark feelings. I concentrated harder on maintaining that wall in Chemistry class than at any other time; no one besides Ms. Lacusta talked to me in that class anyway, so I wasn't missing anything by keeping my head down and my mind closed.

It was difficult to keep Nell out during History, since I really liked that class and its teacher, Mr. Frame. Most of the time she kept her thoughts down to a low roar, but because the subject matter obviously bored her—unlike Chemistry, I guessed—her mind was prone to wander more in this class. I did my best to stay out of its way as it did so.

English class was usually the high point of my academic day. Well, what wasn't to like: there was assigned reading, which was cool, and the only numbers were on the pages of the books. I enjoyed Mrs. Cook, the English teacher. She was interesting and fair-minded. But on this particular day, English was slowly killing me through monotony.

We were reading Shakespeare, which is a totally worthwhile pursuit. But when you've read all the major plays on your own and done a lot of research on the meanings and nuances, class kind of drags as the teacher tries to explain these things to a roomful of students who couldn't really care less.

The bright spot on the day's horizon was a pop-quiz. That would take up at least fifteen minutes. As Mrs. Cook passed out the papers, Amber Cole slid breathlessly into the seat in front of me. She was flushed and nearly late, and not a little flustered. I empathized, because I hated to come into class late myself. But it seemed more than tardiness that was upsetting Amber. Her hands were shaking slightly, and waves of intense emotion were breaking off her and overwhelming me. I automatically took the quiz paper from Mrs. Cook and tried to block Amber. But she was emanating terror, and as I looked down at my paper, I heard her as clearly as if she were shouting: *What have I gotten into? What am I going to do? She says it'll be all right... but... what do they want from me? I don't know... should I go with them? Trust them? All these years of her torturing me... why should I believe her now? But she changed... she said she changed... I'm so scared.*

I glanced at Amber as subtly as I could. She was bent over her own page, nervously drumming the eraser of her pencil on the desk. Her body language bore out what I was hearing. And what I felt from her was nearly suffocating me.

I redoubled my efforts to tune her out and focus on the quiz. Thank heavens *Julius Caesar* was a play I knew so well. Mrs. Cook's quizzes were simple and predictable: ten short answer content questions and one brief essay question to test our ability to interpret the work. I flew through the first ten, wrote a fairly long paragraph for the last question and turned in my paper up front. Mrs. Cook smiled appreciatively at me and glanced at the clock.

"Five minutes, everyone," she announced. There were some muffled groans and muttered curses. I took my seat and tried not to stare at Amber for the rest of the class. At least it distracted me from the boredom that was English class right now.

I remembered Amber's reaction to me during my first few days at King. She wasn't exactly friendly. I hadn't thought too much of it at the time, absorbed as I was in getting to know Michael. But now I considered her. We only had the one class together, but I saw her here and there throughout the day. I tried to remember if I ever saw her with other girls, with a special boy, but nothing came to mind. I knew that Anne had mentioned Nell's long-time abuse of Amber in earlier days, and I wondered if that had anything to do with whatever was going on today.

I was glad when the bell rang, meaning it was lunchtime for me. Michael and I had fallen into a routine: he always made it to the cafeteria ahead of me because he had a free period for independent study preceding lunch. He chose our food, and I struggled to eat even a portion of what he got. Usually we sat at the table inside with his friends, which I enjoyed, since it gave me a chance to visit with Anne. But sometimes, on particularly pretty days, he would find a table outside for just the two of us.

Today seemed to be one of the outside days. I scanned the lunchroom for Michael, giving a brief wave to our normal lunch table. I didn't see Michael, but I did see Amber. She had beaten me to the lunchroom and was sitting with Nell Massler and her group.

I tried not to gape at that sight as I pushed out through the swinging door. Michael was sitting at our usual outdoor table with two trays. Most of the other tables were empty.

"Is this seat taken?" I asked as I swung my leg over the

bench. His smile was slow but sweet.

"I was saving it just for you. As you can see, I had to fight off the throngs."

"Yeah, it's pretty exclusive out here, isn't it?"

He grabbed a crouton off the salad on one of the trays and crunched on it. "Do you mind eating out here? It's quieter. But I guess it's kind of hot, too, so if you'd rather be inside…"

I shook my head. "No. Quiet is good. I wanted to talk about something kind of private anyway."

Michael raised his eyebrows and looked at me speculatively. "Good private or bad private?"

I gave him a light punch on the shoulder, and he caught my hand and held it. Happiness flooded my heart. I'd have to eat one-handed, but I was willing to make that sacrifice.

"I just have some questions for you. And I want to tell you something."

"Okay, fire away."

"How well do you know Amber Cole?"

Michael was quiet for moment, thinking. "I don't know her really well, but we've gone to school together all the way through. She's a year behind me, but I remember a little. She's always been pretty quiet. I think she had a few friends when we were in elementary school, but mostly they drifted into other groups when we hit junior high. I think she's alone a lot. Seems like a nice girl. No boyfriend I know about. Not one of the high achievers or a loser either. Just in the middle."

"Hmm," I responded. "So would it be kind of odd that she's sitting with Nell and her crew today?"

Michael made a face. "Yeah, that whole thing is odd. I

told you before Nell wasn't the nicest kid when we were in grade school. Amber was one of her targets. She used to bait her, tease her. But I've seen Amber hanging out with Nell this year. It would be pretty out of character for Nell to change her mind about someone, but I guess it happens."

I thought about that for a bit. "Anne told me before that Nell used to pick on Amber. She—Amber, that is—came into English today late and scared out of her mind. We were having a pop quiz on *Caesar*—"

"That would be enough to scare me out of my mind."

I rolled my eyes. "It wasn't test terror. That's different. That's like—'oh, darn, I didn't read the assignment, I'm going to fail this, my mom's gonna kill me'—more like dread or anxiety. This was real fear." I hesitated. Trust was something I was still learning, even when it came to Michael. "I also heard something."

"Oh, yeah?" He was nearly finished his own lunch of pizza and fries and was eyeing the roll that came with my salad. I handed it to him without a word. "Thanks. Growing boy and all that. How did you know I wanted it? Did you hear me?"

"There are some things you just don't have to have special gifts to know," I informed him. "And besides, I never listen to you without asking first."

"Never?" He brushed my cheek with his free hand and tucked my hair behind my ear. My face heated.

"You're getting off-topic."

"What? Oh, yeah, right, Amber and Nell and you hearing stuff. So what did you hear?"

"It was like she's gotten involved in something bad, or something she's afraid about. People she's afraid of, maybe.

And she's second-guessing it. Maybe something that's going to happen. Add that to her new togetherness with Nell, and to me it's weird. And I didn't mean to listen to her, by the way, but it was so loud I couldn't miss it."

Michael finished off my roll and gazed at me thoughtfully. "I know you didn't listen on purpose. You don't have to be defensive about that with me. I'll always give you the benefit of the doubt."

"Thanks. I appreciate that. I guess I am a little paranoid about it, especially now that I'm hearing so much more than I'd like."

"I don't know what's going on with Amber. It seems really out of character, both her actions and her thoughts. You really think it has something to do with Nell?"

I considered briefly and nodded.

"Then maybe you'd get more info if you listened in on Nell, if it's something to do with her that's spooking Amber."

I shuddered slightly. "Nell's mind is not a nice place. I've picked up some vibes from her, and I don't like them. She radiates darkness."

He shrugged. "Just a thought. No pun intended." He smirked.

I sighed. "Yeah, you're a hoot. And you're also right. If I want to know what's eating Amber, I should at least check out Nell." Glumly I poked at my salad. "She's in my History class next period. Perfect opportunity."

"Hey, don't do anything that's going to freak you out. I get that you're worried about Amber, but I'm sure it's nothing big."

I didn't answer Michael right away. I was thinking uneasily about my first day of King, my first day in

Chemistry, when I heard someone thinking about a blood sacrifice. At the time, it had freaked me out, but then I'd had to deal with Nell, and then there had been Michael...

"Are you really that worried?" Michael's question snapped me out of my reverie. I noticed that people were straggling out of the cafeteria and looked at my watch. Lunchtime was nearly over. I stood and pulled my hand from Michael's grip so that I could pick up my tray. He grabbed it from the table, stacked it onto his own and took my hand again, giving me that same sweet smile. As usual, my heart fluttered, and I squeezed his hand in appreciation.

"I'm thinking... maybe it is a big deal. Maybe Nell is involved in... something even more nasty than we might think."

Michael shrugged, but I saw something flash through his eyes and detected a skip in his thoughts. In answer to my inquiring eyes, he shot me a quick smile. "I don't think we should jump to conclusions about Nell. Yeah, she's not a very nice person, but still..."

"What if I told you that on my first day of school, I heard someone in Chemistry class thinking about a blood sacrifice?" I kept my voice low, as there were still some people lingering in the cafeteria as we wandered through.

I couldn't quite describe the expression on Michael's face. I might have said he was stricken, but it passed so quickly that I wasn't sure. "I guess I would have to ask you, are you sure? And if you are, then do you know it was Nell thinking it?"

"I'm sure that I heard it," I said without hesitation. "I don't know who said it, but she seems the likeliest candidate." We turned in the direction of his locker first.

"Sure it wasn't the teacher?" It was no secret that Michael found Ms. Lacusta unsettling and creepy.

"No. That I know. I can't hear her mind. When I'm near her, I just get this weird kind of... static."

Michael snorted and spun the combination on his lock. "And that's not suspicious?"

"Well, it is, but I mean that I've never picked up any of her thoughts. And having heard Nell's mind since then, I *am* pretty sure it was her. What if she's pressuring Amber into something really bad? And what if that's one of the reasons for my talent—to help people like Amber?"

"Ah, so now you're a superhero?"

I knew he was teasing me, but I wanted to be serious. "No. But if someone is given a gift, aren't they meant to use it for good?"

Michael considered that as we left his locker. "I guess I can see that. But I don't want you to make yourself crazy over this, whatever it is."

"I won't. I'll just take a little glance at Nell's mind this afternoon—" I made a face, "—and see if I can figure anything out. I don't like doing that on purpose, but I call these extenuating circumstances."

"The ends justify the means?"

"Not exactly, but I just want to make sure Amber isn't getting herself into something really dangerous."

We were in the thick of the crowd by now, and Michael leaned over to speak softly in my ear. "I really don't think Nell is into anything dangerous. Mean, maybe. Cruel. That's her thing."

I shrugged. "We'll see." We had reached my classroom, and I turned to face Michael. "Wish me luck."

He leaned into me again, brushing my cheek with his lips. "Good luck. See you at my car?"

I nodded with a smile and gave him a quick wave as I went into History.

Chapter Twenty-One

I've heard some dark thoughts before. It's just one of the delightful little benefits to my particular talent. Usually, I can't isolate whose mind is thinking these disturbing things; it happens in a crowd, or on a busy highway, with thoughts flying at me from all the people in the vicinity.

Today I knew exactly where the creepy feelings came from, and it wasn't making it any easier.

I slid into my desk, which was a row over and two back from where Nell was sitting. History was one of my favorite classes, and I was annoyed that Nell was ruining it for me.

We were scheduled to have a lecture on the early battles of the Civil War, which I realized would be an excellent cover for picking Nell's brain. She didn't spend much time paying attention in this class as a rule, and Mr. Frame's lectures bored her silly. Her mind would wander, and with luck, it would move toward Amber and whatever she was doing to scare the poor girl.

Mr. Frame put up the first slide and began to speak. I took some cursory notes, scribbled down his outline points and slid my eyes toward Nell. She was doodling on her notebook and twirling a lock of her dark hair. Slowly and carefully I let down the wall that blocked my mind from probing hers.

It wasn't the sweet relaxation that came when I was alone with Michael. Instead it was like an assault, as the random mind meanderings of twenty-seven high school juniors hit me full force. I tensed, and then concentrated on narrowing down to find Nell.

It was something odd that finally caught my inner ear. It was almost like a chant. My mom had a CD of Gregorian monks doing meditative chants, and this sounded vaguely like it, although I was pretty sure I wasn't hearing Latin. It wasn't English, and though I wasn't completely fluent in French, it didn't sound like that either. Perhaps slightly Germanic? No, too melodious for that. I couldn't be sure.

I was thinking that maybe I wasn't tuned into Nell yet, since she didn't seem like the chant type, when there was an abrupt change in the direction and tone of what I was hearing. Suddenly the darkness I had associated with Nell was there in full force. And while I wasn't hearing concrete words, I began to have flashes of images.

This doesn't happen often. As I'd told Michael, the largest component of my talent is hearing thoughts. The feelings I can detect are also fairly common and harder to block. And every now and then, instead of hearing fully formed thoughts in words, I get flashes of images. It's harder to understand and interpret these images, since often they are impressions or memories, frequently out of context.

That's what I was getting from Nell. I saw a group of girls, sitting outside in the dark. I couldn't see individual faces, but I felt familiarity. I couldn't get a grip on what the girls were doing, but I could feel what Nell was feeling—a mix of cynical pride and odd excitement. Whatever this was, Nell was the originator of the plan, and she saw herself as the one in control.

There was a shift, and I perceived that what I had seen before was memory, while now it was moving to a future image, possibly a plan. It was just slightly less defined; the same girls were there, in the same circle, but this time, someone else was present. I could see her face clearly. With a jolt of dread I realized Nell was thinking of Amber. And she wasn't thinking of her with warm, fuzzy feelings.

Instead there was an intensity of hate, resentment and... envy? Before I could delve deeper into that idea, I could see Nell imagining herself. In her own mind, Nell was even taller, more strikingly beautiful and—powerful. The power of her mind was so intense that for that moment, I was *there*, in the circle, with the other girls. I felt a mixture of excitement and terror as I gazed at Amber's face. And then Nell was behind Amber, both of them facing the girls... and me. It was with a shock of horror that I realized Nell was holding a long and deadly looking knife. As she drew closer to Amber, she raised the knife and...

I shrieked, and in that moment I was back in my seat, in History class. My head was spinning. With real effort, I pulled my mind away from Nell's and threw up my mental wall to protect myself.

The room was still tilting, and I gripped the desk. The buzzing I was hearing wasn't an influx of group thoughts; it was the blood pounding in my ears. I realized vaguely that Mr. Frame had stopped lecturing and that all the students sitting nearby were turned in their seats, staring at me.

"Miss Vaughn! Are you all right?" Mr. Frame's voice seemed to be coming from far away, even though I was dimly aware that he had left the front of the room and was moving toward my seat. I couldn't answer him yet; I was still concentrating on staying upright.

Then I felt a cool hand gentle on my neck. "Put your head down on your knees," the voice belonging to the hand instructed calmly. I followed directions mutely, and soon the room had stilled, although I was still shaking and terrified.

I ventured a glance up and recognized my new friend as a girl who was in a couple of my classes. I knew she was in my French class, but since the teacher insisted upon calling us by our French names in that class, I wasn't sure what her real name was. On the bright side, I was fairly certain that she wasn't one of Nell's followers.

At the thought of Nell, I sucked in another fast breath and tried to raise my head.

"Take it slow," my friend advised. I met her warm brown eyes, full of compassion and concern. I nodded and breathed slowly.

The entire room was focused on me, and I was feeling better enough to be completely mortified by that fact.

"I'm okay, really," I assured everyone, slowly sitting up. I scanned the room quickly to see if anyone believed me. My gaze tripped over Nell's and stuttered there. She was staring intently at me, and it wasn't concern I saw on her face. Suspicion and curiosity narrowed her eyes. I tore myself away as Mr. Frame spoke.

"Miss Pryce, would you please escort Miss Vaughn to the nurse's office? She's still looking a little green around the gills."

I realized Miss Pryce must be the girl kneeling next to me, who had taken care of me and kept me from fainting dead away. She stood and put her hand under my elbow, helping me stand.

"Sure, no problem." She turned to me. "Can you walk it, do you think?"

I nodded and tried to stand slowly. "Really, I think I'm okay. It was just—I got a little dizzy. I'll be fine. I don't think I need to go to the nurse."

Mr. Frame was already shaking his head. "No, better safe than sorry. Go ahead."

We moved out of the room and I breathed in the fresh air gratefully. Humid it might be, but at least I was away from Nell.

"Okay?" my escort questioned me.

I nodded again. "Sure. Just enjoying the air." I glanced at her. "I'm really sorry, I don't know your name. I'm new and I'm still figuring everyone out."

She laughed. "That's okay. I was new last year. I know what you mean. I called one girl Melissa for months, and then I found out her name was Miranda. I was so embarrassed! My name's Cara Pryce."

I nodded, smiling faintly. "Good to meet you. I'm Tasmyn Vaughn."

"Yeah, I know. We have French together, too."

"I thought so. Well, thanks for rescuing me. I don't know what happened. One minute it was all battles and the next I was going down."

She shrugged. "It happens. I volunteer at the hospital, in the blood bank area, so I deal with a lot of fainting. You might have a virus or something."

"Maybe," I replied. Cara paused beside an opened door. The inside was like a mini-doctor's office, with a cot, a scale and a vision chart. A red-haired woman was seated at the desk along the far wall.

"Can I help you ladies?" she asked.

Cara took charge. "Tasmyn kind of passed out during our History lecture and Mr. Frame asked me to bring her to you." She followed me inside and closed the door behind us.

"Tasmyn Vaughn, Mrs. Heiger, our school nurse."

I smiled. "Nice to meet you."

"Same here, although I'm sorry you're feeling bad. Why don't you go lie down on the cot? I'll take your blood pressure and see how you're doing." She turned to Cara. "Thanks for bringing the patient. You need a pass to get back to your classroom?"

Cara shook her head. "No, thanks, I'll just go right back and it should be fine. Anything else I can do for you?" she asked me.

I shook my head, and then something occurred to me. "Oh, wait, maybe." Perching on the cot, I turned to Mrs. Heiger. "Are you going to let me go back to class or are you going to send me home?"

"Our general protocol with fainting is to send you home. If you're going to be passing out, we want it to be in the comfort of your own home, where you're not a law suit waiting to happen. If you have a big test or something you don't want to miss this afternoon, we can see how you feel after you lie down. I might be willing to negotiate."

This was a first; I was upset *not* to have a test that might keep me in school. "No, I only have a Math class left today—and it's just another lecture."

"Then I foresee a trip home. Do you have a parent who can pick you up?"

I nodded. "My mom works at home." I turned back to Cara. "Is there any way you could let Michael Sawyer know I'm going home early? He'll be waiting to drive me. He's in English right now, in building three."

Mrs. Heiger seemed amenable. "Go ahead, Cara. Take this pass and get the message to Miss Vaughn's ride." Her voice was wry, and I flushed.

I felt stupid sitting there on the cot as Mrs. Heiger bustled around me. She took my blood pressure, pronounced it borderline low but not dangerous and decided my malady was either hormonal or viral. While I rested, she telephoned my mother and assured her that I was fine but in need of a ride home.

As I waited for my mom to arrive, my mind wandered back to Nell and what I had seen and heard in the scary place that was her head. I shivered and hoped Michael would be sufficiently concerned about me to come by the house after school. I needed to talk about this with someone, and he was my favorite candidate.

Chapter Twenty-Two

My mom is not the type to freak out about little stuff. She was very calm when she picked me up at the nurse's office, and she didn't say much on the ride home. But after we parked in the driveway, she turned to me.

"Anything you care to share with me?"

I opened wide and innocent eyes. "What do you mean?"

"You've never been the fainting type or the faking type. The nurse says you don't have a fever, and you said you're not feeling sick. Is there... something else going on, something I should know about?"

I wasn't trying to hear my mom think, but I did pick up a few of her stray theories. "Mom! No! How could you think that?" My face was burning with embarrassment.

My mother had the good grace to look slightly abashed, even as she defended herself. "Tas, I trust you... but you have a boyfriend now. I think you and Michael are responsible, but you're still... teenagers. Who fancy themselves in love. It's not that far-fetched to follow that line of thinking to a logical if unpleasant conclusion."

I barely contained an eye-roll that would have gotten me in serious trouble. "I can assure you that this had nothing to do with Michael. And I'm not—we don't—really, Mom!"

She shrugged. "Okay, okay. Well, then, what was it? What made you pass out—or nearly?"

I squirmed a little in my seat. "I was picking up some nasty vibes from a girl who sits near me, and I think it was just too much." That was true, and right now it was all I wanted to share.

"What kind of nasty vibes? Are we talking dangerous stuff or teenage girl petty stuff?"

"I'm not sure," I replied slowly. "I think just mean girl type of stuff. You know, picking on other kids."

She eyed me. "You'd tell me if it were something more?"

"If it were an emergency situation, and you could do something, I would definitely tell you. I promise." That much was true. I knew my mother was imagining school shootings or girl gang warfare. What I had seen would really freak her out, and I couldn't imagine anything she could do to prevent it.

"Okay," she sighed. "But remember, Tas—no listening to people. No matter how tempting it might be—it's not the right thing to do."

I nodded, and we went inside, to the cool of the house. I was relieved to be safely home.

"Why don't you lie down for a while and see if you feel better afterwards?" my mother suggested.

I hesitated. If Michael came by and I was asleep, I knew my mom would send him home. On the other hand, I was pretty exhausted by the afternoon.

"If I do go to sleep, you've got to promise to wake me up if Michael stops by. Okay? I really need to talk to him."

My mom's eyes flashed brief hurt. It wasn't hard for her to guess that I wanted to talk to Michael about what I'd heard and seen this afternoon, and she was feeling left out. I gave her a reassuring smile. "I just want to make sure he knows I'm okay."

"All right, I promise," she said at last.

I opened my eyes and felt a moment of disorientation.

My room was nearly dark, with just the faintest late afternoon light coming through the closed wooden shutters. I was lethargic with sleep, and with a sigh, I rolled over and eyed the clock.

Five twenty-three! I bolted upright on the bed, giving myself a momentary flashback to the afternoon's dizziness. I shook it off. Now I was annoyed, either at Michael for not coming over to check on me or at my mother for breaking her promise to wake me.

Before I could work up too much of a mad, though, my door opened and I saw my mom's inquisitive face.

"Oh, good, you're awake!" she exclaimed. "How are you feeling?"

"Much better, just fine," I assured her. "Didn't Michael come by?" I was risking getting a load of mom-sympathy if he hadn't even called.

"Yes, he came by," she began. And as I started to interrupt, she raised her hand between us. "And yes, I tried to wake you up. As a matter of fact, both Michael and I tried. But you were out like a light."

I tried not to be disappointed. I couldn't be mad at anyone, it turned out... except for Nell, who had such an evil mind that it apparently sapped all of my energy.

"But I knew you wanted to see him, and he was very worried about you, so I took pity on you both and invited him for dinner. He should be here any—" the doorbell rang, and she raised her eyebrows. "That would probably be him now."

"I'll get it!" I bounded off the bed.

"Hey! Slowly there, kiddo. Don't forget you were an invalid this afternoon."

I rolled my eyes and waved her off. "It was nothing. I'm

fine."

I dashed to the door and opened it. Michael was standing on the porch, looking off down the block. I had a moment to take him in before he turned to me, and for just a second, I felt weak at the knees again. He was simply gorgeous, and once again, I was amazed that it was me he had chosen.

When his eyes met mine, I could feel the worry he had been experiencing all afternoon. Without a word, he reached out and pulled me into him. I felt very safe and very grateful.

He leaned back, still holding me. His fingers grazed over my forehead and along my cheek as his eyes searched my face.

"Are you okay?" he demanded. "No bruises, no cuts or scrapes..."

"I was sitting down when it happened, and I never actually went under. It was a second of faintness, and everyone is making much more out of it than it was."

He pulled me close again. "I am so sorry. It's my fault. I've felt horrible all afternoon."

"What do you mean, your fault? You had nothing to do with it."

"I was the one who suggested you listen to Nell. It was something to do with her that knocked you out, wasn't it? When that girl from your class came in to tell me you had passed out and were going home—" He closed his eyes and laid his cheek on the top of my head, stroking my back. "I knew it had to be something to do with Nell."

I leaned back slightly and held up my hand. "Hold on just a minute. I don't want to get into this here."

Opening the front door, I leaned inside. "Mom! How long til dinner?"

She appeared in the hallway that led to the kitchen. "About half an hour. Why?"

"Would it be okay if Michael and I went for a quick walk before we eat? I want to get out in the air a little bit."

"Do you think that's a good idea after today?"

"Mom, Michael will be with me the whole time. I promise, if I get even the tiniest bit dizzy, he'll throw me over his shoulder and bring me home."

She smiled. "Okay. Be careful, and be back in half an hour."

"I promise."

I closed the door behind me and offered Michael my hand. "Shall we?"

We turned down the sidewalk. "First of all, it wasn't your fault. It was a good idea, and I would have done it anyway. And it's not your fault or mine that Nell is evil."

"Evil?" he asked, surprised.

I filled him in on what had transpired that afternoon in History class. I watched his face carefully and was relieved to see not a hint of disbelief there.

"A knife? Are you sure it was a knife?"

"Positive. A big and nasty knife."

He was very serious now. "I don't know what to make of it. Could it be just Nell—I don't know, fantasizing or something?"

"Well, yuck, even if she's fantasizing, the girl needs help. And if I had wandered onto this image by chance, I might have thought the same thing. But adding it to what I heard from Amber today, I have to say, no, this was more of a concrete plan than wishful thinking."

"So what do we do? Can we tell a teacher or the police

or something?"

I had been mulling this over all afternoon. "I don't think we can. We'd have to lie in order to do it. I can't risk telling anyone exactly how I came by this information, even if I thought they might believe me. I considered telling my parents, but I'm afraid they'd overreact and pull me out of school. And then probably out of the state."

Michael's brow furrowed. "We definitely don't want that. So can't we just say we overheard Nell making these plans?"

"I don't even know what the plans are, exactly, except they're not good. And Nell will know that we never overheard her, because she probably never talked to anyone else about this. Whatever 'this' is."

"The chanting you mentioned... that was weird. Do you think you remember any of the words? Maybe that has something to do with it."

I wrinkled my forehead. "I don't know. Maybe. I know I can't tell you any of them right now, but if I heard it again, I might recognize it."

He seemed troubled, more so than he had before.

"What? What are thinking that you don't want to tell me?" I demanded. I could only feel an usual reticence and reluctance.

He shook his head slowly. "I don't know. I've lived here all my life, and there's been talk, but I always thought that was all it was. Like tourist hype, you know. My parents always told me it was just that. But they also won't live in town."

"What kind of talk? I don't know what you're saying."

"I told you about how the town was started, with King

bringing his carnival people here to settle. And he played up the whole mystical angle, remember?"

"Yeah, you mean like the people in town who boast about being the descendants of the bearded lady or the sword eater?"

"Right. So the town still plays up that part. You've seen the shops downtown, with the crystals and the books and all that stuff?"

I nodded.

"If that was it, if it was just play—well, you understand that it brings people in and makes money for the town. Whatever. But there've always been undercurrents—rumors and talk—that there's more to it than that. That maybe there's still people who take it seriously."

I felt a chill run down my spine. "What are we talking about here? Cults?"

"The occult, definitely. Witchcraft, I guess, for lack of a better word."

"Do you know anyone involved in this?"

He hesitated. "Not really. Like I said, it's mostly talk. You hear things, but you don't always buy it."

I blew out an exasperated breath. "I feel like you're hedging. Like there're things you're not really saying."

Michael had slowed his walk and now he stopped completely and turned to face me. He moved his hands to my shoulders and rubbed my arms.

"I'm not trying to keep anything from you. I just don't want to say something that's going to frighten you, because I'm not even sure it's true." He glanced around, seeming almost uneasy. "And call me crazy, but I don't really want to talk about this out here."

I glanced at my watch and sighed. "It's time to head back for dinner anyway. But do you promise you'll tell me more later?"

He smiled in that way he had, with his eyes and his mouth, and leaning into me, dropped the lightest of kisses on my lips. "I promise."

My mother had been kind enough to invite Michael for dinner, but she hinted broadly after dessert that I needed an early bedtime after my rough afternoon. Michael took the hint, perhaps a tad too easily for my liking, and after offering to help with the dishes (and my mom turning him down), he made the excuse of homework and said good night.

I walked him to the door. "Homework?" I asked, one eyebrow raised.

"Actually, it's true. I do have to finish up some Math problems."

"But you promised to tell me more about—the town."

He smiled and pulled me out the door with him onto the porch. "I will. But not tonight. We'll talk tomorrow."

"I guess I can wait."

Michael took my face in his hands gently and leaned down to gently touch my lips with his. I moved my arms around his neck to deepen the kiss, and his hands dropped to my neck. I opened my mind to him and felt the most heartbreaking tenderness I had ever experienced. The urgency and passion I usually detected were still there, but much farther below the surface, buried under the leftover worry.

Slowly he pulled back, his hands back on my face, stroking my hair away from my eyes. "Good night, " he whispered. "See you tomorrow."

Chapter Twenty-Three

There was still residual worry hanging around the next morning, both at home with my mom and in the car when Michael picked me up. I was feeling fine, but the two of them looked at me as though I might drop any minute.

"Are you sure you're okay to come back?" Michael asked me for the third time as we drove through town.

"I'm beginning to think you don't *want* me to come back," I complained.

He sighed impatiently. "You know that's not true—or at least, I hope you know it's not. I just worry. Not only about whether you're recovered from yesterday, but also—you know, Nell. What if she tries to pull something?"

"I don't think she has any reason to be suspicious," I said slowly, trying not to think of her narrowed eyes watching me the day before. "So in her mind she wouldn't have any more reason to hate me today than she did yesterday."

"She seems to be able to hate you without any specific cause," Michael observed archly.

"True enough, but that means I'm in no more danger from her today than I was before. I'll steer clear as much as I can." I was already dreading Chemistry, but I decided to keep that to myself. I bit the side of my lip, trying to think of a legitimate excuse to miss that class.

"I actually had a thought about the whole Nell situation,"

Michael said, interrupting my scheming.

"What's that? Does it involve humiliation and mortification on her part?"

He rolled his eyes at me. "You talk big, but you know you'd never let me really do anything fun to her. Problem is, you're way too nice a person."

I raised my eyebrows and blinked slowly. "Unlike you, of course?"

Michael furrowed his brow and tightened his jaw. "I'll do whatever I have to, if I have to." He glanced sideways at me, to see if I was buying it. I wasn't, still gazing at him with lifted brows.

He relented, grinning. "So maybe it would be a last resort." Then his grin faded, and the worried look returned. "But if she keeps messing with you, I won't hesitate to more than humiliate and mortify. I'll do what I have to do, to keep you safe, under any circumstances."

I believed him. I could feel the determination in his words. Tactfully I changed the subject.

"What was your idea about Nell?"

"It's not so much about Nell as about Amber. We know that approaching Nell isn't going to do any good. And we know that our hands are tied right now as far as any outside authorities, teachers or the police. Nothing's happened for us to report. But why can't we talk to Amber, see if she'll spill about what's going on?"

This was so obvious that I wondered why it hadn't occurred to me. I considered for a moment. "Not a bad idea at all. But what if Amber goes to Nell and tells her what we're saying?"

Michael nodded, and I knew he had already thought of

this possibility. "She might. We'd have to approach her. . .carefully. Say nothing about anything except what anyone in the school might have observed, like Amber sitting with Nell at lunch. If you just casually mentioned that subject, maybe she'd open up to you."

I gaped at him, panicked. "Me? I thought it would be you—or even *us*. Amber won't speak to me under normal circumstances. It would be really weird if I just starting asking her stuff out of the blue."

We had pulled into the parking lot, and Michael switched off the car and turned in his seat, laying one wrist over the steering wheel. "Can't you just start talking with her casually? Girls do that, right?"

I was exasperated. "Girls might do that, but *I* don't, and even if I did, Amber really doesn't like me, I don't think."

He looked at me steadily and shook his head. "How is it that two girls could dislike someone like you so quickly? I don't get females."

I patted his arm. "Don't feel bad. Most boys don't."

Michael sighed. "I guess it would make more sense for us to talk to her together. I could ask her why she's pals with Nell all of a sudden."

"Or maybe it would be better for *you* to talk to her alone. I'm telling you, she really doesn't like me. She won't even look at me in class."

He swung open his door and climbed out of the car. I did the same on my side, grabbing my bag from the backseat. "I'll see if the opportunity presents itself, and if it doesn't, we'll find her this afternoon. Okay?" He met me on my side of the car and reached out to grab my hand.

Happiness flooded through me, as it always did when

Michael touched me. The simple act of holding his hand still amazed me. My smile must have given me away, because when he caught sight of my face, he pulled me closer to his side.

"Hey, remember what I said about that smile. It's only for me."

I laughed. "You can't fool me. I know you're not that insecure." I leaned my head against his shoulder briefly. "Besides, you know that all my smiles are for you."

We were quiet as we walked into school, wrapped up in our own cocoon of contentment. As we approached my locker, I heard a voice call my name.

"Hey, you're looking more alive today." It was Cara Pryce, my rescuer from the day before.

"Hey!" I greeted her. "Thanks again for not letting me humiliate myself more than I did yesterday. If you hadn't been there, I think I would've gone down."

"No problem." She glanced at Michael, and I remembered my manners.

"Cara, do you know Michael Sawyer? Michael, Cara took care of me yesterday and got me to the nurse in one piece and upright."

Michael smiled briefly. "Yeah, Cara came into class to tell me where you were." He nodded to her. "Thanks again for that. I would've been wondering what was going on."

"Glad I could help," Cara replied. "Are you feeling better, then?" This was addressed to me.

"Yes, thanks. It must have been just a temporary. . .thing." I tried to keep my tone vague.

"Well, that's good. I guess I'll see you in French?"

"Sure, see you there," I answered, and Cara turned to

walk away.

Michael reached out to tuck a curl behind my ear. "She seems nice. I'm glad she was there to help you yesterday."

"Yeah, me too. She was cool about it, didn't make a huge deal. And she talked to me, which is more than I can say for most of the people here." I gave him a half smile. "Present company excluded, of course."

Michael returned the smile absently, his mind obviously elsewhere. "It would be good for you to have a friend to watch your back when I can't be there. I don't know much about her, except that she moved here last year. Her dad is the pastor at that new church right outside of town."

I frowned. "Really? She's a pastor's kid? Huh. I wouldn't have guessed."

We had walked to Michael's locker, and I leaned back against the wall as he sorted through his books. He poked his head out to look at me quizzically. "Do you have something against pastors' kids?"

"No, not exactly. I've known a few—went to school with them, I mean—and usually what's inside their head doesn't match up with what's outside."

"That's a very cynical attitude."

I shrugged. "I don't like hypocrisy. And I'm in the unenviable position of knowing more about it than most people. I always know when people's real motives don't match their actions. We went to churches sometimes when I was younger, and it was usually the most pious people who had the most wicked thoughts." I looked down at my watch. "I've got to get to French. That's one teacher who really likes me, so I don't want to ruin her impression of me. See you at lunch?" I still asked the question every day, not quite believing that I never had to eat lunch alone again.

"I'll be there. Hey." He grabbed me by my backpack and pulled me back toward him. His face was very close to mine, and all I could see were his eyes. He moved his hand from my bag to my neck, stroking lightly, and then used his other hand to gently brush my hair away from my face. "Have a good morning. Be careful. Stay conscious. And give Nell lots of room, okay?"

I could hardly breathe for his nearness, but I managed a brief nod before he released me with a smile. I tossed him a brilliant grin in return and headed to French.

Cara had an empty seat next to her when I entered the classroom, and I hesitated, wondering if it would be pushy to choose to sit there. Before I could decide, Cara saw me and smiled, gesturing to the desk beside her. Gladly I slid into the seat just as the teacher turned to begin class.

Today we were working on written translations as a group. We took turns doing sentences, each one going up to the board in turn to write the English equivalent of the French words. When Cara went up for her turn, I contemplated her thoughtfully. I wouldn't have pegged her as the daughter of a minister. She was pretty in a way, with her dark blonde hair worn in a short bob. Her eyes were brown, and her features were not remarkable. I realized it was the gentle twinkle in her eye that made her look likable. She was dressed like the rest of the girls, in jeans and a short-sleeved shirt. I tried to remember if I had seen her hanging out with any particular crowd, but I couldn't recall.

We finished the translations, and Madame assigned our homework. She called a student to her desk to go over some missed work, allowing us to talk quietly among ourselves.

Cara turned to me, smiling. "Are you adjusting to life in Florida yet?"

I smiled, too, ruefully. "Well, it's different. But I think I'm settling in, thanks."

She raised her eyebrows at me significantly. "Maybe with a little help from a certain senior?"

I flushed. I had seen looks from some girls, both seniors and juniors, who seemed to resent my relationship with Michael. I remembered Anne telling me that Michael had been the object of much unrequited love. And I knew that those girls were wondering what I had done to ensnare him. It would be impossible to explain that I hadn't pursued him at all, and I doubted any of them would believe it.

I wondered if Cara could be counted in the numbers of the girls who had sighed after Michael from afar.

"Michael… has been a big help," I answered carefully. "He was friendly to me from my first day here, when I was feeling very alone."

I waited to feel skeptical waves coming from Cara, but instead, there was only interest and friendliness.

"It's hard to be the new girl, isn't it?" she mused. "Last year was the first time for me. I'd lived all my life in Pennsylvania, and then we moved here. I didn't know it would be so hard."

"I've been moving all my life. I don't think it ever gets easier."

"The worst part was lunch. I didn't have anyone to sit with, and I decided to just be bold and find a table." She widened her eyes for dramatic effect and leaned toward me, dropping her voice. "I sat down with *Nell Massler* and her group. Whoa!" Cara rolled her eyes. "Talk about the deep freeze. They totally ignored me. I went home that day and cried for an hour. I told my mom I was hitchhiking back to Pennsylvania."

I nodded sympathetically. "I know what you mean. Lunchtime is the worst at a new school. What did you do the next day?"

She grinned. "I went in that morning to my first class and sat down next to a girl who didn't look threatening. I made myself talk to her until she talked back, and when she did, I groveled and asked if I could sit at her lunch table. I guess she felt sorry enough for me, because she said yes. I've been sitting there since, even this year." She paused, and then went on, "I wouldn't say I've made any best friends, but I don't sit alone at lunch."

I smiled. "That was very brave of you. I would still be sitting at a table by myself if it were me." I glanced up at the clock. Class was nearly over, and I was pleased; I had managed to have a normal conversation without hearing anything from Cara's mind. Maybe I could pull this off after all.

I thought about inviting her to eat lunch with Michael and me, but before I could, the bell rang. I gathered my books and gave her a quick wave. "See you in History?"

She smiled. "Sure! Try to stay conscious for Mr. Frame's battle lecture today, okay?"

I laughed and made a face before heading off to Chemistry.

I was determined to maintain a low profile in this class today, but as it turned out, that wasn't necessary. Nell's seat was empty.

I sat down next to Liza, who appeared completely

engrossed in her Chemistry book. Casey didn't turn from her desk either. I looked over the notes from the day before, preparing for class. Chemistry was still a challenge to me, even when Nell was absent.

"Tasmyn." The voice startled me from my absorption, and I jerked my head up sharply. It was Ms. Lacusta, standing quite close to my desk and smiling in her odd way.

I fought to keep myself calm. Ms. Lacusta rattled me almost as much as Nell did sometimes, and today she was much too close to me for comfort. I could feel the troubling waves breaking from her direction.

"I wanted to speak to you about your last quiz," she continued. "You did very well. I'm impressed with how quickly you've caught up here." She paused, seeming to expect some reply from me.

"Thank you," I said faintly.

"I think you would be an excellent candidate for my chemistry club," she continued. "We meet once a week, and we do some—extracurricular Chemistry work. Participation can potentially enhance your class grade, and it will also give you the opportunity to… get to know some of your classmates."

The idea of spending more time with Ms. Lacusta *and* Nell (whom I was certain was active in this club) really didn't sound like fun to me; in fact, it sounded like a nightmare. But I really couldn't afford to offend this teacher. Not only did she control my grade, she spooked me for reasons I couldn't explain. I wondered how I could delicately decline. I decided on my old fall back: parental authority.

"I would have to check with my parents first. They're very strict about my activities. Thank you, though, for the invitation," I added.

Ms. Lacusta gazed at me for a moment, and then she merely nodded. "Of course. You'll let me know, then." She swept up to the front of the classroom and took her normal, ready-to-begin-class stance.

I breathed a careful and quiet sigh of relief. I was absolutely sure that I wanted nothing to do with Ms. Lacusta's club, and I was fairly certain that my parents would back me up if I presented it to them the right way. They had never forced me to participate in anything, and I doubted they would begin now.

I wondered suddenly if Ms. Lacusta's invitation had been prompted by Nell's absence. The weird relationship between teacher and student gave me the creeps, the way Nell stared at Ms. Lacusta, with an odd mixture of awe and cunning, and how often Ms. Lacusta's gaze rested on Nell.

I caught Casey and Liza exchanging furtive glances, and in my anxiety I heard Casey thinking, *Can't believe she did that... Nell is going to be livid. Marica knows she hates that girl... do I tell Nell? If I don't, Liza might... Nell will think I'm keeping secrets... so nasty when she's annoyed...*

It was interesting to hear how Nell's closest friends thought of her. There was more fear than affection, reminding me of the hypocrisy Michael and I had discussed earlier. I didn't exactly feel sorry for Nell, but it made me wonder about her whole group. Perhaps even sadder than having no friends at all was knowing that the people around you were motivated by something other than friendship.

Chapter Twenty-Four

Michael was sitting outside again today, and I joined him, shaking my head in quiet resignation as I looked at the trays of food. He greeted me with the smile that lit up his face, grabbed my hand and gave it a light squeeze.

"Hey," he said, looking up at me. "How was your morning?"

"It was good," I replied, realizing that it had been. "Nell isn't here today, so that is one excellent piece of news... you don't think she left for good, do you?"

Michael laughed. "No, I don't think she did. Even Nell takes a day off every now and then. I'm glad you got a break."

"Me, too," I agreed with heartfelt fervor. "And not only that, I think I might be on my way to another first in my life."

"What's that?" He took a big bite of the pasta on the plate in front of us.

"I think I might be making a new friend, all on my own. Not that I don't love Anne," I hastened to assure him. "I do, and she's been so terrific to me. But she's your friend too, and for me to actually meet someone on my own makes me feel good. I sat next to Cara today in French, and we talked a little bit. I almost asked her to sit with us at lunch, but I wasn't sure if we'd need some privacy." I shook my head sadly as Michael leaned toward me in a mock leer. "C'mon, you *know* what I mean. I thought you might have some news about Amber."

"I knew what you meant... but you can't blame a guy for hoping," he sighed, then sobered. "I'm glad to hear about

Cara. She seems nice. She'd probably be a good friend for you, I think. And actually, I did get a chance to talk with Amber."

My eyes widened. "Really? You did? I thought you were going to chicken out on that. I'm amazed."

"Chicken out?" Michael's voice raised in disbelief. "That's crazy. I told you I'd talk to her if I got the opportunity, and, well, I got the opportunity. She came into the library when I was there for independent study, and I managed to get her by herself."

"That must have been interesting," I commented.

"Oh, it was," he agreed. "I had to turn on the charm."

"Ahhhh..." I nodded. "I see. So she never stood a chance."

"Nope," he said smugly. "Never. Fate threw us together and gave us a study hall monitor who couldn't care less if we talked, as long as we were quiet about it. So we did. Talk, I mean."

"And...?" I prompted.

"And... apparently this friendship with Nell isn't as new as we thought. Amber says Nell has been talking to her, asking her to sit with them at lunch, since the beginning of school. I asked her why on earth she'd want to be friends with Nell, after all the years of torture. She just kind of shrugged and looked—I don't know, almost guilty. She said Nell explained a lot to her, and now she understands more. And she said Nell can be almost sweet."

I choked on the fries I was nibbling. "*Sweet?* Are you kidding me? Are we talking about the same girl?"

"Yeah, I kind of felt the same way, but I covered it up. Amber says Nell has introduced her to all her friends and now, after a few years of being pretty lonely, Amber has friends. And I thought you'd find this interesting, too—Nell has gotten Amber involved in some club that your Chem. teacher runs."

I was surprised, but I shouldn't have been. Whatever Nell was up to, I had a strong feeling that it involved this club.

"Isn't that a coincidence?" I remarked to Michael. "Ms. Lacusta invited me to join her chemistry club today."

Michael raised his eyebrows. "And what did you tell her?"

I gave him an innocent look. "Why, I have to ask my parents, of course. I would never commit to something without checking it out with them."

"Of course," he nodded. "Good idea. Will they back you up?"

"Oh, I think so. I'm not joining their cozy little group, don't worry. Ms. Lacusta creeps me out big time."

Michael frowned. "You think she's involved in this, somehow?"

I shook my head. "Not sure. But speaking of coincidences, I don't think it's one that Ms. Lacusta asked me about the club today, when Nell was absent."

"Do you think she's afraid of Nell?"

"Not afraid, no, but maybe she thought Nell would throw a fit if she heard her inviting me, and she wanted to avoid..." I searched for the right word. "Unpleasantness."

"Got it," Michael said, nodding again.

"So did you ask Amber about anything going on with Nell that's scaring her?" This was the real crux of the matter, in my opinion. If Amber was stupid enough to want to pal around with a girl who used to make her life miserable, that was her business. It was her safety that concerned me, not her sanity.

"I tried to hint around as much as possible. She starting getting real uneasy when I asked her about the chemistry club and what they do. I said that Nell strikes me as someone who'd be dangerous with chemicals, and Amber—well, she got a little freaky. She told me I didn't know what I was talking about, and then she blew my cover."

"What do you mean?" I asked, bewildered.

"She said she knew Nell despises my girlfriend—that was her word, 'despises'. She said she didn't know what your problem was, but Nell said you were making trouble in Chemistry class. She said you blamed Nell for things that were your own fault. I couldn't get her to give me specifics, and then she just clammed up."

"So do you think I'm crazy?" I asked him. "Now that you've talked to Amber?"

Michael shook his head. "I never did think you were crazy," he reminded me. "But I could tell something's going on with Amber. When I asked her if Nell would have a problem with her talking with me—because I'm your boyfriend—" even in the midst of this, he smiled at those words, "—she got very upset. She said Nell would never believe me, that Nell trusted her, and she started shaking. And then she just got up and walked out of the room."

I shuddered. "So she does seem to be afraid of Nell. That fits into place."

Michael nodded. "Seems to." He finished the last morsel of food on our trays. "I think we made a good start today. No matter how it ended, I hope she knows that she has someone she can talk to now, if things with Nell get too intense."

"She's not the only one who's living in fear of Nell. I picked up some interesting tidbits from Casey in Chemistry. I get the feeling that Nell's is a reign of terror, not of love."

Michael frowned; something was troubling him, but it wasn't anything he was going to share with me at the moment. He stood, stretching, and I watched him stack our trays. Lunch was almost over, and I was actually looking forward to History today, knowing Cara would be there and Nell would *not*. It was shaping up to be a decent afternoon.

Michael had to work at the nursery that afternoon, so our ride home was brief. As I slid out of the car, he caught my arm and pulled me back, cupping his hand around the back of head and drawing me closer for a brief kiss.

"I'm glad you're feeling better today," he murmured. "Wish I could come in with you... are you sure you don't want to come over to the nursery with me?"

I smiled against his lips but shook my head. "First, my mom is still a little jumpy after yesterday. She's going to insist on an after-school nap, I just know it. And second, you know I'd only be a distraction if I went home with you. That's not fair to your parents. I want them to *like* me, not resent me."

Michael chuckled softly. "No way they could resent you. They might harass *me*, but they think you're perfect." He caressed my neck and rubbed his nose against mine. "Of course, I tend to agree with them."

The glow of happiness and contentment that always appeared when I was with Michael surrounded me. I could sit in the car with him all afternoon... but reluctantly I pulled back. "You've got to go to work," I reminded him.

He sighed. "I know. I'm going. I'll call you tonight, okay?"

"Yeah..." I moved to the door again, and then turned back. "I haven't forgotten that you owe me a conversation from yesterday. About the occult in King, and what you didn't want to say when we were out."

Michael nodded, his smile fading slightly. "I haven't forgotten either. Can it wait until this weekend? You could come out to the nursery with me, and we could talk there. I'd rather it happen out of town."

"Now you're scaring me," I said.

"Nothing to worry about. I'll talk to you tonight," he repeated. "Have a good nap."

I rolled my eyes at him as he drove away.

Chapter Twenty-Five

My mind was racing, and I tried to calm down. Where would Amber be right now? And would she believe me even if I did find her?

The first thought that leapt into my mind was: find Michael. He'd know what to do. Where would he be? What class did he have this period?

And why was it so dark if we were in the middle of the school day?

With a jerk and cry, I came awake, still breathless, my heart racing. It was a dream. Just a dream. But it had seemed so real. I tried to remember what I could of the content, beyond the terror that had overtaken me near the end. There was something to do with Amber. Somehow in the dream I knew she was in grave danger, and no one could help her but me. I recalled feeling helpless as I tried to figure out what to do.

The bedside clock read 3:17. I took a deep breath, closed my eyes and tried to stop the shaking in my arms.

Could my subconscious be trying to tell me something? It wasn't strange that I would be dreaming about the Amber situation, given that Michael and I had spent a good part of the day discussing her. But what I had dreamed seemed not so much a memory or the jumbled flotsam of the day as it did… something else.

I was wide awake and not a little spooked. Jumping out of bed, I turned on the bedside light, which instantly comforted me a little. My room was exactly as it should be, everything in place. I grabbed my laptop from the desk and climbed back under the covers. It was too quiet, I decided, so I found some headphones in the drawer next to my bed, plugged them into my computer and flicked the music onto shuffle. Perfect.

The music reminded me of the chant that I had heard coming from Nell's head, right before the scary stuff started. Michael had suggested it might be helpful to know more about it, and I hadn't followed up on that yet. I opened the Internet to my favorite search engine, and then paused. What to enter? Weird chanting? I thought about it for a few seconds before I typed in, "Chanting and the occult".

Over two hundred thousand options appeared. My eyes widened. Most of the links were new age information pieces, which of course it might have been... maybe Nell was into crystals and all that? Somehow it didn't seem likely to me. These seemed to be mostly innocuous articles about lightness and goodness and peace, and none of those applied to Nell.

About halfway down the first page, I saw a simple line reading "The Occult and Music/Chanting". I clicked on it, scrolled down through several pages of musical history, skimming it to see that nothing related to what I had heard. Finally, a line caught my eye: *Chanting can be an integral part of spell casting and the working of magiks. Most spell chanting is performed in the ancient languages such as Latin, although there has been a recent movement toward using a primitive Egyptian as well as other African tribal tongues. Some smaller sects utilize their own mother tongues, including Russian, Greek or Romanian.*

Something clicked. I was sure that Nell had not been thinking of Latin chanting; I knew it wasn't Egyptian or African, and I didn't think it sounded Greek. I thought

Russian or Romanian might be stronger possibilities.

I copied that part of the article and pasted it into a blank email. Above it, in bold print, I added,

Found this online. Maybe it was Russian or Romanian? Any thoughts? See you in a few hours.
Love,
Tas

I typed Michael's address in the TO: section and hit send.

I closed the computer and put it next to the bed. Sleep was what I needed now, even if I was still a little jumpy. I knew the sleepiness would end up hitting me in mid-morning if I didn't catch at least another two hours. So I burrowed my face into my pillow and wrapped the blanket around my shoulder, up by my ears.

But I left the bedside light burning. Just in case.

When I got into the car the next morning, Michael was looking at me speculatively.

"Insomnia?" he inquired.

I sighed. "Bad dream, which led to about an hour of missed sleep. So I made the most of it."

"Well, as nice as it was to wake up to an email from you, I'm sorry about your bad dream. At least you accomplished something while you were up."

"What did you think my information?" I asked.

"Hard for me to say, since I didn't hear the chant."

I frowned slightly. "I wonder if there's any way for me to hear Romanian and Russian, to see if either sounds familiar."

Michael's face brightened. "I bet if you searched 'Romanian' under video or audio, you'd find some site in that language and could listen to it."

"Good idea. I'll check after school today."

"What was the dream about?"

I blew out a breath. "Amber, Nell... bad scary stuff. I was trying to find you, but it was night. Really dark." I shuddered a little, remembering. "I knew if I found you, I'd be okay."

He reached over to grip my hand briefly. "You'd be right."

We were both quiet for the rest of the ride.

At my locker, I pulled out my books while Michael crammed for a History test.

"I can never keep the order of the British monarchs in line," he was complaining to me, when abruptly I felt a change in the air around us.

"Michael." I knew the voice, and it seemed my nightmare was suddenly upon us. Nell stood behind me, turned to face Michael. She was wearing jeans that hugged her body, and a light black shirt. Her hair fell straight down her back, and her odd blue eyes were icily livid.

Michael didn't move from where he leaned against the lockers next to mine. "Nell," he returned, gazing at her levelly.

"I was very disturbed last night when I spoke to some of my friends." Nell kept her own voice modulated, even as her face clearly displayed anger. "Apparently you were harassing one of them."

Michael made a show of innocence and ignorance. "I

don't know what you're talking about."

"I'm talking about Amber," Nell all but hissed. "You cornered her in the library yesterday and intimated some not very pleasant things about me."

"I did talk with Amber yesterday in the library, but what we said really had little to do with you. I've known Amber for as long as you have, remember. And maybe *my* memory of the past is even a little clearer than Amber's."

Nell regarded him steadily for a moment. "What happened in elementary school was a long time ago, Michael. And I wouldn't expect you to understand the female mind and how it works. Amber and I are past all that, and we're friends now. Would you take that away from her?" For the first time, Nell shifted her gaze to me. "Is this a way to strike back at me for what your—your *girlfriend*—" she snarled the word, "—imagines I've done to her? What's the matter, Tasmyn, can't you fight your own battles?"

Up to this point, Michael hadn't moved from his relaxed position. Now he stood up and moved closer to me, so that he towered over Nell.

"Leave Tasmyn alone, Nell," he instructed tightly. "I don't know why you're threatened that I talked with Amber yesterday, but Tas didn't have anything to do with it. And as for fighting her own battles, if I really thought that, do you think I would have let you get away with half of what you have? Tasmyn is very capable of standing up for herself."

Nell's withering eyes swept over both of us. "As long we understand each other. Stay away from my friends." She pinned me with her glare. "*All of them.* And mind your own business." She turned and disappeared into the crowd moving on the sidewalk.

I slowly closed my locker and looked at Michael with wide eyes. "What was *that*?" I asked in a whisper.

He gave me a half-smile and took my hand as we began walking. "I think we rattled some cages yesterday. Nell is feeling just a tad insecure, I'd say."

I shivered. "Is that it? It felt more like an attack than a defensive move."

We stopped at the corner, where I had to turn toward French and Michael had to cross the grass to his classroom. He dropped my hand and stroked my hair back away from my face.

"Remember the most dangerous creature is a cornered animal. Give Nell lots of room today, okay?" When I opened my mouth, possibly to protest, he put a finger on my lips. "I know you can take care of yourself. But I'll feel better if I also know you're not going to be in any form of danger this morning. I'm not sure anymore what Nell is or isn't capable of doing, and I don't really feel like putting it to the test today." He replaced his finger with his lips and lightly brushed a kiss onto my mouth. "See you at lunch."

A light rain began to fall about mid-morning, so I knew that we would be eating inside today. Because I felt I needed a little relief from the whole Nell and Amber drama, I made a point of inviting Cara to eat lunch with us. We had just a minute to talk at the end of class, since I just barely made it into my seat before the first bell rang and Madame taught right up to the closing bell. Cara brightened at my invitation and promised to see me in the cafeteria.

Nell had returned to her ignoring-me mode in Chemistry. Her back was stiff and straight, and her head never turned. Ms. Lacusta was lecturing again, and although I noticed her eyes rest curiously on me as well as on Nell several times, she didn't directly address me at all. I was relieved. I had the sense that when Nell warned me away from *all* of her friends, she had been including our Chemistry teacher. A little weird, but I was beginning to realize that was the way Nell's mind worked.

When I arrived at lunch, slightly breathless from rushing, I found Michael sitting at our regular table, with the requisite two trays overflowing with food. Everyone else was already there, too, including Cara, who was sitting across from Michael. When she saw me, she gave a wave and then, oddly, flushed a little.

Senses prickling, I slid onto the bench next to Michael. He smiled his greeting, leaning in to kiss my cheek and whisper in my ear. "This morning go okay?"

I smiled in return and nodded. "Uneventful." I turned to Cara. "I'm glad to see you found the table! I always get to lunch later than everybody else. Mrs. Cook keeps us until the bitter end."

Cara nodded, and I could feel something coming from her—was that relief? I wasn't sure. "I have her in the afternoon for English, in seventh period, and we're always the last class out. She packs a lot in each day, though." She took a bite of the hamburger on her tray.

That reminded me of my own lunch. "So what are you forcing down my throat today?" I asked Michael in mock resignation.

He spread his hands over the trays. "Anything you like. Take your pick. And if you eat all this, I can always get more."

I laughed. "As if! You're just trying to cover up your

own massive appetite. I'll take some pizza, thanks."

He handed the slice to me and also pushed over a bowl of salad. "Here's your rabbit food, too."

"Thank you." I smiled up at him again. It was still such a new experience to have someone other than my parents who knew me, who cared about my wants and needs. I liked it.

Further down the table, Anne leaned back to see me around Michael. "Hey, Tasmyn. I keep meaning to ask you. Are you and Michael going to the Harvest Moon Dance?"

Taken completely by surprise, I wasn't sure what to say. Michael hadn't asked me, but I hadn't thought about it either. I'd heard about it from Anne, who was on the committee planning the dance, and I had certainly seen the posters advertising it that lined the outdoor hallways and the cafeteria.

I was interested to notice a look that I couldn't read in Anne's eyes. It almost felt like a warning, and in the low buzz that occupied my head nearly constantly these days, I caught a few words: *watch out... wouldn't trust that Cara too far... she seemed too chummy with Michael...* I frowned, looking more intently at Anne and wondering exactly what had made her so suspicious.

Michael glanced over at Anne but kept eating his fries. "We haven't talked about it yet," he answered her. Then he smiled at me directly and added, "But thanks for reminding me. I'd better ask her before someone else beats me to the punch."

I laughed. "Yeah, because they're lined up around the corner to ask me."

He regarded me seriously. "You really have no idea. I am the only one standing between you and the possibility of a stampede of boys who'd happily take you to the dance."

"Well, thanks for putting yourself at risk for me," I said dryly.

I saw that Anne was watching Cara curiously during this exchange, and though I wondered what she saw, I purposely redirected my inner ear to Michael. I didn't want to deliberately invade Anne's private thoughts, and I was also reluctant to think too badly of Cara. Maybe Anne was jumping to conclusions. Cara *had* looked a little uncomfortable when she first spotted me, but maybe she had just felt funny that I had seen her laughing with Michael before I sat down. I didn't worry about Michael at all; my trust in him was complete. And while Cara hadn't given me any legitimate cause for concern, I appreciated Anne looking out for me.

As lunch neared its end, Michael and I headed out to our lockers as usual. I told Cara I'd see her in History, and she nodded, smiling.

In the outside corridor, Michael took my hand and I smiled up at him as we walked.

"Will you always want me?" I asked him suddenly.

The question didn't seem to startle him. "Always," he answered without hesitation. "From now into eternity. I promise."

"But how do you know?" I persisted.

This time he did consider. "I don't know how I know, but I *do* know. Maybe the whys and the hows aren't as important as just the knowing."

I thought about this, and then nodded in agreement. "Okay, I guess I can accept that."

"Good." Michael glanced up and down the sidewalk,

which was still deserted, and then abruptly stopped walked and swung me around, pulling me close and dropping his hands to my back. We were both careful about over the top displays of affection in school; neither of us liked making a spectacle. But no one was near us now.

"So," he said softly, looking down into my eyes. "What about you? Will you always want me?"

"Forever," I promised.

"Then," he continued, "will you go with me to the Harvest Moon Dance?"

I made a face. "Do we have to go?"

"Why wouldn't we? Are you opposed to music, autumnal decorations and seeing my cool dance moves?"

I laughed at that, resting my forehead on his chest. "Not opposed to any of that. But I've never been to a dance. I have no idea what to expect, and I know my parents will make a huge deal out of it."

Michael's hands stroked my hair down my back. "It's nothing to worry about. It'll be fun, I promise. We'll dress up, dance a little and then we can go home. Okay?"

I sighed in martyrdom. "I guess so." Michael laughed at me, and then tilted my head up so he could see my eyes again.

"Remember," he breathed. "Always."

Chapter Twenty-Six

The rest of the week passed quickly and quietly. Nell continued her trend of pretending that I didn't exist. Although we had a lab in Chemistry at the end of the week, Liza managed to get through it with a minimum of interaction with me. Ms. Lacusta didn't mention her invitation to the chemistry club, and I was very relieved.

Cara continued to eat lunch with us. I didn't see anything odd about the way she reacted to Michael, and this too was a relief. She began to chat with the others who sat at our table, and I thought I noticed that Dan Hillinger, one of Michael's friends, seemed to particularly like her. I wondered if he would ask her to the upcoming dance. Michael had told me that through high school, the six of them usually went to the formal dances in a group, although now and then one of them would include an outside date.

I knew that Brea was toying with the idea of inviting a boy from my class to be her date. She thought he liked her, but he didn't seem to have the nerve to actually ask her out. Brea was so much the opposite of Anne that it was sometimes hard to believe that they had been best friends for years. Brea was tall and athletic, and although she might have been considered striking, she was not exactly pretty. She eschewed any makeup or hair fussing, which annoyed Anne to no end. I knew that Anne and I had more in common when it came to primping and cosmetics, but Brea didn't seem threatened by me at all. While we didn't have the instant rapport that I'd felt with Anne, Brea was kind to me, pleasant to talk with, and very secure with her role in the group around the lunch table.

I had observed too that Jim Shuller seemed to rest his eyes on Anne more than on anyone else. I remembered her telling me that he had been the one to warn her about Nick, the loser who'd broken her heart last summer. I wondered idly if Jim had had a greater motivation than Anne realized for wanting her to stay away from Nick. It was tempting to listen to his mind for a bit in order to get Anne the inside scoop, but I knew meddling could be dangerous. I decided to watch only with my eyes and hope that Jim would act on his feelings toward Anne sooner rather than later.

Craig Donalson was the quietest of the group. He was a football player, and Michael had told me with pride that Craig had won a scholarship to a Florida state school. Apparently, he was not only an athlete, but also an excellent scholar. He and I had had our longest conversation to date about Shakespeare; I was amazed that he knew the plays so well.

It was mind boggling for me to realize that I actually had a small group of friends. Michael had definitely helped by introducing me to Anne and the others, but Cara I had found on my own. Or rather, she had found me, thanks to Nell. Irony abounded.

We had come to the end of October, and the weather was still beautifully warm each day. The daily afternoon thunderstorms that I had come to expect had disappeared. I missed the changing of the leaves and the chilly evenings that were common in the north this time of year, but I knew I wouldn't miss the long winters.

I broke the news of the Harvest Moon Dance to my mother after school on Friday. Michael had dropped me off on the way to work, with the promise to pick me up before lunch the next day for our date at the nursery.

My mom was sitting at the kitchen table having iced tea and flipping through the mail. She had been preoccupied lately with one of her projects; it was a more involved children's book, with lots of intricate illustrations. She loved the work, but sometimes she seemed to be in another world.

"So…" I cleared my throat as I wandered into the room. "Ummm… there's a dance at school, some kind of harvest dance, I guess, and Michael asked me to go with him."

My mother shook off her absent look immediately. "A dance? Like a real, dressy dance?"

"Yeah, I guess so," I mumbled, hoping against hope that she wasn't going to let her excitement get too out of hand.

"Oh *sweetie*!!" My hopes were dashed as her voice rose several octaves. "That's wonderful! We'll have to go shopping for a dress and shoes… I haven't found a good hair place yet, but maybe I can ask around. . ."

"Mom!" I needed to nip this in the bud. "Listen. We can get a dress and shoes, that'll be fun, but no hair appointment, no big deal, okay? I want to keep this low key."

"Why?" The vibes of excitement and giddiness were still rolling off her, and I felt guilty once again for not being the daughter I could have been.

"Because… just because. This is my first dance, and I'm looking forward to it, but in the grand scheme of things, it's not that big a deal."

She looked at me in exasperated confusion. "Every other dance, at every other school, I got the feeling you wanted to go. I always thought it was Daddy and me keeping you from getting involved."

"No... not exactly. I wanted to be asked, because I wanted to be... normal. Even when I knew I couldn't be. Maybe it was easier to blame you than to admit that I was never going to be like the others. But now here, for the first time, I'm part of things. I don't need a dance to make me feel that way."

My mother was still slightly puzzled, but she nodded anyway. "So then why are you going to this dance, if you're not really excited about it?"

I still wasn't sure of the answer to this one myself. "It's important to Michael. It's something we can do with his friends. It's not that I don't want to go, it's just that I don't want to make a big production of it."

"Okay. No hair. Just dress and shoes. When is the dance, anyway?"

Good question. "I think it's next Friday night."

My mother shook her head and sighed. "Doesn't give us much time. We'll have to hit the mall this weekend..."

"Actually, Mom, I'm spending Saturday afternoon with Michael out at the nursery, if that's okay."

"Oh..." Momentarily deflated, she frowned, and then brightened. "Well, how about Sunday afternoon?"

"Umm... yeah, I think I can do that," I agreed, trying to tamp out the reluctance and feign some enthusiasm.

"Good! We'll go early enough to have some lunch out, just the two of us; we haven't done that in forever." My mother's happiness made up for a little of my own lack, and I smiled in spite of myself.

Alone in my room, I thought about the dance and why I wasn't as giddy with excitement about it as other girls seemed to be. It wasn't that I didn't want to go; it was more the idea that I might be terribly out of place and embarrass both Michael and myself. And of course, I was also worried about my parents and the fuss they were bound to make. I knew it was a big first for them too, but the thought of flashing cameras and doting parents made me want to cringe.

I wondered if Anne would give me some pointers on what happened at the Harvest Moon Dance, just so I could be somewhat prepared. It seemed like a good idea to ask her.

Chapter Twenty-Seven

I was up fairly early the next day, for a Saturday. I spent the morning dusting and vacuuming my room, doing laundry and working on what little homework was assigned over the weekend.

When Michael knocked on the front door, I was ready and waiting. He made sure to say hello to my father, who had come out of the kitchen to see what I was doing. My mom was sequestered in her office, working.

Finally, we were off. Michael had put the top down on the car, and I leaned my head back against the seat, enjoying the rush of wind in my face. My hair blew wildly, and I felt Michael's hand smooth it back away from my eyes. I pivoted my head to look at him.

"It's no use, it'll be a mess anyway when we get there."

He laughed. "Should I put the top up, then?"

"No! I love to ride with it down. I don't care about my hair. I can brush it out and hope for the best."

We were nearly shouting to hear each other over the rush of the wind. So when Michael said something else, I didn't hear him at first.

"What?" I asked.

"I said, today would be a good day for another driving lesson."

I rolled my eyes. "What, so you can get some more material for your stand-up act? No, thank you. I am perfectly content to drive automatic."

"That's ridiculous. It's so easy, Tas. You know you can do it."

"I'll think about it." That was as much as I'd give him. I hoped he might forget about it once we actually got to the nursery.

As Marly had predicted, Sawood was becoming a second home to me. I spent as many weekend days out there as my parents would allow, and I was getting to know some of the people who worked with the plants and in the shop. Sometimes I hung out with Marly in the greenhouse, and other times I tagged along with Michael while he worked in the fields. And now I was not only allowed but actually encouraged to help with dinner prep and clean up. It made me feel warm and accepted. And because Marly, like Michael, seemed to be someone I heard with particular ease, I knew that she was fond of me, too.

The nursery was particularly busy right now, because their pumpkin patch was open. Each Saturday, they offered free hayrides to groups of children who would then choose their pumpkins. Michael sometimes got roped into being the driver, which he didn't particularly enjoy. I'd ridden along a few times and laughed at his long-suffering expression as we waited for each child to select just the right pumpkin.

Today, he told me as we pulled carefully through the crowded lot to park near the cabin, he had only had to drive one circuit. His mother had relented and allowed him to work elsewhere until it was time to fetch me.

We watched the families milling about, buying fall decorations from the shop, while their small children struggled to hold onto the huge pumpkins.

"Strange to see so many people here, isn't it?" I remarked.

"Yeah, and it'll stay this busy through Christmas. I know it's what keeps us going—we need the walk-in customers as much as we need the landscaping jobs—but I have to say, I kind of like it better when it's quieter."

"I understand." I turned to smile up at him. "So what are we doing today? Do you have to work first, or can we talk?"

"I'm clear for the afternoon. I'm going to pull an extra afternoon shift this week to help out, in exchange for taking this afternoon off."

I frowned. "Are you sure that's okay? I don't want your parents to get mad at us."

He tousled my hair, which was still completely windblown. "No, don't worry. They were fine with it. I thought maybe we'd pack a picnic and take it to our spot in the Christmas tree field."

This was an appealing plan. I was hungry, and I loved that Michael felt as attached as I did to our little area between the pine trees and the citrus field. We blew through the kitchen at the cabin, throwing together sandwiches, chips, fruit and drinks. Michael's idea of a small picnic was of course much different than mine. By the time we left, the basket was heavy, and we could've lived off that food for a week.

It was such a beautiful day. A light breeze fluttered the leaves around us and cooled us from the intensity of the sun. Michael spread a blanket on the ground, and we set up our lunch. He kicked off his work boots and stretched out on the blanket while I sat cross-legged in a corner, enjoying my sandwich.

"You're going to eat more than just the one sandwich, right?" he questioned as I finished my lunch.

I shook my head. "I'm dress shopping tomorrow with my mom. Won't you be mortified if you end up having to take me to the dance wearing a tent? I have to watch my caloric intake."

"You look fantastic, you always do. You don't need to diet. I already know I'll have the most beautiful girl as my date."

I decided it wasn't worth arguing. Especially as I could feel the self-satisfied and relaxed vibes flowing from him, which meant he wouldn't be moved anyway. Instead I extended my legs in front of me, rolled to the side and propped myself up on my elbow, facing Michael. He was still flat on his back, eyes closed, soaking up the sun.

"So…" I began, not wanting him to nod off to sleep quite yet.

He opened one eye and looked at me. "So?"

"So, are you going to fill me in on the history of occult practices in the town of King? You promised."

"I know."

"So…" I repeated, exasperated.

He rolled to his side, mirroring my own position, leaning his head on his hand. "Tasmyn, it's not that I'm keeping something from you. If I'm hesitating at all, it's because I'm a little afraid we're making a lot out of nothing. What if I tell you all this—some of which I'm not really sure about—and it does turn out to be nothing?"

"Then we'll do nothing. But how can we make that determination if only one of us knows the whole story?"

He sighed, and I knew he still wasn't happy about this

idea. I was getting frustrated.

"You know, if you don't want to tell me, I could just listen to you and find out on my own." I didn't mean it to be a threat, but it ended up sounding like one.

His eyes widened. "You wouldn't. I know you. You feel guilty about listening to me even when I ask you to do it. You wouldn't purposely listen to something that I'm not ready to tell you."

"Probably not." I wasn't ready to abandon this position just yet.

He sighed again, heavily.

"I really don't get why you're being so difficult about telling me this. If it's just rumors and hearsay, couldn't anyone in town tell me? I could ask Anne."

"No, you don't need to ask Anne. And maybe anyone in town *could* tell you, but they won't. No one wants to talk about the less savory side of King's mystical aura."

I giggled in spite of myself. "That sounded like the opening line of a bad news expose'."

Michael smiled too. "It did, didn't it? Well, it's the truth, however it sounds." He paused, and I could sense the struggle. "Okay, I'll tell you what I know or what I've heard, at least. But promise me you won't let your mind run wild, all right?"

"I'll do what I can to rein it in," I assured him.

"Well... I told you about King and the families who trace their lineage back to the original carnies. Some of them don't live here anymore, but they tend to be the less flamboyant descendants—you know, like the more mundane acts in the carnival.

"What was unique about King's Carnival back in the day

was that he always claimed to have some kind of corner on the really mystical stuff. He not only had a fortuneteller, he claimed he had a real witch—she would sell charms, potions, whatever. Cast spells, maybe. And he had magicians who he said were the descendants of the original alchemists—they weren't just doing tricks, they were actually making things appear out of thin air. That kind of thing.

"Well, while that fascinated some folks, others were afraid of it. So they started getting run out of towns, more and more. The women in the towns weren't happy that their husbands were visiting the witch's tent at night, getting charms or whatever... I think it was probably the *whatever* that bothered them more than the charms, but they used their righteous indignation to rally the churches and chase the whole carnival out of their town.

"King was getting older, and he was tired of the life on the road. Plus I'm sure he was beginning to see that the audience for his kind of carnival was drying up, as people were getting more and more caught up in religious fervor. Maybe he was really that much of a visionary, or maybe his fortuneteller clued him in. Who knows? Whatever it was, he decided he wanted to leave that kind of life behind.

"He had heard about the land in the central part of Florida being wide open, warm year around and pretty isolated. He decided to buy a big parcel of that land and start his own town. He invited all the people who worked for him to come down and begin a new life. He promised them the chance to live freely, without fear of persecution or prejudice.

"So they all came down here and started the town. For years it was just them, then as the surrounding area started settling, more people moved in and opened up businesses, started families. And at first, I don't think they worried about the past or about their reputations as carnies. The people who moved here from other places knew how the town had started and were either okay with that or were willing to overlook it.

"And although I don't know, I imagine that the real mystical stuff was still going on at that point. I'm not saying that I believe in any of that, because I don't, but I think that they were still practicing what they saw as their magic. I'm also fairly sure that it was getting passed down to the next generation around that same time.

"When King finally died—he was pretty old, in his nineties—he had it written into his will that the town belonged to the original families that had settled it with him. He wanted it clear that it belong to them not only in the legal, physical sense, but also in the metaphysical sense. His will is still on display in a glass case at town hall, so you can see right there that the roots of this town were... well, let's just say less than traditional."

"All of this is really fascinating, and I truly am excited to learn about the history of King. Seriously. But I don't get how what happened, what, over a hundred years ago, has anything to do with Nell and Amber."

Michael smiled at me. "Patience, my dear," he said, in an affected drawl. "You have to understand the basis of all this to see why what you saw in Nell's mind made me think of the rumors."

I gestured with my free hand. "Then, by all means, continue. I am your—" I searched for the word, "—devoted student."

He gave me a reproving look in answer to my sarcasm.

"Thanks. Well, I guess during the years right after King's death, the town chugged along much as it had while he was alive. The fortuneteller, or witch, if you will—her name was Sarah—died eventually, but her daughters continued practicing her craft, as she had taught them. There are minutes of town meetings that very matter-of-factly talk about the practices of the witches.

"But I think following Sarah's death, the people who weren't part of the original carnie family starting getting a little bolder. They began protesting some of the more extreme mystical elements. Other towns were beginning to form closer to King, and I imagine no one in King wanted it to be known as the crazy witch town. So things began to change, slowly. As I said before, some of the original families either left town or died out over the years.

"However, the majority of them stayed here. They had land they owned, and really, they still maintained control of the town itself. They might have allowed the outsiders to push some of the more extreme practices underground, but in the end, I think it was just that—they *allowed* it. Probably because they were smart enough to know that the change would make King more attractive to others who might want to move here, and they knew that the town had to grow or die.

"That didn't mean that the other stuff stopped. It just got—hidden. Most people knew about it, or at least had an idea. But they turned a blind eye. It was kind of a live-and-let-live situation, you know?

"Every now and then, though, something will happen and it flares out into the open. Kids will talk about seeing a group of women in the forests, or someone finds a burnt circle... that kind of thing. It makes the paper, and everyone talks about it for a month, then it fades away again. Apparently, if the witches are still practicing, they don't mind a little publicity, and they just maintain a low-profile until it goes away again."

I wasn't trying to listen to Michael, but I was so attuned to his moods and feelings that I naturally picked them up, trying or not. I could tell right now that he was indecisive. There was something more, but he wasn't sure it was right to share it.

"That's all very interesting, but it's still sort of general," I told him. "I can tell there's something specific you're worried about telling me."

"Again, it's not because I don't trust you, but because it almost falls into the category of gossip. All of what I've told you so far is history and real, confirmable happenings. The rest... well, part of it is real enough, but at least some of it is—rumor and talk."

"Tell anyway," I commanded. "I promise not to do any jumping to conclusions." I made a show of crossing my heart and looking earnest. Michael made a face at me.

"All right," he acquiesced. "About... oh, let's see, I was in second grade, I remember, so that would have been what, ten, eleven years ago? Somewhere around then. There was an incident. King has excellent crime statistics, you know, and so when something does happen here, it's big news. There was a prominent attorney who lived here in town. He was part of an old Florida family from outside of King, and he had married into one of King's oldest families. There was talk he was interested in politics, was going to run for office in the county, maybe the state. He had a big future ahead of him. Then his wife—well, she was arrested. She was accused of trying to kill another woman in town. Turned out, according to the newspapers, that she had fallen in love with this other woman's husband. He was a doctor, and whether or not he returned her affection or if they were having an affair—that was never clear.

"What caused all the uproar, though, wasn't the affair or even the crime. It was *how* the attorney's wife had intended to hurt her rival. She was using witchcraft. She had apparently been practicing for quite some time, and she had everything in place to... disable the woman and then eliminate her.

"And what made it even more of a story was that this woman, as it turned out, was a direct descendant of the original King Carnival witch—Sarah. And all of a sudden, all the mystical stuff that had been pushed underground or ignored all those years was news again. There were newspaper articles about the origins of the town, we had the big television news magazines here doing stories... it was a mess.

"My parents kept Lela and me away from most of it, but you couldn't escape it in school. Especially... because it affected someone we knew."

Realization was dawning on me. "Someone you knew?" I repeated slowly.

"Yeah. And this is where the gossip part comes in, and I feel uncomfortable talking about it. It was Nell's mother who was arrested."

I nodded, breathing out slowly. "Nell. Okay, I get it."

"It was horrible. I remember a little of Nell from before, and if you could have seen the little girl she was then—well, you would never guess how she's turned out. That whole time must have been so painful for her. She lost her mother, everyone was talking about her family... and she was only in first grade. So she would have been about six, I guess."

"She lost her mother?" I questioned.

"Yes. Her father had enough connections that he was able to have her put into a very exclusive mental hospital out of state. She was declared incompetent to stand trial and that was that."

"What happened to the doctor and his wife? The one she was in love with?"

"They moved out of town, and fast. I think they knew they'd never have any kind of life here. They weren't from an original family, so it was easy for them to just leave. I heard they ended up getting divorced later, so maybe there was something more than just obsession between him and Mrs. Massler. But again, that's gossip, and I don't want to go there."

For the first time, I felt something more than fear and dislike for Nell. I could picture the little girl she must have been, and I knew that the pain of losing her mother at such a vulnerable age must have been crushing. No wonder her mind was so dark.

"Poor Nell," I whispered.

"Yeah, poor Nell," Michael echoed. "Most people have forgotten it now, or at least it's not in the front of their minds when they think of Nell. But I remember that first year was rough. It was all anybody talked about. And of course, kids are cruel. They called her "witch girl", and they told her that her mom was crazy—which was probably true of course. But Nell had always kind of worshipped her mother—you know, they were always together. My mother thinks too that Mrs. Massler was probably unstable for a while before everything hit the fan, so that would have affected Nell, too."

"Did your mother know Mrs. Massler well?" I questioned. I couldn't picture pretty, down-to-earth Marly being friends with someone who would consciously hurt her child in any way.

"No, she didn't know her except through work—my parents did some landscaping for the Masslers. The family lived in Mrs. Massler's old home—a big house with lots of land. Mr. Massler liked to entertain in that huge garden at their house, and he had my parents redesign it for them, about a year before his wife was arrested. But I was talking to my mother about Nell the other day, and she said that even then, although Nell followed her mom around everywhere, Mrs. Massler seemed very... disconnected, I think, was the word she used."

"Why were you talking to your mother about Nell?" I knew that Michael would never betray my confidence in him regarding my extraordinary talents, but I was curious about their conversation.

"I told her that Nell was really giving you a hard time," Michael answered. "I said I was worried about you. My mom reminded me that Nell has her own issues, and that they probably... what did she say? Oh, yeah—'those issues inform who she is and how she acts today.'"

"I'm sure she's right," I responded. "Not that it makes it any easier to deal with her, but at least I'm not going around wondering why she's so nasty. I still don't know why she hates me, particularly, though."

"There might not be any reason. Once you've become

that kind of person, the kind who hates, I think it takes on a life of its own."

We were both quiet for a time, thinking about Nell and the injustices of life.

Abruptly I broke the silence. "Why didn't you tell me about Nell before? She's been making me miserable since I moved here."

Michael raised his eyebrows. "Would knowing Nell's story have changed the way you dealt with her?"

I thought about it. "No. Maybe. I don't know. I might not have been so—you know, I might have been more sympathetic..."

"And Nell would have hated that. She would have known you felt sorry for her, and she would have hated you even more than she does now. Besides, as I said, I don't like gossip, and at that point, it would have been simply that."

"But now it's not?"

"Now... well, I'm still not sure, I told you that. But you tell me. Does knowing what I told you about Nell and her past impact what you think Nell is up to with Amber?"

Reluctantly I nodded. "I think it does. Whatever was in Nell's mind that day has got to be related to witchcraft. It had that feeling. Girls in a group, in the woods... and the chanting. I wanted to think it was just something like... I don't know, hazing. But it was heavier than that. It was dark."

Michael lay back on the blanket. "See, that was what I was afraid of. Now that you know her history, you think it's a given that Nell would get involved in something like her mom did. But we don't have any proof of that. I'm not saying that Nell isn't playing Amber. I'm not saying Nell isn't bad news. But I really think that given what she saw her mom go through, plying the family trade is the last thing Nell would do."

I looked at Michael in surprise. "Are you mad at me because I don't agree with you about this?" He didn't *feel* mad, as far as I could tell, just maybe a little frustrated.

He rubbed his hand across his eyes, wearily. "No, I'm not mad at you. I'm—concerned. More about you than about Nell. I don't buy any of this mystical occult stuff, I've told you that. But anyone who messes with it, who goes against the carnie families, seems to come out the loser. I don't know why. I don't want you to get involved and get hurt."

"I promise not to do anything yet, or say anything. I'll keep an open mind. I want to think about it. But, Michael, I want *you* to keep an open mind too. If Nell looked at her mom the way you described, if she idolized her—well, it wouldn't surprise me at all if she wanted to follow in her footsteps."

Michael sat up, reached over and tucked my hair behind my ear. "Okay. I'll try. Now—" he stood and offered me his hand to help me up, "—Mom put something in the slow cooker for dinner. She was hoping maybe you'd whip up one of your famous salads to go with it. Are you game?"

I smiled, happy to be needed. "Sure. Want to be my sous chef?"

He pulled me into his arms and kissed me soundly. "Best offer I've had all day."

Chapter Twenty-Eight

I worked contentedly in Marly's kitchen, mixing several varieties of lettuce from her garden and sending Michael for other ingredients. I like an interesting salad, with as many different tastes and textures as possible. While I waited for Michael to bring me some tomatoes, I put together balsamic vinaigrette dressing, leaning out onto the back deck to pull leaves from Luke's potted herb garden.

As I puttered and mixed, I let my mind wander over our conversation that afternoon. I thought of Michael talking with his mother about Nell and about me. He had never asked me if he could tell his parents that I could hear minds, and I knew he wouldn't without my express permission. As unhappy as my parents would be, I was tempted to share my secret with Luke and Marly. Although I wasn't sure I bought into Michael's belief about the men in his family, I hoped that one day the Sawyers would be my family, too, and I felt they deserved to know the truth.

No, my parents wouldn't like that. Of course, they didn't realize that Michael knew, either. My mother questioned me frequently about how I was doing in maintaining my mental wall without making Michael suspicious. I hadn't had to lie outright yet, and I didn't think I would. I just hoped that by the time I had to confess, they knew Michael well enough to trust him to be discreet.

When Marly and Luke arrived at the cabin, tired from a

long day with plants and people, Michael and I had dinner on the table. Marly greeted us with a grateful smile.

"Oh, aren't you the best children any parents ever had!" she exclaimed, and I glowed at both the praise and the inclusion. "Just let us wash up and we'll be ready to eat."

Conversation around the table was as lively and varied as it always was. Marly was talking about Lela and her upcoming fall break when I suddenly made a connection.

"Oh!" I exclaimed. "Michael and Marly, Lela and Luke. Did you do that on purpose, give them your initials?"

Luke and Marly exchanged glances and Michael rolled his eyes. "Now you've done it. You're going to get the name story."

"There's a story?" I asked eagerly. I had my own name story, and it occurred to me that I had never shared it with Michael, let alone with his parents.

"Yes, actually, there is," Marly said. "We named Lela after my great-grandmother. When I was little, she told me that one day I would have a daughter, and she asked me to name my little girl after her. So we did." She smiled. "Then there's Michael's story…"

"He told me he was named after an archangel, isn't that right?"

"Well, yes, named after and quite possibly by an angel."

"Mom!" Michael protested.

Marly was unfazed. "Michael, it's true. Pipe down and let me tell her." She turned to me. "When I was pregnant with him, I had a dream—well, at least I *think* it was a dream, but sometimes I'm still not sure…" She looked thoughtful, and then shook her head. "Anyway, I dreamed that I saw a huge, tall man. He looked like he was glowing. And he told me that I was going to have a son, and that we should name him Michael, after the archangel. And so when Michael came, we did."

"It was a name we liked at any rate," Luke put in. "We'd given Lela my first initial, so we were leaning toward M names. And an archangel seemed like a good idea, right?"

Michael was shaking his head. "Have you ever heard anything like that?" he asked me.

I shook my head. "No, but I can see you as an avenging angel." Michael grinned and struck a noble pose.

"Your name is very unusual, Tasmyn," Marly remarked. "Where did your parents find it?"

I hesitated only a moment. After all, they'd shared their stories; it seemed only right to tell them the truth about mine. "I usually just say my mom read it in a book, but actually, a fortune teller gave her the name."

"Really?" Marly was intrigued. "Tell us about it."

"It was before my mom knew she was pregnant with me. They went to a fair or something, and they ended up at the fortune teller's tent. My parents are so completely not into that kind of thing... I can't imagine why they did it. But when she read my mom, she told her that she was going to have a daughter named Tasmyn. Both of them liked the name, so they decided to give it to me." I grimaced. "Of course, they don't have to live with telling everyone how to spell it and teachers mispronouncing it at every new school."

"Very interesting," Luke remarked. "A story you can tell your kids someday—how mom and dad got their names. Wonder what *their* names will be?"

"Luke!" Marly exclaimed. "Good heavens, they've only been dating for a little over a month. Don't rush them." She rolled her eyes at us, but Luke just laughed.

"With my family history, I don't think it's too soon to talk about the future," he observed confidently.

"Luke, really," Marly laughed, but I could tell she wasn't truly annoyed with him.

"Tasmyn's not upset at me, are you?" he asked me.

I shook my head. "No, of course not."

"Nothing to worry about. I was just saying, it's a funny coincidence that you two kids would be drawn together, given the history of your names."

Marly tactfully changed the subject. "So, what did you do with your afternoon? I assume you didn't hang out in the pumpkin patch."

Michael made a face and we all laughed. "No, we took a picnic to the Christmas tree field and talked about Nell Massler."

I was startled, since I had no idea he was going to be quite so honest with his parents.

Luke sighed. "Yes, that's a very sad story. The whole family was essentially destroyed."

That reminded me of a question I had meant to ask earlier. "Did Nell's father ever pursue his political career?"

"No, after the incident with his wife, he knew it was all over. There was just too much uproar, not only locally, but across the whole region. No one would touch him, professionally speaking, after that."

"What's even sadder," Marly put in, "is how he reacted to Nell after everything was over. It was like she reminded him of her mother... she does look very much like Alyse—that's her mother. And so he's pretty much left her to her own devices all these years. They had a nanny until Nell got too old to need one, but I imagine it must have been a very lonely existence."

"She hasn't helped much, the way she treats people," Michael remarked.

"A little compassion, please, Michael," his mother admonished. "I know Nell hasn't been kind to you, Tas, and I'm sorry about that. But I try to remember that her life has been difficult. Maybe she'll be able to come to terms with that as she gets older."

"I was wondering," I began, "whether... well, Michael said her mother was planning to harm this other woman using witchcraft. And if you believe in that, then I can see it being a threat. But if it isn't real, then wouldn't it have been pretty—I don't know, harmless, in the long run?"

Luke nodded thoughtfully. "Well, she wasn't exactly harmless. Apparently, she had a knife she planned to use on her victim. But the crux of the matter is how much what you believe affects your actions, I think. If Alyse was completely convinced that she had the power to pull off whatever she had planned, I'm not sure how harmless she would have been. I don't know that I believe in witchcraft, but I do know that the power of the mind is quite strong. I don't think that we've even begun to tap into its true potential." He smiled at me, his eyes crinkling at the corners, and I wondered if he somehow suspected the power of my own mind. My mental block was so slippery these days anyway, that it would be easy to just take a little listen... but no, that would be wrong.

As if he realized what I was thinking, Michael squeezed my hand under the table. But when he spoke, he addressed his father. "Are you saying you might believe in witchcraft, Dad?"

It was Marly who answered. "Your father and I try to avoid some of the darker elements in King, you know, Michael. We won't live in town. I knew that from the first time we came here to look at property. This nursery sits on land that was never part of King's property. I don't give a lot of credence to the rumors that go around town, but I also know there is far more to the world than meets the eye."

I nodded in agreement.

Chapter Twenty-Nine

My Sunday was wholly consumed with the dreaded shopping. My mother dragged me out of the house and to the mall before noon, and she had me trying on dresses of every style while she examined each with a critical eye.

"Too young," she would proclaim. Or, with more urgency, "Too *old!*" Some were too long, others too short. I was getting worn out.

Finally, in the fifth store, she handed me a dress in the softest, silkiest material I'd ever touched. It was a deep green, and it shimmered as I dropped it over my head. The thin straps rested lightly on my shoulders, and the bodice draped loosely but tastefully. The skirt swirled to just below my knees, and as I stood in front of the mirror, I actually felt a stir of excitement when I considered wearing this dress to the dance.

"Oh, Tas! It's beautiful. It's perfect! Do you like it?" My mother was effusive in her pleasure when I stepped out of the dressing room stall.

I gave a dramatic little turn in front of the larger mirror. The dress danced around me.

"Yes, I do. I think this is it. Now can we go eat?"

"Shoes first. Eating later."

Thankfully for my empty stomach, shoes were much easier to locate now that we had the dress decision made. I squealed with true girlish delight when I saw the dainty silver heels. They were simply made—just straps and heels—and delicate. I knew they would set off the dress to perfection.

"And I have a brand new silver purse you can borrow if

you like," my mother offered.

"Sold! Now let's please eat before I pass out."

We found a small restaurant in a corner of the mall. The Sunday after-church crowd hadn't yet arrived, so we had our pick of the tables. We decided to share a chicken and fruit salad and sipped sweet iced tea.

Before my mother even opened her mouth to speak, I sensed that she was feeling reminiscent.

"I can't believe that you're going to your first dance," she sniffed. "It just seems like yesterday that you were my tiny little girl, toddling around..."

"Mom," I muttered in embarrassment. "I'm just going to a dance, not getting married or joining the foreign legion. Most girls my age have gone to loads of formals. I'm just backward."

"You're not backward. You're just right. Don't ever think that."

I smiled at her over my forkful of fruit. "I don't, really. I just think it was a matter of finding the right person." I thought of Michael, and my smile deepened.

My mom sighed. "I do worry. I've never seen anything like it. You... actually light up when you talk about Michael, or whenever he's around. It's not just your expression, it's like a glow from inside you."

"Why would that worry you?"

"Because you're seventeen years old. You're not supposed to have this happen so young. You're supposed to finish school, have a life, and *then* find that special person."

"But maybe I *am* supposed to have this happen now. Maybe that's the way my life is supposed to work. And I do have a life, already," I added.

She was quiet, eating and thinking. "I don't want you to be hurt, and I can't see how it can be avoided. I can tell that you feel strongly about Michael, but you're very inexperienced. So much of life is in front of you. Circumstances are bound to pull you apart. Look, even next year, Michael's heading for college. You have to accept that things will change." *He's going to go off to school and leave her here, with a broken heart. I don't know how to stop that from happening.*

Panic filled my heart. "I can deal with change. I've been handling that all my life. But did you ever think that maybe we won't be pulled apart—we might be able to handle it, together?"

My mother nodded. "We'll see. Tasmyn, I just want you to remember that this is your first relationship. So have fun, be young while you *are* young. Try not to be so intense. That's all I'm saying."

It might have been all she was saying, but she continued to think pretty loudly for the rest of the afternoon.

Chapter Thirty

Chemistry had been so quiet for so long, in terms of Nell and Ms. Lacusta, that I had gotten lulled into a sense of complacency. Ms. Lacusta hadn't mentioned her chemistry club to me again; I hoped she had either forgotten about it or decided I wasn't the right material after all. Nell never turned around, never looked at me; it was as though I had ceased to exist in her mind. And Liza had perfected the art of completing a lab without speaking a single word to me.

So I was totally unprepared on Monday when Ms. Lacusta approached my side of the table, her eyes focused on me. I had come into class a little early that day, since we'd had a test in French and Madame had let us go when we finished. I was still feeling challenged by the pace of Chemistry, and I was glad to have a few extra minutes to prepare for the day's lesson.

The room was empty when I sat down in my chair, and I was so absorbed in the reading that I hadn't noticed when others began trickling in for class. Even the growing buzz of thoughts didn't distract me; I was becoming used to hearing it as my ability to maintain that mental curtain was slowly fading.

I didn't see Ms. Lacusta coming toward me, but I sensed her. The strange and unsettling aura she carried wrapped around me, and I shivered as I looked up at her.

Although knowing the future was definitely not my gift, I had one of those moments where I knew exactly what was about to happen. Nell, Casey and Liza were sitting in their respective places; I hadn't even noticed their arrival. Ms.

Lacusta was about to bring up my possible involvement with the chemistry club again, and Nell was going to respond in one of two ways: either she would melt down right there, in front of the class; or she would bide her time and plot to somehow destroy me.

Ms. Lacusta was standing next to me. "Ms. Vaughn," she purred, in that exotically-accented voice, "it occurred to me this weekend that you never responded to my invitation to join my chemistry club. I assume you did not forget?"

I held my breath for just about ten seconds, waiting, my eyes on the back of Nell's head. She was motionless, except for the almost-imperceptible stiffening of her shoulders, but a spurt of angry thought erupted from her mind.

"I... I did speak to my parents, actually. And they feel that with me just starting out here and trying to catch up academically, I need to limit my extracurricular activities. So—thank you, but for now, I think I have to say no."

I spoke in such a rush of words that I was sure she could tell how she unnerved me. I was glad that I had indeed mentioned the chem. club to my parents and convinced them that it wasn't a good idea. So I wasn't lying.

Ms. Lacusta's gaze never wavered from my face. "What a shame," she murmured. "You would have been a wonderful addition to our little group. I've been thinking lately that we needed some... new blood." She smiled thinly and her eyes flickered briefly over the girls sitting around me, none of whom had acknowledged her presence or her words. "Perhaps your parents will reconsider after you've been here a few months. Let me know. The invitation stands."

I didn't know how to respond, which was all right since she had turned quickly on her heel and moved to the front of the room to begin class.

I was shaken as I buried my head in the Chemistry book again. I tried to focus on the words before me, and on the teacher as she began class, but the low buzz had grown into a roar in my head. I could pick out words here and there from the indistinguishable drone. And then, a coldness crept over me.

She wants new blood, does she? Well, I'll be happy to be oblige. When she sees what I'm going to do, there won't be any need for people like that idiot behind me. She'll see that I'm all she needs. The rest are just around for window dressing. Amber is going to be a perfect sacrifice, and then there won't be any stopping me. The fullness of time is within the fullness of the moon. Blood equals power, and I'm not afraid to spill blood to gain power. That's what makes me unstoppable. When she realizes that, everything will be perfect. It will be just the two of us... and the power...

A familiar wave of nausea swept over me, but I was determined this time not to let her knock me out. I gripped the edge of the table and drew several deep, slow breaths until my vision cleared and the sick feeling had subsided.

I had been on the right track, all along. I was certain of it now. There was no ambiguity in Nell's thoughts today, and their vicious nature hadn't left much to my imagination. *A blood sacrifice... it must be blood...*

Now the only question was what I was going to do with this information. I knew that Michael was loathe to act on anything that wasn't precise and specific. I still didn't have any proof to back up what I had heard, so I couldn't go to any teachers or to my parents with what I knew. I was positive that my parents would be more upset that I was giving any credence to someone's private thoughts than about the very disturbing direction of Nell's mind.

I didn't hear one word of the rest of the class. The hum of thoughts stayed with me, but I concentrated on tuning out everyone but Nell. I didn't want to listen to her, but I was hoping to get some more information on her plans. Any little thing might help. But although her anger simmered just below the surface, Nell was paying attention to the lecture and only the occasional image flitted through her mind. I recognized a fleeting glimpse of Amber, standing in the dark. But nothing else concrete emerged.

When the bell rang, Nell rose before I had even gathered my books. She swept past me with only the smallest icy glance. As frustrated as I was that I hadn't pulled more information from her thoughts, it was a huge relief to have her away from me.

It was tempting to go in search of Michael, to tell him what I'd just heard. I wracked my brain to think of a legitimate excuse for getting out of my next class—the dreaded Speech and Debate—that would also allow me to pull Michael out of calculus, but nothing came to mind. And our classrooms for this period were at opposite ends of the school campus as well, so I couldn't even count on a chance encounter.

I decided instead to concentrate on putting the information I had into some semblance of order so that I could present it to Michael at lunch as reasonably and unemotionally as possible. While the teacher introduced the topic of the week—it was political speeches, I guess because we were getting close to election day—I tuned him out and thought about chemistry club, Ms. Lacusta, blood and full moons.

Luck or something like it was with me, and Speech actually ended a few minutes early, with the teacher encouraging us to watch as many televised candidates' speeches as possible in preparation for presenting our own on Friday. Lovely, that was what I needed. But I didn't have time to dwell on it yet; I had the opportunity to waylay Michael before I went to English and at least ask him to save us an outside seat at lunchtime.

I saw him heading toward the library. It was rare for me to see him before he saw me, and I took advantage of the opportunity to observe him unnoticed. He moved through the crowds on the covered sidewalk, not rushing, yet not meandering, either. He had purpose in his stride, but I saw him catch the eyes of several classmates, giving a quick wave or a grin. The breeze ruffled his hair, and I felt the pleasure of watching him, and knowing he belonged to me.

This feeling was so warm and positive after what I had experienced with Nell today, and it reminded me that I wasn't alone. Michael might not have the answers right away, but I knew that he would listen to me with an open mind and support me no matter how I decided to handle this.

I was so caught up in appreciating him that I very nearly let him pass me without accomplishing my mission. Fortunately he saw me even before I opened my mouth to call his name, and I was treated to that instant brightening in his expression, the full smile that I knew was only for me.

"Don't tell me. You ran away from Speech and Debate, and now you're looking for a safe place to hide out?"

I grimaced. "If only. I did think about it actually, but I decided you wouldn't appreciate me pulling you out of calc.

So instead I'm lying in wait for you here."

He brushed my hair back over my shoulder. "Do I need to smuggle you into my independent study? I'm researching hybrids, and I could use an assistant."

"You'll have to muddle through without me, I'm afraid. I just wanted to ask you to take our lunch outside today. We need to talk about something."

Michael looked at me seriously. "Does this have anything to do with our conversation from this weekend?"

I heard the bell ring and glanced in the direction of my English classroom. "It does. There've been—developments. I have to get to class. I'll see you outside?"

He nodded. "I'll be there."

Chapter Thirty-One

It didn't take long for me to share with Michael my most recent brush with Nell's mind. He listened, pushing food in front of me every now and then. His expression was grave.

"So it sounds like it was your chem. teacher who pushed her over the edge with this," he observed when I had finished.

"It didn't make her happy," I agreed. "She's planning something drastic for Amber. I wish I could believe it was just a figure of speech—well, thought—but I really don't think it was. What I heard was just so *black*."

"What do you mean?"

"It wasn't pain, and it wasn't fear. It wasn't even really fury. I just heard intensity. Hate, definitely. But she wasn't really angry with me—she only feels contempt toward me. I'm hardly a blip on her radar. But she's determined to show Ms. Lacusta that she's..." I furrowed my brow, trying to describe what I'd heard. "Worthy, maybe? Worthwhile? I don't know. She's trying to prove something, and that's more important to Nell than anything else."

"But you still think it has something to do with—" he lowered his voice, "—witchcraft?"

I had to be honest about this. "She never thought anything specifically about that," I admitted slowly. "I never heard anything about spells or powers in so many words. But given her history—what you told me on Saturday, what your parents told me—it just seems obvious."

Michael's eyes were steady on mine. "The obvious answer isn't always the right answer. Didn't you once tell me that when people don't understand something, they look for the most reasonable explanation, even if it's the wrong one?"

I raised my eyebrows. "I just told you what I heard Nell thinking today. I didn't give you any of my own commentary. But admit it, your first conclusion was the same as mine. And you call witchcraft reasonable?"

He was quiet as he ate the last piece of fruit on my plate. I closed my eyes and leaned toward him, trying only to feel his mood, not to hear his thoughts. What I felt was deep concern and a brooding indecision. I understood. On one hand, he wanted to agree with me, to tell me he had my back. On the other, he worried that doing that would put me in danger, either real physical peril or the less worrisome risk of humiliation.

His concern warmed me, but at the same time, I was impatient. I knew without a doubt that Nell had deadly intents toward Amber. It was hard to explain to someone who couldn't hear thoughts how different it was from overhearing that person speak or even talking to her directly. Most people speak with an audience in mind, even if that is just one person. But unvoiced thoughts are so primitive and gut-level real that second-guessing motives is an exercise in futility, particularly if that person doesn't know that what she's thinking is being heard by someone else.

"I want to explain something to you," I began. "When we've talked about my talent, we've mostly discussed technique, its limitations and so on... how I can control it or not. But I'd like you to consider this: my parents have known for most of my life what I can do. Even though I extend them the courtesy of not listening on purpose and really try not to hear anything accidentally even, they know that it's a real possibility that I might slip up. I might relax my mental curtain and hear something. So taking all that into consideration, wouldn't you expect their thoughts would be very guarded? But I can tell you that I have heard, completely by accident, some things that I never wanted to hear from either of them."

Michael looked puzzled. "Okay. I understand, I think, but I don't get what this has to do with Nell."

"Remember when we first met, after you knew what I could do? Weren't there times you thought things that you wished you hadn't, because you weren't sure if I were listening or not?"

He made a face that I knew was embarrassment at the memory and ducked his head. I wondered how often he still tried to censor his thoughts on the off chance I might be tuning into them.

"My point is, if you and my parents, *knowing* there was a real possibility that your thoughts aren't always private, cannot control what you're thinking, what makes you think Nell can or would? When I hear something from her—from anyone who doesn't know about me—you can bet it's a pretty reliable source. She doesn't have any motive to think dishonestly. Add that to what I can pick up from her mood and feelings, and I tell you, this is serious, it's bad and I'm willing to bet Nell is trying to follow in her mom's footsteps."

"Would you be thinking that if you didn't know her past?"

I didn't hesitate. "I might not have gotten it right away, but I think I would have come around to it eventually. It makes absolute sense when you consider what I saw her thinking and what I heard today."

"But what if it's just—kind of wishful thinking on Nell's part? Just something that crossed her mind, not a real plan?"

I shook my head. "No. Not this time. When she first thought about a blood sacrifice, it was new. It had just occurred to her. Last week, it was less... formed. It was something that she was considering. Today there was real intent. It was a concrete plan." I rubbed my hand over my forehead, remembering. "And even more, there was a sort of madness there I hadn't really seen before. She's beyond reason now."

Michael took a deep breath. "So what do we do? We're back to that. Nothing has changed as far as evidence."

I nodded my agreement, but something *had* occurred to me that morning. "The thing is, now we do have a clue as to the timing. Something in what Nell was thinking—it was a strange way to phrase it, but I remember it clearly—*the fullness of time is within the fullness of the moon*. That sounds like something she might have read—or maybe a spell?" I tilted my head questioningly.

"*The fullness of time is within the fullness of the moon...*" Michael mused. "So you're assuming she plans to do something to Amber during the next full moon."

"Something that involves spilling blood. When is the next full moon?"

Michael laughed, without humor. "It's this weekend. Remember, the Harvest Moon Dance?"

I groaned. "I didn't know they actually timed the dance according to the moon." Then I perked up. "Hey, if we have to worry about watching out for Amber, that means we'll have to miss the dance, right?"

"Now how can you say that, after I know you spent yesterday dress shopping? Your mother would be crushed. No, we'll still go. It'll probably be a really good opportunity to keep our eyes on both Amber and Nell. Didn't Anne say Nell was on the planning committee? So she'll almost definitely be there."

I sighed in resignation. "Yes. Oh, well. Do we know if Amber is going? I could ask her, but it's a safe bet she wouldn't answer me."

"Can you pick it out of her mind?" Michael questioned.

"I can listen to see if she's thinking about it, but no, you know I can't just go around getting random information from people's minds."

"I can probably ask around and find out. So that's our plan? Watch Amber during the full moon? I'll need to check a lunar calendar to see how many days the moon is going to be full, when it starts. And of course technically the moon is only full for one night, so it would be good to find out if Nell's idea of the full moon is scientific or mystical."

"What do you mean, technically?"

Michael looked at me, shaking his head in mock sadness. "Science, my dear. Astronomy. Although the moon *appears* to be full more than one night each month, actually only on one night is it technically considered a genuinely full moon. So if Nell is going by science, we'd have to find out which night is the true full moon."

"Can you do that?" I queried.

"Of course I can. But how can we be sure whether or not Nell will go by that?"

"We can't. We'll have to find some way to keep an eye on her each of the nights that the moon is full, scientifically nor not. I'll keep listening to her this week, too, to try and narrow it down."

Michael scowled. "I don't like that idea. Messing with Nell's mind isn't good for you."

"But it's our best way of getting information and keeping track of what she's planning. And she just might give me something that'll narrow down that window of time." I reached across the table and laid my hand over Michael's. "Really, I'll be careful. She won't know, and now that I'm more prepared, I can deal with it. I didn't even almost lose consciousness today."

"Maybe not, but you're still very pale—don't think I didn't notice—and you've hardly eaten anything. It makes me crazy to think about you putting yourself at risk." He glanced at his watch and expelled a long breath. "Lunch is just about over. You've got to get to class. Listen, be careful this afternoon, and we'll talk more after school. I'll see you at my car."

He looked so troubled that my own resolve faltered a bit. I climbed off the bench and leaned over to touch my lips to his cheek. He grasped my shoulders and held my face close to his. He looked at me intensely, as though trying to see into my soul. Then he relaxed slightly and pulled me close to him.

"Hey, I love you, okay? Don't forget."

I stood up and threw him a saucy look. "As if I could. See you in a couple of hours."

Somehow I made it to History on time. I slid into my seat moments before Mr. Frame began handing out thick packets of white paper, each stapled in the right-hand corner.

History test! It had completely slipped my mind all morning, preoccupied as I had been. I was fairly confident that I knew the material, but still, it made me jittery to face a test I wasn't mentally prepared to take.

Mr. Frame was still in the front of the room, so I closed my eyes and concentrated on pushing the drone of thoughts out of my head. I had almost done it when I felt a tap on the shoulder.

"Hey," Cara whispered. "Are you okay? I wondered where you were at lunch."

I hate getting in trouble for talking in class, particularly in a test-taking situation. But I also knew I couldn't be rude to Cara. I leaned my head back slightly, keeping my eye on Mr. Frame's progress.

"Sorry, sometimes Michael and I eat outside," I murmured in answer. "I'll talk to you after the test, all right?" Without waiting for a response, I moved forward again and pulled out a pencil.

The test was challenging, but it wasn't as bad as it could have been. I finished about ten minutes before the end of class, and then I spent the rest of the time trying to listen to Nell carefully. It was hard to hear her when so many other people were thinking so loudly, I observed crossly. Every time I lowered my mental block, all I could hear were complaints about the test, people mentally hyperventilating about questions they couldn't answer and the meanderings of those who had finished or already knew that they didn't have a chance of passing. I sighed in frustration.

Nell was bent over her desk, and I couldn't tell whether or not she had turned in her test. I closed my eyes and focused on her boldly this time.

...Casey is poking her nose in where it doesn't belong. She's really beginning to annoy me. They all have to see that

I'm in charge, I'm the one who knows everything. Maybe she'll be the next one. She wants to know why we bother with Amber. She has no idea. And I saw her talking with Marica, trying to turn her against me... ah, soon they'll understand.

The bell rang, making me jump and effectively ending any chance of hearing more from Nell. Instead I was overwhelmed by the sudden noise of twenty-two students thinking loud thoughts of relief, dread and resignation as the test ended. Nell was up and out of the classroom so quickly that I hardly saw her leave.

I nearly forgot to finish my conversation with Cara. She was looking at me expectantly as we moved to the door.

"Sorry," I apologized. "I'm paranoid about getting yelled at for talking in class."

Cara raised her eyebrows in amusement. "Does it happen often?"

"Not for good reason. I've gotten in trouble for answering people who asked me for a pencil or whatever, and that annoys me."

She laughed. "I know what you mean. Sorry. I just wondered about where you were at lunch."

"Yeah, I'm sorry I didn't warn you. Every once in a while we eat outside, especially when we need to talk."

Cara's eyes were unreadable as she asked me, "Is... everything all right with you two? I mean, I hope nothing is wrong." I felt mostly curiosity coming from her, even though I found her questions a little odd.

"No, everything's fine. We just sometimes like to have a little privacy. The lunch table crowd is fun, but it can get a little loud!" I laughed.

"I guess so," Cara agreed. "But I really like them. Did

you know I'm going to the dance Friday with everyone? Dan told me they usually go as a group."

"I'm so glad," I told her, and I meant it sincerely. "I hope you have fun."

"You'll be there, too, won't you? You and Michael?"

I smothered a sigh and nodded. "Yes, we'll be there," I replied, trying to keep the note of grimness from my voice. "I'm heading for Math. See you later!"

I spent most of my Trig class brooding over what I hadn't learned from Nell. So I knew she was miffed at Casey. That didn't help with anything. What was interesting, I realized, was Nell's reference to Marica. I knew she was thinking of Ms. Lacusta—there weren't two of that name in a small town like King—but it was the context, the jealousy once again, that struck me. Michael had been right. It was Ms. Lacusta's attention to me that had enraged Nell this morning, and in History she had been annoyed, remembering that Casey was chatting up the teacher.

I thought about Nell's mother, deserting her young and vulnerable child. Maybe she hadn't seen it as such, in the grip of her madness, but in effect, she had chosen her obsession with the married doctor over the needs of her small daughter. I had seen enough afternoon talk shows to recognize that Nell would still have abandonment issues. I wondered if those issues could have anything to do with her current relationship with Ms. Lacusta. And that relationship seriously creeped me out.

Chapter Thirty-Two

By the end of the day, Michael had determined that the scientifically real full moon was in fact on Friday night. That didn't help us too much, since we still weren't sure whether or not Nell would know that and my generic calendar showed three other possible dates when the moon would be considered full by us non-scientific folk.

Through deceptively casual questioning of Anne, Michael had also learned that Amber, Nell and company were all going to the dance together.

"So," Michael announced to me on the way to school the next day, "this means that not only *can* we go to the dance, we *must* be there. We are morally obligated to attend, in order to protect Amber." Whatever reservations or concerns Michael had had earlier, he seemed to be much more relaxed today.

I, on the other hand, was grumpy and frustrated. My listening the day before hadn't netted us any more hints on exactly what Nell planned to do or when she planned to do it. I knew I would have to spend more time today trying to tune everyone else out while I tried to hear only Nell's thoughts. I pushed out an aggravated sigh.

Michael shot me a sympathetic glance. "You do know, right, that if something happens and we can't stop it, this doesn't fall on your shoulders. Amber isn't your responsibility—and neither is Nell, for that matter. If you didn't have your—ability, your gift, we wouldn't know anything about this."

He wasn't helping my state of mind. "But I do have the

ability. I did hear what Nell's planning. Like I said to you before, what if this is why I can do what I do? What if it's not just a fluke, a weird anomaly in my brain? What if it's got a purpose, and I'm supposed to use it to help people?"

Michael frowned. "You're not a fluke, and you're not weird. And I don't know that you're that far off in what you're saying—aren't we supposed to use all our gifts for the betterment of ourselves and others?"

I stared at him. "Well, that's deep."

He shrugged. "I do read, you know, even if I'm not quite up to your caliber of books."

"So if you agree with me that I should be using my extra hearing to help other people, and I've heard—not by seeking it out, but just by accident—that someone is in very real danger, doesn't that mean that Amber is my responsibility? And Nell... well, no one has taken responsibility for her for a long time, I think. That's part of the problem."

"But Nell has chosen this path. Which means that we'll do our best to make sure no one gets hurt, but you are not going to beat yourself up about any of this."

"Easier said than done," I muttered as we pulled into the parking lot.

We were quiet as we walked into the school, each preoccupied with our own thoughts. I could feel Michael's worry, and I understood it. But at the same time, I knew that I had to everything in my power to be prepared for what Nell was going to do.

We were at my locker, and Michael stood close to me as I exchanged books.

"So let me ask you something," he said abruptly. Uncertainty wavered around him. "You said before, and then again just now, that maybe you have your abilities for a reason. We've never talked about why you can do what you can. Do you think there's a higher purpose?"

I closed the locker and leaned against it. "I've thought about it quite a bit. You know, I've had plenty of time, before we moved here, to consider stuff like this. I believe we're all given gifts, and maybe some of those gifts are just different than others. So you have a way with plants, you can make things grow. And my mom can draw and paint. And I can hear extraordinarily well.

"You and my mom can use your gifts in a more open way, to make a living even. I can't do that, but maybe I can—and more than that, maybe I'm *supposed* to use it to help make the world a better place." I glanced at Michael sheepishly. "Does that sound incredibly corny?"

"Not at all. I get what you're saying. But you keep saying that you were given this talent—who do you think gave it to you?"

I tilted my head thoughtfully. "If we had time to get into a long discussion about this right now, I could tell you how I came to this conclusion. It's not really that interesting, just a lot of soul-searching and long hours to mull things over. But we don't have time—the bell is about to ring, I think—so I'll just say that I consider my talent just as God-given as yours and my mom's. And since I believe that God does work all things for the good, if He gave me my gift, He must expect me to use it for something good. Does that make any sense?"

He nodded slowly. "Yeah, it does. But I want to talk about this more when we have time. I've got lots of questions for you."

"Hold onto them, and after we make the world safe

again, we'll have a long talk. But this morning, I'm a woman with a mission. I'm going to possibly sacrifice my budding Chemistry career on the altar of doing-good."

Michael looked at me as though I'd lost my mind. "Huh?"

I shook my head impatiently. "I'm going to concentrate on listening to Nell during Chemistry class instead of paying attention to Ms. Lacusta. C'mon, try to keep up with me, okay?"

He rolled his eyes and pulled me alongside of him as we walked. "Whatever. Just be cautious about the superhero bit, okay? We don't have any indication you're invincible, and I kind of like you upright and walking around."

"Right." I gave his arm a light squeeze as I broke away from him to head for my classroom. "See you later."

To my utter frustration, I wasn't able to pull anything constructive from Nell during Chemistry. She was concentrating completely on the lesson Ms. Lacusta was teaching. Her only stray thoughts involved her obsession with impressing our Chemistry teacher and being annoyed with a variety of people around us. As far as I could hear, she didn't think about me at all, nor did I hear anything about Amber.

After the lesson, Ms. Lacusta handed out a worksheet for us to work on during the remainder of class then complete at home. I stifled a sigh, thinking that not only had listening to Nell instead of the teacher been a bust, but now I had homework and no idea how to do it. I was counting on Michael to help me out with it, science whiz that he was.

As I sat at the table, trying to look busy even when the numbers and letters on the paper in front of me were gibberish, I glanced up and noticed Ms. Lacusta sitting at her desk, gazing around the classroom. And it occurred to me that it wouldn't be a bad idea to listen to her, especially if I wasn't getting anything from Nell. While I was almost positive that she didn't have any knowledge of Nell's plans for Amber, hearing her thoughts might give me some insight somewhere, particularly if she happened to be thinking about Nell.

It was harder to tune her in than it was to hear the thoughts of those around me. I bowed my head and closed my eyes, using my hands to shield my face, so it looked as though I was just concentrating hard on my worksheet. At first the buzz of student thoughts grew louder, and I struggled to push them down, mentally moving closer to the front of the room and to the teacher.

Again I was hit with that same uneasy feeling. Whispered thoughts in a language I couldn't understand swirled around me. I caught Nell's name here and there, but I couldn't comprehend the context. And then I froze, as I heard my own name surrounded by that unfamiliar tongue.

I forced myself not to pull away from Ms. Lacusta's mind. I realized that I wasn't going to understand the thoughts I heard from her—obviously, she still thought in her mother tongue, which wasn't unusual. But if I could pick up an image or two, it might help me in some way.

I concentrated harder, pushing my mind even closer to hers. The foreign words grew louder and clearer, and suddenly something clicked. This language was the same as the chant I had heard from Nell last week. Knowing that the two were connected shouldn't have surprised me, but feeling the link ran a chill up my spine. Nell must have learned the words from Ms. Lacusta, although I supposed it was possible that she had taught herself in an effort to please her idol. The bigger question was why?

As I considered all of this, suddenly an image from the teacher's mind appeared in my own head. It was Nell, and she was standing somewhere—it was outside, part of me realized I could see trees—and there were other girls standing apart from her in a loosely grouped cluster. But Nell was not with them. She was looking up, and I saw an eagerness and joy in her expression that was so foreign to me it was startling. Of course, with the picture coming from Ms. Lacusta's thoughts, it must have been Nell looking at the teacher. And this supported my suspicion that Nell saw Ms. Lacusta as the mother-figure she had been missing.

The image shifted, and Nell's expression had changed. The eagerness was gone, and in its place was a desperation, a need. I wondered if this represented a different time, or if Nell's mood changes were this mercurial. The pictures were accompanied by feelings, which from past experience I knew came through Ms. Lacusta. She was annoyed with Nell, almost bored by her. At first Nell's infatuation had flattered her, and she had used it. Why? That wasn't clear. But once Nell had moved from simply appreciating her attention to demanding it, Ms. Lacusta had pulled back. And now her feelings toward Nell were... I forced myself to probe deeply. Impatience... anger... perhaps a small bit of fear?

A sudden blast of unintelligible thought assaulted my inner ears. I sucked in a breath and with effort stopped myself from clamping my hands over my ears, as if that would help. The language was the same that I had heard earlier, but the words were whip sharp and so fast they blended together. My mind was being pulled into the storm, and for a terrible, terrifying moment, I wasn't sure I could escape. With real, painful effort I yanked myself away, and the ensuing mental silence was deafening. There was no baseline buzz of thoughts, no underlying murmur. The relief was palpable but short-lived.

My heart was pounding. I kept my head down and tried to slow my breathing. I was amazed that the whole room hadn't noticed my distress, but even Liza, sitting next to me, continued to scribble on her worksheet, somehow solving the problems I couldn't even understand.

I was afraid to look up and meet Ms. Lacusta's eyes, in case somehow she knew what I'd been doing. And in fact when I was brave enough to shift my hands away from my face and look up, the teacher was gazing at me with interest. She didn't look angry or suspicious, only curious. When I didn't immediately look away, her lips curved into a slight smile. I acknowledged her with a small nod, as I would if any of my teachers had caught my eye. And then blessedly, the bell rang, ending the class period.

It took me all of the forty-nine minutes of Speech and Debate to settle down my heart and jumpy mind. Something—either the stress or Ms. Lacusta's frightening brain—was playing havoc with the volume control on the thoughts I heard, and all during class, they went from a nearly imperceptible murmur to a loud roar. I took deep breaths and tried to pull up my increasingly-hard-to-control mental wall.

Michael's friend Jim, who sat at lunch with us, was the only person I knew in that class. I saw him looking at me with concern, and when the teacher was occupied elsewhere, he leaned toward me from his desk.

"Are you okay? Are you sick?"

I shook my head. "Thanks, no. I just have a headache."

Jim nodded, looked at me unconvinced. He was a good friend to Michael, and because he knew Michael cared about me, he did too. While I didn't know Jim as well as I did some of the others in the group, I was aware that he had a wicked sense of humor. And of course, I also suspected that he had more than simple friendly feelings toward Anne.

Thinking about that distracted me from the Ms. Lacusta after-effects. I wondered if Anne realized how much Jim cared for her. And I toyed again with the idea of saying something to her about it. I wouldn't even really have to listen to Jim, since I could tell just by watching them together that he wanted to be more than just another friend. Considering all of these possibilities kept my mind busy until the end of Speech.

When I walked into English class, I could feel that Mrs. Cook was unhappy about something. She was uncharacteristically brusque with all of us as we straggled into the room, and I heard her think, *Not in the mood for this today. Should have just stayed home... I'm not worth much right now anyway.* Mrs. Cook was one of my favorite teachers, and it worried me that something might be really wrong. Of course, it was also entirely possible that she was just having an off day. Sometimes it was hard to tell.

Whatever the cause, she announced that instead of discussing Shakespeare's sonnets today, she was putting us into pairs, and we were to work together to re-write a sonnet in modern language.

I hate group projects, and I stifled a groan. The rest of

the class seemed to share my sentiments, but Mrs. Cook ignored us all as she counted everyone off into twos.

"Joe, with Kevin. Amber, with Tasmyn." She moved through the rows, pointing at each of us in turn.

I saw Amber stiffen. I wasn't surprised. Given her new and treasured close friendship with Nell as well as her talk with Michael last week, I imagined that being paired with me for anything was a worst-case scenario in Amber's eyes. But I was also fairly confident that it wasn't in her personality to buck the teacher's instructions.

And I was right. Slowly but quietly, Amber moved out of her chair and back toward my desk. The girl who sat next to me had gone to sit with her own sonnet partner, and Amber slipped into her seat just as Mrs. Cook came by again, this time to give us our assigned sonnet, number twenty-nine.

"Oh, that's one of my favorites!" I exclaimed. Mrs. Cook gave me a quick but genuine smile, and Amber looked at me as if I'd lost my mind.

"Your favorite?" Her voice held all the skepticism in her eyes.

"Yeah, I kind of read these things for fun, sometimes…" I trailed off my voice, realizing in embarrassment how that made me sound. "Anyway, this one's good, and it'll be easy to translate."

"Good," Amber said, relief evident in her voice. Then she frowned, and I knew she was remembering that I was the enemy. I smothered a sigh and opened my book to find the sonnet.

We worked in relative silence for a while. I didn't want to do all of it, but Amber was very reluctant to offer any of her own insight. I could feel her confusion and doubt doing battle. My frustration level made it even harder to avoid hearing her.

"So this line—'Desiring this man's art and that man's scope'—what do you think? What should we put down?" Amber shrugged, but her eyebrows were knit together, and I could see that she was at least trying.

She knows all this, why doesn't she just tell me or write it down... not like I can figure it out anyway... stupid assignment... who needs this? Nell is gonna freak when I tell her. Or if someone else tells her... so scared when she's angry, like she's not the same person... don't want her to get mad before the dance with them... going to be a wonderful night, if Nell's happy.

I gave in as much for my own sanity as for Amber's. "Do you think it could be... I don't know, something like, 'wishing I had the talents that my friends do'?"

Her eyes cleared and the lines in her forehead smoothed. "Ohh... okay. I think I get that." She ventured a quick glance at me, still not quite meeting my eyes. "How do you know this stuff? It's impossible for me."

I smiled at her. "I moved around a lot all my life, and I haven't made many friends. So I had a lot of free time for reading. I know it sounds weird, but I actually enjoy Shakespeare."

Amber shook her head, amazed. "It just doesn't make any sense to me." She ducked her head shyly. "But I do like to read. Just not this—whatever it is. I like other kinds of books."

"Really? What do you read?" I felt as though I was on the verge of a breakthrough here. If Amber realized that I wasn't the monster Nell had painted me to be, maybe she'd feel more comfortable confiding in me.

"Mostly fantasy—you know, what they call science fiction, sometimes. I like the futuristic books and even some of the space ones." Her eyes lit up, and I thought in surprise that she really was quite pretty.

"Books are easier than people, aren't they?" I observed.

Amber frowned, and her eyes lost the glow. "Sometimes. When you don't have anyone to talk to, you know you can always count on the characters in books to be there for you."

"When you're lonely, it can be a lifesaver," I said softly.

Suddenly Amber seemed to remember who I was. "I'm not lonely, not anymore," she retorted. "And it doesn't look like you are, either. Not many people can come into a school and be dating the most popular boy within a week or so." She looked at me meaningfully. "So I guess you're not reading that much Shakespeare these days."

"What happened when I moved here doesn't make all the other years of being alone go away," I returned. "I still read plenty of Shakespeare. Finding friends shouldn't change who you are. It should make you even more of that person."

Now her eyes blazed, and I could hardly hear her spoken words for the thoughts that were shouting from her head. "If you're talking about Nell, you have no idea. I haven't changed, except the parts that I should have lost long ago. Nell has helped me become stronger and more powerful than you'll ever know—" *and if she knows I'm talking to you about her, she'll be so angry. And she always knows. Somehow she always knows. Sometimes I think she can hear me even when she's not here. She scares me but she's my friend, and I haven't had a friend in so long. You could never know.*

"Powerful?" I interrupted, trying hard to ignore her thoughts and only answer what she said out loud. "What do you mean? That's an odd thing to say."

Amber flushed. "I just mean, more sure of myself. That's all. What else would I mean?"

The temptation to tip my hand and tell Amber what I knew was strong, but I realized that it was much too dangerous. While I didn't think that Nell had any real power, the idea that Amber was under some sort of spell didn't feel that far-fetched right now. Her loyalty to the girl who used to make her life miserable was perplexing.

I leaned closer to Amber and lowered my voice. "I don't know, Amber. Why don't you tell me? Is Nell messing with something she shouldn't be?"

Amber jerked back. "You're seriously deranged, you know that? I see what Nell means. Just leave us alone. You don't have any idea about—about what all of us have together. People always make sick assumptions when girls can be friends and can be supportive to each other. You're just jealous Nell didn't want to be friends with you."

Now that was actually amusing. "If that's what you want to believe, be my guest. You're wrong. But you should listen to me about this. You need to be careful, Amber. If something is frightening you, it probably isn't a good idea. If you have doubts, you should take some time and think about what you're doing." That was as much as I could say without actually telling Amber what I'd heard. I was afraid that if she told Nell that I had warned her more specifically, it might push Nell to act earlier.

Now her mood had shifted from anger to fear. She

looked at me wordlessly, her lips pressed together and her eyes wide. "I can't," she whispered, so quietly that I had to bend close to hear her. "She would never let me pull back now." She sat very still, looking trapped and defeated.

Neither of us moved, and our eyes were locked. As the bell rang, Mrs. Cook raised her voice, telling us to finish the assignment for homework. I finally stood, closing my notebook and gathering my books, but keeping my gaze on Amber, who hadn't moved at all. Before I left, I touched her shoulder lightly.

"There's always a way out," I murmured to her. "I'm here if you need to talk." When I turned to leave the classroom, she was still sitting there.

Chapter Thirty-Three

I was later than usual to lunch, and as I went into the cafeteria, I saw Michael looking worriedly toward the door. His face cleared when he saw me. The lunch table was its normal noisy, chaotic place, and I tried to play along as usual, although my mind was still on Amber.

Jim caught my eye as I nibbled on some carrots. "Is your head feeling better?" he inquired. Michael turned to me, frowning.

"Do you have a headache? Are you okay?"

I sighed and rolled my eyes. "I'm fine. It was just a little one, and it passed after I left speech."

Jim smirked at me. "Yeah, that class hurts my head, too. But you looked pretty out of it there at first."

I gave him my finest shut-up look, disguised by a brilliant smile. "Thanks, Jim. I am fine." I enunciated clearly, in case there was any doubt.

Michael was looking at me suspiciously, and I turned my smile to him. "We'll talk later. Nothing to worry about," I muttered, just loud enough to reach his ears. And then I heard him, quite clearly.

I hate that she's getting mixed up in stuff that might not be safe. I hate that I don't know what happened this morning. And I hate that I can't hear what she's thinking like I bet she's hearing me right now.

I looked away, fast, trying to keep him from seeing the red in my face. I hadn't been trying to hear him; it just happened the way it did so often these days.

Michael leaned over to bump up against my shoulder.

"It's okay," he said quietly. "Nothing I wouldn't have said to you anyway."

"Sorry," I said in the same tone. "I didn't mean it."

"I know. But I'm starting to realize when you're listening. It's a different look than when you're concentrating on *not* listening."

"How is it different?" Our heads were very close, and to anyone sitting around us, it looked as though Michael was just leaning into me, playing idly with my hair.

"When you're trying to block, you look almost… blank. Your face is nearly expressionless. When you're listening, you're intent. And you look—conflicted. Maybe almost guilty."

My face warmed. "Hmmm, too bad," I said, regretfully.

Michael leaned his forehead against mine. "How so?"

"Now that you've figured me out, I must eliminate you. Not that I won't miss you, of course…"

"Of course…" he echoed. "Eat that grilled cheese, while you're figuring out how to get rid of me."

I sat up away from Michael and picked up the sandwich. People were meandering out of the cafeteria, and I saw that Brea had left. Dan was talking to Cara, I saw with satisfaction, and Jim was looking at Anne, who had her head bent over some last minute homework. The yearning in his eyes convinced me that I was right about his feelings toward Anne. Something had to be done there.

I finished the grilled cheese in just enough time to rush off to class, with a quick promise to Michael that I'd see him after school.

Chapter Thirty-Four

I had decided to compromise with my mother on the issue of the upcoming dance and my hair. I didn't want a fussy hairdo for that night, and my mom had agreed that a simpler style would suit the dress. However, she strongly suggested that at least I should have my hair trimmed before the big night. Since this was something I had been thinking about anyway, it was easy to give in.

I knew that Anne's mother owned a hair salon in town, and so on Wednesday after school, Michael dropped both of us off at the corner of Main Street and Second Avenue. Anne had promised to stay with me and make sure nothing radical happened to my hair.

"My mom is pretty good about listening to people and what they want," she promised. "But still, sometimes people get talking and get carried away... I'll have your back."

Second Avenue Rose was a small but quaint salon, tucked on a side street and bearing only a simple wooden sign over the door. Two operator chairs sat along the wall, and in the corner, a waiting area was furnished with small, overstuffed benches.

As we entered, a bell tinkled over the door, and a woman emerged from the back of the salon. She was an almost exact replica of Anne, only with smooth platinum blonde hair in place of her daughter's darker curls. Her face lit up with a smile when she caught sight of us.

"Hello!" she called in greeting. "You must be Tasmyn. Anne has told me so much about you. Welcome to King—welcome to Second Avenue Rose!"

She was so bright and lively, I couldn't help but smile in return. "Thanks, Mrs. Lewis. I appreciate you fitting me in at short notice."

Mrs. Lewis brushed away my thanks with a wave of her hand. "No problem at all. Look at you—you're just lovely. And this hair—" she held a length of my hair away from shoulder, "—why, it's gorgeous. Such a pretty shade!"

I flushed. "It's just brown, really," I mumbled, embarrassed.

"Nonsense! I have customers who pay big money for this shade, and you can never exactly re-create it, no matter how expert a colorist you might be. See how the light picks up the golds, the reds... no," she sighed, shaking her head, "Never could duplicate this. But I can help you out with a trim. Even beautiful, healthy hair needs a little pick-me-up now and then."

In no time at all I was seated in one of the chairs, with my hair wet and streaming down my back and in front of my face. Mrs. Lewis was busily—and carefully, I hoped—snipping away at my split ends.

"So," she said as she moved around me, "how are you liking King High School?"

"Oh, I like it," I assured her. "I've made some good friends already. People have been nice, mostly."

"Yes, you've made at least one pretty special friend, haven't you?" she remarked meaningfully, raising her eyebrows.

I repressed a sigh. "Yes, Michael has made all the difference," I agreed.

"He's just the best. He and Anne have been friends for so long—I used to hope, I'll admit, that maybe they'd be more—"

"Mom!" Anne, sitting in the other operator chair, rolled her eyes in protest.

"No, no, listen, it's true, I did hope, but then I could see that they were only meant to be friends. And now he's found you, and Anne tells me you're perfect together."

I was silent, not sure how to answer. But Mrs. Lewis didn't wait for one.

"And how about classes? Do you like your teachers?"

Now here was an opening I could use. Since listening to my Chemistry teacher's thoughts, I had been curious about her and how she had come to be at King High.

"Well, I like English and History," I began. "Speech is not my favorite. I'm staying afloat in Math mostly thanks to Michael. And Chemistry—" I made a face. "I guess it's okay, but the teacher is a little odd."

"She has Ms. Lacusta," Anne put in.

"Oh," Mrs. Lewis nodded, understanding on her face. "Yes, I've heard she's a little different. She hasn't been here that long, you know. This past spring, Mr. Hennings got really sick. It came on him all of a sudden. So the school hired Ms. Lacusta. She's from—where is it, Anne? One of those Eastern block countries…"

"Romania," Anne supplied.

"That's right. Romania. She did okay, I heard, but a couple of my customers said she was funny about the boys."

I frowned, perplexed. "Boys? What do you mean?"

"She didn't seem to like boys in her classes. One of the women who comes in here said her son complained she never called on him, wouldn't answer his questions, either. When the mom complained to the principal, Ms. Lacusta claimed the boys weren't letting the girls participate, and she was just trying to keep things fair. Most of the boys ended up transferring out of her class."

"That's strange," I mused. "You know, there's only two boys in my chem. class, and I don't think they participate much, either."

"She gives me the heebie-jeebies," Anne said. "And I'm not the only one. You remember me telling you about Nell Massler and her boyfriend Kyle? She broke up with him because he didn't like Ms. Lacusta, said there something strange about her."

"Hmmm..." I was thoughtful. We were all three quiet for a time, and then Mrs. Lewis pulled out the blow dryer, effectively ending conversation while she moved around the chair, twirling her brush through my hair.

"Voila!" she finally announced, spinning the chair to face the mirror. I smiled as I examined my head from one angle and then another. "It's perfect, Mrs. Lewis! Thanks so much."

"I had good material," she replied.

As I paid for the haircut, she asked, "What are you girls up to now?"

"I'm going to walk home with Tasmyn, if it's okay. We're going to try out new makeup for Friday night."

"And I'll drive Anne home afterward," I added.

"Well, have a good time, girls. Tasmyn, you come back any time."

I thanked her again, and we left the salon.

"I love your mom," I told Anne.

She laughed. "She can be a little much sometimes, but she's got a good heart. I think she's happy to see me back with all my friends. She worried when all that was going on last year with Nick."

That reminded me of something else. I knew it was meddling, but...

"Anne," I ventured as we crossed the street and walked along the sidewalk, "what do you think about Jim?"

An odd expression crossed her face, and then she glanced at me sideways. "He's a friend. He's one of us. Why?"

"Oh, nothing. I just noticed..." I bit my lower lip, considering. "Did you know some days at lunch, he can't take his eyes off you?"

Anne's eyes widened. "What do you mean? He's staring at me?"

"Well, not exactly. He tries not to let you catch him at it. But I've seen him. And the *way* he looks... I think he has more than friendship in mind."

Her face pinked, and I hid a smile. "He never really forgave me for last year, though," she murmured. "He hardly talks to me anymore."

"I don't think it's about forgiving you," I said slowly. "I think it might have been more that he was worried about you with Nick, and then when it happened like he thought it would, he was hurting because *you* were hurting. And now, he's just waiting for you to be over Nick..."

"Wait." Anne wheeled around to face me and stopped walking. "Did he tell you all this? Did he put you up to talking to me?"

"No!" My denial was horrified and honest. "No, he doesn't have any idea I even know how he feels. And maybe 'know' is too strong a word. I'm just guessing, really." I hadn't realized how close I was to saying too much of what I'd sensed in Jim. The line between observation and supernatural hearing was very fuzzy, even when I hadn't actually listened to Jim's thoughts.

"Those are pretty specific guesses." Anne was still suspicious.

"Look, I'm really good at intuiting what people are feeling. All those years of moving and having to size people up—it's paid off, I guess, because I get a good sense of what others are thinking." That was putting it mildly. "You could ask anyone else who sits with us at lunch, and I bet they'd tell you the same thing. It's pretty obvious how Jim feels about you."

We had resumed walking, and I could feel Anne considering, rolling this new possibility around in her head.

"Could you—do you have any feelings for Jim?" I ventured finally.

Anne knit her brows together. "It's hard," she said. "I've always known him, as long as I've known all the others. And it made me so sad this year, when he didn't seem to take me back the way everyone else did. It's been like a hole in my life. I used to think—back, before Nick—that maybe Jim and I could have something together—but he never made a move. So I figured he didn't feel the same way I did."

"Well, now's your chance," I encouraged her.

"But how?" Anne moaned. We were turning onto my street, and I slowed my steps and considered.

"You're both going to the dance," I pointed out. "Neither of you has a date—you're just going with the crowd. So once you're there, ask him to dance. On a slow dance. They have those at dances like this, right?" I asked, suddenly remembering that I really didn't know.

"Yes, of course they do," Anne answered. "But what if he says no?"

"Trust me. He won't," I promised her with complete assurance.

"But what if he says *yes*?" she asked, her voice rising in panic. "What do I do?"

I thought about it as we walked up onto my front porch. "I think, once you ask him to dance, you won't have to do anything else. Once he finally gets the hint that you're over that other loser and that you like him, I don't see Jim letting much grass grow under his feet. And—" I smiled at her. "If he doesn't do anything, use your feminine charms. I have faith in you. It'll all work out perfectly."

Chapter Thirty-Five

If only I had the same faith in myself. After Michael dropped me at home on Friday, I spent hours in pre-dance prep. I bathed, washed my hair, deep conditioned it, gave myself a facial and painted my nails, both finger and toe. My dress hung on the outside of the closet, and as I lay in bed waiting for my nails to dry, I looked at it in wonder. Could it really be me going to a big formal dance, and not just with any boy—with the boy of my every dream?

I closed my eyes and tried to calm my quivering nerves. Ironically enough, I was more nervous about the dance itself than about the possible trouble that Nell and Amber might get into tonight. The rest of the week had been quiet, even when I really focused on Nell or Amber and their thoughts. I had left Ms. Lacusta alone, deciding that one encounter with her mind was more than enough. Nell had been thinking mostly about dance details and her growing annoyance with Casey, who was apparently continuing to buck Nell's leadership of their little group. Amber's thoughts skittered about as usual, at some moments euphoric when she considered the dance—it was her first time to go to a formal, too—and at other times uneasy when Nell crossed her mind. But I hadn't seen anything that gave me a hint as to the exact time, date or location of Nell's plan.

The shadows advanced across my room as I rested. I must have dozed off and on, because my dreams mixed with my drowsy thoughts, creating weird and disturbing images in my head. When my mom opened the door about an hour after I'd lain down, I shot to my feet in a panic.

"Hey, calm down!" She smoothed my hair back from my face and peered at me anxiously.

I was disoriented. The blinds were closed, but sunlight still peeked in the edges of the windows. I glanced at the clock and groaned; Michael would be coming to pick me up in two hours.

"I was just coming in to see if you wanted to have a snack," my mother explained. "I know they feed you there, but you probably won't eat until later."

The way my stomach felt, eating later was a much better idea. I compromised with my mom and agreed to a cup of tea and some toast.

"So, are you excited?" My mother's eyes shone; there was no question that she was looking forward to the evening with anticipation. That made my stomach jump all over again.

"I guess so." I nibbled my toast. "I just don't know what to expect. And I really don't want to make a big deal about it, okay?"

"Yes, Tas, we all understand that," my mother replied dryly. "I feel badly that we didn't invite Michael's parents here to take pictures of the two of you, though. I hope they don't think we're rude."

"They don't. I explained it to them last weekend, and we're all cool," I assured her. "They'll see the pictures afterward."

"They sound like very nice people," my mom commented. "I'm looking forward to meeting them. I've been tempted to just drop by the nursery on the pretext of buying plants, but I didn't want to be a pushy mother."

"We'll make sure you meet, don't worry. At least one

time before the wedding, anyway." At the look of shock in my mother's eyes, I made a face at her. "Kidding, Mom. Just kidding."

"Thanks. You must be feeling a little more relaxed if your sense of humor is back."

"I hope once I get there, I'll be okay," I worried. "I hope I don't stick out and embarrass Michael."

"I think that's one thing you don't have to be anxious about. The way he looks at you—well, I think you could go in old jeans with your hair in curlers and Michael would really believe you were the most beautiful girl there."

I blushed. It was one thing to know that Michael loved me, and quite another for my mother to have noticed. I distracted both her and myself by announcing it was time to get ready.

We spent the next two hours primping, curling my hair and making up my face. While I love to experiment with makeup, I don't like to cake it on my face. I had picked up some new tricks from Anne the day before, and I was pleased with the results.

When I put on my dress and shoes, I had to admit that the overall effect was attractive. The dark green material picked up the shade of my eyes and brought out the auburn highlights in my hair, which fell in loose waves around my shoulders. The length of the dress shimmered when I moved, and I loved the way it swirled around my legs. And my silver shoes made me feel like a true princess.

"Very nice," my dad approved from the door of my room, as I stood in front of my mirror, checking my reflection from every angle.

I smiled at him. "Thanks. Maybe this won't be so bad,

after all."

He laughed. "You'll have a wonderful time. I'm glad you're finally getting the opportunity to do this, Tas."

I felt the sentimentality and regret he was experiencing, and I caught his eye in the mirror. "I never missed out on anything, Daddy. This was the way it was meant to be. Really. I never wanted to go to a dance until I knew Michael. Well, to be perfectly honest, I'm still not sure I want to go to a dance, but I want to make him happy. And maybe I *am* looking forward to it, just a little."

My little girl is all grown up and going out for her first real dance. She looks so lovely... I hope that dress isn't cut too low. No, it's very modest. He better take care of her...

"Daddy!" I rolled my eyes and glared.

"What?" He held up his hands in assumed innocence. "What did I do?"

"It's not what you're doing, it's what you're thinking."

"And you know you're not supposed to be listening."

"I'm nervous, so I can't keep the guard up. Plus, admit it, you were thinking so loud you were practically shouting..."

Before we could continue, the doorbell rang.

"That's Michael!" I darted around the bed to the door of my room, and my father stopped me.

"No, you wait here. It's a father's prerogative to answer the door. Plus, you want to make an entrance. Trust me."

So I stood in my room, my knees shaking, and listened to my parents greet Michael and exclaim over how handsome he looked. Finally I couldn't stand it any longer, and I moved out into the living room.

Conversation ceased as Michael spotted me and stopped

in mid-sentence. His eyes grew large and his mouth dropped. I hoped this was a good reaction.

"Well, what do you think?" I asked, timidly.

"Tasmyn... wow," he breathed. "You're gorgeous. You're always beautiful—but you're incredible. Wow."

"I think that's a positive response," my mother laughed.

Michael's eyes met mine and he smiled. Suddenly the Harvest Moon Dance didn't seem like such a bad idea.

My parents, under strict orders not to fuss, did insist on taking several pictures. First, Michael had to take one of both of them with me, then they took turns posing with Michael and me, and then there were the couple only shots. Finally I threw up my hands.

"Enough!" I proclaimed. "That's it. We need to go, or you'll be snapping pictures all night. We're not going to be able to see for hours as it, with all those flashes in our eyes."

Michael laughed at me. "Just one more. I nearly forgot, in the excitement, but I bought you flowers."

They were tiny pink roses, surrounded by a spray of baby's breath. I oohed in spite of myself, and Michael slipped it onto my wrist. I permitted one more picture with flowers, and then I gathered my wrap and my purse.

"Have a wonderful time—be safe—remember, your curfew is 1 AM. Plenty of time to enjoy the dance, have a little snack out afterward, and be home by then."

"I'll have her back in plenty of time," Michael assured my parents. I kissed them each on the cheek and we were off.

Michael had the top up on the car in deference to the formality of the evening. Carefully he helped me into my seat and moved around to join me. Before he started up the car, he turned to face me.

"Seriously, you look incredible. I know you don't want to make a big deal out of tonight, but I just wanted you to know that." He leaned closer, gently and deliberately moved my hair over my shoulder and touched my lips softly with his own. I sensed the depth of his feelings and heard the quiet murmurs of his thoughts, echoing what he had just said. My heart melted.

We drove through the waning light toward King Hall, the building used for all official gatherings in town. Since the Harvest Moon Dance was given for the high school students by the town itself, it was held in what everyone referred to simply as the Hall. Outside, the palm trees were draped with small white lights, and people were walking along the sidewalk toward the front door.

"Are Anne and the others here yet?" I wondered aloud.

Michael turned into the already-crowded lot and looked for a spot. "I don't know. I called Anne this afternoon, and she was acting really weird."

I turned my face away so that he couldn't see me smiling. "Really? That's funny. Weird how?"

He parked the car and turned it off. "Weird in a girl way. Jumpy and kind of flustered. And you know exactly why. I can tell by the tone in your voice."

I looked at him with eyebrows raised and as genuine a look of innocence as I could muster. "Me? Why would you say that?"

"Come on. 'Fess up. I'll find out sooner or later."

I gave in quite easily. "I think Anne and Jim have feelings for each other, and I think tonight might be the time they finally admit it."

"Are you serious? Jim and Anne?"

"I can't believe you haven't noticed."

I could tell he was considering the whole idea for a minute. "He got really mad last year, during the whole time Anne was with Nick. He said it was just because he knew she was going to get hurt, and it turned out he was right. But you're saying he was interested in her that whole time?"

I shrugged. "I don't know about then, but he's been looking at her with what my mom calls puppy dog eyes since I got here."

Michael finally got out of the car and came around to open my door. "And Anne feels the same way?"

"I think she always liked Jim more than she realized, and now that she knows how he feels... it'll all work out." I held Michael's hand as we walked toward the Hall.

"So just what part did you play in this whole situation?" I noted the suspicion in his voice.

"Not what you think. I didn't invade anyone's private thoughts at all. I just noticed how Jim looks at Anne. I admit I picked up some feelings, but I didn't tell Anne that. I merely pointed out what anyone else might have. I used my observation skills, nothing else."

"Hmph." I don't know what else Michael would have said, but we were in the doorway and heading into the main part of the building.

The decorating committee had done an admirable job of transforming what must have been a relatively non-descript hall into an autumnal scene. Faux trees lined the walls and brightly colored silk leaves were scattered on the floor here and there. The light was dim, and a large, yellow circle was hung on the far wall and spotlighted. I assumed that was supposed to be the titular harvest moon.

The music was loud and thumping. It pounded in my ears and heart and made me feel slightly dizzy as my eyes adjusted to the lack of light. At a table just ahead of us, I saw my English teacher, Mrs. Cook. She was collecting tickets and directing people to seats.

"Hello, hello, you two!" she exclaimed merrily, raising her voice over the level of the music. "Find a table here anywhere. The buffet is set up there on the far end of the dance floor—" she gestured with her arm, "—so help yourself. Drinks are in the corner on that end. Have a lovely time!"

I smiled at Mrs. Cook's uncharacteristic giddiness. Michael led me toward a table where I spotted Dan, Cara and Craig. They greeted us effusively and Cara exclaimed over my dress. I returned the compliment. She was wearing a short, ruffled satin dress in a deep royal blue. It suited her, and I didn't think that had escaped Dan's notice.

"Where's everyone else?" Michael asked when there was a pause in the music.

"Brea was out dancing with that junior who moons around her all the time. He finally got up the guts to ask her to dance. I don't know where they are now." Dan craned his neck to look around. "Jim is getting something to drink and Anne isn't here yet."

I frowned. "I thought she was driving over with Brea."

"I guess she got held up, so her mom is dropping her off, then she'll get a ride home with someone."

"Oh..."

Michael lightly elbowed me in the ribs. "Look who's at the next table. That's convenient."

I turned, trying to look as though I were simply admiring

the decorations. A flash of bright red caught my eye, and I saw that it was Nell, wearing a skin-tight scarlet dress that stopped just short of her knees. Her dark hair was swept up and away from her face, and the effect was very striking. Amber and the rest of her friends were sitting at the table, too. Amber wore a rather modest dress in tawny shade, and she actually looked quite pretty, despite her evident uneasiness sitting among the most popular girls in the school at her first major dance.

I leaned toward Michael and murmured, "That's good. We can keep our eye on them all night."

He smiled. "That's not going to give you an excuse to avoid dancing, you know."

I shook my head. "That shows what you know. I actually love dancing. It was just the possibility of a fuss over it being my first big event that I didn't want. I intend to dance and have fun all night."

He laughed. "Okay, big talker, how about a dance right now?"

I was telling the truth, I did love to dance, but I really wasn't ready to join the throng on the dance floor just yet. Before I could think of a good excuse, one walked right in the door. Anne, looking lovely in her strapless deep purple dress, hesitated a moment, looking around the room. At that very second, as though it had been perfectly orchestrated by the powers that be, Jim returned from the buffet and set his plate down. He followed my gaze and spotted Anne. I saw his mouth drop open, and he stood completely still for the span of several minutes.

Anne found us and began walking across the room, giving me a little wave and smile. Her steps only faltered when she saw Jim staring at her.

By now everyone at our table was watching this drama unfold. Anne seemed to have to force her legs forward until she was at our table. She tore her eyes from Jim's and smiled just a bit too brightly at all of us.

"Hi, everyone! Sorry I'm late. Hair trouble, can you believe it? With *my* mother?"

Brea, followed by her dancing partner, returned just then and greeted Anne. "About time. But you look great, so it was worth it, I guess! Do you all know Alex?" She indicated the boy behind her, whom I recognized vaguely from my Trig class. We all nodded and mumbled greetings, and they both took seats. Everyone was sitting except for Anne and Jim, and I noted with satisfaction that the only two empty seats were next to each other. Anne took one, and Jim finally seemed to come out of his thrall and sit down next to her.

He ate silently and steadily, not taking part in any of the conversation that flew about the table over the music. Anne was flushed and animated, and she cast me an amused look when I caught her eye. I tried to send mental encouragement her way, wishing again that someone else could hear *my* thoughts.

Finally the music changed from the up-tempo fast songs to an older slow song that I recognized. I saw Anne lick her lips, take a deep breath, and turn to Jim.

"Would you like to dance?" she asked.

He gazed at her as though she had spoken a foreign language. "Me?" he said, incredulously. When she nodded, he looked stunned and then gestured to his plate. "But-but I'm eating."

I thought for the space of a heartbeat that she was going

to shrug and turn away from him. But instead she smiled at Jim, a full and understanding smile I'd rarely seen on her face.

"Jim," she murmured, "I would really, really like it if you could dance with me now. Please?"

I had to smother a laugh at the expression on Jim's face. He was a goner. She could have led him through fire at this point, and he would have followed without complaint. Slowly he rose and offered her his hand. They moved onto the dance floor, and I turned to Michael, beaming in triumph.

"See! I told you!"

"And about time, too," Brea leaned over Alex to address me. "I don't know how it happened, but I'm glad they finally both realize it. The two of them were really starting to bug me."

"Then why didn't you say something?" I asked her in surprise.

Brea lifted a shoulder. "Not my business. I might have had to, if Jim hadn't made a move soon. Now I don't have to worry. Come on, Alex, let's dance."

As they left the table, Michael rose, too. "Are you ready to eat?" I asked, looking up at him inquiringly.

He gave me an intimate smile that robbed me of my breath every time. "No, I'm ready to dance. Let's get out there so I can show off the most gorgeous girl here."

I made a face at him, but I got to my feet and took his hand. This part was nothing I had been dreading. Dancing in the arms of the most wonderful, handsome boy in town, if not in the world? I had no complaints.

Chapter Thirty-Six

Following two slow dances, the DJ played several fast songs. After the third one, I pulled Michael off the dance floor, fanning myself with my hand. "I can't believe how warm it is in here!" I fairly shouted to be heard over the thrumming music.

Michael pulled me closer to him and bent his head over my ear."Do you want something to drink? I can get us some sodas or water over there in the corner."

I nodded. "Please. I'll just sit right here." I plopped down in the nearest empty chair. "Recovering."

"Resting up for the next dance, you mean," he teased.

I rolled my eyes. "Just get me something to drink, please!" As he strolled off toward the refreshment table, I scanned the room quickly, looking toward Nell's table. Even through the dark, I could make out Liza and Madeline sitting there along with a few other girls I didn't recognize because they had their backs to me. But I could clearly see that neither Amber nor Nell were at the table. I looked at the dance floor, then all around the room. As far as I could see, there was no sign of Nell's flaming red dress. I jumped out of my seat and met Michael on his way back to me, holding two bottles of water.

"Couldn't wait? Just had to get back out to the dance floor?" he teased.

I shook my head. "Did you see Nell or Amber over there anywhere?"

His smile fading, Michael shook his head. "No. Why?"

"They're not at their table, or anywhere I can see in here.

I'm going to check the ladies room, and if they're not there...." I met his eyes anxiously. "We've got to assume the worst."

He didn't hesitate. "Go check, I'll make the rounds in here, just to make sure they're not just hanging out in the shadows."

The girls' rest room was small, with a long line outside. I paused, considering the best way to find out who might be inside. Desperate times, I decided, called for extreme measures, so I stood in line, closed my eyes and relaxed my mind.

The murmur of minds coming from the line was the first thing I heard before I stretched out my parameters. Inside the bathroom itself, it sounded as though there were three people, including one at the sink. I winced as I tuned into their very private thoughts, but it was fairly simple to be sure that none of the girls were Nell or Amber.

As I turned to leave the line and find Michael, I nearly ran right into Casey. Her light red hair was gelled back away from her face, and the short green dress she wore made her look even more like an adorable pixie than usual. The look on her face as she stepped away from me was far from cute, though.

"Do you mind!" she exclaimed, annoyance dripping from her voice.

I didn't have time for the niceties. "Casey, I didn't see you. Sorry. Where is Nell?"

Her perfectly shaped eyebrows lifted in surprise and sardonic amusement. "Excuse me?"

"I don't have time to explain right now. I just need to find her."

Even as her mouth opened to stall me further, I shook my head in impatience and concentrated on listening to her, ignoring what she was saying out loud to me.

What is the deal with this freak? Like I would tell her anything about Nell. If I tell her Nell left, she'd probably rat her out to some teacher.

"Did she leave alone?" I interrupted Casey's sarcastic reply to my last statement.

She looked at me, startled into honesty for once. "Yes. She was alone. She said she had to get something ready. I don't know, Nell can be... cryptic sometimes. I just thought she was preparing—well, never mind. Why would you be looking for her?"

I didn't bother to answer, just walked away from Casey and looked around frantically for Michael. I spotted him across the room, moving away from the table where Liza was still sitting.

"They're not here," I reported as soon as he was near me.

"I know. I just got it out of a very reluctant Liza, that Nell left about half an hour ago, and then Amber got a call and said she had to leave, too. It's too much of a coincidence. It's got to be tonight."

"But where?" I was panicking, feeling helpless. "The only ones who might know are Nell's friends, and they're not going to tell us any more than they have."

Michael looked as stressed as I felt. "If I start asking them, can you listen, to hear what they might be thinking and not telling?"

I nodded, and we both turned back toward their table. Liza was walking past us, and Michael grabbed her arm.

"What is your *deal*?" she shrieked at him. "You know, you used to be halfway normal, until *she* got here. I don't know what your problem is."

"I need to know what Nell's been up to, Liza. I've been hearing rumors, and I want to know where she is right now."

I closed my eyes and focused on Liza's mind. *How could he know, what does he know? Is he bluffing? Can't say anything to him, Nell will kill me.*

"I don't know what you're talking about. Like I told you when you dragged it out of me, Nell said she had to leave a little while ago. Maybe she wasn't having a good time here. Who knows? What do you care?"

Could Nell be up to something the rest of us don't know about? She's been so secretive lately, even more so than usual. Maybe she's planning something.

"Where do you hang out, all of you? Is there a special place Nell might go?" I knew Michael was trying to get information without giving away too much of what we suspected.

"Look, I don't know what your problem is. I'm not going to tell you anything about Nell. We both know that. So why don't you just leave me alone and get back to whatever it is people like you do at dances?"

Would she go to the woods? Without the rest of us? I thought before she might be going there more often than just when we had our meetings, but she told me I was wrong. It's not safe for her to be there by herself.

I saw a flash of images in her mind, pine trees, girls in the dark, but it could have been anywhere. I thought of the acres of wooded fields and forests that lay between the boarders of town and Sawood Nursery, land I saw every time

Michael drove me out to his house. It would be impossible for us to find Nell and Amber there, and I wasn't even certain those were the woods Liza was remembering. The entire town was surrounded by trees like that.

I shot Michael a pleading look. "I need more," I whispered. "She's not being specific enough."

Liza was looking at the two of us suspiciously. "What's going on?" Her voice had lost some of its rancor.

I could tell that Michael had decided we had to risk a little more, in order to get what we needed from Liza.

"Nell's involved in something, and it's putting both her and Amber in danger. You need to tell us what you know, so maybe we can stop anything really bad from happening. That's all I can tell you."

Liza was unsure. Her eyes darted back and forth between us, and her thoughts were scattered and sketchy.

"I don't know," she breathed. "Nell will be so angry at me. If you're lying to me—if you're trying to use me to hurt her—"

"Liza." I put all the urgency I was feeling into my voice. "I promise you, we're trying to help. This is serious. You've been suspicious about what Nell's been doing. You're right. Please, tell us where she would go."

I could feel the moment she gave in. "We—we sometimes meet in the forest out by Lake Rosu. You park at the lake, then follow the trail at the east end. There's a large rock in the middle of the trail that divides it in two. You turn off the trail at that point, just walk straight to the east. There's a clearing about—oh, I don't know how far it is, we always just know when we get there." She dropped her head and sighed. "That's all I can tell you."

Michael grabbed my hand. "I hope it's enough. Come on, Tasmyn."

Chapter Thirty-Seven

As it turns out, while the dress my mom and I had chosen was perfect for the Harvest Moon Dance, it wasn't quite the thing for walking in the woods.

Michael had broken every speed law getting us from the town hall to Lake Rosu. It was on the other side of town, still within the borders of King.

"That makes sense," he muttered to himself as he drove. "They'd want to be on King property for anything supernatural they're trying to do. And Rosu is the only lake completely within town."

"I'm not even sure where it is," I admitted. " I think I've seen the signs for it, but I couldn't get us there."

"Luckily I can. Listen, Tas," he abruptly shifted the tone of his voice. "When we get there, you stay here in the car, and keep my cell phone, in case you need to call for help. I'll go in and try to find them—"

"No way," I shook my head emphatically. "You're not doing this without me. And who am I going to call, anyway?"

"The police. Tell them we heard that Nell was planning to hurt Amber. I don't know, you'll think of something. I'm not dragging you out there and putting you in more danger."

"No, you're not dragging me anywhere. I'm going of my own free will. Arguing isn't going to change that."

His hand tightened on the steering wheel, and I heard a sharp intake of breath.

"Fine," he spit out. "But you stay behind me, and don't get near Nell—"

I knew it was his worry that was talking and not a lack of confidence in my ability to take care of myself, so I let it pass.

We turned into the lake parking lot, just a small gravel patch between the lake itself and the woods. There was only one car in the lot.

"Nell's," Michael nodded toward the sleek black vehicle. We both climbed silently out of the Mustang. I stumbled on the gravel, catching high heels between the rocks. Michael steadied me, holding my elbow.

"How are you going to walk in the woods in those?" he inquired in a low voice.

"Very carefully. I'll take them off if it gets too bad," I promised, and then shuddered at the idea of what I'd be walking on in my bare feet. Michael rolled his eyes at me as he pulled me toward the start of the trail.

"You insist on walking into potentially life-threatening danger without blinking, but you're afraid of stepping on— what, fire ants? Bugs?"

"Or scorpions," I agreed in a whisper. "Yuck."

He shook his head. *She's the strangest girl I ever knew. If she weren't just adorable about it... it would probably frustrate me to death.*

I snorted quietly. "I'm not adorable. Remember? I am elegant and sophisticated." I indicated my dress with a flourish of my hand, and then ruined the gesture by losing my balance again and clutching a tree to keep from falling.

Michael stepped in front of me. "Here," he whispered. "Jump on."

"Your back? I'm too heavy, I'll hurt you."

"Tas, we have no time for this. You're not going to hurt

me. Please, you're insulting my manhood."

Without another word, I leapt up onto his back. He caught my legs around the knees and gave me another boost to secure me as I held onto his shoulders. I laid my head down on his back as he moved much more quickly down the trail.

I raised my head only when I felt him take a sharp left. He didn't slow down, only turned his head slightly and whispered, "Boulder." So I knew we had come to the point where we veered off the marked trail.

My heart was pounding, with fear that we would be arriving too late and with trepidation that we'd have to figure out some way to stop Nell once we got there. I took deep breaths and quieted my head, straining to hear any thoughts that might be coming from up ahead. I purposely ignored the undertones I could hear from Michael—now was not the time—but there was only silence until—

No no no no no... please no... someone please save me... oh, God...

It had to be Amber. I leaned closer to Michael's ear. "I can hear Amber—what she's thinking. We must be getting close. She's alive, but I can't tell if she's already been hurt or if she's just afraid."

He nodded and increased his speed. I listened harder, and this time, over the screaming fear of Amber, I could hear Nell, too.

They'll see, they'll all see. My power is going to be greater than anything they've known. I'll be the most powerful witch in generations. Even my mother... A flash of painful memory flew across her mind at that, and I winced in shared pain. And then we could hear both of them, just in front of us.

"Nell, please... don't do this. You're my friend—"

Nell's unpleasant laugh cut across Amber's words. "Shut up. This is *why* I'm your friend. Did you really think I spent all this time and attention on you because I liked you? Please. This has been my plan from the beginning. I need a blood sacrifice, Amber. You're the one whose blood I've chosen to spill. You really should be honored—your sacrifice is going to go a long way to making me more powerful. Once she sees what I'm capable of doing, Marica won't be able to ignore me. She'll see that I'm the one who deserves all her attention. Now, please, step into the sacred circle. I really don't want to cut you until you're within."

Amber's laughter was hysterical. "You think I'm going to do *anything* you ask me to? Are you crazy, Nell?"

The answering screech was pure pain and fury. Michael stepped into the clearing just in time to see Nell launch herself at Amber and knock her into a tree, still holding onto her. He released my knees, and I dropped easily to my feet, sliding down his back. The minute I was clear of him, Michael was across the clearing. He grabbed Nell from behind and pulled her off Amber, who immediately fell to the ground at the base of the tree.

I ran to Amber as quickly as my shoes would allow me. She was lying against the tree, and I could tell she was breathing. I pulled her up to me, leaning close to her ear.

"Amber, are you okay? Are you hurt?"

She grabbed onto me with a grip of steel. "Don't leave me here, she wants to hurt me, please don't leave me!"

I held her close, instinctively rocking as I would a young child. "Shh, we're not leaving. It's okay."

About five feet away, Michael was still holding a struggling Nell. She twisted, trying to kick him, attempting to get free. He had her hands restrained, and I looked about wildly for the knife, terrified she might break free and stab him. But I didn't see it anywhere.

"Amber, did Nell have a knife with her?" I asked her urgently.

I could feel her head move against my arm, nodding. "Yes. She had the athame—but she was going to use it for more than just drawing the circle this time. She was going to use it on me—"

"Shut up!" Nell screamed. "Keep your stupid mouth closed! You know the secrets don't go beyond the clearing—and now you've ruined our sacred place. The presence of a male within the sacred—" She clamped her mouth shut abruptly, and then turned to hiss at Michael. "You don't know anything. Let go of me. I'll tell everyone you came here to attack Amber and me—"

"Oh, yeah?" Michael's voice was amused, even as he tightened his hold on a still-struggling Nell. "So I brought Tasmyn along, what, just so she could watch?"

"You have proof of nothing. Nothing any of you says will mean anything. What Amber and I choose to do out here is our own business and you interfered."

Another hysterical laugh rose from Amber, and she pushed away from me. "What I *choose* to do, Nell? You were going to kill me. I didn't *choose* that."

Nell stopped moving for a moment and rolled her eyes. "It was all metaphysically speaking, Amber. I was never going to really hurt you—how could I? You're my friend—haven't I shown you that you can trust me?"

Amber stood up, slowly. "I should never have listened to anything you said to me. I knew, down deep inside, I knew it wasn't real. But I wanted it to be, so I didn't pay any attention to what I knew. And that almost killed me."

Nell laughed. "Again, I remind you, there's no proof of any of this. How was I going to kill you, Amber? I don't have a gun, do I?"

"The knife. You had the athame. You were going to use it on me."

Nell's eyes glittered in the moonlight. "Really, Amber? A knife? What knife would that be? Do any of you see a knife around here?"

I had been looking around, all this time, and she was right. There wasn't a knife anywhere on the ground, and it wasn't in Nell's hands.

"Check her," Michael instructed me. "She's got to have it on her somewhere if it's not on the ground."

But Nell's well-fit blood red gown really left little to the imagination. I could tell that she didn't have it hidden beneath her dress. I clumsily patted her down, ignoring both her spitting-mad thoughts and her verbal noises of outrage.

I closed my eyes and listened to Nell, which should have been simple, given the volume of her thoughts. But Amber's were nearly as loud, as her fear still screamed, and even Michael's were interfering.

They'll never find it, and without a weapon, they don't have any proof. And no witnesses, so it's their word against mine. Everyone knows that no one will go up against a Massler. It'll backfire on them, and the whole school—the whole town—will be talking about them, laughing at them.

I was quiet, thinking. She was right. Without the knife, it

was just two girls in the woods, maybe fighting, maybe not. There was no proof that Nell had lured Amber here, and we hadn't alerted the police or teachers to what we suspected. It was, as Nell pointed out, our word against hers, and who was going to believe us? Michael might hold some clout, but Amber and I were at a distinct disadvantage. And knowing Nell, she would figure out some way to turn things around to hurt Michael. I wasn't going to let that happen.

I moved to stand in front of Amber. "Michael, let her go," I said wearily. "As much as I hate to say it, she's right. We don't have any proof."

Behind me, Amber sucked in a breath. "But she was going to kill me. She had a knife and she was going to—" she stopped, unable to continue.

"Amber, I'm sorry," I answered. "I know what you're saying is true. We believe you. But there's nothing we can do."

I saw the same realization cross Michael's face. Grimly, reluctantly, he released Nell. She stumbled forward, surprised, and then she righted herself. Her eyes narrowed as her gaze flickered among the three of us. For the briefest moment, I could hear, she considered going ahead with her plan. But Michael's presence had truly sullied this spot for her. Instead, she spun to face all of us, backing toward the trail.

"I'll have to think about what I'm going to do. I might still press charges." Her voice was smooth, but I could sense it was mostly bravado.

"Give it up, Nell," Michael said dismissively. "You don't have proof any more than we do. Only difference is, we all know what went down here. And we're not going to forget it."

Nell stood there for another silent minute. And then she turned and disappeared into the woods.

Michael shook his head, looking at Amber. "Amber, I'm sorry we had to let her go. You know you can still press charges—"

"No!" I nearly shouted. "No, Michael. If Amber pursues this, Nell is going to go after you. And I'm not going to have that. She's not going to ruin your life."

"So we're just going to let her get away with all of this?" Anger and frustration tinged Michael's voice, and I could feel the depth of it emanating from him.

I was suddenly so tired that I could barely stand. "We stopped her from hurting Amber. That was our real goal, right?"

"We stopped her for tonight. What's going to stop her next time?"

I stifled a yawn. "Amber's not going to put herself into a position to be hurt again by Nell, are you, Amber?"

Amber was leaning against the tree, looking from Michael to me in bewilderment. I could hear that she was struggling with the same fatigue I was—a reaction to the extreme stress, I imagined.

She shook her head slowly, in answer to me. "No. I don't want to have anything to do with Nell, not ever again." Her head dropped and her voice lowered. "You tried to tell me. You didn't even really know me, but you were warning me. And I didn't listen, and it could have cost me my life…" She shuddered, and I began to worry that she was going into shock.

"Michael, we need to get her out of here," I said, my

voice low but intense. "We all need to get out. Amber, how did you get here? We only saw Nell's car in the parking lot."

She was attempting to keep her focus, but it was getting more difficult. "I—she told me not to park there—she said to leave my car alongside the woods, in a pull-off, and then I walked into the clearing from there."

"Okay, you'll come back to the parking lot with us, then we'll drive out to your car and Tasmyn can take you home. Let's go—can you walk it?"

Amber nodded, and Michael reached out to take my hand, leading us through the trees, onto the trail.

Chapter Thirty-Eight

As we drove into the darkness, Amber began to shiver. Her dress was sleeveless, but the air in the backseat of the car wasn't that cold. I found a blanket Michael kept on the floor and wrapped it around Amber, rubbing her arms in what I hoped was a soothing way. Her thoughts were running in quick sporadic bursts, followed by long, frightening blanks.

I leaned forward. "Michael, do you think we should take her to the hospital? What if she's going into shock?"

"N-no," Amber protested. "I just want to go home. If I have to explain to my parents—no. Please just take me home."

Michael met my eyes in the mirror. "We could go out to the nursery, try to get her settled down. It's still early enough, believe it or not. The dance won't be ending for over an hour. What time were you supposed to be home, Amber?"

She shook harder. "Not-not tonight. I was supposed to spend the night at Nell's. She said-she said we would have a slumber party." Of course. That would have bought her some more time, hours during which no one would miss Amber. I shivered at how close she had come to succeeding.

"Do you want to go out to Michael's house, Amber?" I asked her softly. "I promise you, it's a safe place, and Michael's parents won't say anything to anyone. They'll just help us take care of you. We can all settle down a little bit."

She hesitated, and I knew she was overwhelmed. Twenty-four hours before, Michael and I were her enemies—or so she thought. Now she was clinging to us for dear life.

"Okay," she finally answered. "But you'll take me home afterward?"

"Definitely," Michael affirmed.

We found Amber's car where she had left it, and I got into the driver's seat, bundling Amber into the seat next to me, still wrapped in the blanket. We followed Michael through the dark roads until I saw the familiar nursery sign.

The red taillights led me through the deserted nursery back to the cabin. Amber looked around as we climbed out of the car. She shot me a look of terror, and it struck me that coming back into the woods might not have been such a great idea for Amber. I patted her shoulder comfortingly.

"It's really okay. Look, there's Marly and Luke at the door."

It was impossible to be with the Sawyers and feel ill at ease. Marly took over instantly, pulling Amber into the warm living room and putting a mug of hot tea into her hands. The lights were low, and a fire in the corner fireplace gave off a comforting glow.

I culled from Marly's thoughts that when we had stopped at Amber's car, Michael had called ahead to warn his parents that we were coming. Nobody brought up anything beyond the ordinary during the first half hour; Marly guided the conversation deftly, asking us about the dance, the decorations and fussing over both my dress and Amber's.

"You girls are beautiful," she smiled. "What a treat to be able to see you all dressed up after all. I thought I would have to wait for pictures."

Michael shook his head with a smile. "That's my mom, always looking for the bright side."

We were quiet for a time, watching the dancing flames

and each keeping our own counsel. My mind was exhausted, but I still picked up the occasional thought floating about. Michael was thinking very specifically, so that I knew he was actually speaking to me in his head.

I didn't tell my parents any more than what they needed to know. I told them Nell had caused trouble, Amber needed to get some place safe to recover and that we were all pretty shaken up. What we choose to tell them now is entirely up to you.

I caught his eye and nodded to indicate I'd heard him and understood. Marly and Luke were controlling their curiosity, but I heard the questions that kept ringing in their minds. Amber was still trying to process everything.

"Amber," I began softly, "I think we need to talk a little about what happened tonight."

She looked at me dully. "You saved my life tonight, you and Michael. I still don't get how you knew what was going to happen. Did the other girls tell you?"

"No," Michael said. "I think Nell's friends were out of the loop on this one." He glanced at me. "Or they made a good show of it, anyway."

"They didn't know," I answered with certainty. "They suspected, maybe, that Nell was up to something she hadn't shared with them, but I don't think any of them knew what it was. Or even guessed at what she really had in mind."

Marly looked from Michael to me. "Which was…?"

Michael shot me a questioning glance before I answered his mother. "Nell was planning to kill Amber tonight."

The room became completely still. Luke was the first one to speak.

"That's a very serious accusation, Tasmyn. I know you

wouldn't make it lightly. What exactly happened?"

This was the trickiest part. "I can tell you our part, but Amber knows more than we do," I replied. "Michael and I suspected that Nell intended to do something to Amber, but we didn't know it was going to be tonight. Then they both disappeared from the dance, and we got anxious. We convinced Liza to tell us where they usually met, and somehow we got there in time. Nell had attacked Amber. She had a knife with her—" this news elicited a gasp from Marly, "—but we don't know where it went in the confusion of getting her under control."

"Michael, why didn't you call for help? You could have both—all—been badly hurt, if Nell was as out of control as you say." Luke's voice was rough with anxious concern.

"There wasn't time, Dad. And in the beginning we didn't have any proof. Turns out we still don't. We had to just let Nell leave and get Amber out of there."

"You did the right thing," Marly interjected. "We can always call the police now."

"And tell them what?" Michael asked. "Nell threatened to turn it all on us, and she's right. We know her friends will back her up on anything she says. Unless we find that knife, there's nothing we can do."

"I'm a little confused about one thing," Marly said slowly, and my heartbeat quickened. I knew what she was going to say, because it had been rolling around her head all during this conversation. I had a decision to make.

"How did you two know what Nell was going to do? If someone told you, that person could be a witness. Or if you overheard Nell telling someone else…"

Michael didn't answer; he simply looked toward me.

And I knew what I had to say. It was awkward with Amber here too, but I decided that after all we had been through, she deserved to know as well.

"Nell's been planning this for a long time. She's been thinking about it. And—" I took a deep breath. "I could hear her. I could hear her planning to do something horrible to Amber."

Again the room was quiet. "What do you mean, you could hear her?" Marly queried.

"I mean, I could hear her thoughts. I can do that. I can hear what people are thinking. I try not to, most of the time, but sometimes I can't help it." I looked at both Luke and Marly, pleadingly. They were staring at me, blankly. In her chair in the corner, Amber looked bewildered.

"Mom, Dad, this doesn't change who Tasmyn is. She just has a talent you didn't know about. She's still the same person you know and—"

"Michael, don't be stupid." Marly's voice was impatient. "We know that. Just because we're a little surprised doesn't mean it changes how we love Tasmyn, not one iota."

Relief flooded my heart. I hadn't realized how much it mattered to me, what Luke and Marly thought.

"So..." Luke spoke. "You... heard... what Nell was planning, and you decided to try to stop her yourselves?"

Apparently we weren't going to deal with my rather unusual gift just at this moment. Actually, I was kind of grateful that they seemed to be taking it so matter-of-factly.

"We didn't know what else to do," Michael answered his father. "We handled it the best way we could."

"Tasmyn, do your parents know about this?" Marly wanted to know.

I hesitated, not sure of what she meant at first. Luckily I was still picking up thoughts, and I realized that she was referring to the Nell situation.

"No," I replied. "My parents—well, I know Michael told you how protective they are. Now you know the biggest reason. They worry about people finding out about my gift and taking advantage of me." I made a wry face. "If they find out about tonight, they won't let me out of the house for the next century."

Michael reached across the space between our chairs and took my hand. His parents exchanged glances.

"We can discuss that later," Luke said. "What I'm more concerned with right now is where Nell went after she left you. And Amber, how are you doing?"

Amber hadn't said a word during the entire conversation. Her eyes had widened at my revelation, and she had let the blanket fall from around her shoulders. Now, in response to Luke's question, she nodded slowly. "I'm not so cold and shaky anymore. Thanks." She turned to Michael and me. "I didn't say this before, but thank you for being there tonight. It sounds so silly and stupid, but you saved my life, I know you did. Even if the knife wasn't there—I swear she had it. It was the same athame that she used each time before, but she only drew the sacred circle with it then."

"You used that word before—athame? What's that?"

Amber closed her eyes and leaned back in her chair. "It's a knife. A-a witch's knife. But we never used it for anything —Marica said we had to—" She flushed red and dropped her chin.

"I think, if you feel up to it, you should probably start from the beginning and tell us everything, Amber. Tas and I only know what she's heard from you and Nell, and that's pretty sketchy," Michael said.

Amber drew in a deep breath. "I can tell you what's happened since Nell started talking to me. That was right after school began this year. But she and the other girls…" she trailed off, and then she squared her shoulders.

"Okay. I'll tell you what I know."

Chapter Thirty-Nine

Amber swallowed hard as she met my eyes.

"I'm sorry, it's just that they told me so many times how important it was to keep everything quiet. Marica—that's Ms. Lacusta—she said it was very dangerous to tell anyone what happened when we met."

"Wait." Marly held up one finger, her eyebrows pulled together over astounded eyes. "Ms. Lacusta—a teacher is involved in this?"

Amber's eyes slid to me. "I thought you would know that."

"I suspected. Nell seems to be a little, um, obsessed with our Chemistry teacher," I explained to Luke and Marly.

"Okay. Hmm. Go on, Amber," Marly nodded.

I could tell that it was extremely difficult for Amber to share all of this with us. The rule of secrecy must have been pounded into all of them, both by Nell and Ms. Lacusta. But Amber was beginning to trust us—that much I could feel—and trusting us made it all easier.

"It was right after school began. Maybe the second or third week—I don't know. It was just the same for me—I hated school, I hated being there. And then one day I was at my locker, and Nell came over to talk with me. I was—shocked, and kind of suspicious. She'd been leaving me alone since we left junior high. I really just wanted to get through the rest of high school without more problems. You remember how it used to be." Amber pointed at Michael.

He nodded at her. "I do. Nell made your life miserable."

"Yeah. And so I didn't really trust anything she said or

did. Even though she was very nice to me that day at my locker—and she kept on being nice, I didn't want anything to do with her. She invited me to eat with her friends at lunch, but I figured that was the trap—you know, I'd go there, and then they'd all pretend Nell hasn't asked me and use it to make fun of me.

"So then one day, Nell showed up at my house after school. She was standing there on the porch, and when I answered the door, she said she needed to talk to me. I still didn't trust her, especially because my mom wasn't home, and I didn't want her in the house with me alone. So I went out onto the porch and just stood there, and Nell—she apologized. For everything. She told me that when she was younger, she never knew how much her actions had hurt other people. And she said she wanted to be my friend."

Amber paused, lost in thought. "I didn't want to believe her. It was easier to go on hating her. But she said that she'd really changed, that she had—I remember clearly how she put it, she'd found a new way. And it required her to make amends where she had left hurt. I thought she meant she'd found religion, and when I asked her, she laughed. Not a mean laugh, like before, but real, genuine. She said, no, it wasn't precisely religion. She'd tell me more about it later, but she wanted to make sure we could be friends.

"So that's when I started hanging around with her at school, eating lunch with her friends—and we'd even do things after school. It was—" she drew in a deep breath, and even now, after all that had happened tonight, her eyes were bright, remembering, "—the best time. For the first time in so long, I had friends."

She turned pleading eyes on me. "So you understand,

Tasmyn, right? You know what it's like to be lonely. We talked that day in English, and you said you knew what it was like. And then to suddenly have friends—the world opened up to me. I didn't hate school anymore. I started to do better in my classes. It was what I dreamed high school could be.

"I knew that they were all involved in some kind of club. There were days when they met after school, and I knew there were things they weren't telling me. But they weren't mean about it.

"Then one day Nell asked me if I wanted to join their chemistry club. She said Ms. Lacusta had started it up last spring, when she first got here, and they were learning so much. I wasn't much into Chemistry; I barely passed the class freshman year. But Nell said it wasn't like that. She convinced me to try it, and she was right. It wasn't like any class I'd ever taken."

Amber stopped again. We were getting into the more intense part of her story, and I knew it would be difficult for her.

"Ms. Lacusta—she told us that Chemistry was so much more than just formulas and test tubes. She told us there was real power in it. I remember that. Real power. And the other girls, they were so enthusiastic about it all. It was easy to get caught up.

"Nell told me that they were meeting one night. She told me that Casey would pick me up, because she had to go early to talk with Marica—outside school, Ms. Lacusta wanted us to call her by her first name—and we were meeting in the woods. I was a little spooked, but more than that, I needed to keep these friends.

"So Casey and I got there—it was where we were tonight, the clearing near Lake Rosu. And I saw that the girls were different. Everyone was in a circle, and they were wearing dark robes. Nell gave me one, and I joined the circle. I was scared, sure, but I was also kind of excited.

"Nell drew the circle—that was the first time I saw her with the athame. And then they all started chanting—not in English, and I didn't know what it was at first, but Nell told me later it was Romanian. She said it was something Marica had taught them. After the chant, in the middle of the circle, Nell started a fire. I don't know how she did it—I didn't see matches or anything—but suddenly there was a fire there. And Marica handed her a pot that she hung over the fire. They chanted some more, then Marica stood up. She told us that what was in the pot was what we'd been working on in Chem. club that week, and that it was a potion that would make us more powerful.

"She said something else in Romanian over the pot, and then she scooped some out. We all had to dip our fingers in it, then touch it to our lips. I was scared—I kept thinking that I had no idea what she was giving us. So I didn't actually touch it. It was dark, and I figured no one was really going to notice."

Amber took a long drink of her tea and closed her eyes over the mug. I could feel her exhaustion.

"Amber, was what they were doing—was it like a Wiccan ceremony?" Marly was doing an admirable job of keeping her voice steady.

Amber shook her head. "I don't really know anything about that, but I asked Nell once if we were Wiccan, and she said no. What Marica taught us was ancient magics, from her homeland. Marica said that her family had been powerful for many generations, and they had passed on their secrets. We didn't worship anything; there was no mention of demons or anything like that. And I know that wiccans usually worship the elements, right? We didn't do that."

"How often did you have these ceremonies in the woods?" Luke too was remaining calm.

"Every other week or so. Marica would tell us when we were meeting. Of course, the Chem. club was happening almost every day after school. My parents were starting to get worried, but then, on the other hand, for the first time I was happy and involved, so they didn't tell me I couldn't go."

"What else happened at the meetings in the woods?" Michael asked.

Amber pursed her lips. "Well, they all pretty much started like that, then after we would chant over the potion, each girl would perform something—Marica called it proof of power. It could be something small, like creating fire, or bigger—levitating or whatever. And then after that we danced around the circle, and then we'd chant again, and sometimes Marica would talk, then we would leave.

"I mean, I know it sounds lame. But being part of it… and Marica telling us how our power was growing exponentially… and how we had to keep silent about it, because that was part of the power. She told us we could be unstoppable. She said that we were all her daughters, that she had foreseen that she would come to this place, which was a mystical spot, and that she would pass on her secrets to us."

I caught Michael's eye. "That would be exactly what Nell's looking for—someone who calls her a daughter. I can see how Ms. Lacusta drew her in."

"Yeah," Amber agreed with me. "I could tell that Nell was really... almost possessive of Marica. From what I heard from the other girls, Nell had started messing with witchcraft —they call it the power—about a year ago. I think in the beginning, in her mind it was a link to her mom. She had her mother's books, and of course she probably knows people from her family who still practice it. But she didn't get very far, and she wasn't happy with the spells she'd found. Julie said they thought Nell was getting bored with that and was finally going to stop making them play along. She had started dating Kyle, and they were all relieved.

"But then Marica arrived. She sought Nell out, spent time with her, and convinced her to help start up the chemistry club. Nell was... I think it was Liza who said that Nell had been infatuated with Ms. Lacusta from the beginning. She was—and is—possessive of her, even among all of us. She hated her to give attention or time to anyone else."

"That's one of the reasons Nell hated me right away— Ms. Lacusta was nice to me that first day."

"It was more than that," Amber said slowly. "Marica talked about you that first day, too. She said there was power in you. She didn't know what it was, but she was excited. She wanted Nell to be your friend, to get you to join us. And Nell—that was the first time I saw her freak out. She screamed at Marica, she said she hated you and there was no way you were joining us. Nell said that if Marica brought you in, all of the rest of us would leave."

My heart accelerated. Ms. Lacusta sensed power in me? Was that just a coincidence, or did she really know something?

Michael frowned and tightened his grip on my hand. I could feel his protective nature leaping forward, and I heard him think darkly that Ms. Lacusta would never get near me again.

"After that, things got worse. Nell wasn't the same nice person she had been. Well, to be honest, she had been getting kind of snappy even before you got here. I think Marica might have been—I don't know, almost getting bored with Nell? Nell followed her around like a puppy sometimes, and although Marica probably liked that at first, Nell was maybe getting too demanding. It might have been that you were just a convenient excuse for her to start to make a change."

"Amber, about two weeks ago you came into English all upset. I could hear you—your thoughts were so panicked you were practically yelling. That was when I started worrying about what Nell was up to with you. What happened that day?"

Amber knit her brows. "So much happened so fast there... two weeks ago. Well, things started getting scarier to me about a month ago. Nell started talking about what could be done to... threaten you. To keep you away from Ms. Lacusta and the chemistry club. And she wasn't just talking about being mean to you—she kept saying she had the power to make it happen.

"That was enough to make me second-guess everything that had happened in the past two months. Then Casey said something to Nell, totally off-topic, about Marica. Nothing important, just like Marica had told her something. And Nell freaked out on her. She wanted Casey to just stay away from Marica, and Casey—she's braver than the others, braver than me, definitely. She told Nell to shut up. I saw the look Nell gave Casey after she turned around, and it was just awful. It scared me to death.

"And I guess it probably was the day you're talking about when Nell grabbed me outside of class. She told me she had plans, and I was part of them. She said we were going to do something, just the two of us, that the others couldn't know about. She told me, 'Just be ready,' and then she smiled—but it was the worst thing I'd ever seen. And I was really frightened."

"That makes sense," I mused. "And it was about then that Nell was thinking about... hurting you, Amber. I saw her thinking about the knife that afternoon."

Amber shuddered, and Marly moved to put her arms around her. "Poor thing," she murmured. "You've been through so much. Let me warm up your tea."

We were all quiet until Marly returned and perched on the arm of my chair. She put her arm around my shoulder and drew me to her, kissing the top of my head. "It must have been so frightening for you, seeing and hearing what you were, and not knowing what to do." She leveled a gaze at Michael. "You know you could have come to us."

It was Michael's turn to look uncomfortable. "I know. But it would have meant telling you how we knew what we did, and that would have meant betraying Tasmyn's confidence. I couldn't do that."

I turned to look up at Marly. "It wasn't that I didn't trust you," I explained. "But I've never told anyone on purpose. Michael guessed. My parents don't know that he knows—it would really upset them. They've been protecting my secret all my life."

Marly smiled at me. "I'm not upset at you," she assured me. "And I'm not mad at Michael either. I can see why you thought you had to do this, but the mom in me is not happy that I couldn't protect either of you."

"Speaking of moms and so on, it's getting pretty late. We should probably take Amber home—and Tasmyn, too."

I turned to Amber. "If you want, you can stay with me tonight, and I'll take you home in the morning."

Amber hesitated, and then shook her head. "I appreciate it, more than I can tell you. But—I kind of want to see my parents. I've been less than honest with them in the past few months. I want to be truthful now."

"What will you tell them?" Michael asked.

"As much of the truth as I can. I'll tell them that Nell really wasn't my friend. I'll tell them that she hurt me—emotionally. And I'll tell them that they were right all along about her."

I touched Amber's shoulder. "I hope you can tell them that you made some new friends tonight. You don't have to go back to being lonely, Amber, just because of what's happened with Nell."

She wasn't sure, I could tell. And who could blame her: between what had happened to her when she did trust someone and now what she had learned about me tonight, she had to be completely freaked out. Which reminded me... I opened my mouth, but Michael beat me to it.

"I agree with Tasmyn, Amber. I hope we'll see you at our lunch table on Monday. But there's one thing. Please remember no one can know about Tasmyn's gift. This is really important. Especially not Nell or any of her group, or Ms. Lacusta."

Amber's eyes were wide. "Don't worry. I won't say a word. I'm not planning to talk to any of them ever again if I can help it. I just want to go back to being normal.

Chapter Forty

Normal would have been nice. And actually, I did have one day of it. I made it home on Friday before my curfew, even with all of our extracurricular activities. Michael and I decided on the way back into town with Amber that telling my parents loosely the same story that Amber told hers would be the safest way to go. The only difference was that I admitted to my parents that I had actually heard Nell planning to humiliate Amber but assured them that my secret was still safe.

My mom and dad were more surprised than angry, at least initially. I was so tired that I barely knew what I said to them before I shuffled off to bed with the promise to explain more the next day.

I slept until nearly noon on Saturday and stumbled out into the kitchen. My mother must have heard me poking around for something to eat because she came out of her office and sat at the kitchen table.

"I was just about to go in and make sure you were breathing," she commented.

"Sorry," I mumbled. "I'm not used to being up so late... or all the excitement, I guess."

"Yes, it sounds like you had quite the night," my mom observed.

"You know me. Never a dull moment."

"I'm sorry that your first dance turned out this way, though."

I picked up my bowl of fruit and joined my mother at the table. "You know, it was fun. I did have a good time. The part with Nell and Amber didn't ruin it for me."

"Well, good, I'm glad to hear it." She was toying with a napkin, a frown on her face, which I knew meant she had something to say. I picked at my fruit and waited.

"Your dad and I are worried. You heard something from that girl's mind, and then that you acted on it. That was a real risk."

I didn't answer right away. I knew this was coming. What I had done, or at least what my parents knew I had done, went against everything they had taught me about controlling and concealing my gift.

"I don't know how else I could have handled it. I couldn't have let Amber be hurt—in any way."

"But Tasmyn, we've talked about this so many times before. What you hear people think—you cannot base judgments or actions on that. And you're not even supposed to be putting yourself in a position to hear those thoughts. You know how to protect yourself from hearing things. How did that happen?"

I cast my eyes down unhappily. "It's been harder lately. It seems like the happier and more relaxed I am, the more difficult it is to keep up my guard."

My mother sighed. "Well, that's a dilemma. Obviously, your dad and I are glad that you're happy, and we don't want you to lose that. It's been very gratifying for us to see you make real friends here. We felt that you were finally old enough to have those friends and still keep your secret. But you're going to have to work harder, Tas, to learn how to maintain your mental block even while you're more relaxed."

"But what if I can't? What if this is just the way I was made and I'm really supposed to be using this gift, not trying to suppress it?"

My mom's mouth dropped slightly, and she stared at me. "Tasmyn, that idea is very frightening to me. That's why what happened last night scares us. You cannot go around interfering with lives just because you think that your talent gives you that right."

My temper was rising, and I struggled to remain calm. "I wouldn't say it gives me any rights. I look at it more as an obligation. If I heard someone planning a crime, wouldn't I be right to do something about it?"

"But the question is, where do you draw that line? How do you determine that someone is merely considering versus someone who is seriously planning?"

"I can tell the difference," I insisted. I remembered Nell's first vague idea about blood sacrifice and then her very specific planning of this past week. It was quite clear to me.

My mother shook her head. "We need to talk about this more, when your dad can be part of the conversation."

"Mom, look at this way: you've raised me right. You taught me how to manage this talent of mine. Now in less than two years, I'm going to be leaving home anyway and making my own choices about how I adapt my life to my particular circumstances. Wouldn't you rather I start doing that now, when I can come to you for advice and guidance, than when I'm completely on my own?"

She reached out and laid her hand over mine on the table. "Tasmyn, as long as Daddy and I are living, you'll never be alone. We'll always be here for you. And I don't think I agree that there are choices to be made. It's just a matter of controlling your mind…"

"Then you've lied to me all along. In your eyes, it's *not*

a gift or a talent, like you and Daddy have always said. It's a handicap. A curse."

Something flickered in her eyes, and I knew I had hit on a nerve. But her voice was steady. "Don't be ridiculous. We don't think of it that way."

I stood and picked up my empty bowl. "You're right that we need to talk about this, all of us. But today, I'm still too worn out. I need a little peace and quiet." My first instinct was to call Michael and ask him to come take me to the nursery, but I knew that wouldn't work. This was the last weekend of October, one of the busiest days all year. And I doubted my parents would be very enthused about me leaving at this point, either.

Instead I spent the better part of the day in my room, working on homework and doing laundry. I carefully folded my dress from the dance and put it in a bag for the dry cleaners. It gave me a pang of regret to think that my first dance would always be associated with Nell.

Late in the afternoon, I heard the phone ring and hoped it would be Michael, offering to come and rescue me. And my mother did come to my room, carrying the cordless handset. But when she handed it to me, she whispered, "It's Amber."

Surprised, I took the phone and settled on my bed, the door closed behind my mom.

"Hello?" I answered.

"Tasmyn? Hi… it's Amber."

"Hey! How are you doing today? Did you sleep okay?"

"Well, once I got to sleep, I pretty much passed out. I was up for a long time, talking with my parents."

"How did that go?" I wondered, thinking about my own recent conversation.

"It went... well, it was incredible, actually. They were so understanding, and worried... we talked a long time about how I can change things in my life, so I'm not so easily taken in by someone like Nell again."

My heart warmed. "I'm so glad, Amber. It sounds like your parents are pretty terrific."

"They are. I never really thought about it until now. I've always felt so sorry for myself because of how bad things are at school, but lots of kids don't have parents like mine. That's a good thing, right?"

"It's a very good thing," I agreed. "And I don't think things will be so bad at school anymore. You know Michael and I were serious about wanting you to hang with us. You'll be surprised how fast Michael's friends accept people. Hey, they took me in, didn't they?"

"As long as none of them are into... other stuff, I'm in."

I laughed, without too much humor. "No, I can assure you that no one in that crowd is into anything wacky. Just the typical stuff. You'll like them."

"Okay, good, I'm looking forward to Monday. Isn't that weird? Probably the worst Friday night of my life, ever, and I'm excited about Monday."

I laughed. "I'm glad you called, Amber. I was thinking about you today. What are you doing tomorrow?"

"Well, my parents have been going to that new church outside town. You know Cara, that girl in our class whose dad is a minister? It's his church. So I was thinking I would go with them tomorrow. They've wanted me to go, but Nell always made fun of it, so I didn't go. If Nell doesn't like it, I figure it's probably a good thing."

"Yeah, I think you're onto something there. I know

Cara. She's really nice. You'll like her too—she sits at our lunch table."

"Cool! I'm going to go help my mom with dinner. I'll see you Monday?"

"Definitely," I promised, hanging up. The conversation had made me thoughtful about my own situation. I knew that my parents only wanted the best for me. The tricky part, I decided, was that at some point my opinion of what was best and theirs were going to part ways. Could I handle that gracefully, so that my mother and father realized that it wasn't them I was rejecting—just their view of my talent? I wasn't sure yet.

Dinner that night was subdued. Our conversation stuck to the generalities, and I could feel the unease that both of my parents were experiencing. I realized that what I had said to my mother this afternoon went counter to everything they wanted for me, which was only a normal life. I needed them to understand that maybe I wasn't designed for normal.

"So..." I began, trying to keep the nerves out of my voice, "Mom, I'm sorry if I got a little... ummm, testy with you this afternoon. I know that you're just worried, both of you."

They exchanged relieved glances, and I heard, *Oh, good, she's being reasonable. That's the daughter we know. Thank heavens...* It would be so easy to just let it go at that, to let them think that I agreed and was continuing to go along with their guidelines. But I knew that wouldn't accomplish what we both needed in the long run, and if I valued my relationship with them, I had to be as honest as I could be.

"But," I continued with resolve in my voice, "That doesn't change the fact that I'm old enough now to make my own decisions about the best way to use my talents. My ability. You've sheltered and shielded me when I didn't know any better, when I would have gotten into real trouble, not knowing how to use it. But hearing thoughts—that's not just something to hide and try to suppress—it's part of me, it's part of who *I* am. And when I feel ashamed of it, I'm feeling ashamed of myself. I don't want to live my life that way."

There was silence around the table. The unease my parents had been feeling had given way to surprise and confusion. I had never bucked them about anything involving my abilities, so this was completely new territory for all of us.

Finally my dad spoke. "Tas... that's a very interesting point. Your mom and I—we've never wanted you to feel ashamed of what you can do, of who you are. But you're also right that we don't see it as part of who you are—you are so much more than that to us. If you were handicapped in some way, we wouldn't want that to define you. And this shouldn't either. With a little work, you should be able to lead a completely normal life—"

"What if I don't want normal?" I interrupted. "As a matter of fact, *why* would I want normal? Our family has never been typical. We move constantly. I've never had friends until this year. *I can hear what other people are thinking. I can feel what they're feeling.* That's not normal, Dad. And for the first time, I'm thinking that maybe it's a good thing, not something I need to hide."

My mother looked troubled. "But Tasmyn, flaunting your gift could put you at real risk. Things like this aren't the same as—I don't know, being able to speak several languages, or being a math genius. This is a talent that can be so easily exploited. Telling anyone at all is really very dangerous for you."

This was my opening. I drew in a deep breath. "That isn't precisely true, Mom. You're right that making a big deal of it and telling everyone would be wrong. But sharing this—this part of me, of who I am, with someone, with people I trust—it's not wrong. And it's not dangerous. I know that for sure."

Now the silence took on an entirely new depth. I swallowed nervously, as I felt what I'd just said register in their minds.

"Tasmyn... are you saying... you've told someone already?" My mother's tone was frightened and incredulous.

"I hope you mean that you're thinking about doing it, and you know, of course, that your mom and I discourage that as strongly as we can." My father leaned more toward disapproval in his fear.

I bit my lip nervously. "I mean, I didn't necessarily tell someone. But... someone... guessed."

"And am I correct in assuming that someone was Michael?"

I nodded, unable to trust my voice.

My father heaved a long and heavy sigh. I couldn't discern whether it was disapproval or disappointment... perhaps a bit of both.

"When did this happen? Was it part of last night's events?"

I shook my head. "No. Actually, Michael figured it out very early on."

"How exactly?" My mother's voice shook.

"It was the day I spilled the stuff on me in Chemistry. I was upset, and he was talking to me, and I accidentally answered what he thought instead of what he said out loud."

"That could have been explained away," my father remarked.

"Yes, it probably could have," I answered slowly. "But it was my choice not to do that. I knew that I wanted to be totally honest with Michael. It was very important for me."

They digested that statement in silence. "You trust him that much?" my mom queried.

I replied without hesitation. "I do. I trust him, and he hasn't let me down."

"Well, not yet anyway," my father said archly.

"That's a very cynical comment," I shot back.

"The world is a very cynical place," he answered. "I believe Michael will be discreet for as long as he is involved with you. After that... my expectations of him sink considerably."

"What if I tell you that won't be a problem?" I asked.

"Then I'd say you're fairly naïve, which is about what I'd expect of a seventeen year old girl."

"But we've established that I'm not really your typical seventeen year old girl, and you know, I have more insight into the situation—into my relationship with Michael—than most girls my age would have."

"You may think you do—"

"Daddy, trust me on this. Michael has no problem with me listening to him, and although I try not to do it—I really do—I've heard enough to know that he's not going to betray my confidence or break my heart." My face flooded with heat. I hadn't been yet so frank with my parents about my relationship with Michael, and it was oddly unnerving.

I could tell that they both remained unconvinced. Since I was already in so deep, I decided to go for broke.

"I should tell you that as of last night, Michael's parents know the truth about me, too."

My mother groaned and held her head in her hands. My father just sighed again. I could tell he was quickly losing patience with what he saw as my blatant rebellion.

"I'm sorry. I had to tell them. And you don't know Marly and Luke yet, but please believe me, we can trust them."

"Tasmyn, this is the crux of the whole issue. You really aren't mature enough to understand who can or cannot be trusted with a secret that could literally turn your life upside down. You've known these people for less than two months. *Two months.* That's nothing in the greater scheme of things. They could be psychos. They could be completely rational people who just happen to mention to a friend that their son's girlfriend can read minds, isn't that neat? And just like that, it's all over." My father was becoming more and more angry as he spoke.

"You have no confidence in my ability to judge people, do you? Don't you know that all these years, you and Mom have been teaching me how to do that? Because of you, I *can* discern when it's safe to open up to someone and when it isn't. I know for a fact that even if today I told Michael that I never wanted to see him again—" my heart skipped a beat at even the thought of that, "—he wouldn't ever tell anyone about me. And I know that his parents love me. They haven't known me for a long, but they do. And since they didn't know until last night that I could sometimes hear them think,

I feel pretty secure in trusting my intuition about that."

I paused, looking at my parents for a minute. They were both shaken and somewhat appalled by what I had shared with them. I knew it would take time for them to digest it all and understand what I was trying to tell them.

"I want you both to understand that I love you, and I will always appreciate how you brought me up. I know it wasn't easy. You faced challenges that most parents wouldn't be able to handle. And I want you to know that everything you did, all the time you took—it was worth it! I'm able to control my listening, for the most part. And when I do slip, I'm able to discern what's serious and what isn't. I don't make rash decisions and I don't jump to conclusions.

"But I don't think you raised me to stay the same little girl who was afraid of what she could do, who was scared to have friends in case they guessed the secret. I think you raised me to be able to go out on my own and live a full life. And I'm telling you, this is the beginning of it. It doesn't mean I'm rebelling against you. It means I'm fulfilling every dream you had for me."

The tension in the room had largely dissipated. My mother sat back in her chair and gazed at me thoughtfully. She glanced at my father, and when she spoke, her voice was low but steady.

"You're right, Tas. We didn't bring you up to be a hermit, or to stay with us forever. Maybe we just thought that we'd have a little more time. It was hard enough to accept that you're ready to have a boyfriend, and we were probably pretty short-sighted not to realize that you'd want to share more of yourself with him."

Now my face was really flaming. "Mom—you're talking

about Michael knowing I can hear minds, right? Because I haven't, um, shared any more of myself with him."

My mother laughed. "That is a relief, and it's also a whole different conversation. No, I meant you telling him. Or him guessing, however it happened. I have to admit, though, that I'm very disappointed that you didn't tell us sooner about him knowing. I won't speak for your father, but it makes me feel left out. I'm also a little upset that you've been lying to us all this time."

It was my turn to feel squirmy. "I didn't really lie to you. You never asked me, and when you asked if I was being careful with Michael, I told you yes. That's the truth. I was being careful. I *am*."

"Tas." My father's rolled his eyes at me. "It's the spirit of the rule, not the letter. You know that. You were fully aware of what we expected."

"And what would you have done if I had told you?"

My mother spread her hands in front of her. "What *can* we do? He knows. It can't be undone. We have to live with it, and hope for the best, I suppose." Her tone indicated that she felt more doubt than hope about the situation.

"Your mom is right. But from now on, we expect you to be honest with us. No more secrets. Got it?"

I swallowed hard, thinking of what I hadn't shared with them about Nell and Amber and our encounter in the clearing. I knew this wasn't the time to do that, but I hated keeping anything from them. I nodded and forced a smile.

"Got it."

Chapter Forty-One

Sunday was a blissfully uneventful day. Michael took me to Lancer Lake, to our special beach, and we spent the afternoon reading and talking about anything that wasn't related to Nell or Amber.

That night, Anne called. I had been curious about how Friday evening had turned out for her and for Jim, and I was excited to talk to her.

"So?" I asked, anticipation in my voice.

"So what?" she replied, all innocence.

"So tell! Tell all!" I insisted. "What happened Friday night?"

"I could ask you the same thing. You and Michael disappeared pretty abruptly. No one knew what happened! We were worried!"

"Oh, yes, so worried you called me right away?" I teased.

"Well..." she giggled. "I have to admit, I slept most of yesterday. And then I had plans last night." The emphasis she put on the word *plans* made me laugh.

"Oh, do tell!!" I insisted. "All the gory details, please!"

"The first thing I have to say is thank you. You were right. And I never would have known or done anything about it if you hadn't said something. I don't know if Jim would've gotten brave eventually, but he had no idea how I felt, so maybe not. Can you imagine? All this time, we've both been feeling the same way and not knowing it or telling each other?"

"No, I can't imagine," I replied, amused. "But what did

he do? The last I saw, the two of you were heading to the dance floor, and Jim looked like someone had hit him over the head. He was positively dazed."

"He was, wasn't he?" Anne was clearly enjoying this. "We went out there, and at first, I wasn't sure he was really going to dance with me. He just kept looking at me like he had never seen me before. But then we did dance, and suddenly, when his arms were around me, and we were moving to the music, Jim seemed surer of himself.

"And then he looked down at me and told me I looked beautiful. He said, 'I've been waiting for you to be whole again.' I asked him what he meant, and he told me that since everything happened with Nick, it looked as though part of me was gone."

"Oh, how romantic!" I exclaimed.

"It was! So I told Jim that maybe the part of me that was missing was him. I told him I'd hated the way we argued, and that I knew he had been right."

"And then what happened?"

"The dance ended, and he asked me if I wanted to go out onto the back porch of the Hall with him. So I did, and we talked... and talked... and then he kissed me. Oh, Tasmyn, it was the best night ever. It was more romantic than any time I ever spent with Nick."

"I'm so happy for you," I murmured.

"After the dance, he took me out to have dessert at a cute little diner, and then he took me home. I slept until noon yesterday, and my mother told me he called three times. When I called him back, he asked me out to the movies last night. He came over and asked my parents if it was all right for us to date—they've known him forever, so it wasn't like I had to introduce them or anything. And then he took me out, and we had a great time."

"Anne, this is wonderful. Oooh, I just thought of something—we could double date sometime!"

"Yeah, or triple date—Brea seems pretty stuck on that junior."

"And have you noticed that Dan seems pretty friendly with Cara?"

"I did notice that. I guess love is in the air!" For the next hour, we dished on all the couples and potential couples in our little group, and then in the school at large. We finally circled back around to Jim, and it thrilled me to hear how Anne's voice sang whenever she mentioned his name. Then she changed the subject abruptly.

"So you never told me where you and Michael went Friday night when you disappeared. Was it someplace romantic?"

I hesitated, wondering how much to share. I decided that we had to have some explanation for why Amber would be sitting with us at lunch the next day, and maybe it was a good idea to lay down the basics for Anne right now, as a sort of trial run for the group at large.

"Actually, no. It was more of a rescue mission." I laughed lightly, to keep that from sounding as grim as it truly had been. "Nell Massler was up to her old tricks with Amber Cole, and Michael and I slipped out to help Amber. Everything's okay now, but I don't think you'll see Amber and Nell hanging around together anymore, and Nell—let's just say I don't think we'll ever be best buds."

Anne was sympathetic. "That's terrible for Amber. How's she doing? How was Nell torturing her this time?" I knew Anne meant that more figuratively than literally, but it was closer to the truth than she knew.

"Amber's fine. Her feelings were hurt, and she's feeling a little betrayed, but she'll recover. I invited her to sit with us at lunch on Monday. I hope that's okay."

"Sure, it's your lunch table, too. We'll be happy to have her. And speaking of Monday, I have a chapter of History I have to read for tomorrow. I better go."

After we hung up, I sat for a while, just marveling at the changes in my life. I had Michael, someone who knew all of me and loved me anyway. I had Anne, a friend who actually credited me—*me!*—with resurrecting her love life. This weekend with Amber, I had used the talent that I'd hidden in shame and fear my whole life to really help someone. And I had been mostly honest with my parents and at least laid the groundwork for a little more understanding and independence.

I remembered that last fall, in Wisconsin, I had spent my weekends wrapped in blankets, alone in my room, devouring all the poetry of Dylan Thomas and John Keats. There were no friends on the telephone or dates to the lakeshore. I had been miserably aware that I was different from other girls my own age and fearful that this difference would make me an oddity for the rest of my life. There had been very little hope or optimism within me, and I had struggled to hide all of this turmoil from my parents.

All things considered, I liked this year much better.

Chapter Forty-Two

I was jittery on Monday morning, wondering if Nell would be in school and how she would act toward Amber, Michael and me. Michael picked me up as usual, but our ride was much quieter than it normally was.

"So, how were your parents today?" Michael inquired. I knew that he was worried about how they viewed him, now that they knew the truth.

I made a face. "They're still not happy about all the changes they see in me. It's my own fault, really. If I had been up front with them from the beginning, they would have had time to process everything little by little. Now it's all hitting them at once."

Michael sighed heavily. "I'm sorry it's so rough on you. Not what you needed after this weekend."

"Well, maybe not. But I think they'll come around. I tried to be as reasonable as I could without giving in completely."

We pulled into the parking lot and walked hand-in-hand to my locker. The walkways were fairly empty; we'd made it in early. I didn't see any sign of Nell or her crowd, but as I pulled books from my locker, Amber approached us.

"Hi," she smiled, almost shyly. "I'm really glad to see you. My mom dropped me off early, on her way to work, and I've been wandering around, afraid of seeing—well, afraid of what was around every corner."

"I think you're pretty safe here," Michael said. "But you should probably watch your back when you're alone outside school. Is your mom picking you up today or are you walking home?" I felt the concern that he was trying to hide, and I picked up random scenarios flitting through his head.

"Yeah, I'm covered," Amber confirmed. "I have a feeling that my parents are going to be a little overprotective for a few days, at least."

"Overprotective is good for right now," I put in. "You'll have plenty of time to stretch the apron strings once things settle down."

"I guess so," Amber agreed. "I can't imagine how bad it would be if I'd told them I was actually in physical danger. They'd have probably shipped me off to boarding school. Or a convent."

We all laughed, somewhat ruefully because we knew how close to the truth it was.

In French, Cara and I rehashed Friday's dance. She told me that she had enjoyed hanging out with Dan but assured me that they were just friends.

"I like him," she whispered as the teacher began the lesson, "but not anything heavy, you know?" I nodded and was suddenly tempted again to listen into Cara's thoughts, remembering the suspicions I had picked up from Anne about Cara's feelings for Michael. If she had some sort of crush on him, that could explain why she didn't want to get involved with Dan. But after the talk with my parents over the weekend, I was determined to keep my motives pure when I decided to use my talents. This would definitely be a selfish purpose.

I was on edge as French ended and I walked to Chemistry. My palms were sweaty, and I felt slightly sick at the prospect of confronting Nell. As I turned the corner of the walkway, I heard my name—not spoken aloud, but thought somewhere near me. I glanced up to see Michael leaning against the building, smiling at me.

"What are you doing here?" I asked, surprised. His Physics class was nowhere near my Chemistry classroom.

"I knew you were going to be jumpy about going to chem. today, so I thought I would hang here, just to remind you I've got your back. She might be nasty, but she won't do anything in front of the class, or especially in front of Ms. Lacusta, I think. Be strong."

My nerves eased, and I smiled up at him. "You know, you're fairly wonderful. What did I ever do to deserve someone like you in my life?"

He grinned back. "That's a topic we can explore later. For now, go on in and deal with Chemistry. I'll see you at lunch, okay?" He planted a swift kiss on my cheek, so quickly that no one watching would realize he hadn't merely leaned down to whisper in my ear. Then he was gone, around the corner.

I knew he was right. I was perfectly safe in class. I lifted my chin and went inside.

Nell was in her seat, facing the front of the room. Casey and Liza had their heads together, whispering, but Nell was ignoring them. In self-protection, I concentrated on keeping up my mental wall and sat down behind her.

Ms. Lacusta began class immediately, and thankfully, it was an intense lecture, requiring all my attention and note taking abilities. Although I didn't hear anything from Nell's mind, it was a relief when the bell rang and I could leave.

In English, Amber smiled at me as she took her seat, and I marveled at the contrast between what I felt from her today and the Amber I had first met nearly two months before.

Despite her underlying anxiety, she was much more peaceful today.

We walked to lunch together after class. Julie DiNardo and Casey passed us, and they both flashed glares of intense dislike at Amber. I half waited for her to wilt beneath their obvious anger, but she merely looked away from them.

Once in the cafeteria, I broke away to join Michael at our table while Amber filled her tray. I smiled at the changes I saw; Anne and Jim were sitting close together across the table, and Brea's junior boyfriend was next to her. Cara threw me a quick wave as I sat down next to Michael.

He took my hand in his and drew me closer to his side. "How did it go this morning?" he murmured in my ear.

"It was fine. Just like you said, nothing happened. She ignored me completely."

"Good. I passed her on the way here, and it was the same story. She didn't even look at me. Maybe she's a little embarrassed by the whole thing. You know, now in the more reasonable light of day and all that."

I snorted. "Yeah, maybe. I don't think 'reasonable' or 'embarrassed' are words that I associate with Nell Massler."

He shrugged. "As long as she's leaving all of us alone, I'm not going to sweat it."

I nodded and began to eat some of the sandwich that Michael pushed in front of me. "I don't trust her. I don't see her being that easily dissuaded. That's why I'm going to check in every now and again, just to make sure she's not still plotting evil and mayhem."

Michael frowned. "You mean purposefully listening in on her?"

"Not all the time. Just now and then. You know, kind of

like when someone's on parole and there's an officer to make sure the rules are being followed. I'm Nell's parole officer."

Amber joined us just then, sitting next to me but looking uncertainly at the rest of the table. I turned to include her in our group. As I had predicted, there was a warm welcome from the whole crowd. Anne was particularly kind, and I could feel Amber's gratitude. Only Cara looked slightly perplexed by the turn of events. I figured I was in for a grilling during History class.

She caught up with me outside the classroom, right after Michael had left for his own class. I waited to walk in with her.

"So… what's the deal with Amber?" Cara didn't waste time with any preliminaries. "I thought she was tight with Nell Massler. Now she's sitting with us?"

"Long story. Basically, Nell finally pushed her too far, and Michael and I happened to be there for her at the right time. Amber's had a tough time of it lately, and she needs friends. That's about it."

"Huh." Cara and I sat down and waited for Mr. Frame to arrive. I could feel that Cara knew she wasn't getting the whole story about Amber, but I chose not to elaborate. My silence provoked her into comment.

"She seemed like kind of a loner, before. When I moved here last year, I tried to talk to her a few times. But she was so quiet, I could never really get a conversation going. She looked completely different today at lunch."

I shrugged. "Who knows? Maybe she just needed to realize that she doesn't have to be lonely anymore."

Cara looked at me with one eyebrow raised, but she didn't push it any further. Mr. Frame came in to begin class, and I was relieved to have an excuse to turn my attention elsewhere. As much as I liked Cara, I wasn't entirely sure that I trusted her yet.

Chapter Forty-Three

After a week of relative peace, I began to feel cautiously optimistic about Amber's safety. Nell continued to ignore all of us, and if her friends shot Amber dirty looks or made loud, derogatory comments in our direction, it was easy to pretend we didn't hear. I listened to Nell as frequently as I could stand it, in both Chemistry and in History, and I didn't hear anything beyond her normal dark thoughts. Her little spites toward the girls in her group, her continued worship of Ms. Lacusta and her general disdain for the rest of us were always there, but that didn't concern me. I figured that was just who she was.

Only one thing troubled me slightly during that week. In Chemistry, on the Wednesday after the dance, I noticed that Casey and Liza were both very tense. Nell refused to acknowledge their attempts to talk with her; she sat staring straight ahead in stony silence. I wondered if I had interrupted an argument.

Sensing that this might pertain to the Amber situation, I didn't have any qualms about lowering my mental curtain and listening to Casey and Liza. Nell's mind was eerily silent, though I could feel the unpleasant mood flowing from her.

Don't know why Nell keeps harping on this. Haven't we told her everything, like, a million times? What happened at the dance after she left one more time... all she talks about... gonna scream... know I'm not the only one... Casey sighed in frustration and turned in her seat, away from Nell.

Why she blames me... something with Amber... not my fault. Won't tell us what happened... she keeps going on and on... what did Tasmyn say, what did Michael ask, how did she ask it... crazy... starting to think that's what Nell is, too. Liza frowned and fingered her pencil nervously.

This was worrisome. I cast my mind back to those minutes before Michael and I had left the dance, when we were madly trying to discern where Nell and Amber had gone. I hadn't been completely discreet at that point about listening to Liza's mind. In fact, some of the things I had said could be quite damning. At the time, my focus had been on finding and saving Amber, so I hadn't worried about what Liza might think. And left to her own devices, she might not have thought anything other than I was exactly the freak she'd suspected me to be.

But the fact that Nell was questioning both Liza and Casey about what happened at the dance made me nervous. She was suspicious about how we had figured out her plan. The only possibilities were that one of her friends had spilled the beans or Michael and I had followed her to Lake Rosu. Since it seemed that she had played this one very close to the chest, I doubted that any of the girls knew what her intentions had been. I sincerely hoped not. Though I didn't like any of the girls in Nell's little posse, neither did I want to entertain the idea that they would sit back and allow her to murder another girl in cold blood, in the name of magic and power.

I told Michael about it that day at lunch. We were sitting outside again, enjoying a little time to ourselves. I had worried about leaving Amber at the lunch table by herself, concerned she would feel we were abandoning her, but she was fitting in so well that she didn't even blink when I explained to her where I was going once we reached the cafeteria. She only grinned and gave me an airy wave. Anne caught my arm as I headed for the door, still looking back at Amber indecisively.

"Don't worry about her. I'll look out for her today. Enjoy your private lunch." She gave me a suggestive wink that made me blush.

My cheeks must have still been pink when I reached Michael since he greeted me with one raised eyebrow.

"Something I should know about?" he inquired.

My face heated all over again, and I shook my head as I sat down. "Nope. Just Anne being naughty."

Michael pulled me closer to him and wrapped one arm about my waist. "Remind me to thank her. I like it when you're flushed and flustered."

I rolled my eyes at him but couldn't really work up a good mad. He was just so insanely good-looking, and the teasing light in his eyes reminded me once again that I was the one he had chosen. The unlikelihood of it still caught me by surprise at the oddest moments. This was one of them.

"So what's the status of our parolee today?" he asked me, tearing open a packet of crackers.

I pulled over the salad he'd brought me and added the dressing. "Nothing much going on in Nell's head. However, I got some interesting tidbits from her cohorts."

Michael bit into a sandwich. "Which ones?"

"Liza and Casey. I'd hoped maybe they hadn't noticed anything strange at the dance, when we were giving them the third degree. I don't think they necessarily did. But Nell's been grilling them, and now they're all getting upset. Might not be long until they start getting suspicious, too."

"So what do we do? How can we damage control this?"

I shrugged and made designs in the salad dressing with a carrot stick. "There's not much to do but act as though we think they're nuts if they say anything. And let's face it—they *would* sound crazy. They don't have proof, and Nell would have to tip her hand a lot more than she's willing in order to convince the others."

Michael finished his sandwich and grabbed a napkin. "And you don't think any of the others know what Nell was planning to do? What are they thinking now about Amber?"

Slowly I shook my head. "No, they don't seem to have a clue. And I think they just figure the Nell and Amber thing ran its course. They were probably more confused about why Nell included Amber in the first place than they are about why she isn't part of things now."

"That makes sense, I guess." Michael turned so he was straddling the bench and reached to brush my hair over my shoulder. "How are you doing? You look tense."

I blew out a breath and pushed away the half-eaten salad. "I feel like I'm walking a line. On one hand, I'm telling my parents that I don't want to be afraid or ashamed of my talents anymore. I don't want to live in hiding. But on the other hand, I'd be an idiot to shout the truth to the rooftops. I'm still working to protect myself, and it feels like hypocrisy."

Michael chuckled. "And you hate hypocrisy, I know. But I don't think that's what it is. 'Discretion is the better part of valor', right?"

I sighed glumly. "Actually, it's 'The better part of valor is discretion, in the which better part I have saved my life.'

Falstaff, in Henry IV. And he's referring to his own cowardice there. So what does that say about me?"

Michael groaned and rolled his eyes at me. He reached for my hand and pulled me close to him. Burying his face in my neck, he whispered, "Well, first it says you know way too much about Shakespeare that you can quote it that exactly. That's just bizarre."

His breath tickled my ear, and I shivered. Turning my head slightly so that he could hear me, I replied, "But knowing the periodic table of elements and all that math stuff, that's normal?"

His lips were moving on the side of my face, but he didn't even hesitate to answer. "Absolutely. That's essential information that you can use every day. But you interrupted my point. You are definitely not a coward. Self-protection is just a mark of intelligence. And you're not a hypocrite, either. You're feeling your way through this new territory."

I reached back to touch his face, flooded with gratitude for his love and loyalty. "It's just so strange having more people know about me. With you, it was natural. It didn't feel that odd, because I wanted to tell you everything about me. But now that Amber and your parents are in the loop, too, I'm more self-conscious." I pulled away a little, so I could see his face; even though I could hear him thinking, I wanted to be able to gauge his expression. "I haven't seen your parents since Friday night. How have they been… adjusting to this new information?"

I didn't notice any change in his thoughts or his face as he gave a half shrug. "We haven't really talked about it. I don't think it threw them half as much as you think, Tas.

They like you so much that it's just another element of who you are, so that's okay."

I studied him for a moment, then turned again and leaned my head back against him. "How did I get so lucky? You know, in all fairness, your parents should be stiff, intolerant people who can't stand me."

He laughed, shaking us both and shifting so that his arms held me closer. "How do you figure that?"

"Because you're so wonderful and perfect that there should be some—I don't know, some fly in the ointment. Something that mars the total picture. But there isn't. You, your parents, your friends—all of you are just right."

"You haven't met my sister yet, so maybe she won't like you," he offered. "Would that make you feel better?"

"Oh, no," I moaned. "You're right. I just totally cursed myself. Lela is going to hate me, isn't she?"

Michael grasped me by the shoulders and turned me around to face him. "No, she is going to love you. Just like my parents do. Just like my friends do. But most important..." he brushed his lips lightly over mine, "—just like I do. That's all that matters. The rest is just gravy."

Chapter Forty-Four

Sometimes events converge in such a way that we just can't help but believe in some kind of higher power. Call it fate, call it God. Whatever it is, I believe in it.

It was the early part of November, and at King High, we were in the midst of mid-term exams. I wasn't at all worried about English or History. French had the potential to be a little challenging. I had to perform a four minute speech for the class of the same name, which didn't delight me but at least didn't involve hours of study.

Trig and Chemistry were going to present my biggest challenges. I was spending long hours pouring over the books and working problems with Michael. He was endlessly patient, never rolling his eyes or even thinking about how surprisingly clueless his girlfriend was.

Right in the middle of all this academia, the publisher my mother was working with on her latest illustrating venture requested that she fly to New York for a few days of face-to-face meetings. My mom vacillated about it for almost a day, worrying about leaving my dad and me to our own devices for a week. In the end, though, she decided to go.

Her absence meant that I now had a car to drive to and from school, which seemed like one of those convenient coincidences: Michael was pulling extra hours at the nursery as they geared up for the holiday season, and his botany professor, impressed with Michael's hard work and natural ability in class, had arranged for his extra hours to count as an internship. It was a wonderful opportunity, but it meant that I had to find my own way home.

A couple of days, I had walked home with Amber and hung out at her house. Her mother was glad to see her making healthy friendships. Their home was warm and comfortable, and I enjoyed the time I spent there, even while I missed my rides home with Michael.

I knew Michael missed our afternoons together, too. He was grumbling about it as we drove into the school parking lot on Tuesday morning of mid-term week.

"I feel like I'm missing something when I leave every day," he complained.

"Well, you are," I replied. "You're missing me. But it's only until the end of the semester. And how cool is it that you're getting school credit for your work at the nursery!"

"Yeah," Michael conceded. "That's true. But it doesn't mean it's easier not seeing you between lunch and the next morning."

"Now that I can use my mom's car, maybe I could ride over and see you tomorrow," I offered. "I could drive myself to school, and then out to the nursery after school. You know, later in the afternoon. I wouldn't bother you while you were working."

Michael turned off the car and smiled at me. "That's the best idea I've heard all week. But how will I last from now until then?"

I giggled. "I guess you'll just have to soldier on."

"Well, then, kiss me well enough to get me through until I see you at the nursery."

I leaned back far enough that my head rested nearly on the steering wheel, my arms wrapped around my heavy backpack. From that vantage point I looked up into Michael's gorgeous eyes and smiled. Then I shifted slightly, raising my head just enough to meet his lips with my own.

I was lost almost immediately in the intimacy of the kiss. In one way, pinned to the seat by my bag, I felt vulnerable, but knowing that I had initiated this made me feel exultant. I could hear Michael's murmuring thoughts, all endearments and croonings. Finally, when I felt my heart would pound out of my chest, he pulled away. Leaning back on the headrest, he blew out a long breath. "Whew. Wow. Okay."

Innocently, I fluttered my eyes at him, still trying to catch my own breath. "Will that hold you until this afternoon?"

"Um, I'm not sure. That might have hurt more than helped." But he gave me a gentle boost up again and brushed a hand over my hair as I got out of the car. I threw him the sweetest smile I could muster as we headed toward school.

Amber was waiting at my locker.

"Hi, Tas," she greeted me. "I was wondering if you want to walk home with me today. Maybe we could study for the English exam."

Michael leaned down and brushed a quick kiss over my lips. "I'm going to get into class early and do some cramming while you two work out your plans. I'll talk to you tonight, Tas."

My eyes followed him down the walkway as I answered Amber. "That sounds good. I can definitely use the extra study time."

"We could do it tomorrow, if that would be better," Amber offered, and I could hear the hesitation in her voice and mind. Our friendship was still new, and she worried about asking for too much.

"No, today would be great," I assured her. "Actually, tomorrow I'm planning to go out and spend the afternoon with Michael. With my mom away, I can use her car, so I thought I'd take advantage of it!"

"Good idea." Amber threw me an understanding smile. "Okay. I'll see you at lunch!" She pushed off the wall and moved away through the crowd. As I closed my locker, I caught the very edge of a darkly familiar mind, and I glanced around uneasily.

Just across the walkway, Nell stood against the wall, making no attempt to disguise the fact that she was staring at me. Our eyes met for a moment and for just a split second, I could hear her clearly.

I wonder...

And then the thought noise of everyone surging around us intruded, and involuntarily, I winced and closed my eyes, putting my hand to my head. When I looked up again, Nell was gone, and I was left with a lingering sense of dread that stayed with me the rest of the day.

Chapter Forty-Five

The next day I drove myself to school in the morning. It was odd to pull into the parking lot without Michael, and I ignored the small voice in my head reminding me that this was what next year would be like.

I had a few precious minutes with him at my locker before we both rushed off to our respective classes. It was only later that I remembered I hadn't told him about Nell and the weird vibe I'd gotten.

My History midterm was that day after lunch. My confidence in Mr. Frame and his straightforward tests was justified, and I turned in my exam well ahead of the rest of the class. With time to kill, I pulled out my Trig notes and tried to make sense of what Michael had added. I was getting thoroughly lost when abruptly something broke the steady hum of mind-noise around me and caught my attention.

It was familiar, the same chant I'd heard in Nell's thoughts weeks before. I glanced over at her. Obviously she too had finished her test; she was sitting with her long hair shielding her face.

I carefully avoided any movement that might make her turn, closed my eyes and concentrated on her mind alone. At once there was sharp swell of sound as the anxiety of the other students hit me. I kept my breathing as steady as possible, ignored the other noise and focused.

It was the same circle I'd seen before, in the same clearing, so much more familiar now that I'd been there in person. This time there were only two robed girls, and I saw them standing hand in hand. Then Nell's perspective shifted, and I saw something else, in the center of the circle. There was pile of rocks, and leaning against it was shadowy figure. Slowly it began to take shape, as Nell's mind clarified, and with horrifying sickening sense I realized that it was Michael.

The room tilted, just as it had the first time I had listening to Nell's mind. But this time I fought to keep steady. I gripped my chair and forced my breath to remain even. I didn't want to lose focus on what Nell was thinking.

The first time was just a trial, and it worked perfectly. Marica wanted to be sure, to know exactly what she could do. And now that we know, it's time for the main event. She may be able to see the future, but will she see her precious Michael again, before we sacrifice his blood to cleanse our sacred space?

Every cell in my body was poised for flight. I clung to the seat in order to keep myself from bolting out of the classroom and running to find Michael. My heart raced and adrenaline surged—where was he now? English. On the other side of the building. How fast could I get there?

And then Nell resumed her line of thought. *Marica has him by now. I could get out of next period, see if I can get out there early. We can take care of him, make sure the clearing is ready for the next part... when she's our sacrifice.*

Before I could react, Nell stood and walked to the front of the classroom. She leaned toward Mr. Frame and whispered something I couldn't hear, not even in her thoughts. In the teacher's mind I detected only resigned embarrassment, and he nodded quickly before handing her a pass and waving her away. Nell didn't even look my way as she moved out the door.

I was stuck. If I tried to leave now, to use an excuse to

leave class early after Nell has just done so, Mr. Frame would become suspicious and probably refuse. I'd just have to leave and deal with the consequences later. I was about to slip from my desk when the bell rang.

I jumped as though electrified and pushed through people to get to the door, ignoring the surprised and disgruntled looks. Once in the walkway, I sprinted around crowds and across the patchy grass, all the while glancing desperately from face to face, looking for Michael. Was there still a chance he was here and safe?

The classroom was empty by the time I got there. I turned around immediately and headed toward the parking lot. If what Nell had been thinking was true, Ms. Lacusta had Michael. I knew that by myself I couldn't save him—not from both Nell and Ms. Lacusta—but I thought I could stall them until help arrived.

But how where would that help come from? Frantically I cast my mind, trying to think of who was where—I didn't know anyone's class schedule. I was alone, I didn't have time to go from room to room looking for someone I trusted—and it would only be a matter of time before a teacher saw me outside without a pass and marched me to the office, where I knew they were less than likely to believe what I had to say.

I have to be calm and think this through, I told myself. *There's an answer, I know.* I turned the corner and nearly ran directly into the pay phone.

This phone was something of a school joke, since virtually no one used it. Almost everyone used cell phones, either their own or, if they were like me and didn't have one, a friend's. I wasn't even sure how to use a pay phone. I dug into my change purse, deep in the bottom of my handbag, and found quarters. Isn't that what they took? I slipped two into the slot, dialed the number of Michael's cell phone and prayed that he would answer.

But instead of a ring, I heard his voice mail, which meant his phone was turned off. I bit my lip and swallowed hard. Not good. And that had wasted two of my quarters. With every ounce of faith I prayed that I had more—and I breathed a silent prayer of thanks when my fingers closed on two.

This time I punched in the familiar number of the nursery. *Marley and Luke*, I chanted to myself. *Marley and Luke will know what to do.*

It was Belinda who answered. She worked in the nursery shop, and I knew her slightly from my visits. I worked hard to keep my voice from shaking as I asked her if Michael was at the nursery.

"No, I haven't seen him," she answered. "Marly and Luke are out working on a landscaping job. You know she doesn't usually go with him, but I guess he talked her into it today—"

I groaned as I interrupted her. "Listen, Belinda. I don't want to be rude, but it's very important that I get a message to Marley and Luke. They need to know that Michael is in trouble. Please tell them it's Nell again, and I'm going over to the clearing, and they have to come fast. I don't know if they have a phone with them or what, but please—this is an emergency."

"Should you call the police?" Belinda's tone was only slightly suspicious and very confused.

"I don't have time. Or quarters. You can call them if you want. Just please get that message to them." I hung up the phone before I could waste any more time. As I turned back toward the parking lot, I realized that I was standing right in front of Amber's locker.

Without taking the time to reason any more, I dug into my backpack and ripped out a sheet of notebook paper and a pen. With a trembling hand, I wrote:

Nell and Ms. L have Michael at the clearing. I am going out there now—send help ASAP. Please.

I underlined the last word and scribbled the time next to my name, folded the sheet and shoved it through the vent in Amber's locker.

I had done all that I could. I wasn't sure what would be waiting for me there, but I knew I had to return to Nell's forest clearing. And this time, I was going by myself.

I stumbled across the parking lot toward my mom's car. My hands were shaking so much that I could hardly pull the keys out of my bag. My fingers had just touched the cool metal when I felt a prickle at my back, and I heard the low insanity of Nell's mind.

Before I could take a breath, her weight was pinning me against the car. I heard the madness of her laughter, and then…

…the pain was sudden and intense. It struck at the base of my neck and I couldn't move. Panic and terror warred for a moment and then there was nothing but darkness.

Chapter Forty-Six

It was the muttering that called me out of the darkness. A low level of incoherent words spoken and ideas half-formed floated around. My eyes were too heavy to open, but slowly I began to pull myself out of the mire of nothingness.

As I became more aware, I realized that I was hearing thoughts, not spoken words. For a moment, I was confused. Who was I hearing? And where was I?

Groggily I tried to turn my head and pain shot through me. I remembered then that I had been in the parking lot at the school... I was looking for Michael... or for Amber. Which? Why? And somehow I had gotten hurt. Tentatively I stretched my fingers slightly, expecting to feel the stones of the gravel. Instead I felt soft grass and dirt.

I forced my eyes open, and the world was out of focus. There was light, but it was blurred and moving, and it made the pain in my head even worse. Squinting, I tried to look around without moving my head.

The blood spells... they're the dangerous ones, but so worth it, because of the power they release... and with her abilities, who knows what her blood will hold. Might make the spell even stronger... out of my way at the very least. Didn't belong here anyway, outsider, not one of us. Never one of us.

The words I heard finally cut through the last vestiges of fog in my mind. It was Nell. She was here, somewhere near me. I had been trying to save Michael from Nell's latest plans of blood and mayhem. And I'd been standing by the car when she came from behind. I remembered her pushing me forward against the hood and then the blow to the back of my head.

My hands groped a bit further and encountered more grass and some pine needles. The forest, then, I decided. Would she have dragged me back to the same clearing? It was possible. She'd been livid before about Michael's male presence sullying the place, but then today she'd thought of a cleansing spell. Maybe she had performed it—without blood. Or maybe Nell was just nuts enough to convince herself it didn't matter after all.

I couldn't let myself consider the other alternative. Michael wasn't here, so I had to believe that he was alive. I didn't hear Ms. Lacusta or sense her presence either; had she ever really been a part of this afternoon's plans? As far as I could tell, I was alone here with Nell, which meant that it was most likely that Michael had gone to the nursery, where he would be expecting to see me later this afternoon. Relief flooded my heart; without doubt I was in a bad way, but at least I knew Michael hadn't been sacrificed in the name of ritual cleansing.

I tried moving my head again. The pain was still right there with me, and I sensed it wasn't going away any time soon. But by taking it slowly, I could shift in tiny increments without passing out again.

I caught sight of a robed figure standing in front of a pile of rocks. I knew it was Nell. My heart pounded, and I tried to calm myself enough to figure out how I could best save myself. It was pretty clear from her thoughts that I was the chosen sacrifice today. And it also sounded as though she was buying into the idea that I possessed some sort of power. I wondered if she knew what it was.

I toyed with the idea of feigning unconsciousness for as long as I could, hoping that might buy me some time. I was growing increasingly uncomfortable on the ground; something was poking me in the back, and I tried to move. But my feet somehow didn't seem to be obeying my mind. I couldn't feel them at all. Wincing in agony, I lifted my head as far as I could and looked at my legs. My feet were bound tightly with rope and fastened to a large wooden stake in the ground. The knot was on the other side of the stake, beyond my reach even if I could ignore the pain long enough to sit up. The binding must have cut off my circulation, I realized, which explained why I couldn't feel my feet.

That was when true, mind-numbing terror took over. I was stuck here, unable to move, completely helpless against anything Nell was planning to do to me. My eyesight was still blurry, and my head throbbed; I assumed that probably meant a concussion. That really wasn't going to matter in the long run, because Nell was going to do something to spill my blood. I was betting on her using the knife again. By the time she was finished, a concussion would be the least of my problems.

My one good chance for rescue was the message that I'd left at the nursery. If Belinda got in touch with Marley and Luke, they would know what to do. And if Michael wasn't here, then of course he must be there, working. He might even get the message himself and understand where I was.

Of course, there was the possibility that Amber would alert him. When she found the note in her locker... if she found the note in her locker... would she call his parents and find out that Michael was not really in danger? Had I told her that I was coming out here by myself? My head was still fuzzy and it hurt to think that hard.

I twisted again, trying to lean away from whatever was hurting my back. Then I froze, because at my movement, the murmurings of Nell's mind stopped abruptly, and she turned to look at me.

Her smile was one of pure pleasure, and suddenly I couldn't breathe. She seemed to float over to me, as the long robe covered her feet to the ground.

"You're awake!" she exclaimed in what sounded like true delight. "Good. We have so much to do. I was afraid I was going to have to try to bring you around myself. Apparently, it's very important that you're conscious when we begin."

Nell sounded as though we were beginning a school project together. Her voice was matter-of-fact, but her eyes blazed with the true madness that I'd been hearing in her mind for months.

I tried to sit up, but the agony in my head was strong enough to make me nauseated, and I fell back.

"Yes, sorry about the head. Probably hurts quite a bit, doesn't it? That was unfortunate. I considered trying chloroform, but it's not as easy to get as you might think, and there's a paper trail, too. I couldn't have that."

I stared at her incredulously. "You don't think you're really going to get away with killing me, do you? You might do it, but between Michael and Amber, I'm going to bet the cops will be at your door before you've had a chance to clean up. If I disappear, who do you think will be the number one suspect?"

She laughed then, a silvery tinkle of amusement tinged with insanity. "Oh, poor Tasmyn. You don't think I've thought this out? It was very complicated, you know. Everything had to fall into place so precisely, and it had to be done in very little time. I had been waiting for an opportunity, I was prepared to be patient, and then yesterday, when I overheard your conversation with Amber, it just fell into my lap. Perfect timing, with your mother away, no one expecting you at home... and by the time your boyfriend starts to wonder where you are, it'll be much too late.

"But there's no worry of me being suspected of anything. I drove you here in your car, and it will appear that you came out on your own. You see, it turns out that your end will come courtesy of a rather hungry alligator that lives in the lake here. I'm sure he'll have help from the other things that live there, too, but I think the gator will be the one to really do the job."

Nell leaned closer to me, and the hood fell off to pool around her hair. "Don't be frightened. In reality, you'll be long gone before they bother with you. I need a fairly large quantity of your blood—more than you can spare, as it turns out. But I know how to do it in such a way that my cuts won't be at all visible by the time your body is found."

I shook my head and then closed my eyes to breathe through the pain. "Doesn't matter, Nell. They'll still know."

"Oh, your adoring boyfriend or that stupid Amber might suspect. But they'll have no proof, and it won't matter. Besides, if they make too much fuss, my father will shut them up. He might not be good for much, but he wouldn't let anyone slander me." Her laugh this time was short and harsh. "Wouldn't want any harm coming to the precious Massler name. Or maybe I should say, any more harm. That's really why he could never forgive my mother..." Her eyes clouded and she frowned. I could feel the hurt and fury coming from her, and the mutterings in her mind cried out in pain, too. Maybe this was my opportunity.

"I'm sorry about your mother, Nell," I said as gently as I could manage. "It must have been very hard for you to lose her when you were so little."

"She was brilliant," Nell murmured. "Simply brilliant. No one was like her. And she loved me. She taught me…" Her voice faded and then she jerked her eyes back to me. "That doesn't matter now. She's put away because she wasn't smart enough to manage things. She let a man ruin everything. I learned that lesson early. No man is worth giving up your power. No man is worth losing what's really important. They can't be trusted." She smiled down at me again. "Not even your precious love. You'll see. Or actually you *won't* see. You won't be around to see!" Nell giggled maniacally. "Maybe I'll offer him some comfort while he's grieving for you…"

A fierce rage shot through me at the idea of Nell anywhere near Michael. "He would never—" I began, but Nell cut me off.

"Oh, he might never—you may be right—but you know, there are spells for that, too. My power will be limitless after I perform this ritual. Doesn't it make you feel a little better to know that your blood is going to such a good cause?"

I turned my face and refused to look at her, but she wouldn't move away.

"Oh, come on now, Tasmyn. Let's not be coy. It didn't take me too long to figure out where your power lies. Marica could sense it from the beginning, you know. She just couldn't isolate exactly what it was. But after the whole

Amber debacle, I put the pieces together. I played you today, made you think I was on the wrong track. And now, if I'm right—which I nearly always am—your blood, with your special gifts, will make me the strongest witch of my generation. And in a way, you'll be part of that. Even if you're not around to see it!" She erupted into laughter again.

I knew I had to be calm. If I could keep her talking, keep her focused on something else, I could be buying precious time, and there was a chance that someone would find me. The thought of Nell with Michael sickened me, but I had to tamp down that anger and try to reach whatever part of Nell's sanity that might be left.

She was standing again in front of the pile of rocks I had noticed earlier. Her mind was focused on them, and then I heard the familiar chanting. She was thinking of the chant as she mumbled some words over the stones.

I felt a burst of energy so strong that it forced me further into the ground and robbed me of my breath. Startled, I realized it had come from Nell's mind. And there, where a mound of stones had been seconds before burned a bright flame.

I remembered that Amber had talked about Nell and the other girls making fire. At the time, I had assumed there was some trick Ms. Lacusta had taught them. But the flash of power I'd felt at the same moment the fire started could not have been a coincidence. Somehow Nell had made those flames.

In desperation, I closed my eyes and opened my mind, clearing all the walls as thoroughly as I could. Combating Nell was going to require every bit of strength I possessed.

Now, the words must be perfect. The athame must be

purified in the flames created by the craft, and then she has to be upright. I'll have to prop her up in some way. And the vessels, they have to be prepared, too—

TASMYN!

Cutting through Nell's musings and ramblings, I heard my name coming from a completely different mind. I caught my breath as I struggled to keep my face expressionless. I could not let Nell look at me and guess what I was hearing.

Tasmyn. I'm coming for you, I know you're around here somewhere. Hang in there, I love you, don't you dare let her hurt you, I'll kill her myself. Stay with me, Tas.

Tears filled my eyes, and I squeezed them shut. With tremendous effort, I choked down a screaming reply. I wouldn't help either of us by taking away the element of surprise, Michael's only real advantage in this situation. But every fiber of my being yearned toward him.

Nell had straightened, and she was coming toward me. One hand was behind her back, and the same beatific smile was on her face.

"Well, Tasmyn, I think it's about that time. Now, I'm going to need your cooperation in some of this. You must be sitting up, so that I can catch the blood in the vessels that have been prepared for this ritual. Oh, it's going to be amazing." She brought her hand in front of her, and in it I saw a long, thin knife. Nell turned it over lovingly, caressing the white bone handle. I could hear her again more clearly.

Amazing. That's right. Just the two of us. The athame will link us, forever.

"That's the athame?" I questioned her softly. I wanted to keep her attention on me.

"Yes." Still smiling, Nell held it out the knife front of

her. "Isn't it beautiful? It was my mother's."

Without thinking, I blurted, "I thought Ms. Lacusta gave it to you—the athame."

Confusion moved across Nell's face. "Marica? My mother…" Her mind bleated distress. Then she shook her head. "It doesn't matter. One and the same. Powerful witches, and both their blood runs in my veins." The idea of blood brought her back to the task at hand. "This athame has served me well. If you feel the back of your head, you'll find a lump in the shape of its handle. Turns out it's useful in more ways than even I had guessed."

"That's what you hit me with?" No wonder my head was killing me.

"Yes. It worked out perfectly. The hardest part was keeping my mind blank. I knew you'd hear me if I started thinking once I got near you. So I had to have it all planned before I was close enough, and I wasn't really sure how far away you can read minds." She knelt down next to me and slid a hand beneath my head. "Now you have to sit up."

Nell's fingers brushed the back of my head, and I shrieked in pained protest. She jerked her hand away, then chuckled.

"Sorry. I forgot that your head must hurt pretty badly. Don't worry, it won't bother you much longer." She giggled again, but this time she gripped me by the shoulders. "Look, I'll swing you around so you can lean against this tree."

She shoved me up, and I moaned again as my head banged against the tree. Moving had tightened the bindings on my feet, and I felt as though I were being stretched.

Nell sprinted back to the fire and returned to me quickly, this time holding two stone bowls. "These are the vessels.

We'll need to tie your hands, I'm afraid, so that you don't accidentally knock anything over." From the folds of her robe, she pulled a length of rope that matched that at my feet.

"Give me your hands." When I merely stared at her, she sighed in exasperation. "Tasmyn, there's no way out now. Let me have your hands. It's for your own good. Delaying this, fighting it, will only make things more painful for you."

Tas, be still. Let her tie your hands. I'm right here, watching. I'm waiting for her to put down the knife. I can't risk her going for you. But don't worry, I won't let her hurt you. Just play along a little while longer. Try to get her to put down the knife. I'm with you.

I swallowed convulsively. Michael was right. Charging at Nell while the athame was still in her hand would be far too dangerous. If she was tying my hands, she couldn't be holding the knife, could she? Hesitantly, I held them out, shaking.

"That's better." Somehow still holding the athame, she threw the rope over my wrists and rapidly tightened it around my hands. Her strength and dexterity both astounded and frightened me. Would Michael be able to overpower her, even if she did put down the knife?

"Now, it's time." Nell's eyes sparkled with excited anticipation. She sat back on her heels, the cloak spread around her, and flipped the hood over her head again. Closing her eyes, she began to speak the chant that I had been hearing in her mind all this time. It was nearly hypnotic, and I resisted the urge to give in to its rhythm.

I wondered if Michael could see Nell. Depending on his vantage point, he might not be able to tell that her eyes were closed. This one-way communication was so frustrating.

Abruptly Nell stopped chanting. She raised the athame above her head and said something else in the same language—Romanian, I guessed. I watched in a combination of fascination and horror as she slowly lowered the knife and brought it to my neck.

"Don't be alarmed," she whispered to me. "They will be only shallow cuts. We don't want gushes of blood. It must flow slowly, into the vessels. Here—" I felt a sudden pain below my chin, "—and here—" another slice on the other side of my neck, "—and here." She moved the knife to my arms.

"NO!!!" The bellow of rage rose from the trees directly across the clearing from where Nell crouched over me. "Get away from her!" Michael charged directly at Nell, as she spun around to face him, knife still in her hand.

"Michael!" I screamed. "She has the knife—stay away!"

Nell looked wildly from Michael to me, and I could hear her mentally vacillating between attacking Michael or coming back to complete what she'd begun with me. Still facing Michael, she backed up toward me, the athame, stained with my blood, raised in her hand.

Slowly she lowered the knife back to my neck. "Go ahead," she hissed, her eyes on Michael's face. "Try it. I know where to cut. She'll bleed out in a matter of minutes. Even if you get to her, it'll be too late."

"Michael!" I kept my voice steady even in its intensity. "Go. Get help. Don't let her hurt you, too—"

"I'm not leaving you!" His anguish was nearly palpable. "Nell, leave her alone. You stop now, we can get you help. You're not thinking right. If you hurt her—more, there won't be anything we can do—"

Her wild laughter cut through his words. "I don't want your help, you weak, stupid *man*. My power is greater than you can imagine, and it's about to be increased a hundredfold. Why don't you stay for the show?"

And before either of us could react, Nell had leaped across the clearing and tackled Michael. Caught off guard, he staggered under her weight and fell backward. She sat astride him and held the knife to his throat as she alternately cackled and crooned.

"Now who's going to help *you*? If you so much as glance at her, I'm going to slice you right here, and she can watch you bleed away your worthless life. Of course, maybe it would be better for you to simply end it now. Obviously I can't let you walk away either, but perhaps after the ritual is over you'd be more open to my suggestions." She ran the flat side of the knife over Michael's face.

Tas, I'm going to fight her off. You've got to try to get free...

"Michael, I can't," I was sobbing openly now. "I can't move." Blood was dripping down my neck, my hands were immobilized, and both my legs and my head were screaming in pain.

"Why, how rude of you," Nell reproved us. "It's very impolite to hold a private conversation when there are other people around. I think someone needs a lesson in manners." She flipped the athame in her hand and with lightening speed, drew it across Michael's face.

My scream filled the woods. I felt Michael's pain as though it were my own skin that had been sliced, and more tears ran down my face to mingle with the blood. I struggled anew to free my feet and hands. Nell only laughed and raised the knife again.

A shout rose beyond the wall of trees. We all three froze, listening, and I heard the welcomed jumble of thoughts—many people's minds, all talking at once and approaching us quickly.

Before Nell could react, Amber appeared next to me, and then Cara was there, along with a tall man I didn't recognize. They all three took in the scene before them with varying degrees of horror and disbelief. Cara's mouth dropped open, but it was Amber who moved first.

"Get away!" she yelled, running headlong into Nell and knocking her off Michael. The athame flew out of Nell's hand and through the air, landing near the fire. Nell screeched and fought back against Amber, grabbing her hair and reaching for her eyes.

"You idiot!" she shrieked. "You've ruined it all again. I'll kill you, I swear I will. I'll never rest—"

The man standing next to Cara moved with admirable speed, considering the shock that was still running through his mind. He reached into the melee of arms and legs that was Nell and Amber and pulled Nell away.

"Enough!" he commanded her firmly. "Stop it." Nell glowered at him, but she stopped talking. He held her by the arms, much as Michael had done the night we'd saved Amber. He nodded toward Cara. "Get the phone out of my pocket and call the police."

Cara obeyed without hesitation, and I realized, hearing her mind as clearly as I was, that this man was her father. I had no idea how he had come to be here, but I was so grateful that I began to sob all over again.

Michael was by my side in an instant. He lifted my

hands and began undoing the rope. "Tell them we need an ambulance, too—she cut Tasmyn. Let me see," he said to me gently. "No, move your hands. I need to see."

"She cut you, too. Are you all right?" As soon as my hands were free, I flung my arms around his neck and pressed my face to his chest, holding him so tightly that I could feel the beating of his heart against my cheek.

"I'm fine," he murmured in my ear, pressing kisses along the side of my face. "I'm sorry, I'm so sorry I didn't get here sooner. I let her hurt you—"

I shook my head against him and noted vaguely that it was still hurting badly. "You saved me. If you hadn't come, I'd be lying here bleeding into her stupid vessels—oh, she's crazy, Michael. If you could have heard some of the things she was saying, or worse, that she was thinking…"

He pressed me more tightly to him and bent his head to whisper to me. "Shhh. It's all right now." More softly, he added, "Cara and her father are here." I realized that he was still protecting my secret, even in the middle of the chaos.

"Tasmyn?" I heard the hesitation in Amber's voice, and I pulled away slightly from Michael to look at her.

"Amber, I don't know how you did it, but I can never thank you—you saved us both."

Tears filled her eyes as she knelt beside us. "Then we're almost even," she said quietly. "But she cut you. The blood—you're covered—"

"They're not deep cuts," I assured her. "I think they look worse than they are. But if someone could untie my feet, I'd really appreciate it."

Amber scrambled down to wrestle with the ropes, as Michael pulled me close to him again.

"Ow," I moaned.

"Where? Where else do you hurt?" he demanded, leaning back to look me over.

"My head. She knocked me out with the handle of athame. I think I've got a pretty good knot back there. And I'm kind of dizzy."

"Concussion," both Michael and Amber pronounced together. We heard sirens in the distance, and I felt Michael's profound relief.

Near the dying fire, Cara was still speaking rapidly into her father's cell phone. Reverend Pryce was holding Nell firmly, but she was muttering still, casting baleful glances of hate and spite toward the rest of us.

I could now hear the minds of the approaching police and EMT's, and a few moments later their footsteps and voices were audible to all. Suddenly the adrenaline that had kept me upright was gone, and the world began to spin. Once again I surrendered to the dark of nothingness. But this time, I wasn't alone. This time, strong arms circled me.

Chapter Forty-Seven

When I opened my eyes again, the world was white. Replacing the filtered light of the forest was a harsh glare of institutional lamps. Someone was holding my wrist with cool fingers.

I blinked and moaned softly as the pain that had been held at bay rolled back over me. My head was pounding.

A warm and compassionate face filled my line of vision. She was dressed in pink hospital scrubs, and she was smiling.

"Hi, there," she murmured, just loud enough for me to hear her without hurting my head any more than it was. "Welcome back. Are you in pain?"

I opened my mouth to speak but found my throat was so dry I could only rasp. "Yes, a little."

"Well, let's get you some water, okay, and maybe something nice for that head. No need for anyone to suffer." She was cheerful without being obnoxious. I heard the clink of ice and then she was holding a cup to my lips. "Can you get this down?"

I gulped the water awkwardly, feeling the relief of it spill over my lips and down my throat. She took the cup away, and then I saw her inject something into a clear tube above my head. I realized that the tube must be attached to me. I moved my hand and could feel the discomfort of the intravenous line.

"There." There was a squeak of something being opened, then the sound of metal upon metal, and I assumed that she had discarded the syringe. "That should help a lot."

I could speak a little more clearly now. "Where am I?"

"Lake County Memorial Hospital. Do you remember how you got here?"

I frowned, and a vague pain moved through me again. It was softened now somehow; the medicine was doing its job.

"You had quite the adventure, I understand. Lots of rumors flying around about what happened out there in the woods by Lake Rosu."

It came back to me in full force then. I tried to sit up, looking about wildly. "Michael?"

"Is that your boyfriend? Well, don't worry. He's fine. He was here all night. We just now convinced him to have that cut on his face seen by our plastic surgery resident. It's not an emergency, but since it's on his face..." Her words trailed off as tears began to flow down my cheeks. "Now, sweetie, none of that. It's okay. Everyone is fine. I know you've been through a terrible time, but it's over now."

She bustled around my bed a few minutes more in silence. I drew a shuddering breath.

"You said—all night? What time is it? How long was I out?"

"It's nearly noon. Thursday. You started to come around in the ER, but you were kind of out of control—yelling about all sorts of things, thrashing around—so they knocked you out again. Safer for you that way, and you missed the worst of getting stitched up and so on."

I raised my hand to my neck to feel the bandages. "No, don't touch those. They're going to be tender for a bit. But you're fine. You can relax. It's going to be all right."

I closed my eyes. I could hear similar comforting thoughts in her mind, so I knew she wasn't lying to me.

"Nell?" I asked, with my eyes still shut.

There was a surge of conflicted emotion in this woman's mind. "Nell… is somewhere safe. A place where she can't hurt herself or others. She's fine." There was indecision, then resolution. "You shouldn't think… well, Nell is a sick person. Her mother was a sick person. What they did… that's not what all witches are about."

I sucked in air and opened my eyes wide. She was looking out the window thoughtfully, fingering a charm that hung from her neck.

"It's all about elemental magic. White magic. Doing good. The vow is that it must hurt none. What Nell did—it was as far away from that as it could be." Her attention seemed to snap back suddenly. "I just thought you should know that. You shouldn't be frightened."

I wasn't. This woman—I assumed she was a nurse—was as comforting as my own mother.

And that made me wonder where my parents were. "Are my mom and dad here?" I croaked, still trying to find my voice.

"Your dad was here all night, too, and he just left a little while ago to collect your mother at the airport. They'll be back shortly." She smoothed the sheet at the foot of the bed. "That medicine should be kicking in by now. Why don't you rest until your family arrives?"

"I don't want to be unconscious again—I want to see them…" I protested weakly.

"What I gave you was only a mild pain med. It won't knock you out; it will just let you sleep naturally. You need that now." She stroked my foot softly. "Go to sleep…"

My mother's voice awakened me next. It wasn't her spoken words; it was the soft hysteria of her thoughts.

My baby, so vulnerable lying there in that bed... oh, her poor neck... shouldn't have gone away. It wouldn't have happened...

I pulled myself up out of the bliss of sleep and opened my eyes. "Mom?"

"Tasmyn!" Gentle hands touched my cheeks, and I could hear the tears in her voice.

"Mom, it's okay. I'm all right. And it's not your fault. Don't think that."

She laughed through her sniffles. "Someone's cheating."

I blinked. "Sorry. S'hard to block when my head doesn't feel like my own."

"That's fine. I was just teasing you."

I could focus on both of them now. "I'm sorry. I didn't mean to make you worry. I'm sorry I got hurt. And that you had to cut your trip short, Mom."

She ran her hand up and down my arm in comfort. "Don't worry about that now. We'll talk when you're feeling better. Just rest for now."

I gazed around the room, searching. "Where's Michael? The nurse said he was okay—that he was here."

My father answered this time. "He is—both fine and here. He's down the hall with his parents. They very thoughtfully gave us some time alone with you, but I imagine that Michael is anxious to get back in here. Should I step out and call him?"

I didn't want to hurt my parents' feelings, but my need to see Michael was overpowering. I nodded carefully, and my father moved through the door.

"Don't be alarmed when you see Michael's face—he's got stitches, but it looks worse than it is," my mother assured me.

But nothing could have prepared me for the flood of feeling when Michael walked into my room. His face was the least of my concerns. Instead I focused on his eyes, and at last I felt whole again.

He moved to the side of my bed and took my hand. "Hi," he breathed. *Oh my God, Tasmyn, I didn't know... I thought... I was so scared. You were so still and so white... I have never been so frightened in my life...*

I smiled up at him. "I'm here," I said. "You don't have to be scared anymore."

My parents exchanged knowing looks and slipped from the room. Michael heaved a huge sigh and dropped onto the bed next to me, still clutching my hand.

"I can't even begin to tell you... I thought, when you went limp on me there in the woods... I thought you were gone. I've never seen anyone just... slip away like that."

"Sorry," I whispered. I tried to say more, but my throat was dry again. "Water, please?"

"Oh, sure." He jumped up and found the cup of water the nurse had poured earlier. "Here you go."

I drank deeply, appreciating the liquid, and then tested my voice again. "Thanks. That's much better."

"Yeah, they had you on oxygen for a while, so you're probably pretty dried out."

I nodded. "Are you really all right?" I brushed careful fingers over the taped line on his cheek.

"Perfectly fine. The plastic surgeon gave me some cream that should minimize scarring, but I'm not really worried about that. It'll only add to my manliness, don't you think?" Michael winked at me.

I wasn't ready to joke yet. "I'm sorry," I murmured, tears filling my eyes again. "If I hadn't been so stupid... so gullible..."

"Hey." He gripped my hand again, pulling it up to his lips. "None of that. You were so brave. I'm very proud of you." He leaned down to brush his lips against my forehead. "But if you ever put yourself in danger again, I am going to be really, really angry."

"Tell me what happened. How did you find me? How did Cara and Amber get there? And what about Cara's dad?"

"It was pretty wild," Michael admitted. "I got the whole story from Amber and Cara after we got here and the doctors got you stabilized. Your dad and I were sitting here with you, and between both of them—oh, and Reverend Pryce—trying to tell us their parts, and then your dad getting phone calls every five minutes from your mom, who was hysterical at the airport in New York, trying to get a flight out... well, let's just say it took me a while to piece it all together."

I groaned. "Oh, that must have been... interesting."

"I was considering swiping some of your pain meds."

"So, share it. I'll bet you can be much more succinct."

"I'll try. Let's see. I left school right after English. I knew my mom and dad were working at a house on my way home, so I stopped there for a few minutes, just to see if they needed any help. And then I went right out to the nursery. I guess I had been there about half an hour when Belinda found me. She said that you'd called and you sounded odd. She said you told her I was in trouble, and something about a girl and a clearing.

"I might not be quickest mind around, but that one I could figure out. I bolted right back to the car and broke every speed limit getting to Lake Rosu. I tried to call my parents, but I only got their voice mail."

I closed my eyes. "I feel like an idiot. I was just so frightened when I heard what Nell was thinking."

Michael stroked my face gently. "You can explain all that to me later. I know you acted on the best information you had. That's all you could do."

I still felt stupid. "And you got to me, and you saved me."

Michael laughed without much mirth. "I don't think I saved anyone. I ended up at the wrong end of Nell's knife, too, remember?"

I frowned, remembering. "So how did Amber and Cara get out there? Did Amber find my note?"

"Yeah. Amber told me that part. She said she looked for you after school and when you didn't show, she figured something had come up. And then she went to her locker and found your note. That was good thinking on your part."

"At least I did something half-way right," I muttered. Michael ignored me and went on.

"Amber panicked, and she looked for anyone who could help her. She just happened to run into Ms. Lacusta, and Amber figured out that if Ms. L was still at the school, she couldn't be helping Nell out at the clearing. And then get this—our quiet little Amber stopped Ms. Lacusta and demanded to know where Nell was. Ms. Lacusta claimed that she had no idea, and Amber said that you and Michael were in danger. She told her that Nell had tried to kill her—Amber, that is."

My eyes widened. "Oh," I breathed. "What did Ms. Lacusta say?"

"Amber said that at first she thought Ms. Lacusta was stunned, but then again, maybe... not so much. Her sense was that she was surprised about some of it, but not about Nell's intent. She wanted to know details, but Amber told her there wasn't time. She still needed to find help for us. So she ran out to the parking lot, and she saw Cara, whose father was picking her up."

Now things were coming together. "Amber figured Cara was someone who could help."

"Yes. She said she wasn't sure it was all right to trust Cara, but there was no one else—and since Cara's dad was there, this time they'd have someone as a witness if something bad truly was going down."

"Thank God she did trust her. If she hadn't..." I shuddered, thinking of the possibilities.

"I know. She told Cara you needed help. Cara's dad told her to get in the car, and I guess Amber filled them in as they drove. She directed them to the lake. And when they saw your mom's car there—and the Mustang—Amber knew she'd figured right."

"And meanwhile, you'd already come to rescue me." I touched his face again. "Thank you."

"When I got to the lake, I saw your car. And then—there was blood on the door. I almost—Tas, you don't know. I thought I was too late. I just started running into the woods. I tried to think encouragement to you, because I had to believe you were still alive.

"Then I got closer to the clearing, and I could hear Nell talking, and I heard your voice—I can't tell you how relieved I was. I watched her, but when I saw the knife, I knew I had to be careful. She had her back to me, though, and I couldn't see if she had put it down. I moved to a different angle, and that's when I saw her cut you." He dropped his head into his hands and was silent.

Reaching up, I ran my hand over his hair. "It's okay. It turned out all right, remember?"

"But it was too close. I couldn't see her... then when I did, I didn't stop to think. I just reacted."

"You reacted just right. If you hadn't, she would've cut my arms, too. You saved me."

Michael lifted his eyes to mine. The pain and guilt I saw there, combined with the anguish in his mind, broke my heart. He leaned in to lay his cheek next to mine.

"I could've been too late," he whispered, his voice muffled next to my ear. "If I hadn't gotten there in time..."

"But you did. Of course you did. You're my guardian archangel. Michael the Avenger."

I felt a reluctant smile touch his mouth then, and then he raised his head so that his face was very close to mine. "I'm never letting you get messed up in something like this again. The idea of losing you—I can't deal with it." His lips met mine in a soft whisper of a kiss.

"How about we both stay away from life-threatening danger? I can't handle losing you, either."

"Sounds like a plan." He straightened and took my hand again, holding it in both of his. "Speaking of danger, you want to tell me exactly how you ended up out there with Nell? I know you heard something from her, but what made you think I was in danger? That's still the murky part of the story."

It didn't take long to sketch out how I came to be at Lake Rosu. A myriad of expressions crossed Michael's face as he listened to story, and I heard his thoughts clearly enough to know I was in trouble.

"Why did you even think about going out there by yourself? Do you know what a chance you took?" The anguish was still stronger than the anger. I squirmed uncomfortably.

"I heard what she was thinking, and—I just reacted. I thought you were in danger. I never for a moment thought that Nell was setting *me* up to be the sacrifice."

There was a rustling at the door, and Marly leaned into the room. "Tasmyn! Oh, it's good to see your eyes open!" She moved to my bedside and hugged me carefully. I could see the weariness etched on her normally unlined face. "We've been so worried."

"I'm sorry," I murmured, chagrined to be apologizing yet again.

"Don't be silly. There's no reason for you to be sorry. You're a hero, don't you know?"

I rolled my eyes. "Some hero. I put other innocent people-including your son—in danger, and I needed rescuing. That's just stupidity."

Marly looked at her son. "Clearly that's the head trauma speaking. The Tasmyn I know and love is much smarter than that. She would know that we're only happy and relieved that she's all right, that we're proud of her for being very brave." Her eyes flashed at me, daring me to contradict her. I blushed and lowered my eyes.

"Your parents are heading back down here," she announced. "They've been so sweet to give you two time together, but your mom is going to self-destruct if she has to be away from you any longer. They're lovely people, by the way. Such a pleasure to meet them."

Michael chuckled. "Yeah, most couples introduce their parents to each other over a nice dinner. We do it in the hospital after a crazy witch almost kills us both. We're definitely unique."

"We bonded," Marly said smugly. "I've already spoken to your mother about coming out to the nursery for coffee one day soon, Tas, and your dad is chomping to come and look over our bushes. But now," she said, turning to Michael and fastening on him a gaze that brooked no nonsense, "I am taking my son home to get some sleep, and to let you visit with your parents and rest."

Michael protested, but to no avail. I could see exhaustion lying just below the worry in his eyes, and I joined his mom in insisting he go.

"I promise not to do anything exciting or dangerous while you're gone," I teased. "I'll just sleep and recover."

He finally left, with the promise to return first thing in the morning. My parents sat next to my bed until sleep claimed me once again.

Chapter Forty-Eight

I was released from the hospital late the next afternoon. My head seemed to be recovering; the dizziness had subsided, and the headaches were duller. The cuts on my neck were healing, too. The worst physical issue was the residual soreness from the ropes and a few bruises from Nell's less-than-tender handling of me.

Before I was discharged, the doctor reviewed my litany of injuries and treatment. He pointed out that the backs of my legs were pretty scraped up; they assumed that Nell had dragged me across the gravel parking lot and forest floor.

In the twenty-four plus hours since I had awakened, we had ignored the circumstances that landed me in the hospital. My parents diplomatically avoided bringing it up, and I wasn't in any rush to talk about it with them. But the doctor's words seemed to end that moratorium. My mother shuddered slightly, and I felt leftover fear and wild worry coming from both of my parents.

The ride home was quiet. I concentrated mainly on keeping up the mental block; I wasn't ready to hear my parents' thoughts yet.

My mom insisted on a nap once we arrived home. I knew that Michael had returned to school that day; he didn't want to miss any more mid-term exams than he already had. I figured a nap was the safest way to wait until he was free to come and visit me.

But the house was silent when I opened my eyes. I could tell that it was late afternoon by the angle of the sun through my window. I lay still for a moment, listening. I could hear vague thoughts from my parents; it sounded as though my mother was sketching in her office, and my dad was reading reports from work.

My stomach growled, and I decided to seek some sustenance. The food at the hospital had been less than extraordinary, and I hadn't really been hungry there anyway. I poked around in the refrigerator and came up with a bagel that looked mildly appetizing.

I had it toasted and was just sitting down with my plate when I heard both parents approaching. I could tell that they had decided I was sufficiently healed to offer some explanations. I bit into the bagel to buy myself some time.

"How was your nap?" My mother needed to be sure I was feeling well enough before she attacked—psychologically speaking, of course.

I swallowed before answering. "Good." I was cautious.

My father took the seat across the table from me. "Tasmyn, the detective investigating this mess with Nell Massler called while you were asleep. I guess he'd gone by the hospital hoping to see you and learned you'd been released. He wants to come by and ask you some questions."

My heart was racing. "The police? What does he want to know? Why does he need to talk to me?"

"Obviously because you are a witness—really, their best witness. He's already spoken with Michael, Amber and Cara... oh, and of course, Reverend Pryce. But he needs to get the details of how Nell—well, how you came to be in the clearing."

Distress must have been evident on my face, because my mom reached out to cover my hand with hers.

"Don't worry, honey. They just need to get the facts

straight. You didn't do anything wrong. You're the victim here."

"But how am I going to explain everything to them? You know, about how I knew what Nell was planning."

Both of my parents' faces were grave. It was my father who answered me. "That *is* going to present a problem, Tasmyn. If you tell this detective that you overheard Nell sharing her plans with someone, he's going to want to know who that was. And you can't give just any name; that person would then be implicated in Nell's crimes."

My anxiety was rising. "So what do I do?"

My dad hunched over the table. "You're going to have to tread carefully. It's possible that you can use your gift to know what he's going to ask before he does and be ready for it." He sighed, heavily. "And of course, if it comes down to it, you're going to have to tell the truth, and hope for the best."

My head was beginning to pound again. "When's he coming?" I asked dully.

"Tomorrow. I persuaded him you needed a little more rest before you could deal with the interview."

"Thanks. I guess that gives me some time to figure it all out."

My mother spoke this time. "Maybe if you told us what happened, we could help you."

I toyed with the bagel still on my plate. "I thought Michael and everyone told you."

"They did. Well, of course, Cara and her dad were fuzzy on some aspects, since they don't know the full story. But we heard their side, at least. Now we'd like to hear it from you."

I drew in a deep breath. "I assume Michael told you that

I wasn't completely honest with you about what happened with Nell at the dance. I know you're upset about that, and I'm sorry. But I was afraid that you'd over-react—that you'd pull me out of school, or keep me away from Michael—something like that."

"Have we ever given you cause to believe that we'd be so unreasonable, Tas? I can't think that we have."

"You haven't exactly been completely supportive about my relationship with Michael, and we don't see eye to eye on my abilities lately. I was afraid it would be the last straw."

"Of course we would have been very upset, Tas. The idea of you and Michael taking something like this into your own hands—well, it's irresponsible."

"But what would you have done if I'd come to you with the information I had? You would have told me to stop listening to Nell. You would have probably sent me off to boarding school."

My father sighed in exasperation and my mother rolled her eyes. "No need for melodrama, Tasmyn."

"You want the story, and I'm just telling you how I feel. That's why I did what I did. So then when I heard Nell again on Wednesday…"

I shared the entire story, from overhearing Nell in History to when I passed out in the clearing, after all my rescuers had arrived. My parents were silent throughout the telling; if a few questions flared now and then in their minds, I was able to block them. When I finished, we were all exhausted.

Finally, my father spoke. "Tasmyn… what you did was extraordinarily dangerous. You put yourself at risk, and consequently you put other people at risk. I'm trying to look at it from your perspective, trying to think of what in your background, in how we raised you, would make you think that you could handle this on your own or that you couldn't tell us the truth. But I have to tell you, I'm having trouble figuring it out."

"It's not that we're not proud of you, on some level," my mom interjected. "You were incredibly brave, and very resourceful. But you risked so much—not once, but twice—and it could have ended so differently." She closed her eyes against the sudden tears I saw leaking out the corners and covered her mouth with her hand. "Tas, I have never been so frightened in all my life."

I swallowed hard over a lump in my own throat and tried not to cry. "I'm sorry," I whispered.

We were all quiet for a time, and then my dad cleared his throat. "I think we've had enough for today. We're all tired and more than a little emotional. Let's wait and see what happens tomorrow after you talk with the detective."

I nodded. "Can I ask just one more thing?"

My father patted my arm. "Of course you can."

"Where is Nell now? What happened to her?"

My parents exchanged glances, and the buzz factor of their thoughts went up several notches. I frowned and tuned them out with a great deal of effort.

"As far as we know, Nell is in police custody. However, apparently she was pretty out of control after they took her in, and the detective said something about moving her to a mental health facility."

"But she's—she's not just out there, right? She's not free?"

"No, Tas. Don't worry. I promise, you're safe from Nell.

She won't be able to hurt you again."

Chapter Forty-Nine

That was true in theory. Actually, though, Nell still had the power to haunt my dreams.

Michael arrived just after dinner, having promised both his parents and mine that he would only stay for one hour. We sat on the front porch; I knew my parents weren't letting me out of their sight any time in the near future.

He held my hand and kept his eyes glued to my face, as though I might disappear at any moment.

"How was school? Was it weird?"

Michael hesitated, and I could feel him searching for the right description. "It was… different. First of all, I missed you all day. It felt wrong without you there."

"You've been going to school there for over three years without me," I reminded him.

"Yes, but that was before I knew what I was missing," he retorted, lightly rubbing the back of my hand with his thumb. "Aside from that, of course everyone was talking about Nell and wanted to know what had really happened. The rumors going around are pretty wild."

I groaned. "That's great. Just what I need."

"Don't worry, it'll die down. But you should've seen all the people stopping by the lunch table—you know, just to ask about you of course." He rolled his eyes. "I didn't need to hear their thoughts to know what they really wanted."

"What did you tell them?"

"The truth. It's an on-going police investigation, and none of us are at liberty to say anything." Michael smiled smugly.

"Good answer," I said.

"Thanks. Like I said, pretty soon everyone will have something else to talk about and they'll leave us alone."

"How are Amber and Cara doing? And did Liza or Casey say anything to you?"

"Amber and Cara seem to be doing fine. I think they're getting to be pretty good friends—I guess they bonded over this whole thing. And I only passed Liza in the hall. She made a point of not even looking my way."

"Hmm." We sat in silence for a few minutes, as I digested all the news. "They must be shaken up by this whole thing."

"Amber said that Nell's group was questioned by the police, so I'd say you're right about that."

"What about Ms. Lacusta?" I had nearly forgotten about the teacher until then.

Michael shrugged. "As far as I know, she was in school today. And I didn't hear anything about her in all the talk going around."

I leaned closer to Michael and lay my head on his shoulder. The night was peaceful; through the cooling air I could hear the chirp of crickets and cars in the distance. His fingers tightened around mine, and when he spoke, it was hardly above a murmur.

"Are you worried about tomorrow? Talking with that detective?"

I frowned. "A little. I think my parents are resigned to the fact that I'm going to have to tell him the truth."

"Will you?"

"If I have to. I'm not going to lie and implicate someone else just to protect myself, and that's what I'd be doing if I said I overheard Nell talking to someone. Even if I claimed not to know who she was talking to—they'd still think there was another person who knew. I can't do that."

"I know. What do you think they'll do?"

"Will they believe me, do you mean? I'm not sure. It might make me sound more suspect. I guess we'll have to wait and see."

And the waiting was the hard part. I tossed and turned in bed that night; I hadn't been active enough to be worn out, and my anxiety about meeting with the detective intensified when I was alone in the dark.

When I finally did fall into a troubled sleep, my dreams all centered around Nell. I was back in the woods, and she had the knife. My nightmares didn't allow for rescue; instead, I was powerless as I watched Nell stab Michael over and over again. My own screams woke me, and my mother was immediately at my side, soothing me.

She stayed next to me the rest of the night, but I remained restless. When dawn broke, I was more tired than I'd been the night before. I dozed on the sofa in the living room, reassured by the familiar sounds of my mother preparing breakfast. In my half-asleep state, I could hear her thoughts and those of my dad, as they worried over me.

I roused myself mid-morning to shower, carefully protecting the bandages on my neck and avoiding the lump that still ached on the back of my head. The detective was scheduled to arrive at noon, and I was jittery as I tried to fill the time until the meeting. I sat in my mom's office with her as she sketched; she kept up a constant chatter about her shortened visit to New York, describing the hotel, the buildings and the author with whom she was working.

"She was so understanding when I had to leave. I guess I'll have to go back once everything is settled down here." My mom cast a concerned glance my way. "No rush, of course. I don't have to go anywhere for now."

I sighed, more in frustration with myself than with my mother. "Mom, I'm okay. I know I had a bad night, but it'll get better. Once I get this police thing out of the way-"

As if on cue, the doorbell rang. My heart pounded in my throat, and nausea overwhelmed me. My father was working at home again today, and I heard him answer the door.

"Come on. Let's go out there and get this done," my mother said softly, rising and taking me by the hand.

The man standing in our living room was tall. He wore jeans and a collared shirt with the letters "KPD" embroidered on the pocket. In his hand he held a baseball cap. I judged him to be in his early thirties. He regarded me with thinly veiled interest, and his eyes swept over my bandaged neck.

Still looking shaky. Girl did a job on her neck, no doubt. Hate to put her through more, but it's gotta be done. Procedure, if nothing else... covers us... get this started.

He greeted my mother in subdued tones, and then held out a hand to me. "Tasmyn? Detective Sam Lawrence. Good to see you up and about. I saw you after they brought you into the hospital. You were pretty roughed up."

I nodded, unable to work my voice yet. He turned to my father again. "Is there some place Tasmyn and I can speak privately?"

My dad scowled. "Does she have to be alone? She's not the criminal here; I don't see why her mother and I can't stay with her."

"Daddy." I laid my hand on his arm. "It's okay. I'll be

all right. I can handle it."

He hesitated for a moment and then nodded. "Why don't you stay here, and we'll go into the kitchen. Sit down, please," he offered belatedly.

We sat across the room from each other, the detective holding his hat between his hands and looking at me with a not-unkind smile.

"Been through a tough time, huh?"

I cleared my throat and tried to keep my voice steady. "Yes. It was very frightening, and I was very lucky."

He squinted at me and thought, *She's not going to give anything away easy.* I kept my face as impassive as I could.

The detective shifted in his seat. "I've spoken to some of your friends, to the others involved in this situation. It's quite a story they tell."

I waited again. That wasn't really a question, and until he asked me something directly, I didn't feel the need to volunteer information.

"I'd like to hear your side of things. How did you end up in those woods with Nell Massler?"

I took a deep breath. "I thought my boyfriend was in danger. While I was in the parking lot at school, about to get in my car to go out to him, Nell hit me in the back of the head. When I came around, I was in the clearing, and I was tied to a stake."

His face revealed nothing, but I could hear him clearly. *That agrees with what her friends said. Doesn't answer the questions they couldn't.*

I tensed, waiting for him to ask those questions. Instead he nodded slowly. "And she cut you there, on your neck, with the knife?"

I was confused by the direction of his question, but I answered. "Yes, with the athame. The same one she used to hit me in the head."

"Athame... that's a witch's knife?"

"Yes. I guess... as far as I know, most of the time it's used to draw the circle."

"Yeah... that sounds right. Not that I know that much about it, of course." He sat quietly for a few more minutes, turning his hat over and over in his hands, examining it closely. I couldn't get a clear line on his thoughts, but when he spoke again, there was a different intensity in his voice.

"You should know, Nell Massler is going away for the rest of her life. She's not going to be hurting anyone else again." His head dipped so that his eyes were shadowed, and I couldn't see them. "She's not going to prison. There won't be a trial. She's been declared mentally incompetent. Her father has agreed to commit her to an out-of-state hospital."

My breath caught in my chest. Battling with the relief I felt in hearing that Nell wouldn't be a threat to me again was the horror at hearing her fate, so eerily reminiscent of her mother's. An unexpected surge of anger toward her father choked me. Nell's crimes fell at least partly at his feet. How could he abandon her yet again? I couldn't reconcile these two reactions, not yet.

"So you see, most of what I would normally ask you really becomes superfluous. No need to waste time setting down all the details. Not that I don't have questions, because I do. I'm curious about how you came to know what Nell was planning. And if there were a case here, I'd have to ask you those questions." Detective Lawrence raised his eyes to meet mine levelly. "But since it seems there's no case, since that's all been taken out of my hands by powers way above mine, I guess I don't have to do that. I'm just here to wrap up paperwork. Unless, of course, you want to tell me about it."

I didn't blink. "No, I don't think so. As you say, there's no case, no need."

He stared at me deeply for another few seconds before he exhaled and leaned back. "All right then. Seems like that's all I have for you. If you think of anything else you feel I should know, your parents have my card. Just get in touch." He rose to his feet, and then turned back to me abruptly. "Is there anything I can answer for you before I go?"

Something *had* occurred to me in the last few minutes. "What about Ms. Lacusta?"

I sensed his surprise at my question, and he looked down at me, eyebrows raised. "What about Ms. Lacusta? I talked with her. Said she knew Nell from some chemistry club at school. She told us Nell's behavior lately had been more and more erratic, and that she'd been worried. Nothing else. Is there something we should know?"

I shook my head slowly. There was nothing I could say; I had no proof of the teacher's involvement in Nell's actions, only Nell's own word.

"No, nothing," I murmured. "I just... wondered. She seemed pretty close to Nell." It sounded lame even to my own ears.

Sam Lawrence eyed me thoughtfully. "I'll keep that in mind. Not much I can do right now, but I can keep my ears open."

"Thank you." This interview could have gone much differently, I realized. I was grateful that I hadn't had to reveal anything, grateful that the detective hadn't satisfied his own curiosity at my expense.

"Okay, then." He turned again toward the door, and this time I stood and followed him. As he stepped out, he looked back over his shoulder at me. "Try to keep your head down. King's a good town, a decent place. You don't ruffle too many feathers, and you'll get along. Call me if anything else comes up. Don't try to handle everything on your own again, you hear?"

I heard the not-so-subtle chastisement, and meekly I nodded. He met my eye for one more instant and then he was gone.

Chapter Fifty

Michael came over after school, and I filled him in on the meeting with Detective Lawrence.

"So he didn't ask you directly how you knew about Nell's plans?" he asked, frowning.

"No. He made it clear that he was curious, but he also gave me the option of not telling him. And obviously I took that option."

Michael was silent, thinking. I picked up some of it, a few random, incomplete thoughts.

"What is it?" I prompted, puzzled by what I was hearing.

"I just remembered that Sam Lawrence's daughter was in Lela's class. They weren't really good friends, but she came over every now and then. She was very proud of the fact that she came from one of King's original families."

Things were falling into place. "Which carnie member did she come down from?" I asked, and then nodded before Michael could answer out loud. "Ah, I see. So how closely is he related to Nell?"

"Not too close. Maybe third or fourth cousins? But they're in the same family."

I sucked in a deep breath. "That explains a lot. I almost got the feeling..." I trailed off, thinking about our conversation. "I think he might have known more about me than he let on. But he was cool about it—like he didn't really want me to say it."

"It would have complicated matters for him to have been forced to pursue that angle. As it stands, Nell's been quietly put away, and it's all very tidy."

"All the loose ends tied up," I agreed somberly. "Just like with her mother." I closed my eyes and leaned my head back against Michael's arm. "I know she wanted to hurt me—to kill us. I think she would have done it. But I can't help feeling that I failed her somehow. I knew what she was planning, what she was thinking. Is there something I could have done, some way I might have helped her?"

"You can't look at it that way. You gave her every chance to change her mind."

"Maybe." I wasn't ready to concede.

"On another topic, I hate to mention this, but it might be that *all* the loose ends aren't tied up. Amber and Cara asked if they could come to visit you this afternoon."

I smiled. "I don't call them loose ends."

"That's not what I meant. Amber caught me between classes and told me that Cara's dad was very curious about the details of our little adventure. I guess once he had time to process everything, he realized some of the pieces didn't fit. I think he's afraid that maybe you were involved in Nell's— uh, extracurricular activities. Not as the sacrifice, but as a participant. He's been grilling Cara and Amber about you."

I blew out a sigh and rolled my eyes. "Geez, I can't catch a break. If it's not an insane wanna-be witch trying to exsanguinate me, it's a preacher trying to burn me at the stake."

Michael softly rubbed my shoulder. "I don't think it's that bad. No stakes yet. He's just curious. Apparently he told Cara he didn't want her spending too much time with you until he was sure about—who you are."

"Well, when he figures it out, maybe he can let me know," I muttered. "Between how my parents are feeling about my recent actions and my guilt over Nell, I'm not sure if I'm the superhero or the villain anymore."

"Hey." Michael lifted my chin to look into my eyes. "You're neither. You're a beautiful girl with a good heart who tries her best to help others—and if they don't want help, there's nothing you can do about it. More importantly, you're the one I love—my one and only. Never forget that."

I needed that assurance when I returned to school the following week. Although I was happy to be with Michael, I was dreading the inevitable talk and questions—both what I would hear verbally and what I'd pick up from mind-buzz.

There were curious looks and I knew people were talking, but no one approached me directly. In French, Cara was happy to see me. She and Amber had visited me over the weekend, and she hadn't said anything about her dad or his questions. A few of her thoughts went in that direction, but there was nothing concrete. Mostly she seemed to think he was overreacting.

I was dreading Chemistry most of all. I dawdled along the walkway, timing my arrival for the last possible minute before the bell rang and sliding into my seat just as Ms. Lacusta began her lecture.

Her eyes moved over me with only the slightest change in expression, but otherwise, she didn't react. I kept my eyes down and took careful notes. Beside me, Liza shifted uncomfortably, and in front of us, Casey, now sitting by herself, didn't even look my way. I couldn't help feeling the same unease they were both experiencing, and I focused on not hearing their thoughts.

At the end of class, as we all put away our books, Liza half-turned in her seat so that she was facing me. Not meeting my eyes, she said quietly, "We had no idea what—what she was planning to do. I never—if I *had* known—"

In the same low tone, I replied, "I know. But you suspected. You had to have wondered what was going with Amber, why Nell suddenly wanted her in the group. And you didn't do anything about that." I stood slowly and my hands went unconsciously to the bandages still at my neck. "It could have ended much worse than it did."

Liza nodded, and as Casey turned, their eyes met. The troubled expressions they wore were identical. I wasn't worried about them; without Nell to act as ringleader, I had the sense that her former friends would leave me strictly alone.

I couldn't say the same about Ms. Lacusta. Michael had heard through the town grapevine that she had been reprimanded by the administration for being too involved with a student, but that her job was not in jeopardy. I wasn't sure how I felt about that. In my mind, she bore a great deal of responsibility for Nell's actions; even if she hadn't introduced the idea of witchcraft to her, I had no doubt that Ms. Lacusta had encouraged Nell to push the envelope. Whether she knew it or not—and I had dark ideas about that—the teacher had played on Nell's longing for a mother figure in order to manipulate the girl. Now Nell was paying, and Ms. Lacusta had received a figurative slap on the wrist. It wasn't fair, and that frustrated me.

I also worried about how much Ms. Lacusta knew or suspected about me, and how long she would keep quiet. I had a sense that she would use the information if she had to. For the immediate future, though, I was fairly certain that she was going to maintain a low profile, at least until the whole

Nell situation had died down.

The nursery had extended hours through the holiday season, and Michael offered to work later that night in exchange for some free time after school. It was a rare dreary day, with spotty showers, so we drove over to Lancer Park and sat in the car. I was just glad for some peace and quiet away from the inquisitive thoughts at school and the anxiety of my parents at home.

We held hands and gazed out at the lake, gray in the dim light. Michael's eyes were half-closed as he leaned his head back against the seat. A small flesh colored tape still covered the wound on his cheek, and every time I saw it, a trace of the panic I'd felt when Nell had cut him surged through me.

"Do you ever wonder what it all means?"

I wasn't surprised by his words, since I'd been picking up his brooding thoughts since we left school.

"Maybe you should be more specific about 'it'," I suggested. "You've been thinking about quite a few things. Do you mean everything that happened with Nell, with what goes on in King... or do you mean us?"

His hand tightened around mine, and he lifted our joined fingers to lightly stroke my cheek.

"I think I mean all of it. But not—I don't mean that I have doubts about you and me. That's the one thing that seems completely *right*, without question. I was just thinking about all the circumstances that put us here, together, in this time and place."

I shifted in my seat and pulled my feet up to curl under me. "What brought this on?" I wondered.

"I don't know. I guess some of it is my parents. They got talking the other night, about everything that had happened, and my dad said that maybe it wouldn't hurt us to check out Reverend Pryce's church. I thought my mom would freak out a little, but she actually said that he might be right."

"Why are they thinking about church right now?"

"My dad said that after seeing some of the real evil that's out there, the stuff that Nell was messing with, he thinks it wouldn't hurt to find out what the good guys are up to. That's how he put it. Maybe they're looking for reassurance… don't know. He sat with Cara's dad for quite a while at the hospital the day everything went down. Mr. Pryce was talking about demonic spirits and all that. I guess he thought that Nell's witchcraft involved that kind of thing."

"So now that's got you thinking, too."

"Yeah, I guess. I was remembering you said maybe your gift was given to you for a reason, that you're suppose to use it for the greater good. So you think that it came from God. And I thought about how we met. Could that really be a coincidence? Or were we meant to be together—were we brought together by some higher power—like God?"

I leaned my head against the seat, considering. We'd skirted around this conversation before, but Michael had never seemed so troubled by the possibilities.

"Are you feeling manipulated? Are you questioning. . .why we were brought together?"

"No!" He was emphatic. "No, I told you, I don't have doubts about us."

"I'm not suggesting that you do. I'm only saying that it wouldn't be wrong for you to feel—to feel that you didn't really have a say in this. If things work in your family the way you've told me—well, it's occurred to me before now that eventually you might resent your lack of choice. And I would understand that."

No longer leaning back, Michael fastened his incredulous gaze on me. "So you're saying that if I told you now, today, that you're right—that I feel like fate or God or whatever pushed me into this relationship—you'd be perfectly okay with that?"

"No!" This time it was my voice that rose several octaves, and tears threatened behind my eyes. "Of course I wouldn't be. I would be—it would devastate me. But maybe the idea that you were with me under duress would be even worse." I turned away toward my window, pulling my hand away from Michael's and pressing my fingers against my eyes. Shaken, I couldn't help but hear him quite clearly.

No. That's not it. There's no duress. It's true that something powerful drew us together at first, but I wouldn't change that—not for anything. To give this up—to not have her—it would be like someone taking away my ability to breathe. I couldn't live.

"You lived before," I mumbled, my voice muffled against my arms and my back still turned to him.

"But not well. Not like now."

"You don't know that."

"I know that as well as I know my own name."

I wrapped my arms around my knees and leaned my forehead against the glass. The stiff bandages still on my neck poked up into my chin. He meant it, I was sure. Nothing in his thoughts rang false; if he was deceiving me, he was also lying to himself. But could he really be so certain?

I felt his hand sweep down my back, the lightest touch. I shivered and for a fleeting moment thought that nothing else mattered; I needed him. The whys and hows weren't important. That he wanted me was the miracle of my life, and perhaps that was good enough.

But I knew it wasn't true. I couldn't keep him with me out of my own great need. I loved him too much to do that.

"What about you?" Michael interrupted my reverie. "What if you're the one who really didn't have a choice? I never gave you a chance to make up your own mind. I just swept you along, because I knew—I know—that I wanted only you. That I could love only you. But maybe you're second-guessing that now." He radiated uncertain misery, and my heart ached for his pain.

"I wasn't ever unsure. I never felt like you forced me into anything. I was frightened, because it was all new. And I'm still scared now—I'm still afraid that you're going to wish fate picked someone else for you—someone beautiful and smart and *normal*."

Michael grasped me by my shoulders and gently pulled me across my seat, over the gearshift and onto his lap. My back was against the driver's door, and my face was inches from his.

"You are so beautiful that more often than you know, I can't take my eyes off you. I stop breathing each morning when I see you for the first time. You're the most well-read, intelligent person I've ever met. And normal—who wants normal? What you can do, your gift, it's part of who you are. It's part of your compassion, your tender heart. It's why you're still mourning over Nell, even after she tried to kill us. You work so hard to keep from listening to people—it's because you're a good person, a kind person.

"Maybe it *was* fate or God who brought us together. If it

was God, and He has a plan for us and for your abilities like you think, then I'm just grateful. Because if I didn't have you in my life..." He swept his hands over my hair and carefully held me still. "If we didn't have this, I couldn't go on. You are as essential to me as air and water. Never think I didn't have a choice. I did, and I chose you. Every day, every minute, for the rest of my life, I choose you."

He traced my lips with his finger. "You don't have to be frightened. You're not alone. Trust me."

"I do," I murmured. "How could I not? You have the most open, honest mind, and I know you mean everything you say. But if you ever want to change that mind—"

"I won't." He kissed me then, packing into it all of the passion and emotion of our conversation. It was impossible to doubt him, impossible not to feel the depth and sincerity of all his words. His thoughts exploded into my head until I couldn't separate mine from his, and I lost myself in the intimacy and intensity of the moment.

When he pulled himself away from me, it was with considerable regret. My arms were still entwined around his neck, trapped between the headrest and his body, and we were both trying to catch our breath.

I don't want to stop. I could stay like this, right here with her, forever and never get tired of it...

My mouth was still close to his, and I smiled against his lips. "I think you might change your mind after your legs go numb."

"Nope. I told you, there will be no mind changing here."

"I think someone would miss us, eventually. And find us."

Michael stroked my back. "Probably. We could lock the

doors."

I giggled. We didn't often take time to be silly like this, just in love and talking nonsense. And after the intensity of our conversation, the levity was a welcome relief.

But even as I rested my head against his shoulder, smiling in the simple joy of being with him, a thought crossed my mind. It had been skirting my memory for a few days, refusing to stay down.

"Michael," I murmured against his neck. "I was thinking about something."

He brought my lips to his again and whispered, "Something like this?"

"No. But that was very nice, thanks. No, I was thinking about that first time in the woods, with Nell and Amber."

He straightened a bit, shifting me slightly so that my head lay against his arm. "What about it?"

"What do you think happened to the knife?"

Michael didn't ask me what I meant, and I knew that it had been troubling him, too.

"I don't know. I told myself that she'd thrown it somewhere, but I don't see how she could have done that without me seeing it. I was on top of her so fast."

"Did you even see it in her hand that night?"

He hesitated, frowning again. "I think—I think I did. Just a flash of it. But then again, maybe I didn't. It happened so quickly."

We were both quiet, considering.

"You know, when she had me tied in the clearing, she made fire." I spoke as evenly as I could. I hadn't mentioned that to anyone before now.

"What do you mean? She lit a fire?"

"No, I mean there were rocks, then—I could feel this shot of power going out from her—you know, I was trying to stay really attuned to her mind then, trying to keep a step ahead of her. So when that power went out—it was like nothing I'd ever experienced. It knocked the breath out of me. And then there was fire."

I could feel Michael's thoughts, troubled and uncertain. "If she did somehow make that knife vanish... and manage to conjure fire from nothing, what does that mean?"

I shivered, even safe in the circle of Michael's arms. This was the disturbing possibility that had been eating at me for days.

"I guess... I guess it means there really is a lot more to the world than meets the eye. And going back to what you said earlier... maybe it means that we were *supposed* to be here, in this time and place, to fight what Nell was doing."

Michael's arms tightened around me. "If that's the price we pay for having each other—then it's worth it. As long as it's over. As long as you're safe. As long as we're together."

We clung to each other, a tiny island of serenity amidst the storm that blew around us.

Chapter Fifty-One

Thanksgiving was late that year, at the very end of November. The news reports from Wisconsin showed several inches of snow and temperatures hovering around the freezing mark.

In Florida, the sun was shining, light breezes stirred the palm tree branches, and the grass was green.

We were celebrating the day with the Sawyer family out at the nursery. This was new territory for my family; since my grandmother had passed away when I was ten, our holidays had been quiet affairs involving just the three of us. Occasionally one of my father's co-workers who was far from home or single would join us, but I had always thought wistfully of the large family gatherings I'd seen on television shows or read about in books.

Michael's paternal grandparents had driven down from the Panhandle for the holiday, and I had met them the day before. They reminded me of Luke with their easy-going ways and warm embraces. Both insisted that I call them Gram and Poppy, and I loved feeling so much a part of the family.

On Thanksgiving Day, Michael arrived at our front door promptly at noon to collect me. My parents would follow later in the afternoon, and my mother was in the kitchen baking pies for dessert.

I had dressed carefully that morning, trying on and discarding several outfits before settling on a simple brown cotton skirt and a loose weave sweater in a coordinating tan. I blew my hair dry until it was straight and then pulled part of it back with a pretty clip.

My time and attention were rewarded by the light of admiration in Michael's eyes when I met him at the front door. I grabbed my bag and shouted a good-bye to my parents.

"What's the rush? Dinner isn't until four. I was going to wish your parents a happy Thanksgiving," Michael protested as I pulled him by the hand down the front walk.

"You can do it when they come out to the nursery. I didn't want to get held up with all the small talk."

His long-suffering sigh was mostly in jest, and I pointedly ignored the teasing thoughts I could hear coming from him as he helped me into the car.

"I put up the top, since I figured you wouldn't want to be wind-blown today," he informed me as he climbed into the driver's seat.

I glanced up at the roof in regret. "Yes, you're probably right." I really loved riding the country roads with the top down and the wind rushing through my hair. I had given up on learning to drive stick shift—and I hoped that Michael had given up on teaching me--but I was always a willing passenger in the Mustang. I brightened. "Maybe we could put the top down on the way home tonight."

"Count on it." Michael slid his hand around my neck and pulled me closer to him. My heartbeat accelerated as it always did when he was this near. My eyes slid halfway closed, but I didn't feel the touch on my lips that I expected. Instead, Michael was looking down at my neck. He moved the hand that wasn't around me to brush over the scars there. His eyes were troubled.

I laid my fingers against his cheek, turning his face

toward mine. "Hey. What is it?" I asked softly.

"Nothing. I just... I don't think about it all the time. But then I see these..." he traced one scar from below my chin down to my collarbone. "And it all comes back to me. How close I came to losing you."

I grabbed his hand and held it in my own. "Stop. It's over, and we're both here. Nobody lost anyone." Even as I said it, I felt a twinge of guilty regret, knowing it was untrue. Nell had lost all, again.

We sat there, both deep in thought. Michael pulled his hand from mine and framed my face with his hands.

"You're right," he whispered. "I'm being silly. This is a happy day. A day to be thankful, especially knowing all that might have been." He kissed me then, first a light brush of lips, then deeper, longer and more involved.

He leaned back just when I had forgotten to breathe, and his lips curved into the smile I loved.

"Lots to be thankful for," he observed before he put the car into gear and pulled away from the curb.

It took me several minutes to catch my breath and gather my scattered wits. But once I did, I remembered the primary reason for my nerves today.

"So, is she there yet? Did she get home?"

"Who?" Michael asked in all assumed innocence.

"Don't play dumb with me. You forget I can get hear you thinking, and consequently I know that Lela did in fact arrive home late last night while you and I were at the movies with Jim and Anne."

"I don't know why you even bother to ask me," he muttered.

"Because you don't think it if I don't ask it, and I can't

hear what you're not thinking."

"Okay. Well, now you know. Yes, Lela was home when I got there last night."

I listened for a few more minutes, knowing that he really didn't object. I was becoming so tuned to Michael's mind that our conversations were frequently an amusing jumble of shorthand as I answered questions before he asked them.

"And she was waiting for you up in your room? It was pretty late when you dropped me off."

"Yeah, well, she ambushed me. And then grilled me for over an hour."

"Really?" I was only slightly apprehensive. "About…?" I heard the answer before he spoke it. "Oh. Me."

"Yes, you had the starring role. We did touch on a few other topics."

"And did you handle it the way we discussed?" After a long talk with my parents, Michael, Luke and Marly, we had decided it would be unfair to keep Lela in the dark about my mind-hearing gift. Michael was nominated to explain everything to his sister.

My parents hadn't changed their minds on being more open about my talent, but they *had* gotten to know the Sawyers well over the few weeks; consequently, they trusted that neither Luke nor Marly was likely to be indiscreet. That trust extended to their daughter now as well.

"I told her all about you—that you're beautiful, intelligent, funny and caring. Oh, and the most important thing—that you're desperately, hopelessly in love with me."

I rolled my eyes but couldn't help smiling in spite of myself. He might have been smug, but he was also telling the truth.

"But did you tell her about—all of me?"

"I did, eventually."

"And what did she—oh. She didn't believe you."

"Not at first. And even when she said she did, last night, I don't think she really bought it. But then this morning, while my grandparents were out for a walk, my mother convinced her that we weren't just pulling some enormous prank."

"How did she react after she finally knew you were telling the truth?"

Michael didn't answer immediately, and I frowned, my heart sinking. "She thinks I'm a freak."

"No!" Michael was emphatic. "That's not true."

"You don't know that. You can't hear what she's thinking. But she said something like it—your mother was angry with her?" I turned questioning eyes to Michael.

"Not angry, exactly. She just corrected some misconceptions my sister might have had. In a very firm way."

I sighed heavily. I loved the Sawyers. Already they felt very much like my family. The last thing I wanted to do was cause hurt or division.

We were quiet until we turned onto the nursery property. I had been brooding, shutting out Michael's thoughts, but suddenly I recalled something that had crossed his mind earlier.

"You were thinking that Lela— about her being hurt. And that made me think of something that never occurred to me. You've told me all about the men in your family and how once you meet the one woman you're destined for, it lasts forever. What about the women in your family? You know, the ones related by blood. Does the same go for them?"

Michael smiled wryly. "Not really. Matter of fact, things don't always go so well for them."

I knew there had to be a downside to this whole soulmate deal. "Tell me."

We had entered the empty nursery parking lot, and after the bustle of the busy autumn season, it was almost eerie to see it deserted. Michael pulled over in front of the gift shop.

"If I drive back to the cabin, they'll all descend on us," he explained. "Here's the deal with the women in my family. The first answer to your question is yes, they do tend to find the one person who's meant for them. They fall in love just once. But it doesn't always last."

"Why not?"

"I don't know, exactly. I guess maybe the men they love aren't... up to the challenge? Hard to say. But it never ends well."

"Examples?"

"Oh... well, my great-aunt Lyn. She met her husband right after college graduation. She *knew*, she said. He was the one. They got married a year later. Had three kids. Then one day he just... left. Disappeared. She was devastated. Eventually she met someone else and got remarried, someone who loved her and the kids. She seemed pretty happy. But when she passed away a few years ago—it was her first husband's name she spoke as she died. Her daughter told me that she'd never stopped loving him."

I stared at Michael. "That's one of the saddest things I've ever heard."

"We don't have that many girls on my dad's side of the

family, so it's hard to say if what happens is the flip side of what the men experience or if it's just bad luck."

"And Lela—it's got to be on her mind, right?"

"Yeah. Here I tell her that I've found the one person I'm going to love for the rest of my life, and I know she's worried about whether she'll ever feel the same about anyone—and if she does, will he be worthy of that love? Or will he leave her?" Michael reached over to take my hand, linking our fingers tightly. "So that's part of why she might seem a little distant at first."

"I understand." What Lela feared wasn't that different from how I'd pictured my future before Michael.

He pulled the car into the driveway, and I took a deep breath as we headed toward the house.

The tempting aroma of a cooking turkey greeted us as we opened the door. Luke was sprawled on the sofa, a plate balanced on one leg. His father sat in a chair near him, and they were both absorbed in the football game on television. They barely looked up as we entered, but Luke called a cheery happy Thanksgiving to me.

"Where's Mom?" Michael asked.

"All the women are in the kitchen, discussing the pros and cons of stuffing versus dressing. It got too intense, so we decided to come out here and enjoy the serenity of football." Luke spoke without moving his eyes from the screen.

Michael smiled and pulled me toward the kitchen. "Come on, I want you to meet Lela." I tried to quiet the trepidation that zinged through me at his words.

Over the last few months, I'd had opportunity to spend a great deal of time in the Sawyers' kitchen. It was usually peaceful and well ordered. Today there were bowls and pans on every surface; steam rose from pots on the stovetop, and there was a steady buzz of conversation, which halted abruptly when Michael and I entered.

"Tasmyn! There you are. Happy Thanksgiving, sweetie!" Marly swooped across the room to embrace me warmly.

"Thanks—same to you." I returned the hug with equal affection. "Everything smells good in here!" I gazed around the room, taking in the chaos.

Gram sat perched on a stool at the counter, a cutting board and a bowl of green beans in front of her. And standing at the sink peeling potatoes was a beautiful girl who was perhaps an inch or two taller than me. Her hair was much lighter than Michael's chestnut tones; she was very nearly blonde, with the merest hint of auburn in her curls. As she turned to look at me, I saw that her eyes were the same deep brown as Luke's, although hers were surrounded with the long eyelashes that I envied in her brother.

Those eyes were cautiously assessing me now, showing no emotion at all. And although I had promised myself that I wouldn't listen to her mind—certainly not before I'd gotten to know her better—I heard Lela's first thoughts about me anyway.

So this is her. Michael's right, she's pretty. No, wait, he said unbelievably gorgeous. I felt her fleeting amusement here as she recalled her brother's enthusiastic words. *Well, he's not wrong. You don't see it right away, but then—oh, crap. Can she hear what I'm thinking? I forgot. Blank mind, blank mind, blank mind...*

I kept my face composed as Michael led me across the kitchen. "Lela, this is Tasmyn. Tas, my sister."

I smiled as genuinely as I could. Shaking hands seemed to be way too formal for this situation, and she wasn't opening her arms for a hug, so I settled for a small inclination of my head. "Hi, Lela, it's good to finally meet you. I hear so much about you from your parents and Michael."

She wasn't sure how to respond at first. I could feel it. I could also hear her continued efforts to keep her mind blank.

Finally Lela smiled in return. If it was a hesitant, guarded smile, it was at least real. She wasn't sure about me yet, but she had decided to give me a chance. That was the most I could hope for, under the circumstances.

"Hi. It's nice to meet you, too. My parents have been raving about you. On the other hand…" She swung her gaze around to Michael and archly raised one eyebrow. "My brother never seems to have time to talk to me anymore."

Michael was unfazed. "Sorry. Life's been a little busy." He winked at me, and I felt my face heat.

"I'll try to make sure he does better on that," I promised Lela. "He's lucky to have a sister, and he needs to treat her right." I shot him a reproving glare.

He surrendered, throwing his hands in the air. "Okay, if you're both going to gang up on me, I'll just give up now. One decent phone call a week, I promise."

Lela's laughter was genuine, and the wariness she'd been feeling earlier was melting slowly.

She actually seems nice. And normal. My brother can't take his eyes off her, that's for sure. And he's different, too. Is this what love looks like? Will I ever know?

My face must have reflected what I was hearing, for Lela frowned at me and her mind slammed shut. I looked away, hiding sympathy I was sure she didn't want.

Ever observant, Michael rescued me. "Mom, do you need to put Tas and me to work? What can we do?"

"Not a thing right now. Turkey's in the oven, potatoes are boiling away... everything else is ready and waiting. In a little while you can send Tasmyn in to help us finish up." Marly sank into a kitchen chair and waved a hand at us. "Gram and I are going to sit down and have a rest here for a bit. Why don't you three go for a walk or something? Give Tas and Lela a chance to get acquainted."

I knew we all saw through Marly's shrewd manipulation, but despite that, we filed obediently out of the kitchen and onto the deck. Once there, Lela turned to Michael.

"I can stay here. I don't need to tag along with you. It's okay."

Michael opened his mouth to protest, but I spoke first. "Lela, I would really like the chance to talk to you, to know you. I know this whole situation is new, but it would be wonderful if we could be friends." I knew I was blushing again; stepping out of my comfort zone to make a speech like that was still difficult for me.

Lela's face was inscrutable, and I carefully blocked her thoughts, purposefully concentrating on Michael's mind to avoid hearing Lela.

Finally she nodded. "Okay. Let's sit out here. It's warm enough today in the sun."

Michael pulled me into the double glider with him, and Lela curled into a nearby chair. We were all quiet, and over the thought buzz coming from inside the house, I could hear birds calling to one another. Michael used the hand he held to tug me closer so that our bodies were fused at one side. He swung one arm around me, and I nestled my head into the crook between his neck and shoulder.

I knew he was making a statement here, presenting his sister with a unified front. It was a "love me, love Tasmyn" gesture, which I appreciated in one sense; but in another, the last thing I wanted to do was purposely provoke Lela.

She was gazing at me steadily, without either antagonism or warmth. I was working hard to keep up my mental wall, since I knew that at least part of Lela's uncertainty arose from her distrust of my abilities.

"Do you hear… everything?"

Her question was so soft that I might have missed it. I smiled to assure her that I didn't mind answering.

"If I opened myself up, relaxed, yes, I'd be able to hear just about everything. I might not understand it all because it would be like hearing everyone in a crowd talking at once."

"What do you mean, if you opened yourself up?"

I shifted slightly in the swing, so that my back lay against Michael. He slid his arm down and linked his two hands around my waist. That core part of me that still wondered at the miracle of Michael and his love for me sighed in contentment. I tried to bring my focus back to Lela's question.

"I have the capacity to block most of it. At least, I used to be able to do it. It's not easy. It would be like you trying not to hear anything that I'm saying right now. You could do it; you could focus really hard on not listening to me, and you probably would miss most of what I say. But it takes lots of practice and concentration to block thoughts on a regular basis.

"I could do it more easily, before I met Michael. But it's

much harder now."

"How come? I mean, I know my brother complicates things—" she saucily stuck out her tongue at Michael, "—but why particularly with this?"

I was relieved to see that Lela seemed to be coming to terms with me and with my abilities. Michael was unruffled. He tightened his grip around me, and I felt his lips brush my hair. *My sister's such a brat,* I heard him think affectionately. *But she's coming around.*

"I don't know that it's all Michael's doing. The main difference is that I never had friends, never had anyone other than my parents close to me. Now that I do have these relationships... well, it's the most wonderful thing in the world, but it does mean I can't focus all the time."

It was Lela's turn to look at me with sympathy. "Why didn't you have friends?"

"For the very reasons I just explained. I had to focus on not hearing thoughts, which made me seem like a pretty anti-social person."

Lela rested her head against her hand, in a gesture very reminiscent of her mother.

"I'm not trying to be difficult," she said slowly. "I know I must seem like a real pain. I was a little anxious coming home anyway, because of the way Michael and my parents have been talking about you. I'm used to being the only girl around here. But I was prepared to get to know you, even to like you. Then when Michael told me last night... or maybe more when my mom convinced me this morning that he was telling me the truth... it really threw me. The idea that you can hear what I'm thinking—" She flushed and looked down, twisting her fingers in the weave of her sweater. "Sometimes

I don't always think the nicest things."

"Lela, please, don't. I really don't want you to be uncomfortable around me. I can avoid hearing you under normal circumstances. And I promise, I don't judge people based on anything I might accidentally hear." The memory of Nell flickered through my mind, and guiltily I pushed her aside. Michael stroked my arm comfortingly, and I wondered if he suspected what I was thinking.

"I won't say that it doesn't bother me anymore. It's something I'm going to have digest for a while. But I do want to get to know you. If my family's history accounts for much, it's a fairly good bet you're going to be around for a while." Her smile was warm and genuine, even if a hint of wistfulness remained.

Michael spoke for the first time since we'd come outside. "I'm glad you feel that way, Lela. Because you're right, Tasmyn isn't going anywhere. She's with me—for always."

Dinner was over, and Michael and I helped with the table clearing and dish washing. My father settled down in the living room with Luke and Poppy, and my mother was relaxing over a cup of tea with Marly, Gram and Lela.

When I would have joined them, Michael took me firmly by the hand. "Mom, if you're sure we can't help anymore, Tasmyn and I are going for a walk," he announced. "We need to work off some of that excellent food."

Marly laughed. "Good idea. We should probably all join you." At the look on her son's face, she laughed again and flapped her hand at us. "Don't worry, I'm not going to ruin your time alone. I don't think I could move from this chair anyway."

Without discussing our destination, we walked to our favorite spot in the trees, in the small, protected border between the citrus trees and the evergreens. It was a treat to have it to ourselves today; in the past weeks, this section had been crowded daily as families stopped in to tag their trees for Christmas. Michael assured me with a roll of his eyes that it wouldn't change any time soon, since those same people would be coming back to cut their trees or to buy the imported pre-cut trees. I had already committed my out-of-school hours to working at the nursery beginning the day after Thanksgiving. It was a dream job for me: I would be earning a little money for Christmas shopping, I would be able to see Michael, even if I couldn't be with him the whole time, and I had the best bosses in the world.

But for today, our little section of this world was paradise. The sun was still shining warm, even as a light and chilly breeze fluttered the leaves around us. I hugged my sweater around me while Michael spread a blanket on the ground.

"And," he said with a flourish, "I even scored us some dessert." From the inside of his jacket he pulled a small plastic container with two slices of pie.

I groaned. "You cannot possibly be hungry, or think that I might be, after the meal we just ate. I can't imagine eating for the next week."

He looked offended. "I'm not saying we need to eat it now, I'm just saying we have it in case we need sustenance before we walk back." He dropped to the ground and sprawled on the blanket. With his eyes still on me, he gestured to the empty spot next to him.

"Oh, am I invited to sit on the blanket, too?" I teased as I dropped down beside him.

Michael pulled my hand across his chest, so that I had no choice but to fall onto him, with my face inches from his.

"Of course you're invited," he murmured. "Who else would I want here?"

The wind drifted over us, and a faint scent of oranges filled the air. I lay my head down on Michael, my ear against his heart. I didn't have to reach to know what he was feeling; it was the same thing that I felt. Utter contentment.

His hand brushed my spine lazily. "Did you have a nice Thanksgiving?"

I shifted so that my lips were just under his chin and moved them against his jaw. I could smell his unique scent, warm and inviting.

"What do you think? It was only the very best Thanksgiving—the very best holiday, bar none, that I've ever had in my life."

"Was it the food or the company?" His hand had moved up to toy with my hair.

"Hmm... let me think. Well, the mashed potatoes were delicious... ow!" I protested as he gave my hair a playful tug. "Okay. So it was the company. It was your grandparents, specifically—"

Suddenly I was on my back, flipped over with a smooth move that left my head spinning. And Michael's eyes were directly above mine, his hands on either side of my head. He was attempting a threatening expression, but his eyes were smiling.

"My grandparents? They're what made this the best Thanksgiving of your life?"

I pretended to consider. "Okay, okay. It wasn't the

potatoes or Gram and Poppy, though I do love them." I framed his face with my hands. "It was you. But you knew that already."

He nuzzled my neck and moved his lips along my throat. "No, I'm not the one with the mind-hearing ability. So I like to hear it every now and then—that you still—" His eyes smoldered. "That I'm still the one. The one you want to be with."

"The one I love." I pulled his lips to mine, and the kiss left us both short of breath. "You're what I'm thankful for today."

His fingers traced my scars, as they had earlier. "I was thinking of that at dinner—how differently things might have ended. I was—am—so grateful that I found you… and that I didn't lose you… and that I still have you." He punctuated each pronouncement with a quick kiss on my eyes and nose, and then rolled to lie on his side next to me, one arm still across my ribs.

I heard a calling bird in the distance and closed my eyes against the dappled sunlight. It was perfect… but a part of me was anxiously asking how long it could last.

"You're frowning." With the tip of his finger, Michael smoothed my forehead.

"I was thinking. About the future. About next year." My chest tightened and my eyes were damp.

"There's nothing to worry about. I promise you."

"But you don't know. What if you go away to school, and you realize how much better you could do… if you meet someone else, and you find out that I'm really not the one? Or worse, if you didn't go and then you resented it forever?"

"Hey." Michael's fingers were firm beneath my chin.

"Open your eyes. Look at me." I blinked, hoping the tears would disappear even as they rolled down the side of my face. He gently wiped them away.

"You know that none of that is going to happen. I love you, and even if I have to be away from you for a little while, that's not going to change. Of all people, you should know that—you can see into my head."

"But I can't see into the future," I whispered. "And what's in your head could change then."

I expected him to protest, to offer me more assurances. Instead, he leaned into my ear and murmured, "Listen..." then covered my lips with his own.

Tasmyn, you are mine and I am yours. For yesterday, for today and for tomorrow. For as long as time goes on, and longer still. I might not know the future, but I do know this— you were made for me, and I was created for you. Trust me. Trust this. Don't be afraid.

And lying there, in that time and in that space, with him so near I could feel his every breath, I wasn't afraid.

About the Author

Tawdra Thompson Kandle lives in central Florida with her husband, children, cats and dog. She loves homeschooling, cooking, traveling and reading, not necessarily in that order. And yes, she has purple hair.

Coming Soon

Tasmyn Vaughn is not having the senior year she expected. Her boyfriend Michael leaves for college, she's being stalked by a suspicious preacher, pursued by the hot new boy at school and blackmailed by her chemistry teacher – who just might be a witch. Tas needs all of her many talents – and a little help from unexpected sources – just to keep her head above water…

literally

Chapter One
- Halves -

The sun shone warm on my face, and even with my eyes closed, I could still see its brightness. A breeze blew gently over me, and then, in its wake, I felt the lightest touch of a single finger running down my cheek.

"Are you awake?" The finger stroked along my hairline, and I concentrated on keeping my face immobile and my breathing even. He waited a moment, and then his hand moved down along my chin, tracing the contour of my jaw. He hesitated only the briefest second before brushing over the scars that I knew were still fairly visible along my neck.

Tasmyn... come out, come out, wherever you are...

His fingers moved along my collarbone, and I shivered involuntarily. I heard a quiet laugh.

"Or," he continued, speaking out loud now, "suffer the consequences." With lightening speed his hand moved to my ribs and tickled mercilessly.

I gasped and my eyes flew open. "All right, all right! Geez. I was just about asleep."

"Why don't we take a walk before you nap? I need to stretch my legs."

I reached up and slid my sunglasses into place over my eyes. Michael was still sitting next to me on the beach blanket, leaning one arm across my ribs as he gazed into my eyes.

"I think I can do that," I answered, stretching. "What

about Anne and Jim?"

"What about them?" Michael gestured to the blanket next to us. Anne was lying on her stomach, flipping through a magazine, listening to music through ear buds. Jim was clearly asleep; he lay on his back, mouth slightly open. Anne glanced up at us and smiled, then leaned over to brush her lips over Jim's cheek in a gesture that warmed my heart. It gave me undeniable pleasure to see my friends so happy.

"Okay." I moved to sit up, but Michael didn't budge. Instead he leaned closer to me, covering my lips with his own until I lay back again. He flattened his hands on either side of my head, and his thoughts became louder and more intense. My heart was pounding almost painfully.

When I thought I was about to either implode or lose consciousness, Michael pulled away and fell half across me, carefully avoiding putting any weight on me and burying his face in my hair. I could feel his breath heavy against my neck, and I turned my head slightly to whisper to him.

"I already said I'd go for a walk with you. But as far as persuasion goes, that was very convincing."

Michael laughed again and slowly sat up. I found the oversize shirt that served as my beach cover-up and pulled it on over my head. Michael offered me his hand and pulled me to my feet.

Anne pulled one ear free and leaned to look up at us. "Everything okay?"

"Just going for a walk," Michael answered her. "We'll be back in a little while. Better make sure Sleeping Beauty there gets some more sunscreen pretty soon, or he's going to be in a lot of pain."

Anne grinned. "I'll take good care of him, don't worry."

We walked along the very edge of the water, letting it lap at our feet.

"It's so warm!" I marveled for at least the third time that day. I had only known the frigidly cold ocean of the northeast Atlantic or the Pacific; the Gulf was a totally new experience, and I loved it. During this incredible summer, we'd made the drive to the west coast as often as possible, sometimes with a large group of friends, several times on our own.

"I'm sorry now we didn't bring the snorkel gear," Michael remarked. "It would've been a good day for it." He tightened his grip on my hand, and I could feel the anxiety banked just below the relaxed front he was putting forth.

We walked in silence for a while, although I could easily hear what was going through Michael's head.

This is our last beach trip. For this summer, at least. Maybe I can work it out to drive down a few times before it gets too cool. It's four hours to get home from the school. That's not too far for a weekend. But then you add in the drive over here... maybe if it were a long weekend...

He was frowning now, and I reached over to smooth his brow.

"Hey," I said softly. "I thought we weren't going to think about anything but today. Wasn't that your rule for this trip? No talking about the future."

Michael shook his head at me ruefully. "I wasn't talking about the future. I wasn't *talking* at all."

"Well, you were thinking awfully loud." The hollow feeling in my stomach that I'd been holding at bay threatened again, and I deliberately pushed it away.

"Ouch!" Michael stopped suddenly, looking down at his foot. "Stepped on something. Maybe a broken shell or..." He leaned over and picked up something white that was sticking out of the sand. "Huh. Look at this."

He held something white in his hand, studying it. When he turned it over, I saw that it was half of a sand dollar.

"Pretty," I commented.

"And kind of unusual. I've found lots of pieces of sand dollars here, but never a half like this one."

We walked on, slowly. I scanned the sand carefully, looking for shells. I had found some exquisite ones this summer, and I had planned to add to my collection today. Michael's find had jogged my memory.

"But you know, we could." It took me a moment to realize that Michael was continuing his earlier train of thought. "I can drive home from school on a Friday, after my last class, then we could come down here on Saturday."

"That's a lot of driving for you," I observed. "And I don't care about the beach. I mean, I've enjoyed it this summer, obviously, but as long as I can be with you, it doesn't matter where we are."

I was unprepared for Michael's sudden stop. He used the hand he was holding to tug me back to him and pull me flush against his chest.

"We're going to make it work," he whispered. "I promise you we will. We were made to be together, and this next year is just a little detour. We're going to be fine." He covered my lips again, but this time, there was more desperation lying beneath the intensity.

The water rushed over our feet, and I felt something hard against my ankle. Breaking away from Michael, I looked down at our feet and sucked in my breath.

"Look at this!" Stooping, I picked up the flat white shell.

It was another half sand dollar. I turned it over in my hands. "I can't believe we found another one. You didn't drop yours, did you?"

"Nope." Michael held out his hand, with his half still visible. I took it from him and joined it with the piece I'd just found, and we both stared. The pieces fit together perfectly.

"See, it's a sign," Michael murmured. "Just like us. Two pieces of the same whole."

"What are the chances that the two of us would find these two halves, and not even in the same section of beach?" I marveled.

About the same as the chances that the one girl in the world who is the other half of my soul would stroll into my school one day. Michael smiled at me and closed his hand over mine, which still held the sand dollar.

"Keep this. It'll remind you that it was more than chance that brought us together, that keeps us together."

"No, I have a better idea. You keep the half you found, and I'll hold onto my piece. That way we'll both have a reminder." I smiled up at him, hoping the tears weren't visible behind my sunglasses.

"Good idea."

We turned then to look out over the Gulf. In the distance, dolphins were playing in the rolls of surf. The sun's reflection glittered over the blue water. It was a perfect scene in a perfect day.

But perfection isn't meant to last.

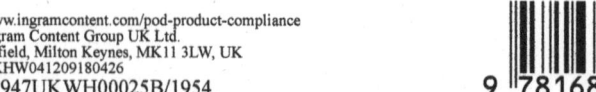

www.ingramcontent.com/pod-product-compliance
Ingram Content Group UK Ltd.
Pitfield, Milton Keynes, MK11 3LW, UK
UKHW041209180426
11947UKWH00025B/1954